EVIL, INC.

EVIL, INC.

GLENN KAPLAN

A Tom Doherty Associates Book

New York

EVIL, INC.

Copyright © 2007 by Glenn Kaplan

This book is printed on acid-free paper.

A Forge Book
Published by Tom Doherty Associates, LLC
175 Fifth Avenue
New York, NY 10010

www.tor-forge.com

Forge® is a registered trademark of Tom Doherty Associates, LLC.

Library of Congress Cataloging-in-Publication Data

Kaplan, Glenn, 1950–
    Evil, Inc. / Glenn Kaplan.—1st ed.
        p.   cm.
    ISBN-13: 978-0-7653-1618-9
    ISBN-10: 0-7653-1618-8
    "A Tom Doherty Associates book."
    1. Businessmen—Fiction.   2. Ambition—Fiction.   3. Success in business—Fiction.   4. Business ethics—Fiction.

PS3561.A557 E95 2007
813'.6—dc22

                                                                2007009595

First Edition: July 2007

Printed in the United States of America

0   9   8   7   6   5   4   3   2   1

To the memories of

EVAN HUNTER, for his talent, unstoppable joie de vivre, and generosity in helping this book early on

BRUCE HENDERSON, business thinker of genius, who planted the seed of this story in one of our unforgettable conversations

EVIL, INC.

PROLOGUE

The woman screamed and slammed the bedroom door shut. The wall of smoke and blast of heat from the flames on the ground floor nearly knocked her over.

"Where's Timmy?" she shrieked as she pulled up her flannel nightshirt to cover her mouth, not caring that she exposed her flabby belly and thighs.

"He's in his room," her panicked husband said, coughing from the invading smoke. He pulled his T-shirt up over his mouth, revealing his hairy paunch and tattered briefs as he dropped to his knees. "Down," he mumbled through the cloth, and pulled at his wife. "You're supposed to stay low."

"Timmy!" she shouted hoarsely. "Timmy!" She collapsed in a heap and started sobbing. "Earl," she whimpered through her tears, "goddammit, I told you I heard a noise! I told you I smelled something! Why didn't you listen?"

The fire beneath them roared like a train barreling through the small house. The floorboards were heating up. Smoke burned their throats and cut into their lungs like a thousand small daggers.

"Mommy!" a little boy's voice sounded through the din. "Mommy!"

"Timmy!" she howled, and jumped to her feet, only to collapse again. "Go get Timmy!" She coughed. "Go get Timmy!" She punched her husband. "Go get him!"

Earl crawled to the door. "I'm coming, Timmy!" he tried to shout through his T-shirt. "Stay where you are." The doorknob was hot as he turned it and flung open the door. Suddenly, a huge column of flames roared up the stairs through the corridor of open air he had just created, incinerating everything in its path.

Down the block, at the far side of a small snow-covered park, a teenage boy crouched behind a mailbox. He watched the flames light up the night, consuming the modest two-story house. He watched neighbors in pajamas pouring out of identical houses around it. He watched the fire engines arrive, too late to save the mother, father, and little boy.

He thought about the key to the padlock of the old-fashioned cellar doors at the side of the house. He had tossed it down a storm drain. He thought about the books on electrical wiring and fire prevention he had studied so carefully. He thought about everything he had done with such care. How he had waited for the family to go to bed. How he had placed the penny under one fuse in the socket and screwed the fuse back in. Then pulled some slack from the two wires in the ceiling above the old slate set tub and lowered them to just a few inches below the level of the faucet. Then peeled back just a hint of insulation on both wires, put the plug in the drain, and turned on the water. Then left the cellar silently and, once outside, carefully locked the padlock on the doors.

He did not need to see what happened down there to know that it worked.

When the rising water met the two exposed wires, the current passed between the positive and negative wire, creating an arc. The tampered fuse let the current surge in. The wires on that line smoldered in the darkness, then sparked, crackled, and burst into flames. The brittle lathing and pre–fire code insulation inside the walls ignited like kindling. The fire spread quickly. As he watched the firemen try in vain to bring the blaze under control, he extracted a dog-eared paperback book from the pocket of his winter coat. The boy had read and reread *Success Can Be Yours!* countless times.

Holy shit, he thought, it's true. Holding the book before him in the flickering light, he recited the author's words: "Start by working harder than others could ever imagine. Then find the courage to take risks others only dream of. And you, too, can ascend the pinnacle of success."

He gaped at the scene across the park, amazed at what he had accomplished. Then he disappeared into the night.

1

The crash sounded like a small bomb going off in the kitchen.

"Shit!" said Sandra Olson, watching the puddle of orange juice grow beneath the spout of the sippy cup.

"Sit! Sit! Sit!" little Sara cried with delight as she pounded the tray of her high chair.

Ken Olson looked up from his coffee and *The Wall Street Journal* as his wife and child engaged in that daily ritual of mortal combat called breakfast. "Sandy, are you trying to instill *all* your bad habits in our daughter before she turns three?"

Sandy knelt down with a paper towel to clean up the mess. With her other hand she picked up the sippy cup, licked the spout as if to remove the germs it acquired on the floor, and handed it back to Sara. "I think for now, we're okay. You can't tell what she's saying because her elocution sucks."

"Sucks! Sucks! Sucks!" the two-year-old sang out.

Sandy winced and silenced little Sara with a spoonful of cereal. "Ken," she said quietly, "I have a confession to make."

"I've got to be at the airport at eight," Ken said as he gulped down the last of his coffee. The tall, thin thirty-four-year-old executive with blond hair and pale blue eyes was focused on making his getaway. "Pennington wants me to pick him up at the company jet. Me. Just me. After months of sitting in crowded conference rooms trying to make an impression on this guy, I've finally got time alone with him. I've been working on this town meeting of his for two weeks, and today is the big—"

"Kennnn!" Sandy insisted as she pushed her dark shoulder-length hair off her forehead and flashed her big brown eyes. "You're not listening to me." Even barefoot in old sweats, wearing no makeup and half her baby's breakfast, she had the power to stop him dead in his tracks. She cocked her pretty oval face to one side and stood up straight, making her short buxom body as tall as she could, her hands resting defiantly on her full round hips. A pose that just dared him to ignore her. "I said I have a confession to make."

Ken froze in place. "Okay, Sandy," he pleaded, and raised his watch arm in the air, "please make it fast."

"I don't know why you're in such a hurry to go pick up the bastard who's coming to fire everybody's ass."

"Listen," he said, exasperated, "I know for a fact that he's interested in my turnaround plan. He made that clear at the last meeting of the Leadership Circle. And besides, I hardly think he'd be videotaping himself and all the employees at the town meeting if he were going to announce that everyone's getting laid off."

She gave him the big brown eyes again, full blast. "Ken, I've been job-hunting for you on the Internet." He started inching toward the door. "I sent your resume to a bunch of headhunters. Made a pretty impressive presentation of your career."

Ken stopped in mid-slink. "You did *what*?"

"I'm trying to get you a new job."

Ken fought a wave of anger. "Jesus, Sandy! You can't just send my resume around. You have no right. If word got out, do you know what that could do to my career? We get graded on commitment! How do you think I've gotten a promotion every year? *And* made it to the Leadership Circle *and* got Tom Pennington to notice me and read my reports? I'm really starting to make some headway. Don't you get it?"

"What about your commitment to our life?" Sandy demanded. "What about our freakin' life?"

"What's wrong with our life?" Ken gestured at the well-appointed kitchen of their three-thousand-square-foot mini-McMansion on the quarter-acre lot in the new subdivision of Beaver Creek Estates, in Beaver Creek, Ohio, just outside Dayton. "My parents never even dreamed of living in a house this nice. It's bigger than our last house, and it's got a new designer kitchen."

"What's *wrong*?" Sandy asked. "What's *wrong*? That company moves you to a new job every time you turn around. This is what? Our fifth house in six years? We've got boxes in the living room we haven't unpacked from the last move. I should have my teaching certificate already, but we've never stayed anywhere long enough. So instead, I'm, I'm, I'm assistant head of the goddamn company day care center. We're such nomads; even I have no choice but to work for that company, too. It's like growing up in the army with my father all over again." With her free hand, she gave an exaggerated salute.

"That's not fair," Ken said. "We are *not* your father and mother. For one thing, I don't drink. Two, you are not clinically depressed. And three, I don't think we're headed for a divorce. Or is there something I don't know about?"

Sandy took a deep breath. "I don't give a flying you-know-what about the countertops. And FYI, our glorious new designer dishwasher is on the fritz. Ken, I want us to have a real life somewhere, with real roots, and real friends, and a real community."

Sara started fussing. Sandy stuck a spoonful of cereal in her daughter's mouth.

"Sandy," Ken said quietly as he reached for the door, "everybody moves around a lot these days. That's just the way it is. The people in the company, they're our community."

"You call those corporate robots people?"

Ken replied quietly through clenched teeth, "Sandy, I don't have time for this right now."

"Ken," Sandy said through equally clenched teeth, "wake up. They're going to shut down your freakin' plant and close your division, and all we're gonna get is a crummy severance package and then it's going to be twice as hard to find a new job. So I started looking for you now."

"Sandy," he said, "I really have to go. This could be a very big day in my career."

"Listen, I hear company gossip, too. You think the other mothers who come to the day care center just sing Barney songs? I promise you, that company is going to screw us all."

Ken stood in the open doorway, one foot tapping nervously. "I really have to go now. Will I see you at the town meeting?"

"I don't think so. That's not exactly a great field trip for twenty kids under the age of four." Ken turned to leave. "Ken, wait a minute, I want to finish our discussion."

"Sandy, I have to go to the airport."

Sara started crying. Sandy picked up the child to quiet her, bouncing the baby girl on her hip. "Ken, I just want to protect us."

"What do you think *I'm* trying to do?" Ken said over his shoulder.

"I still love you!" she shouted at the closing door. "Even if some-times you are an asshole."

"Ath-hole!" Sara blurted happily, spraying a mouthful of cereal onto her mother.

2

Like a limo driver meeting the private jet, Ken got a pass from the General Aviation security desk at Dayton International Airport and drove his Chevy Blazer onto the tarmac just in time to watch the Ayvil Industries Gulfstream 350 descend out of the bright blue sky. It was a lovely spring morning; the gentle rolling hills of the Great Miami River valley were just starting to turn green. To Ken's surprise, there was also a van from WSJK, the local ABC affiliate, with a camera operator and newsman Cliff Reynolds waiting beside it.

"What brings you guys here?" Ken asked, trying to hide his irritation. "Our PR people didn't issue a release about anything."

Reynolds, a familiar figure on the local news, nodded in the direction of the private jet just as its wheels screeched and smoked upon touching down. "I know," he said smugly.

"So why are you here?" Ken did not want his first solo meeting with Pennington to be tarred with an unpleasant and avoidable incident involving the press. "We're here on routine company business. What makes you think there's a story?"

"Anonymous tip," Reynolds said. "Phone call to the station late last night. Told us to be out here to talk to the guy coming in on the private jet. Said we might hear some good news for Dayton." Reynolds sized up the airplane. "That's a G350, if I'm not mistaken. 'Bout thirty million a pop, aren't they?" He was not really asking. "Caller ID screen read 212 area code. That's New York City. We checked the number. Turned out to be a pay phone."

Ken said nothing and watched as the white jet, with its blue Ayvil logos on both sides of the nose and tail fin, crept toward them. When the Gulfstream came to a stop, the door opened out and down like a jackknife and the airstair unfolded. Tom Pennington stepped out and walked directly to Ken. In his navy blue suit, white shirt, and red-striped tie, the handsome fortyish executive looked like a movie star playing the role of a young presidential candidate.

"Ken Olson," Pennington said warmly, extending his hand and seeming not to notice the news crew. "I'm so glad we can have this time together. We've got a lot to get done today."

Cliff Reynolds cleared his throat noisily. "Uh, Mr. Pennington."

Pennington seemed confused. "Ken, did you arrange for them to be here?"

"Absolutely not," Ken answered. He was about to reprimand Reynolds when Pennington cut him off.

"Well, you should take credit for it. It was a great idea." He turned to Reynolds. "I assume you'd like a statement from me. I'm sure everyone in town is concerned about the fate of Ayvil Plastics."

"I'll say," Reynolds replied, "it's been a big employer in Dayton for a good hundred years."

"One hundred and seven years, to be exact," Pennington said. "Horace Ayers founded his pipe fabrication company here in 1900. You rolling?" he asked the cameraman. Reynolds showed Pennington where to stand. They did a sound level check. Then Pennington took command. He was relaxed in front of the camera, likeable and warm but without sacrificing the gravity befitting a senior executive on the road to becoming a Fortune 500 CEO.

"A thousand people work at Ayvil Plastics here in Dayton," Pennington said, gazing confidently into the glass eye. "They are not just numbers; they are people. What started here as Ayers & Vilmont Piping has grown into Ayvil Industries, the twenty-seven-billion-dollar diversified global company. As the executive in charge of this division, it is my responsibility to protect the company's investment." He stopped and took a deep breath.

"Now, most people assume that means our investment in plant and equipment, dollars and cents. But I'm talking about the kind of capital that's much harder to replace. I'm talking about the value of our *people*. They are not something you throw away when you hit a rough patch."

He leaned his head forward ever so slightly. The cameraman picked up his cue and zoomed in tighter on his face. "Dayton is our company's birthplace. Dayton also gave the world the Wright brothers, the automobile self-starter, the headlight, the electric cash register, the parachute, frost-free refrigerators, liquid crystal displays, and the ink-jet printer. It's a place where American workers make things that make the world a better place." He paused again. "I believe that the purpose of business is to serve the greater good. And that greater good demands that we give our workers in Dayton the chance to reclaim their birthright." He smiled warmly, stepped out of the camera's view, and made a slicing gesture across his throat to signal that he was done.

3

"I need multiple copies of that segment as it aired," Pennington said as they got into Ken's Blazer. "DVDs or dubs of their DigiBeta. But please not VHS; the sound loss is awful and they get worse with each successive dub."

Ken was not sure what the video tech talk was about, but he understood the part about not getting VHS. He had never seen an executive at Pennington's level who knew or cared anything about television.

As they drove out of the airport, Pennington looked into the backseat. He noted Sara's car seat and the little Ernie doll wedged beneath it. "How many kids you got, Ken?"

"Just one. Little girl. She's two."

"What's her name?"

"Sara."

Pennington smiled and took a deep breath. "I was married once. But Katherine died. Terrible boating accident. She was pregnant. Doctors said it would have been a boy."

"I'm sorry," Ken said awkwardly.

"After that," Pennington mused, "I guess I married my work. It's been, uh, effective. But maybe not the healthiest way to live."

Ken was silent, hoping the subject would soon change.

Then Pennington asked brightly, "Now what should we do about this turnaround proposal of yours? You really think it's viable?"

In his glance sideways, Ken could not read Pennington. "Of course I do," he said, sounding more tentative than he wanted to. "Those numbers aren't blue sky. They're real. I, uh—" Ken could not tell if Pennington was skeptical or probing for his level of confidence. He took a deep breath and said firmly, "I'd stake my career on that plan."

"Really?" Pennington asked, and stared out the window, just long enough for Ken's stomach to twist into double knots. Then he reached across the seat and delivered a mock punch to Ken's arm. "You're on. I'm going to give you the chance to do just that."

Ken stared at Pennington as they stopped for a red light. Pennington was smiling. "You know, Ken, you remind me of myself ten years ago. You and I have a lot in common, don't you think?" Ken nodded emphatically. "We're driven, we're impatient, we're impossibly demanding, more of ourselves than of others. As that guy said in *Good to Great,* a successful corporation isn't about the people; it's about the *right* people. You've read *Good to Great,* I assume."

"Twice," Ken said eagerly.

"Me, too. See, I told you!" Pennington went on cheerfully. "You mean you can turn up savings like that just by attacking capital expenditures with your new criteria? You're saying we can actually save *more* money *and* still keep the business alive?"

"I'm convinced of it," Ken said, trying to erase any doubt in his voice and wishing he did not have to keep his eyes on the road. "Look at all the costs of downsizing; they really add up. The savings my budgeting disciplines can produce are real. I've run the numbers every way possible."

"I thought you're marketing by discipline, not finance?" Pennington asked.

"Tom," Ken said solemnly, "I think of myself as a *general* manager."

"Right again!" Pennington declared. "That's exactly what I said when I got my first big corporate job. I *knew* you and I were on the same wavelength the first time I saw you at Leadership Circle. We're two peas in a pod, you and I. I just knew it."

Ken could hardly believe his ears.

"What was your last job assignment?"

"Auto Parts in Des Moines."

"That was good training—obviously. This rotation in Plastics will really help round you out as a manager. Of course," Pennington said, changing to a more conspiratorial tone, "you'll need more authority than you have in your current position." Ken did not dare to react. "You know . . . a promotion? I'm promoting you to Divisional Director in charge of this whole Dayton operation."

Ken was dumbstruck.

"Pull over here," Pennington said as they approached the entrance to the Ayvil complex. "We need to talk before we go inside."

Ken steered the Blazer to the curb.

"Look, Ken, I don't have to tell you that there are people at corporate who think we should just cut our losses and get out of this business. But I'm not one of them. As the new guy hired from the outside, I've had to take on some of the problems other people haven't been able to fix. But I'm the kind of person who, soon as you say something can't be done, I say I can do it. My sense is that you're the same way."

"Absolutely," Ken said enthusiastically.

"Ken, you know what really drives me? It's the next thing. Soon as I reach the top of the peak, I ask myself, what's next? Not that I don't appreciate what I just accomplished—it's just that, that next peak, well, that's the one I really need to conquer."

"The next thing," Ken said, nodding. "Me, too. I'm all about the next thing, too."

Pennington clapped Ken on the shoulder again. "Like I said, two peas in a pod."

"Yeah," Ken said, "two peas in a pod."

"Here's the plan. I want to implement your turnaround proposal. Uh, with some modifications from me, of course."

"Of course," Ken said deferentially.

"From now on, you report directly to me." Pennington extended his right hand. Ken took it and gave Pennington his most sincere, virile, empowered handshake. "I don't have to tell you that adopting your plan—pardon me, *our* plan—is going to raise eyebrows back at corporate. There is risk involved here. But no risk, no reward, right?" Pennington gestured for Ken to put the Blazer back in gear. "Now let's go in there and start a history-making turnaround."

They passed the big sign on the lawn: AYVIL PLASTICS, BIRTHPLACE OF AYERS & VILMONT, AYVIL INDUSTRIES WORLDWIDE. In the distance, in the middle of the fenced-in hundred acres, was the sprawling one-story building. It was a bland boxy artifact of 1950s industrial design, about the size of two and a half football fields. Most of it was the factory space. At the back loomed tall white tanks, the pressurized silos of chemical feedstocks. In the front were the offices. A large glassed-in atrium had been added to the main entrance in the mid-1990s.

"How's the security here?" Pennington asked idly as they slowed down for the series of speed bumps on the long drive to the parking lot.

"Not exactly state of the art. But better than we'll probably ever need," Ken said. "We added those magnetic door locks last year. I suppose we could seal ourselves off from the outside world completely if ever we needed to."

"Hmm," Pennington muttered, "you never know these days."

4

The atrium was jam-packed. The buzz of nearly one thousand nervous employees filled the air. Ken showed Pennington to the makeshift stage with the podium and microphone.

Pennington turned to the man with the video camera on his shoulder. "You shooting 24p?" he asked.

Steve Washington, a black man in his late thirties, was surprised and pleased that Pennington knew about his equipment. He lifted the camera. "Panasonic DVX-100," he said proudly.

"Excellent." Pennington smiled. "Twenty-four frames per second."

"You bet," Washington said, "a better look, more like film."

Pennington extended his hand. "Hi, I'm Tom Pennington."

Washington took it. "Steve Washington," he said.

"Steve, you're in charge of history here," Pennington said.

"Thanks, Mist—"

"It's Tom, okay?"

"Okay," Steve said.

"If I say anything wrong," Pennington whispered conspiratorially, "fix it in the mix, okay?"

"You're on," Washington said cheerfully as he stepped back to get his shot of Pennington on the stage. Pennington motioned to Ken to join him.

When he got the nod from the cameraman, Pennington took the portable microphone. He stood casually beside the podium and gestured for the crowd to quiet down. In a few moments, the atrium fell silent.

"People, I know what's on everyone's mind." His sonorous, amplified voice filled the hall. "So let me get right to the point. I am not, repeat *not*, here to close this division and lay off all the workers." There was a collective gasp as a thousand people let out their breath. Pennington put the microphone down and let his words sink in.

Slowly, applause began to build, then cheers, then the noisy, happy hubbub that comes after a sudden-death, overtime touchdown. Then Pennington raised his arm. There was immediate silence.

"You know, firing people is easy. And mass firings are even easier. Because, unlike firing your buddy Joe down the hall, it's impersonal. It's just numbers. Two thousand downsized here, ten thousand laid off there. But they are not just numbers. Every one of those lay-offs is a person and a family. It shatters careers. It destroys communities. And more often than not, it doesn't even end up helping the businesses over the long haul. That has been documented time and again. Now, I'm not here on a mercy mission. I'm here because I'm convinced this can be made a viable business."

Applause started up again. Pennington cut it off.

"Now comes the tough part," he announced in a more formal tone. "There was a great company in this facility. I say *was*. Because it isn't a great company anymore. In fact, this division has become a drain on the rest of the Ayvil Industries. I'm not here to assign blame. All that ever leads to is people running around to cover their asses."

Nervous laughter spread around the atrium.

"I want to talk about what happens from this day forward. I want each and every one of you to make a declaration of war against failure, against complacency, against old habits and sacred cows. Now, in every war, there are sacrifices. A year from now, not every one of you will still be working here. But if we wage this war successfully, there will be a business here and it will be healthy, growing, and profitable."

Whispers ran through the atrium.

"This is the oldest of all the Ayvil companies. And this is where the new spirit of the company is going to be born. No, *reborn*. From this moment forward, no one in this building is an ordinary employee. Everyone is on a special emergency task force with a single goal—to reinvent this division and bring it back to profitability.

"I spoke to Don Batiste last night. Don has graciously accepted an early retirement package. I'm appointing Ken Olson from marketing to be your new Divisional Director."

Buzz and chatter filled the atrium. Some people shrugged with indifference. Others asked who the hell Ken Olson is. Others were angry—especially the older men, the engineers from whose ranks the leaders of this division had always, *always,* come. Off mike, Pennington whispered to Ken, "Go ahead, you're in charge now."

Ken took the microphone. He cleared his throat, thinking he was off mike, but he wasn't. The embarrassing sound effect quieted the crowd. "Uh, I've got great news. Great news. Tom has okayed my, uh, *our* turnaround plan. We are going to turn this business around. We can do it!"

While the crowd clapped, Ken looked at Pennington, who beamed with support. Borrowing the gesture from his boss, Ken raised his arm to silence the room. The crowd quieted, but not as quickly as it had for Pennington.

"Uh, there, uh, there, uh," Ken mumbled, "there will be some cuts. But"—his voice brightened—"we'll do everything we can to minimize them. We're going to have a new budgeting process, new strategies, and new product initiatives. There'll be a detailed memo later today. There's a lot of hard work ahead and some tough choices, but we have demonstrated to management that there is light at the end of this tunnel."

Applause filled the room again. Ken clutched the podium.

Pennington took the microphone. He raised his arm. Again, the room fell silent instantly. He waited to let the silence ripen. "As I look around at your faces, I do not see ordinary people leading ordinary lives. I see extraordinary people with extraordinary capabilities that come out in this workplace. Look to your left. Look to your right." The crowd did as it was told. "That's not just the guy in the house down the street or the woman you run into at the supermarket. That's the person with talent and drive who is going to give us their best. That's how we're going to turn this company around."

Pennington pulled his suit jacket away from his chest as if to relieve a case of the sweats. "Whew, is it hot and stuffy in here, or is it my imagination?" He got a laugh and some catcalls exclaiming that it was the old ventilation system.

"You mean it's always like this?" he joked at no one in particular. He got cheerful complaints from around the atrium. "We can't turn this company around if no one can breathe properly. I'd say the first item on your cap-ex list, Ken, is to fix the ventilation. I'd look into a new system from your sister company, Ayvil Control Systems." He smiled at Ken, who made a check on an imaginary pad in his hand. "They've got a great product line. I know, because they report to me as well. And I think I can help you get a good price." More laughter from the crowd.

Pennington looked at his watch. "But I'm already running late. It's in your hands now. It's not going to be easy, but if everyone delivers his best and her best—and I mean every single day, nights and weekends, too—you have a real chance of making it. Do your best for all the people who depend on you. And I promise, this company will give you what you deserve."

More applause.

Pennington raised his arm slightly. Instant silence. "Look to Ken Olson for leadership going forward. And now I've got to get back on the plane and get to Denver."

He handed the microphone to Ken and whispered, "There's a car out there waiting for me. It's all arranged. You take it from here."

Pennington stepped down off the little stage and headed for the door. The crowd parted to make way for him.

Ken cleared his throat, this time unamplified, then spoke into the microphone. "This is the start of a brand-new day. We owe it to ourselves and our families and to this great company to make the most of it."

5

Ken lay in bed, watching the late news on American News Network. Sandy was in the bathroom brushing her teeth. The reporter on screen was a sexy double-process blonde with high cheekbones, angular features, and lush, full lips, probably puffed up with collagen. Behind her were three giant tapered cone-shaped cooling towers of a nuclear power plant, steam pouring from two of them. Protesters marched in front of the plant's security fence. They carried signs and chanted slogans: TICKING TIME BOMB. WEAPONS OF MASS DESTRUCTION IN OUR BACKYARD. THERE IS *NO* NUCLEAR SAFETY!

The reporter spoke in her most serious newscaster voice. "The Nuclear Regulatory Commission today ordered an investigation after the emergency shutdown of the Perry's Bend nuclear reactor Number Two here in Ames, Colorado. The shutdown and emergency declaration of an alert were reportedly caused by the failure of a steam generator tube here in this plant that has seen more than its share of operating problems in recent years. The statement, issued by the NRC's resident inspector, Gerald Davenport, stressed that the small amount of radiation released was well below the so-called technical specifications, which means there was no danger to the public. Just this week, Dynergetix, the plant's owner and operator, agreed to be acquired by General Industries, the giant conglomerate that makes everything from jet engines to dishwashers. Michael Guillaume, executive vice president of General Industries, rushed to the scene today."

The report cut to a handsome middle-aged black man in a dark suit and tie, standing in front of a dozen microphones. He was trying not to blink at the flashbulbs going off all around him. "At General Industries, public safety is our first priority. Effective immediately, we will institute General Industries' Total Quality Management procedures here at Perry's Bend. We will do whatever it takes to safeguard the thousands of people who live near this plant and the millions who depend on it for clean, safe, affordable power. As we head into the summer season, with its peak needs for electricity, we will keep this plant running to meet those needs. I give you my word and the word of everyone at General Industries."

The pretty reporter closed the segment. "This is Kat Pierce for ANN at the Perry's Bend nuclear power plant."

Ken called to Sandy, "Hey, I just saw an executive in deeper yogurt than me." Sandy came out of the bathroom wearing a purple V-neck nightshirt from Lands' End. With her damp hair pulled back, her big dark eyes looked even larger. "Impossible," she said with a smirk, sticking a finger into one ear to flick out the water. "No executive in America is in deeper yogurt than my husband, the new Divisional Director."

"Seriously," Ken said as he turned off the remote, "General Industries just acquired this nuclear power company, and no sooner than the deal closes, all these problems with the plant start cropping up. This guy Guillaume is getting blamed for stuff he didn't even do."

Sandy jumped onto the bed with a little bounce. "Sounds about right for corporate life. Blame the innocent; promote the guilty. Liberty, injustice, and politics for all."

"Oh, come on, Sandy," Ken protested.

"It isn't exactly the cream that rises to the top. At least from what I've seen."

Ken turned sideways in the bed, playfully pressing his face against hers. "What about me and my promotion? Huh?"

Sandy turned away. "I didn't mean you. I think you're too good to be in that place. I'm just waiting for *you* to reach that conclusion and," turning back to him, she said urgently, *"get outta Dodge."*

Ken sat upright. "Sandy, I'm not going to 'get outta Dodge.' I've got a great job in Dodge and a future like we couldn't even imagine a few weeks ago. Can't you see?" Ken beamed with macho pride. "I'm really kicking ass."

"Ken," she said, "don't you get sick of those phony people with their platitudes about teamwork, running around stabbing each other in the back, wearing those big smiling corporate happy faces?"

Ken did not respond.

"Do you know some of the rumors people have started about you? Especially the old guard engineers. They hate you, Ken. They really hate you."

"Come on, it's not that bad."

"Yes, it is. You just don't see it, because you're such a good person inside. They resent you because you're not an engineer like them. And being twenty years younger than most of them—well, that just gets them even more pissed off."

"What are they saying?"

"Well, I don't get the whole scoop, naturally. But I overhear enough."

"Like what?"

"Like they've started rumors about your relationship with Pennington. You know, like the two of you are . . ." She made a fist with one hand and inserted her index finger into it.

"Oh, come on!" Ken guffawed.

"I'm serious," she insisted. "You call your career the fast track; they call it something else. They're still loyal to Don Batiste, and they feed nasty shit back to him and the powers in New York that hate Pennington. If they don't have stuff to report that's for real, they make it up. Believe me, you are in the middle of a political rat's nest."

"I've come this far without stooping to that kind of thing, and I don't plan to start now."

"Ken, it's lucky you haven't come up against a really slick operator who's smarter than you. At least not yet." She took his hands in hers. "Oh, Ken, I love you, but I'm afraid you won't see it coming. You only look at the good side of people."

"And I usually find it," he said. "That was my management style in those personality assessments we did at the Leadership Circle."

She shot Ken her "cut the crap" look.

Ken backed off. "Look, it's all a game. I know that. But I'm winning now, Sandy, I'm winning *big-time*. I know enough to keep my eyes wide open. Really, I do."

"It's a sucky environment," she said. "And the higher you go, the worse the people are. Just be careful. Please! I love you and Sara loves you and we both need you." She pressed her face in front of his, her eyes wide. Then she leaned in for a kiss. Just as her lips were about to touch his, she whispered, "And we both think you'll be happier outside that giant corporation."

Ken kissed her lightly, then turned away. He rolled over and turned off his light. "Not till I'm ready. I've got a lot to accomplish first."

"I'll keep workin' on you, babe," she muttered to herself. She pinched his butt under the covers and turned off her light. "You'll come around."

6

"From this moment forward, no one in this building is an ordinary employee." Arch Paulson pushed a button on the remote. The image of Pennington on the television dissolved to black. Paulson threw the remote on the floor, sending it bouncing off the antique Persian rug and skittering into the corner of the private den beside his office at Ayvil headquarters in Manhattan. The CEO's cavernous corner suite of rooms on the forty-third floor looked out on the tops of other skyscrapers in Midtown Manhattan, an eagle's perch in the middle of the densely packed range of steel-and-glass mountains.

"Jesus H. Christ," he muttered, "what the hell does he think he's doing? I hired him to shut that operation down. Not to instigate some stupid turnaround." Paulson was a bald, burly, powerful six-footer who looked younger than his sixty-two years. He wore dark pinstripe suit pants and a custom-made Turnbull & Asser dress shirt with bold blue stripes, white cuffs and collar, and matching blue necktie.

Keith Macmillan and Paul Czerwinski, both about fifty, in dark suits with their suit jackets on, stood by expressionless, revealing none of the elation they were feeling at checkmating Tom Pennington, their corporate rival, so early in the game.

"We wanted to give you the heads-up, Arch," Macmillan, the gaunt finance man, explained. "I got the tape from Don Batiste."

"Yeah, it didn't seem like the strategy you had in mind," said Czerwinski, the former college lineman gone portly, "unless something's changed since the last meeting of the executive committee."

"Has it?" Macmillan asked.

"No," Paulson said with annoyance, "nothing's changed. I put my balls on the line to bring in this outside guy and give him a shot. I checked him out every way short of a colonoscopy, and he seemed like our kinda man. Now I'll have to neutralize him or reassign him or . . . Jesus, we just negotiated his contract. Explaining this to the board is going to be a real pain in the ass."

"Arch, to be honest with you," Czerwinski ventured, "hiring Pennington in the first place got a lot of people talking. And questioning. I mean, we've always prided ourselves on growing our own."

"That's right," Macmillan chided his boss, "remember our Ayvil Vision and Values. Rewarding managers who commit to the long term? We paid those McKinsey consultants a fortune to analyze the corporate culture and tell us what we stand for."

Paulson got up from the sumptuous leather couch in the den and strode into his office next door. The two subordinates tagged behind him. "I know, I know." Paulson shook his head. "Justin Hildreth suggested Pennington. And when Hildreth speaks, the rest of the board listens."

Paulson sat down behind his enormous desk and clenched his arms across his chest. Paulson's executive secretary sounded over the intercom. "Mr. Paulson, I found Mr. Pennington. Should I send him in?"

"Yes, please."

A moment later, Pennington, also in a dark business suit, strode in. He was about to make cheerful greetings when he felt the wall of hostility awaiting him. He stopped and stood at attention.

"Hello, Arch," he said, and nodded to his colleagues. Another silence. "What's the matter?" He looked around again. "What's up?"

In his most imperial voice, Paulson said, "I just saw the tape of your town meeting at Plastics."

"Oh, that's good. I was just finishing up the formal analysis that goes with it. You were supposed to see them together, but it's okay. The report has all the details; the tape provides the big picture and the, uh, visuals. Something wrong?"

"Something wrong?" Paulson fumed. "Something wrong? Pennington, I hired you to shut that plant down. Didn't I?"

"Arch, you told me to evaluate the business, report in on my plans, and do what's right. And that's what I've done. Er, what I was in the process of doing."

More hostile silence.

"Arch, I think you'll be surprised at the numbers you can turn up when you really open your mind."

"And when was I going to get to see this report?"

"This afternoon. Or tomorrow morning, first thing, at the latest.

Sorry, but I'm a bit of a perfectionist. I keep revising until the last possible minute."

"How nice," Paulson said icily.

"Arch, you'll see, I've done what you asked me to do."

"Well, that may be true. But you did *not* do what you goddamn well knew I *expected* you to do! Which is to close down that division and get it off our goddamn books! Why is that so hard to understand? What's this about a turnaround? What are you doing giving those people hope? Their business is *dead*. Those people are *dead*. Now, if you don't know how to go in there and kill them off, I'll go in myself and show you how it's done."

He looked at Macmillan and Czerwinski, who were both working hard not to look thrilled. "And you can be goddamn sure I've got other managers with the guts to go do what has to be done. I repeat," he said slowly through gritted teeth, "those employees are . . . *dead*."

"Arch," Pennington said softly, "I just wish you'd read the report."

"Fine, I'll read the goddamn report. But that doesn't change what has to be done." Paulson got up from his chair and stood eye-to-eye with Pennington. "I thought I had you sized up. I guess I was wrong."

The voice of another one of Paulson's secretaries sounded over the intercom. "Mr. Paulson, the car is waiting downstairs to take you to your lunch." Paulson mumbled thank you and strode over to his closet to get his jacket. "You gentlemen will excuse me. Justin Hildreth is waiting. I don't have to remind you he's the second most powerful member of the board. After me."

7

The limos and town cars along West Fifty-fourth Street in front of Le Mec were standing two and three deep, making the street almost impassable to regular traffic. But the police never bothered the illegally parked flotilla of black Lincoln Town Cars, Cadillacs, customized Suburbans, and Mercedes-Benz S-class sedans outside this year's favorite restaurant for power lunches. Here, regular traffic had no clout.

Justin Hildreth was already seated at his corner table when the maître d' showed Arch Paulson in. Hildreth rose and extended his hand. Le Mec was hushed even at busy times like this, its gray minimalist décor screaming understated luxury.

"Arch, it's good to see you." Hildreth was somewhere in his seventies, but with an ageless energy and verve. He had a full head of straight white hair that had once been blond, a strong jutting chin, thin aquiline nose, and the lock-jawed accent of old money.

"You're looking good, Justin," Paulson said, really meaning it. He marveled at Hildreth and his career of spectacular achievement without real work. Hildreth sat on the boards of more corporations, museums, hospitals, and universities than anyone could count. He seemed to be intimately connected with every important event of the day without ever actually doing anything himself.

"I see you've been in the sun," Paulson said as he put his pale hand next to Hildreth's tanned one. Beside Hildreth's long, thin aristocratic fingers, Paulson's stubby hand looked like a catcher's mitt.

"Can't help it down at Lyford Cay," Hildreth said, drawling the three syllables of the tropical enclave of the super-rich, "though the doctor has me under orders to keep covered. I know everything there is to know about SPFs. In my next life, I'll start a sunblock business." The bit of laughter broke the ice.

They sat down, ordered the first of many bottles of sparkling mineral water, and made small talk for most of the three-hundred-dollar expense account lunch. Both men passed on dessert. Hildreth ordered herbal tea, Paulson a double espresso.

"You know," Hildreth said, "when you've been on as many boards as I have for as many years as I have, you gain a certain perspective on the life cycles of companies."

Paulson was getting edgy. He had not figured out how to broach the subject of Pennington.

"Arch, you have done an admirable job building Ayvil over the years. You have grown the businesses and made many wise and profitable acquisitions. But there comes a time when a company reaches the limits of what it can accomplish on its own. A twenty-seven-billion-dollar industrial conglomerate may well be too small for this era of bigness."

Paulson gave Hildreth a puzzled look.

Hildreth drew a deep breath. "I'm talking about letting Ayvil get acquired by a bigger corporation, one of the companies with real critical mass—like a General Industries, for instance. You've had a tremendous run. This could be the time to maximize the share value for everyone."

Paulson's head recoiled. "I-I respectfully disagree. We are not anywhere near done building shareholder value. We've got tremendous upside still untapped. Tremendous. We're not at all ready to sell out. No, no. Not at all."

"There is an irrational side to the stock market," Hildreth said. "Good, solid companies get devalued and even destroyed for little or no reason. Flimsy, worthless companies get inflated beyond all measure of sanity. Remember the dot-com bubble. These fits of madness happen all the time. Believe me, I've been a student of the market since I was a boy in prep school." Hildreth smiled. "And that was a long, long time ago."

"That's why we've built our story on steady performance," Paulson said emphatically, "year after year after year."

"Some people would say"—Hildreth leaned in to deliver his message confidentially—"that Ayvil stock is stuck in the doldrums. That it has become . . . dull."

"Then let them!" Paulson exclaimed, as if daring other diners to overhear him. "If what I've accomplished over the last twenty years is dull, then give me more of it. Other CEOs would kill for a record like mine."

Hildreth leaned in closer to Paulson and said in a whisper, "As CEO in an acquisition, you would stand to make a great fortune instantly. Hundreds of millions."

Paulson leaned back. "I've already done that. Besides, money isn't what drives me. Not anymore. I've seen what happens to chief executives who get acquired. I'm not ready to sit on toothless committees and become a figurehead."

Hildreth did not react.

"I-I-I built this company from a middling domestic manufacturer into a global force. I *am* this company. And I am far from done." Paulson turned his head to look for the waiter to get a refill of his espresso. No waiters noticed him. "Justin, are you suggesting there's a potential acquirer sniffing around to make a run at us?"

"No, not at all," Hildreth said soothingly. "We're just talking. That's all."

"Good, because I would be prepared to lead the board in a fight to keep our independence. And I assume you would be prepared to follow me." Paulson tried not to make his assumption a question, but it was.

Before Hildreth could answer, the waiter interrupted. "More coffee, gentlemen?" Hildreth shook his head no; Paulson pointed to his empty espresso cup. The waiter snatched it up and went to fetch a refill.

Hildreth raised his chin and breathed in through his nose, a gesture people often interpreted as the old aristocrat looking down at them. "Believe me, Arch, I understand—nobody wants out of the game. Why look at me, I'm sixty-eight."

Paulson flinched; he was sure Hildreth had been officially sixty-eight for three or four years. "Someday I'll retire," Hildreth mused, "and, as I like to say, practice the arts of comfort and serenity. But not just yet. Every board I'm on has voted me a special exemption from mandatory retirement age, including Ayvil. So I'm no one to talk about gracefully stepping down."

Paulson jumped at the chance to change the subject and flatter his most senior board member. "We wouldn't have it any other way. You are invaluable to Ayvil, a priceless asset. We are going to need you for a long time to come."

"Thanks." Hildreth folded his large linen napkin with great care while Paulson sat silent. Finally, he looked up and said, "Let me commend you for bringing in new management blood. How is Pennington doing?"

Paulson knew this was the moment. "About that. There's something I, listen, uh, about Pennington . . ."

Hildreth jumped in enthusiastically. "This is no time for false modesty. Hiring Pennington was a brilliant move on your part. I just suggested him as a possible candidate. It was all your decision." Paulson tried to hide his puzzlement. Hildreth beamed. "I assume you've seen the tape of his town meeting."

Paulson put on his best poker face. "Yes, of course."

"Then I'm sure you saw how he managed to turn a potentially ugly downsizing situation into a win-win for everyone."

Paulson listened without reacting.

"It was mailed to me in the Bahamas, no return address, postmarked Dayton. No note, no explanation. I thought it was a bit odd. Then I watched it." Hildreth sat back against the banquette, radiating admiration.

"Pennington," he said proudly, "is an executive with talents this company needs in the world we live in today. He truly understands the power of the image. I think he could be on the short list to be your successor," then added quickly, "uh, when you decide the time is right."

Paulson struggled to keep from expressing his dismay.

"Look at how skillful he was," Hildreth continued. "He didn't promise he would save the business. He didn't underestimate the gravity of the losses. He didn't promise that we would *not* shut it down. He made saving the business *the responsibility of the employees.* That's a stroke of public relations genius!"

Paulson scratched his head in silent amazement.

"He's right about the culture and the history all starting there. What he did was an act of brilliant self-interest on the company's behalf. If they can pull off a turnaround, then he has earned Ayvil the kind of goodwill that can't be bought at any price. And Ayvil profits. If they can't pull it off, the workers are honor-bound to admit defeat and *fire themselves.* Either way, the company wins. I can't wait to share this with the rest of the board."

Paulson collected his thoughts while stirring the slice of lemon peel in his espresso. "You're right. Pennington *is* an exceptional executive. But he still needs aging in the bottle. Under my care, of course."

Hildreth nodded in agreement.

Paulson looked urgently at Hildreth. "You know, *I* was the one who gave Pennington that turnaround strategy. I spoon-fed it to him. All of it."

Hildreth looked deep into Paulson's eyes. Paulson's gaze did not falter. A faint smile formed across Hildreth's thin lips. He reached across the table and patted the CEO on the forearm. "I'm sure you did, Arch," he said. "I'm sure you did."

8

Ken drove the brand-new Pontiac Torrent into the driveway, parked beside their Chevy Blazer, and beeped the horn twice. Sandy emerged from the kitchen along with a man in his mid-forties who carried Sara on his shoulders.

"Hello, stranger!" Ken called to his brother-in-law as he got out of the sporty red SUV with the price sticker still on the rear window. Ken extended his hand. Phil Lambert grabbed Sara's right leg and offered it instead. Ken happily shook his daughter's foot and tossed the keys to Sandy.

"That's some hot car," Phil said admiringly.

"I'm some hot babe," Sandy said as she bumped Ken aside with her hip and slid into the driver's seat.

"Mommy car?" Sara asked.

"Mommy *and* Sara," Ken said emphatically. "You like it?"

"Red," Sara said. "I see red."

"It's called Fever Red," Ken said brightly.

"Considering the effect I have on men," Sandy said, running her hand over the dashboard, "I think that's very appropriate." She finished her cursory inspection, got up, and closed the door. "Okay, we'll take it."

"I don't think you'll have any trouble finding *this* in the mall parking lot," Phil said, jostling Sara on his shoulders. Phil was a head taller than his kid sister and on the heavy side of trim. He had receding short hair going gray at the temples. There seemed to be little resemblance between the siblings until you got to the eyes. Both had the same big riveting dark brown eyes. "What do you say, Sara, will you recognize mom's new car at the mall?"

"Red car! Red!" she cooed as she tried to climb off her uncle's shoulders in order to get her chance to sit in the driver's seat and blow the horn until she had annoyed absolutely everyone in the neighborhood.

Later, the grown-ups had coffee at the kitchen table while Sara napped upstairs.

After a little small talk, mostly about Sara, Sandy said, "So, big brother, long time no see. No hear. No write. Not much of anything except a call. Maybe every couple of years, if I'm lucky."

Phil looked up from his mug. "You trying to lay some of Mom's special guilt on me?"

"Why not?" Sandy said. "It's the gift that keeps on giving."

"Won't work, little sis, not on me. I got out of that family when I had to."

"You sure did. Right in time for the divorce. I got left learning how to practice shuttle diplomacy between Mom, Dad, the U.S. Army, and family court at the age of fourteen."

"Sorry, Sandy, but I protected you as long as I could."

"Thanks a heap for those precious years of childhood while *you* thought you took all the heat from the fighting and the drinking and the pills and the depression."

"Hey, I ran interference for you for a long time."

"Yeah." Sandy snickered. "Yeah, right."

Phil finished his coffee in one gulp. "I did what I could. And from day one, I made you the beneficiary of my insurance policies and government pension. And now you and Sara."

"That some kind of bribe? So if you died young, without us ever knowing you, we'd get your money."

"San-dy!" Ken interrupted. "Come on!"

"It's okay," Phil said with a shrug, "I had that coming. What do you say to me turning over a new leaf? I promise to reconnect with my one and only sister and her family."

"Come on, Sandy," Ken said, nodding approvingly at Phil.

"Hmm," she snorted, "men." She stood up and took Phil's mug and her own to the new Braun coffeemaker by the sink. She put Phil's refreshed mug in front of him and stood behind him, one hand resting on his shoulder. Phil reached up and put his hand over Sandy's.

"I promise," Phil said.

"You gonna be there for Sara?" Sandy asked. "Before she's all grown up?"

"Promise," Phil said softly.

"And for me? Even though it's a little late in the game."

Phil nodded.

Sandy said, "Just as if we were . . . *family*?"

"Yes, Sandy. Just as if you and I were brother and sister, sharing the same DNA, the same dearly departed alcoholic father and pill-popping, twice-remarried mother."

"Promise?"

"Promise."

Sandy patted Phil's bald spot. "Deal," she said, and sat down. "All right, then, big brother, tell you what you can do." She leaned across the table, her eyes wide. "Now that you've started your new life in the private sector, I want the scoop on those years of mystery with the, what's it called? The Defense Intelligence Agency. Come on, spill the beans."

"Sandy," Phil protested gently, "you know I can't talk about that stuff."

"Oh yeah? I've been waiting since junior high."

Phil shook his head.

"Come on!"

"Sandy, if I had told you what I was up to, I'd have had to shoot you. Sorry," Phil added with a little smile. "Let's talk about my new life."

"All right," Sandy said with a sigh, "what exactly does Medusa Associates Worldwide do?"

"We call it risk control. For corporations mostly and private individuals."

"They're corporate private eyes. Like Kroll Associates," Ken interjected knowingly. "We used them to uncover some crooked vendors when I was at Auto Parts. Nailed the bastards red-handed."

"Well, we do compete with Kroll, and Cerberus, and Global Options Group, and some others," Phil said. "We do security, testing, forensics, forensic accounting, political intelligence gathering—whatever clients need to reduce their exposure to, well, risk."

"Ooh," Sandy said eagerly, "hunky bodyguards with big shoulders, little thingies in their ears, and pistols strapped to their calves?"

"Yeah, we got some of those."

"So that means you can bring us juicy tales of vice and corruption from the boardrooms of big business?"

"Sorry," Phil said, and zipped his lips shut with his index finger.

"Your careers, big brother, are no fun at all. Good thing there's so much dirt about crooked executives every day on the front page of *The Wall Street Journal*." She looked pointedly at Ken.

"*San*-deee," Ken said.

Phil cleared his throat. "So, I see you guys are moving up the old corporate ladder. Nice house, new chariot."

"It's all good," Ken said proudly. "I'm now the youngest Divisional Director in the company. I'd been working my butt off to impress this superstar from corporate, and it looks like it really paid off. He gave me a promotion that leap-frogged me three levels up. With this guy as my mentor, I could be on the fast track to senior management." He rolled the last two words on his tongue slowly, "*seeen-yorrr* manage-ment," tasting their delicious glory. Ken was glowing with pride. He reached across the table and touched his wife's hand. "Sandy can even quit her job if she wants to."

Sandy slid her hand away and folded her arms across her chest.

Ken and Phil looked at her, waiting.

"*If* she wants to," Ken offered.

"Uh, that's really nice," Phil said.

"Well," Sandy said finally, "I'm not sure *she* wants to."

"You don't have to quit your job," Ken said defensively. "I'm just saying that it's not a matter of money anymore. If you don't want to work, you don't have to."

"It so happens I *like* working. And even though the day care center is not my ideal job, it *is* a place where Sara and I can go together. It gets us both out of the house. And when Sara's older, I plan to get my certificate and teach for real."

"Oh," Ken said pointedly, "so the company isn't so bad after all?"

"I didn't say that. I still think you need to get the hell out of there."

"Sandy!" Ken snapped. "I just got an amazing promotion! I keep telling you it's a game, this corporate thing. It's all a game. And I'm finally winning at it. Do we have to go over this again? Huh, do we?"

"No," Sandy said quietly, "we'll have the rest of our lives to do that. And I do not consider that a *game*."

Phil looked back and forth between them. "Whoa! Did I walk into the middle of something here? I just stopped in on the way back to

New York to check out this marital bliss thing. You know, see what I've been missing by staying single all these years."

Ken and Sandy stared at opposite ends of the kitchen. "Come on, guys," Phil said. He reached out and touched their shoulders across the table, as if to bridge the gap between them. "You're supposed to be the ones who make *me* feel bad."

9

An angry Arch Paulson stood looking out the window of his office. Macmillan and Czerwinski sat in front of Paulson's desk. Their mood was as grim as the rain outside.

"I admit it, I made a mistake hiring Pennington," Paulson said. "I had no idea he could get this kind of power so soon."

"Yeah, but he hasn't produced any results yet," Macmillan said to the back of Paulson's head. "Paul and I have track records that go back fifteen years."

"And more," Czerwinski added.

Paulson spun around. "Thank you, *Mr.* Macmillan, thank you, *Mr.* Czerwinski. In case you hadn't noticed, the game at this level isn't just about managing the business; it's about managing impressions. And Pennington has a talent for managing the impressions of the people who count. Starting with Justin Hildreth. Believe me, I know what he's doing. I did the same goddamn thing twenty years ago. Hildreth has more influence and more power than anyone has a right to have. But he's Justin Fucking Hildreth, and once you've got him on your side, well, you can't believe the doors that just magically open."

Paulson sat down. He leaned back in his chair and placed his fingertips on his immense mahogany desk. He seemed to be studying the empty expanse of endangered tropical hardwood. "Back then, you didn't have to have yourself videotaped for sound bites like a goddamn political candidate."

"He's got to screw up sometime," Macmillan said. "Everybody makes mistakes. Something always goes wrong. It's got to happen to him, too."

"The problem," Paulson said, looking up, "is if it happens later and not sooner." Paulson stared out the window and mused, "If only there could be a crisis in Pennington's world."

"What do you mean?" Macmillan asked.

"I mean," Paulson said, "some terrible problem that leaves everyone at a loss about what to do. Everyone that is, except me."

"Yeah, there needs to be a crisis like *that*," Czerwinski said quietly.

"That's right," Macmillan said, "something that forces you to step in and take out Pennington. For the good of the whole corporation."

Paulson turned and faced the pair. "Now, gentlemen," he asked, slowly enunciating every word, "what do you think that might be?"

Macmillan shrugged. Czerwinski drew a blank.

"Let's see," Paulson sneered, "between the two of you, I pay you men—uh, let's see now, let me add base and bonus, the stock, the long-term incentives, et cetera, et cetera—five million apiece. That's ten million dollars a year. And the first time I really need you to come up with an idea, you sit there with your thumbs up your—"

"Arch," Czerwinski pleaded, "we're just brainstorming here, talking this through for the first time."

Paulson waved his hand dismissively. "Think, gentlemen! There needs to be a crisis in Pennington's world. Something that makes him look really bad."

"Uh-huh," Macmillan agreed, "a big goddamn crisis. That'd do it."

10

The drive at Ayvil Plastics was quiet. The employee parking lots were full. The little rush of visitors for lunchtime meetings had not yet begun. Four men in business-casual clothes riding in a tan Ford Explorer with AYVIL CONTROL SYSTEMS painted in blue on the front doors swung into the drive and followed the signs to the visitors' parking area, carefully slowing down for each speed bump along the way. They were plain white men who looked like they might be engineers.

The man at the wheel was big and brawny, with dark hair going gray, a grizzled mustache and goatee, black horn-rimmed glasses, and pale skin. "Here we are, gentlemen," he said as he turned into a parking space, "ground zero. The operation begins." He spoke with a slight accent, faintly British but not quite. "Remember, we are all employees from the sister company."

"A-all in the family," the heavyset man in the shotgun seat said. He had a stutter and a smile that he used to charm people into patience with his disability. "Th-think we'll b-be here for the company picnic?"

"No," the driver said curtly.

"Oh," the stutterer said with mock disappointment, "I l-love a b-barbecue and a three-legged race." He turned toward the man in the backseat. "Don't you, Char—?"

"I told you," the driver snapped, "we use work names at all times from now on. Even when we're alone."

The stutterer turned again to the man in back. "D-don't you, *James*?"

"That's better," the driver grunted.

"Yeah, *Casey*," the man in back on the left said with mock delight, "I love picnics. Hot dogs, Coke, and apple pie, too." The man beside him in back smirked.

"Let's get to work," the driver said as he opened the car door, "there's two million dollars for us to split at the end of this job. That's five hundred thousand dollars each."

"Yes!" said the stutterer without a trace of hesitation.

From the back of the Explorer, the men collected two aluminum briefcases, a bulging accordion file, and three sets of blueprints rolled into long thick tubes. They entered the small structure in front of the atrium, walked up to the glass window that resembled a bank teller's station, and set their baggage on the floor.

The man with the goatee spoke first to the guard who sat at the desk behind the hole in the window. "Peter Houghton from Control Systems to see Al Darling, the facilities manager," he said. "We're here to start work on the new HVAC system."

The guard was a paunchy older man in a white polyester uniform shirt and blue clip-on necktie. Perched on the bridge of his nose, he wore half-moon reading glasses on a long string. He sat, unarmed, manning the sign-in sheet. Behind him was a panel of sixteen small black-and-white television monitors, four by four, showing checkpoints around the building. Under the TVs was a small control panel with a few dials. A two-way radio sat on the shelf, crackling and squawking bits of conversation.

"Welcome!" the guard said cheerfully. "We been expecting you. Let me get Al on the phone. Sign in here, please. I'll get your badges." He motioned to the loose-leaf notebook with the pen attached on a chain. The men signed in one by one.

"Hi, it's Mack at the front desk," the guard said into his phone. "The HVAC guys from Control Systems are here to see Al." He hung up. "Al will be right down to get you." Mack got four visitor badges from the desk drawer and inspected the upside-down signatures without turning the notebook around. "Now, which one a you is . . . Peter Houghton?"

The man in the goatee nodded.

Mack, a lefty, wrote the first badge number upside down and backwards for himself but right side up and frontward for the notebook, beside the first name. "Here you go, Peter," he said cheerfully, proud of his small, odd skill. "Now just touch your badge anywhere on those barriers on your way in and way out." He motioned to the four waist-high wooden pillars, spaced four feet apart, that defined the entry space to the atrium behind. "And please be sure to leave your badges here at the desk when you go. People forget and hang on to 'em for weeks sometimes, and I gotta keep puttin' in for new ones. Then my boss gets mad. Promise?"

Houghton nodded.

"We're sure glad you're here," Mack said. "Gonna be a long hot summer."

"We'll take care of you," Houghton said.

Mack looked up quizzically. "Yer accent? Yer a . . . Australian, aren't ya?"

"Yah," Houghton replied curtly.

"I thought so!" Mack said proudly. "I'm pretty good with accents."

Houghton took the badge and clipped it onto his belt.

"Casey Rogers?" Mack asked, reading the next upside-down signature.

The heavyset man with the stutter nodded and took his badge.

"Bill Hunt?" Mack looked at the two remaining men.

Hunt, the shortest of the four, a trim and compact man with wire-rim glasses, approached the window and got his badge.

"And that means you must be . . ." Mack paused. "James Cavanaugh," he announced as he handed over the badge. "Welcome, Jim. I come on at seven most mornings, so I'll be here to see you in. I'm Mack Winston."

"Peter Houghton?" a man's voice asked. Al Darling appeared from behind the barriers. He was another plain graying white man in the business-casual uniform of khakis and button-down shirt.

"Hello, Al," Houghton said.

"Glad to meet you in person, Peter. Finally."

Houghton introduced his men. "This is Jim Cavanaugh, our systems engineer; Casey Rogers, electrical; and Bill Hunt, HVAC expert."

"Gentlemen," Darling said, greeting the others. "I'm glad we could get you the building plans and documentation ahead of time."

"Yeah, it really saved us some time," Hunt said. "We've run our first set of load projections and have some recommendations for the upgraded system. But we do have questions about particulars."

"Yes," Cavanaugh added, "quite a list."

"Excellent," Darling said, "let's go upstairs and go over the drawings. Then we can walk the facility together and get into the nitty-gritty." He gestured for the men to enter. They picked up their briefcases, the accordion file, and rolls of drawings. They tapped their badges against the short wooden pillars and followed Darling.

They were in.

11

The men who called themselves Peter Houghton, Jim Cavanaugh, Casey Rogers, and Bill Hunt sat in the windowless conference room. Al Darling had brought in two other grizzled, middle-aged engineering types, Carl Unger and Jack Lumley, who had been managing the production facilities for as long as anyone could remember. The large round table was covered with the unfurled blueprints of the building and its ventilation system.

Houghton finished unrolling the last blueprint. "Can we begin?" he asked. He gestured at Hunt, who stood and cleared his throat.

"There are three problems, really," Hunt said. "First, it's a closed system, which was fine in the eighties when it was installed. But now, by code—"

"Uh, we should really wait . . . ," Darling interrupted, "for Ken Olson to join us. He's our new . . ." He paused, searching for the right word.

"Our new *leader*," Unger said with a sneer.

"Boy wonder," Lumley mumbled under his breath.

"He's our new Divisional Director," Darling explained with a brightness that seemed to contradict his colleagues' sarcasm but in fact reinforced it. "He's the first man to hold that job who has not been trained as an engineer."

Lumley turned to Unger. "Doesn't MBA stand for Master of Bullshit Always?"

Unger smirked. "I don't think he's got one a those. I think he came here straight from junior high."

Darling looked at his watch. "I think we might as well get started. Ken's a busy guy, and this is pretty technical stuff."

"That's right," Lumley said in a loud mumble. "Ken's strictly a big-picture kinda guy."

Ignoring Lumley, Darling motioned to Hunt.

"Right," Hunt said, "as I was saying, there are three problems.

One, it's a closed system, which was fine once. But now by code, we've got to introduce outside air for ventilation. On top of that, you've got these Advair 6000 units, which were fine when they were new. But when you combine them with the glass atrium you added in, when was it, '94?"

"'Ninety-five," Darling replied.

"'Ninety-five. Thanks. Well, the glass atrium contributes solar heat gain in the summer and heat loss in the winter, so those old units are undersized for the job you're asking them to do. The new units we'll install are much more powerful and energy efficient."

"I see," Darling said.

"So the job," Hunt said, "is to bring in more capacity and a constant stream of outside air to the system. Does that sound right, Peter?"

Houghton nodded.

"More power and a breath of fresh air," Cavanaugh added with a smile.

There was a knock at the door. "Come in," Darling said loudly.

Ken stepped inside. "This the HVAC team?" he asked.

"Sure is," Darling said. "Gentlemen, meet Ken Olson, our new . . ."

"Divisional Director," Ken said, trying not to sound impressed with himself.

Lumley and Unger exchanged smirks. The four men from the HVAC team stood to introduce themselves and shake hands with Ken.

"Pleased to meet you," Ken said, motioning for everyone to sit down again. "I don't want to interrupt you." He nodded at Lumley then at Unger, trying to be friendly. "Jack, Carl," he said with a smile.

Lumley and Unger nodded without the slightest hint of a smile in return. The boy wonder was getting no help from them.

Ken turned to Darling. "How's it looking, Al?" he asked brightly.

Darling obliged with a chipper response for his boss. "Great, Ken, just great! Sounds like what we're going to get—" He paused and looked at Cavanaugh. "—is more power and a breath of fresh air."

Cavanaugh nodded.

"More power and a breath of fresh air," Ken said. "Gee, I like that. I'd say what this whole division needs is just that. More power and a breath of fresh air."

Unger and Lumley exchanged "oh, brother" grimaces. Al Darling lowered his head. Ken did not notice. He spoke as if addressing a much larger audience. "Let me emphasize, gentlemen, we're in a hurry. This project is key to productivity, absolutely key. I don't want our people to suffer through another hot summer with outdated AC. You know, we're trying to turn this business around. We've got a mandate from Tom Pennington, our *executive* vice president. We want to keep this place feeling up. Nothing is more important than employee morale." He looked across at Darling, Lumley, and Unger, who were studying their fingernails. "It's all about the people. But then management always is. Tell me, how long will the job take?"

Houghton looked at the drawings.

"Well, in our preliminary specs, we haven't spotted any major hurdles," Cavanaugh offered, "isn't that right?"

"Right," Houghton said. "The structure of the system and airflow patterns look clear. It's just the power systems that need to be upgraded. And with the new technology, it's pretty straightforward." He looked at Hunt, who was looking at the plans over the tops of his glasses. "Right, Bill?"

"Based on the load programs we've run and barring any problems," Hunt said pensively, "I'd say, uh, we could complete the job in about two weeks."

"Really?" Ken asked.

"Yah," Houghton replied. "Barring any glitches. We *all* want to fast-track this job."

"And how." Ken looked at his watch and sighed—an overbooked leader with too many responsibilities and too few hours in the day. "Al, are you comfortable with the way this is going?"

"Yes, Ken. You can leave the details to us."

12

The four men in the Explorer rode away in silence. Houghton at the wheel waited until the Ayvil complex disappeared from his rearview mirror before he spoke to Cavanaugh, who sat beside him. "So what do you make of the security?"

"They've got Magnalocks for the whole building. That's pretty new. The rest of the system dates from the late eighties. They've got their cameras on five seconds per rotation. With sixteen screens, it gives us just under eighty seconds of safety in any given spot where they've got a camera. Jeez, they haven't multiplexed their video. They've got seven old cassettes that rotate the seven days. Probably nobody's even looked at one of those cassettes in three years."

"What else?" Houghton asked.

"All systems appear to be in the guard shack. The fire- and smoke-alarm panel's an LED enunciator board."

"That good?" Houghton asked.

"Well, convenient. When we run our tests of the—" He cleared his throat to underscore the irony. "—the new HVAC units, we'll put the fire and smoke system off-line. That'll give me an excuse to hang out and spend some quality time with old Mack. I'll figure out the best way to make sure the tape doesn't record what it's not supposed to see."

"Good," Houghton said, and asked the stutterer in the backseat, "and we can get the explosives on the roof close enough to the silos of chemicals?"

Rogers nodded and spat out, "B-b-b-boom!"

"Good," Houghton grunted, and pulled the cell phone from the clip on his belt. Holding it in one hand, he flipped it open and dialed. It rang for a long time before someone answered at the other end.

"This is Houghton," he said quietly into the phone in his flat, almost British accent. "This is the secure line, yah?" A pause. "I am confirming two weeks' time."

He paused and listened. "Yes, we have scoped it out." He paused again, then spoke very slowly and deliberately, holding himself back from the brink of rudeness. "I said, the operation *will* go smoothly. I guarantee it. You understand what my word means, yah?" Houghton nodded at the response. "Good. Yes. That's right." He paused again to listen. "Just make sure the rest of the money arrives on time on the day." Pause. "Yes, on the day."

He snapped the cell phone shut.

"Two million dollars for us to split," he said to his colleagues, then repeated it slowly, savoring every syllable, "two million dollars."

They nodded at each other. Houghton handed the phone to Cavanaugh. "Do me a favor, will you. Remove the SIM card."

Cavanaugh slid the back panel off the phone. He reached inside and extracted the little plastic chip that identified the phone but not its owner, while giving the phone access to the cellular network. From the driver's side, Houghton pushed the button that lowered the front passenger's window.

"Now toss it," Houghton said.

Cavanaugh flicked the sliver of silicon and plastic into the air. It fluttered to the side of the road, another speck of highway litter.

"Thanks," Houghton said quietly, and closed the passenger's window from his side.

"T-t-teamwork," Rogers said with a smile.

13

Sandy closed Sara's bedroom door gingerly, not wanting to wake her after finally coaxing her to sleep. She crept down the stairs and into the little den where Ken sat working at the computer, piles of paper stacked all around him.

"Hey, Mr. CEO-to-be. Your kid is officially down for the count."

Ken grunted.

Sandy leaned down and gently nibbled his right earlobe. "Hey, sailor, can I interest you in a quickie on the couch?" She was barefoot and wearing a worn gray T-shirt, a man's XXL that came halfway down her thighs. AYVIL SOFTBALL was printed in fading letters on the front.

"Come on, Sandy, can't you see I'm busy?"

She reached down and brushed her fingers gently across his zipper. "Ken, unless you're gettin' some at the office, which I doubt, you're not gettin' any. Which means *I'm* not gettin' any." She sighed. "It's been weeks, babe. I know you've got a lot of pressures. But, Ken, *everybody* deserves to be gettin' some. We've only got so many chances before we die. Come on, how about a quickie?"

"How about a rain check?" He shifted away from her and stared harder into the computer screen. "I'm halfway through this analysis. In a couple of hours, I think I'll have it cracked."

Sandy sighed and threw herself down on the couch. She pulled the T-shirt down between her legs to cover her new black lace panties from Victoria's Secret. She picked up a magazine and began leafing through the pages noisily.

Ken stared at his computer.

Sandy threw down the magazine. "Since Pennington showed up, it's like you don't even live here anymore."

"How many times do we have to go over this?"

"Ken, it just doesn't seem real to me. There's something they're not telling you."

"Like what?"

"Honey, I just don't trust them."

"Sandy," he said, still staring straight ahead, "you're not seeing the projections I'm seeing."

She stood up from the couch. "I don't care about your numbers; they're just blips on a computer screen. Ken," she said urgently, "I have a bad feeling about all of this."

He turned from the computer. "Just exactly what do you want me to do about it, this bad feeling of yours? I'm leading this entire division into what could be a history-making turnaround. No, let me rephrase that. What *more* do you want me to do?"

She took his hands in hers. "I want you to go to Cleveland and do the interview with ADF. It's a much smaller company and they're growing like crazy. You'd be getting in on the ground floor."

"Je-sus, Sandy!" He pulled his hands free and turned back toward the computer.

"Ken, I worked hard writing your resumes, composing your letters, pretending to be you in the e-mails. I can do just about everything for you, but I can't go on the interview and pretend I'm you."

He stared at the computer.

"I can't," she said. "The headhunter specifically said no cross-dressers."

Ken could not suppress his laugh.

"Ken, I'm serious. You've learned everything you're going to learn at Ayvil. You need to grow and expand your horizons. For all of us."

"Look," Ken sighed, "given my responsibilities here, if word got out that I was interviewing at another company, well, if *I* heard about that kind of disloyalty—"

"Loyalty?" Sandy threw her hands up. "Jesus, Ken, will you wake up and see what century we're in. The only loyalty your management has is to their comp packages. How much did that guy Paulson make last year? Twenty million? Thirty million?"

"Honey," Ken pleaded, "you're putting me in an impossible position."

"I'm putting you in the position of doing what's right for your career and your family." Sandy took him by the shoulders. "I want you to go on the interview. Just go on the freakin' interview. Please."

"Sandy, don't you see? This is my shot. *Our* shot. This could get me a corner office at headquarters, a seat on the Gulfstream, the works. Someday maybe twenty million a year for us. Wouldn't you like that?"

Sandy shrugged.

"I've told you before. Ayvil rewards longevity. The top guys have all been there their whole careers. I'm right on the brink." He looked at her urgently. "Sandy, I'm so close!"

She had a hint of panic in her voice. "Uh, uh, maybe we could start our own business? Be our own bosses? Yeah, we've talked about that before. Come on, let's ditch the big-company bullshit once and for all. What do you say? Let's move somewhere and start fresh. We'll open a dry cleaner's or a little store. Something, anything. We'll be on our own."

"San-dy! You sound like my father. He said he'd never work for anyone else, and look what happened. He fell flat on his face with one cockamamie scheme after another." Ken shuddered. "So? So there's bullshit in a big company! Of course there's bullshit in a big company. There's bullshit everywhere. So what?"

"Ken, maybe everything will work out great here and you'll be a hero and get all those rewards. I just don't think it's going to happen. Not because of you. But because of *them*. Please, Ken, for the sake of us, please go on that interview. Please."

She touched his shoulder. "Please?" She took his hands in hers and clasped them together. "Please?"

He looked up at her.

She took their clasped hands and pressed them to her heart.

Ken sighed. "Okay, I'll go."

She let go of his hands, smiled at him, and held her arms open. "I love you."

He stood up and embraced her.

As he caressed her back, his hands slid down and cupped her ass. Noting the lace texture against his fingertips, he craned his head to one side and looked down as he raised her T-shirt above one hip.

"Mmmm." He ran his finger over the black lace panties, then reached inside and squeezed.

She looked up at him and they kissed. They walked upstairs touching lightly. At the top of the stairs, they stopped in front of Sara's door. Sandy raised an index finger to her lips and switched off the hall light. Slowly, being careful not to let the doorknob make noise, she opened Sara's door.

Blue moonlight filled the room. Sara lay in her crib sleeping deeply, breathing noisily, her little chest rising and falling in a peaceful rhythm. Ken and Sandy gazed at their child and held hands. Then they turned to each other and kissed once, slowly, making sure their lips made no noise. Silently, they left. Sandy closed the door with great care, again releasing the doorknob very slowly. Holding hands, they walked across the little hallway to their bedroom and closed the door.

14

Hunt and Rogers directed the crew of workers on the roof. Houghton barked orders to the crane operator and the remote crew through the headset of his walkie-talkie. The crane raised the two new HVAC units onto the roof and brought the old units down to the flatbed truck. Out of their big crates, the new units, gray boxy affairs, looked like several enormous refrigerators welded together at odd angles, with huge fans and vents protruding here and there. Metalworkers bolted the units onto their frames; mechanics and electricians finished connecting them to the system. After an hour of intense activity, the crew, drenched in sweat, assembled in front of Houghton.

"Attention," he barked into his walkie-talkie, "we are all piped and wired. Ready to test the system. Over."

Houghton's voice crackled over the headset of the walkie-talkie Jim Cavanaugh wore down in the stifling, un-air-conditioned guard station. Sweaty Mack Winston and Al Darling looked on, munching doughnuts from the white-and-green box of Krispy Kremes on the desk. Only two doughnuts remained in the dozen box that Cavanaugh had brought in that morning.

"We're going to put the alarm and fire systems on test," Cavanaugh said into his radio. "I'll tell you when we're ready. Over."

"Okay," Houghton replied, "over."

"Go on, Mack," Darling advised the guard, "call it in."

Mack put down his half-eaten glazed jelly doughnut, licked his fingers, and picked up his desk telephone. He dialed the number printed in bold letters on a strip of paper under Scotch tape at the top of the phone. CENTRAL MONITORING STATION, the strip read.

"Hello, Central Station," Mack said. He was trying to sound official, but he instantly cracked a smile. "Hey, Billy, it's Mack out at Ayvil." He listened for a moment. "Oh yeah, it was a heck of a game, wasn't it. Listen, Billy, we're gonna put the system on test. Got that new AC going in today. Uh-huh. Yessir. The code is one-three-five-six-dash-eight-B. Uh-huh. Thanks, Billy." Mack hung up the phone and reached for his doughnut. Several lights on the panel above his desk stopped blinking. He nodded to his boss.

"Okay," Darling said to Cavanaugh, "the systems are on test. The Central Station will ignore us for as long as you need. You can go ahead."

"Thanks, Al," Cavanaugh said as he brought the radio to his face. "This is Cavanaugh," he said, "systems are on test. We are good to go. Gentlemen, start your engines. Over." He smiled at Al and Mack and replaced his radio onto the clip on his belt.

On the roof, the new units came to life with a rumble.

From around the units on the roof and from points around the building, crewmen chimed in on their radios as they checked readings of the system.

At first, warm air blew from the registers. Grumbles from people all around the building could be heard—from inside conference rooms, bathrooms, behind cubicles and office doors, and especially in the cavernous factory space. Then, like magic, the air started to turn cool, then cooler, then downright cold.

Mack felt the rush of cold air filling the guard station and celebrated by reaching for another doughnut.

There were bits of chatter over the radio as the crew waited for the building to cool off. After half an hour, Houghton's voice crackled over the radio. "Are we within temperature parameters?" he asked. Responses from around the building chimed in positively.

Cavanaugh looked at Darling and gave him a thumbs-up. Darling returned the gesture and finished off the last hunk of sugary doughnut.

Then the cascade of deliciously cool air suddenly stopped.

Over the radio, voices from around the building called in, overlapping. Sounds of confusion from the roof. Houghton's voice came on shouting, "Unit number two is down! Unit number two is down!" More voices of concern clamoring over the radio.

"Peter! Peter!" Cavanaugh said, trying to break into the chaos. "This is Cavanaugh. What is the problem? Over."

"Jim," Houghton answered, "it looks like the compressor in unit number two is locked. Shut right down. We're looking at it now. Why don't you come up to the roof? Over."

"On our way," Cavanaugh said, "over." Darling looked at him with alarm. "Let's go up and see. I'm sure it's something we can fix. This kind of thing happens all the time. You know, working the bugs out."

Darling led Cavanaugh out to the back of the complex. Along the way, people stopped him to ask him what was wrong.

"Just working the bugs out of the system," Darling repeated apologetically.

Up on the roof, unit number one hummed along, cooling its half of the building. Houghton, Rogers, Hunt, and the crew stood around unit two, its cover paneling removed, its internal workings exposed, stray disassembled parts lying around on the hot asphalt surface.

"What's the problem?" Darling asked Houghton.

"It's definitely the compressor," Houghton said, staring at the machine and not looking at Darling. "She's locked down. Bill says we can't fix it." He looked at Hunt who stood by the dead machinery.

Hunt, looking mortified, said, "Uh, under the warranty we're entitled to get a new compressor shipped here soon as possible. No charge. I just got to make a phone call. It's an in-stock unit, so we should have a new one here in—" His voice trailed off. He looked up at Darling, embarrassed. "—a week, tops."

Darling looked up at the baking sun then back at the dead HVAC unit then back at Houghton. "Mister, we got a heat wave going on here, in case you hadn't noticed. You're telling me half of my building is going to be a sweatbox for a whole week?" His voice was rising with his irritation.

"Well," Houghton said, scratching his head and stalling for time, "you've been without good cooling for some time already."

"It may not have been good," Darling snapped, "but it was cooling. Now we've got nothing for half the damn building." Darling surprised himself with his use of a curse word. "Sorry," he muttered, "this is upsetting. Isn't there anything you can do?"

"Well," Houghton said, "we, uh, we could see about bringing in a temporary cooling unit."

"When?" Darling demanded. "How soon?"

"We'll have to make a couple of phone calls. But I think we could have one here tomorrow. Bill?" he asked of Hunt, who was already on his cell phone. "How soon you think we could get a mobile unit here?"

Hunt had turned his back to them to focus on the call he was making.

"You make it tomorrow," Darling shouted indignantly. "Peter, I know several managers above your level at your division." Darling was bluffing, but he was confident that Houghton would not dare to call it. "Just because this job is in the family doesn't mean we don't deserve the right kind of treatment. I've got a thousand people in there who deserve better than this. And I don't care what it costs. What it costs *you*," he added, jabbing his index finger at Houghton, "because it's going to be on your tab."

Hunt turned around. "Great news!" he called. "We can get a new replacement compressor here day after tomorrow! Whole new unit! I told you it's an in-stock item. How's that for good luck?"

"Just make sure it works," Darling said, and turned his back on Houghton. He took his cell phone from the clip on his belt and started to dial, then stopped. He motioned to the radio headset Houghton wore. "You might as well tell the men in the loading bay areas they're free to open their doors. This test is over."

15

Sandy walked into the front hall foyer from the kitchen. The early morning sun poured in. Ken, dressed in his interview suit minus the tie, was arranging papers in his briefcase. She was wearing sneakers, jeans, and a casual white blouse, her usual outfit at the day care center. In one hand she held a long narrow gift box. She handed it to Ken. "Here, I got you this. It's for good luck at ADF today."

Ken opened the box and removed the necktie from its tissue wrapping. It was navy blue with a small muted pattern.

"Nice," he said dubiously, "very subtle."

"Confident," Sandy said, and chucked him under the chin. "It says, I don't have to try. I've got the stuff and I know it."

"I like that," Ken said. "Without that explanation, I might have said it's kinda dull."

"That," Sandy said, planting a kiss on his forehead, "is yet another reason why you need me—to give you styling sophistication."

Ken held the tie out at arm's length. "You know, ties are kind of a weird thing for men."

"I know," she said, grabbing it back, "they're a symbolic extension of their dicks."

"How'd you know that?"

"*Everything* about men is an extension of their dicks."

Ken smirked.

"Now if they make you an offer, just tell Pennington you have to leave. Period. Tell him I've got family in Cleveland. A dying mother, some bullshit like that."

"I think he'll be pissed. Really, really pissed. He put himself on the line for me."

"Ken, he didn't do a fucking thing for you that wasn't doing something even better for himself. Jesus, Ken!"

Before Ken could answer, a little giggle filled the room. Sara was standing at the bottom of the stairs in her jammies and little bare feet.

"Honey," Sandy said with astonishment, "you climbed out of your crib *all by yourself*?"

Sara smiled and made a big sweep in the air with both arms. "Sara climb!" she exclaimed, and broke into a run, leaping into Ken's arms and squealing with triumph.

"That means," Ken said with shock and distress, "she can climb out of her crib *any time* she wants to."

"No shit," said Sandy, shaking her head with an equal measure of parental horror.

"No sit!" little Sara piped up. Then Ken and Sandy covered their baby girl with hugs and kisses.

16

Sandy drove Ken to the airport in their new Torrent. Ken had one arm slung over the seat in order to play tickle games with Sara in her car seat behind him. She held on to one of his fingers and sang and chattered, announcing all the local sights—the supermarket, the McDonald's, the mall—like a tour guide with a squeaky voice and muddled pronunciation.

"Go get 'em, slugger," Sandy said as she pulled to a stop at the terminal. "Come on, 'Kiss and Drop,'" she said, repeating the words of the sign above. She presented her lips to Ken as if obeying a local ordinance. He gave her a husbandly peck and leaned into the back-seat to kiss Sara.

"Nice tie," Sandy whispered playfully as he opened the car door.

"Yeah," Ken said halfheartedly.

"Hey!" Sandy snapped. "If you're going in with that kind of an attitude, we don't need to bother. I mean, don't do me any favors."

"I know that!" Ken stood up and leaned against the open car door.

"If *I* can see how you're feeling," Sandy said, "don't you think the trained interviewers at ADF will, too? Jesus, what have I got to do to get you to—?"

"To do what? Huh? To do what?" Ken shut the car door angrily, not quite slamming it. He glared at Sandy through the closed window.

Sandy lowered the window with the electric button. "To realize your full freakin' potential, that's what!" she shouted. "If you had let me say it." She raised the window, put the Torrent in gear, and, giving an angry wave with one hand, drove away.

"See you tonight," Ken said to the back of the car.

17

Houghton drove the flatbed trailer with the crane and the new compressor. Hunt and Rogers sat beside him in the cab. Cavanaugh followed in the Ayvil Control Systems Ford Explorer, another box of freshly made Krispy Kremes on the seat beside him. The hot sun in the cloudless sky so early in the morning promised another scorcher.

They met Al Darling in the back of the building. Cavanaugh excused himself and left to visit Mack in the guard shack. Houghton explained to Darling that his smaller crew would get the new compressor up to the roof in the morning. Later, when the sun got a bit cooler, the rest of the crew would arrive to finish the hookup. It had been too difficult for the big crew working in the noonday sun during the first installation. Darling grudgingly admitted that no one should be on that roof unnecessarily and certainly not in the worst of the heat. When Houghton suggested that Darling, too, should stay off the roof, he agreed and waited on the ground in the shade.

Houghton's men disconnected the broken unit, raised it with the crane, set it on several dollies, pushed it to the side, raised it off the dollies, and set it down beside the truck. Then they raised the new unit, still fully crated, up to the roof and out of Darling's view. They set it on dollies and moved it over beside the silos of chemical feedstocks. They raised a second big enclosed crate and set it on the roof, also out of view, and slid it into position beside the silos. If anyone had been listening carefully, and no one was, they would have noticed a slight sound of liquid sloshing around from inside the new crates. But the noise of the crane and the roar of the other functioning air-conditioning compressor covered that odd and inappropriate sound.

Houghton left the truck and joined his men on the roof.

"Sure you don't want to come up here with us?" Houghton called down to Darling.

"No, only you guys deserve that," Darling yelled back.

"Why don't you go back inside," Houghton said. "We're just working on some details up here. When we come back after three, we'll bring the rest of the crew and we'll finish the job. Why don't you go get some real work done. I'll call you when we get back. I've got you on speed dial." Houghton held up his cell phone as if that were proof.

"Yeah," Darling said sourly, "I know." He turned and headed for the door. "See you later."

Cavanaugh unspooled enough coaxial cable to run between the two crates. At the two ends he connected two rods that looked like silver pencils. At the other end, the wires met at a gray junction box about the size of a shoe box but only half as tall—the receiver end of the MAS Zengrange demolition remote firing device, DRFD, approved by the United Kingdom Defence Ordnance Safety Group and fully EMC tested in accordance with Def Stan 59–41. They set the silver "pencils," the detonators, down on the roof and covered them with a small sandbag. Houghton held the transmitter in one hand. It was a bulky gray box the size of an old-fashioned walkie-talkie. He turned the switch from OFF to TEST and pushed the button. The green light lit up.

"We have continuity," Houghton said.

Standing by the receiver, Cavanaugh noted the green light there, too. "Yes, we have continuity." They removed the sandbag and inserted the two detonators, one into each of the crates. Then they lined up the receiver box that connected the coaxial cables and carefully faced it toward the east, making sure no pipes or railings or other mechanical roof objects were in front of the line of sight of its antenna.

When Sandy and Sara arrived at Ayvil, they waved to Mack Winston and the HVAC man in the shack with him; they waved back. She touched her tote bag, with her key card clasped to the handle, to the barrier. Then she trudged down the long corridor to the day care center.

When she got to the door of reception, she put Sara and the tote bag down and pressed her keycard against the pad. It made the familiar clicking sound as it unlocked the door.

"Come on, pumpkin," she muttered to Sara as she picked up the tote bag and motioned for her to go inside.

"No!" Sara insisted, folding her arms across her chest.

"Yes," Sandy countered, not amused.

"No!" Sara stood her ground.

"Sa-ra! What do you want?"

"Sara go home. Go home," she insisted.

"No, sweetie, Mommy and Sara have to go to work."

"Sara go to work?" The child looked confused.

Sandy sighed and suddenly felt very tired. "No, I mean Mommy goes to work. Sara's gonna go play. You wanna go play? Come on, let's go play."

"Okay, Mommy," she said, "Sara go play."

Sandy took a deep breath and put on her best Assistant Director smile as she and Sara walked through the door into the reception room. Sandy punched in the code on the windowed door and ushered herself and Sara inside. "Good morning, everybody!" she announced.

"Gooboningeveeyboddee!" Sara chirped behind her. A little chorus of garbled kiddie greetings responded as they entered the cheery preschool with all its brightly colored paraphernalia.

"I don't feel so good," Mack said, holding his belly. He looked weak and very ill. A half-eaten glazed jelly doughnut sat on the paper napkin on his desk, the open Krispy Kreme box Cavanaugh had brought him beside it.

"You dug into those yesterday no problem," Cavanaugh said, looking concerned.

Mack groaned and stood up with alarm. "Oops, gotta go. Can you mind the store while I go to the john?"

"Sure, Mack, no problem."

Hurriedly, Mack grabbed the logbook with several months of signatures and put it into the bottom drawer of his ancient steel Shaw-Walker desk. Then he dashed out the door and ran for the men's room down the hall.

"Ready to commence operation," Cavanaugh said into his radio. "Over."

"Copy," Houghton replied through the static. "Over."

From his pocket, Cavanaugh pulled a pair of vinyl examination gloves and slipped them on. He lowered the window shades on both windows. The guard station was temporarily closed. Then he reached for Mack's telephone and dialed the Central Station.

"This is Ayvil, we're going to put the system on test again." He listened impatiently. "No, Mack's out sick today. I'm new. I work for Al Darling. Uh-huh, uh-huh. Sorry, we've got work to do. The code is one-three-five-six-dash-eight-B. Uh-huh. Thanks," he said, now trying to sound friendly. "It's Billy, isn't it? Yeah, thanks, Billy." Cavanaugh hung up the phone, looked above the desk, and waited for the lights to stop blinking.

Then he turned the suitcase on its side, opened it, and took out a screwdriver. He walked to the Magnalocks control panel on the wall and opened it. Quickly and expertly, he unscrewed an interior panel. He loosened two screws on the relay, removed the wires wrapped around each screw, and twisted the wires together into a single lead. Then he walked across the little room to the security monitors. He pushed the STOP button on the VCR. The images continued flashing on the monitors, but nothing was recording.

"This is Cavanaugh," he said into his headset. "I am operational. Over."

"Copy," Houghton said. "Return to base. Over."

"Copy," Cavanaugh replied. "Over."

Cavanaugh walked out of the guard shack. As the door closed behind him, he heard it make a little click sound. The Magnalocks were all in place now. For the next few minutes, no one could get in or out of the building.

Cavanaugh joined his colleagues as they piled into the Explorer.

Steve Washington was editing the videotape of Pennington's now-famous visit. It was a loop, a continuous repeating snippet that would be broadcast in-house on the video monitors in the lobbies and public areas. In between the scrolling notices of bake sales, new benefits information, Ayvil press releases, and hourly updates on Ayvil's stock price, Pennington's inspirational speech at the town meeting would appear. Ken had suggested it as a morale builder.

Steve had the edit just about where he wanted it. He rewound the tape at high speed. A fractured image of Tom Pennington streaked across the screen with a high-pitched whine that sounded like Alvin and the Chipmunks in Swedish. He stopped the tape at his edit point and reviewed it at normal speed. Pennington's handsome face filled the screen.

"Do your best for all the people who depend on you at work," the man from headquarters said. "And I promise, this company will give you what you deserve."

Steve pressed the EDIT button and saved the looped segment. He pushed some more buttons and sent it to the master feed for the in-house video channel. In the next instant, Tom Pennington's face filled every TV screen in every corridor and gathering place in the building. In his soothing, authoritative voice, he told everyone within earshot, "Do your best for all the people who depend on you. And I promise, this company will give you what you deserve."

Houghton and his men drove a quarter mile away to an empty hill-top. They stood in the field overlooking the Ayvil plant.

Hunt handed the transmitter to Houghton. "Line of sight with the receiver on the roof confirmed," Houghton said, moving the switch from OFF to TEST to OPERATE.

"Payday, lads," Houghton said as he pushed the firing button.

18

At thirty-eight thousand feet over the Rockies, Tom Pennington sat alone in the cabin of one of the Ayvil Gulfstreams. A stack of reports was piled on the table before him. He was reviewing a thick binder in his lap when the airphone on the wall beside him rang. He pulled it from its cradle.

"This is Pennington," he said, raising his voice against the noise of the jet and sketchiness of the telephone signal at this altitude. "Yes, Jane, it's me. No, I'm alone. Elkins decided to stay behind. Yes, yes, I can hear you just fine."

He held the phone tightly to his ear for a minute.

"What?" he shouted incredulously. "That can't be!"

The cockpit door opened and the steward emerged, looking pale and stricken. "Mr. Pennington! Mr. Pennington!" he shouted urgently. "We just got word on the radio!" He waved at Pennington to listen to him.

"Just a second, Jane," Pennington said into the phone and took it away from his ear. He looked at the steward gravely. "It's the accident in Dayton, isn't it?"

"That's what we just heard!" the steward shouted. "They say hundreds could be dead! This is horrible!"

Pennington took a deep breath. "Tell Paul to reroute us to Dayton, Ohio."

"Does Mr. Paulson know?" Pennington asked Jane. "Yes, yes, I know he's in China. Tell him I'm on my way to Dayton now. I should be there in less than two hours. Uh-huh, that's right. No, Jane, I can't imagine how. Can you alert the authorities on the ground that I'm on my way? Do we know anything else?" He stopped to catch his breath. "Oh, Jane," he said with heartbreak in his voice, "there must be more survivors. There *must be.*"

19

The Boeing Business Jet carrying Arch Paulson, Lew Simons, Ayvil's PR chief, and three crew members took off from Shanghai's Pudong International Airport just after sunset, heading east over the ocean and turning left for the polar route back to New York.

The Boeing Business Jet is the big daddy of private jets, the corporate world's answer to Air Force One. The BBJ is actually a Boeing 737, the commercial airliner originally designed to carry more than 130 passengers and crew, outfitted for the private comfort of a couple of lucky executives. With over one thousand square feet of living space and ceilings over seven feet high, the BBJ has a large main cabin, a private office, gourmet kitchen, private bedroom with queen-size bed and full-size bath plus shower, a bunk room for the crew, airphones galore, and DirecTV. It is a complete executive home and office in the sky.

Arch Paulson had chosen the décor himself, selecting from swatches of cowhide, carpeting, and exotic wood. The BBJ he had configured for Ayvil had the brownish look of a traditional gentleman's club. The airplane cost forty-five million dollars, another six million a year to maintain, and about twenty-five hundred an hour to operate.

Paulson, in shirtsleeves with his French cuffs rolled up, collar open, and tie loosened, leaned back into the leather couch and raised his highball glass. "Here's to cheap labor. Fifty cents an hour and no unions."

Simons, a slight ferret of a man with curly hair slicked back, was still in his suit jacket. He sat facing Paulson in the single leather seat big enough for two. He clinked his glass with the CEO's. "That's right, Arch, fifty cents an hour."

Paulson looked at his watch. "Next year, we'll be able to close those plants in Michigan and Indiana. We're looking at savings of at least ten million right off the bat."

Simons nodded obediently.

"You know what that's going to do to our numbers?" Paulson asked rhetorically. "Czerwinski will get in there and make those cuts. He's got what it takes."

"Yeah, it's going to be great."

"You know what I love about business? It's the future. We live in the present, but we've always got one foot in the future. Building it. Shaping it. Making it happen right here and now."

"That's great," Simons said eagerly, " 'one foot in the future, making it happen right here and now.' " He quickly scribbled the CEO's words in his notebook. "We can use that in one of your upcoming speeches."

Paulson smirked and stretched out his legs to settle in and relax. The two men sipped their drinks in silence.

Then the jet phone rang. Paulson motioned for Simons to get it. "Hello!" Simons shouted. He listened for a moment. Then his jaw fell open. His eyes looked like they were about to pop out of their sockets. "What?" he said, breathless. "What? Oh no!"

Paulson sat sipping his Jack Daniel's and looking out the window.

"Arch, Arch!" Simons said. "There's been a terrible accident at Plastics. An explosion and a fire."

Paulson sat up and gestured for Simons to give him the phone.

"Yes?" Paulson shouted into the phone. He listened closely for a few moments. Then his face went white. "H-how many?" Sweat beads appeared on his forehead. "Oh my God," he said quietly, "how did it happen? How many? No, no, call me back. Use the radio if the phones give you trouble. . . . Just keep me posted."

He replaced the phone into its cradle and pulled a handkerchief from his back pocket to dry his forehead. He grimaced. Then he leaned forward, elbows on his knees, and held his head in his hands. When Paulson finally looked up at Simons, he wore a look of cold determination.

"This is going to be one hell of a shit storm. Marshal the lawyers, call out all the experts, whatever we need. Spare no expense. You hear me?"

The flack sat silent, ashen and quaking from the knowledge that he would be the one facing the firing squads of journalists for months to come.

Paulson spoke slowly and deliberately. "This was a safety violation; I'm sure of it. A goddamn safety violation. And it happened on Pennington's watch." He leaned forward as if to make their private conversation even more private. "I want Pennington to fry for this."

Paulson sucked in a big breath and stared out the window for a moment. "We're going to go back to New York and we're going to get to the bottom of this terrible thing. We're going to take our licks. We're going to do whatever it takes to get this company back on its feet."

He stood and walked toward the back of the airplane. He stopped short of the door to the private bedroom suite and walked back to Simons. He stood, towering over him, one hand gripping the flack's shoulder.

"This company needs me more than it ever has," he said, breathing bourbon into Simons's face.

Simons gulped. "Yes, Arch."

"I can't begin to think about a successor right now. It would be irresponsible. I've never been a quitter, and I'm not going to quit now. I've got to lead this company out of this mess. No one else can do it. No one."

Simons nodded.

"It's a matter of conscience," Paulson said. He turned and headed back to the private bedroom suite.

20

Houghton drove the Explorer to a town called Nelsonville. The roads got narrower, the woods thicker, and signs of people more scarce. Finally, they turned onto a dirt path that went down to a small clearing in the woods. There sat a mobile home. A string of lonely old utility poles along the dirt road brought a power line to it. A tank of water and another of propane at its side rendered it more or less habitable. A dusty late-model Chevy Impala was parked beside it.

"Now can we break open some beers?" Cavanaugh asked as they climbed down out of the SUV.

"Certainly, lads," Houghton said, "beers for everyone. For a job well done."

"I-I-I'll drink to that!" Rogers chirped, and gave Cavanaugh a high five.

"So where's our money right about now?" Cavanaugh asked as he and Rogers and Houghton entered the mobile home. There were three shabby old chairs, a cot, a kitchenette, a small filing cabinet, and a cramped fiberglass toilet compartment. On a card table sat the rolled-up plans of the Ayvil complex and a laptop computer.

"Right now," Houghton said, "our money is moving electronically from New York to the Royal Bank of the Caymans. Then, in little packets, to other banking paradises around the world. Finally, untraceably, all the little pieces land into our own individual secret numbered accounts."

"Five hundred thou," Cavanaugh said as he reached into the fridge and tossed green bottles of Rolling Rock to his companions. The two men flopped down into the chairs and opened their beers.

"It really ought to be less," Houghton said as he caught his bottle and twisted off the cap. He remained standing.

Cavanaugh glared. "What are you talking about?"

"W-what the f-fuck do you m-mean?" Rogers sneered.

"I should get more because I'm management," Houghton explained with deadpan calm.

Cavanaugh and Rogers glared at each other.

Houghton said, "We've been watching the corporate world, haven't we now. Management always gets compensated more for managing— what do they call it?—the big picture. Isn't that right?"

"Fuck you," Cavanaugh said.

"And the horse you rode in on," Rogers added angrily with no trace of a stutter.

Houghton raised his beer bottle and cracked a big smile. "Just kidding, lads. Half a mil for everyone, just like we promised."

The tension evaporated. Cavanaugh and Rogers raised their bottles. Houghton toasted, took a small sip, then set his bottle on the cabinet. "Gotta pee," he said as he opened the door to the toilet, stepped inside, and closed the door behind him. He heard the sounds of the fridge door opening, caps popping, and glass bottles clinking again.

Houghton peed into the fiberglass bowl. Then he worked the chemical toilet pump with his foot while he extracted the gun hidden behind the toilet frame. He unlocked the safety and put the GLOCK 18 machine pistol in the fully automatic mode. He pumped the chemical toilet faster and harder to mask the noise as he snapped the slide back to cock the firing mechanism.

He opened the door and stepped back into the room with a smile on his face and his right arm behind his back.

The two men looked up from their conversation, beers in hand, expecting another round of victory toasts.

In one blindingly fast motion, Houghton pulled his right hand from behind his back, spread his legs and bent his knees in the firing stance, steadied the gun with his left hand, and fired a spray of bullets into their heads and chests. They were thrown backwards into their chairs. Their bottles tumbled to the floor. Dark holes in the front of their heads, splats of blood and brain bits from the back of their heads stained the chair backs, dead eyes open, arms and legs sprawled.

Houghton breathed a contented sigh and put the pistol on the little table. He looked at his dead, leaking colleagues and smirked. "Speaking as senior management," he said, "let me thank you for your hard work and sacrifice. You gave your all for that most worthy of causes—*my* compensation."

He pulled the cell phone from the clip on his belt and dialed. He waited then spoke. "Mission accomplished," he said in a flat American accent. Then he snapped the phone shut and put it in the limp outstretched hand of the man who had been called Jim Cavanaugh. He wrapped the dead fingers around the phone and squeezed the hand shut, then let the hand open and the phone drop to the floor.

Houghton collected the overnight bag from the cabinet, put his GLOCK 18 and the laptop computer inside it. He went to the desk and opened the top drawer. Inside were a collection of receipts for the purchases and rentals the men had made on the mission and a pack of traveler's checks, all one hundreds. He scooped up the checks, put them into the bag, and stepped outside.

Hunt stood waiting by the car. He had rigged a bomb under the gas tank of the Ayvil Control Systems Explorer. Set with a timer, the bomb would go off the next morning and set the truck on fire, something that would be certain to bring the police and firefighters of Nelsonville to this lonely clearing.

"Done," Houghton said. Then the men whose names were not Houghton and Hunt got into the dusty Impala and drove away.

21

Ken was torn by his success in the interviews. He liked the people at ADF and the way they seemed to genuinely like each other. He liked the informality of the smaller company and the apparently real feeling that the people were all building something together. Sandy was right: this young new company was everything Ayvil was not. The vice president of human resources told him he could expect an offer letter in a day or so.

Ken really needed to talk to Sandy. Right now. And he wanted to touch base with his office and his people, if only to see how it felt to talk to them as an outsider. But he was getting nothing when he called. No voice mails. Nothing. Just ringing to nowhere.

Then something familiar caught his eye on the TV screen over-head. It was a close-up of Cliff Reynolds, the Dayton TV newsman. Below him was the super, SPECIAL BULLETIN: INDUSTRIAL DISASTER. Ken pulled the phone away from his face and stared at the screen. What was Cliff Reynolds doing on Cleveland TV?

Ken watched as Reynolds's voice sounded in his brain. "A scene of unimaginable horror here at Ayvil Plastics," he thought he heard Reynolds say. "Mass death as an explosion and fire destroyed this plant and, from all reports, everyone who worked here." Cliff choked and struggled to regain his composure. As the newsman's words began to penetrate, Ken felt his whole body vibrating like a tuning fork.

What Ken saw and heard was a fractured collection of words and images, flying shards of the newsman's report registered in no particular order:

A store manager shaking his head with disbelief. "Deafening. An explosion like nothing I ever heard before. And I was in Vietnam."

Shots of the strip mall near the factory, with all its plate glass windows shattered.

Cliff's voice saying, "Vinyl chloride used by the plastics industry to produce polyvinyl chloride, the plastic resin used in many products."

"A massive explosion. Mushroom clouds."

A home video of a toddler on a swing. Suddenly the handheld camera lurches upward. Autofocus pulls the blur into clarity. A giant black mushroom cloud above the suburban rooftops, fireballs billowing beneath it.

Close-up of Reynolds fighting back tears.

"Coroner's estimates of the number of dead, already beyond five hundred, could go higher. Fire chief Joe Redmond said everyone was trapped inside. . . ."

"I remember when Ayvil management promised to save these jobs in Dayton."

File footage of Tom Pennington's interview at the airport that morning.

The mushroom cloud over the rooftops again. And again.

"State and federal officials will continue to monitor air and water samples, but assure the public that the air is safe."

He stared at the phone in his hand. Then snapped it shut. Horrifying, incredible, unthinkable thoughts were screaming through his head. Sandy, Sara, where are you? Are you safe? Sandy? Sara? He felt his mouth go dry. Trapped inside in an inferno-like hell on earth? Had he really heard that? All sound felt distant and muffled. His movements felt slowed down, as if the air around him had turned thick and viscous.

His thoughts were a broken kaleidoscope—images of Sandy and Sara, the faces of coworkers appearing randomly, the plant as he remembered it yesterday, and the flattened, smoking wreckage he saw on television.

He could not stop the questions from hammering in his brain. Did I cause this? What could have happened? Am I a murderer? Sandy, Sara? Are you all right?

He thought he heard his flight to Dayton being called. He turned in slow motion and walked on padded, tingling feet through the thick, heavy air. A part of him that he could not quite identify told him he had to move forward and get on the airplane.

As he boarded, the steward pointed at his cell phone and asked him to turn it off. He complied, dropped it into his briefcase, and forgot that it existed.

22

It was late afternoon when the commuter plane landed at Dayton International. As Ken climbed down the steps, he recognized one of Ayvil's Gulfstream jets about a hundred yards away on the tarmac. The little blue *A* symbol with the rings around it graced the tail fin and the nose. Like the jet that always brought Pennington to Dayton. Near it was a Lincoln Town Car, the driver closing the rear passenger door.

Clutching his briefcase, Ken broke into a run and headed toward the private jet.

"Sir! *Sir!*" the steward called after him. "You are *not* authorized to go there!" The lone attendant could not leave his post escorting the other passengers, so all he could do was yell at Ken.

Ken arrived at the car, panting. Tom Pennington jumped out. "Ken! Ken!" he shouted, grabbing Ken by the shoulders. "You're alive! Thank God you're alive!"

Ken stood frozen.

"My God, Ken!" Pennington took Ken into the backseat. "Where were you today? I mean . . . thank God you were away."

"I-I was in Cleveland." Ken stared into the darkness.

"Ken, what could have happened? What about our safety procedures?"

Ken said blankly, "My wife and daughter are in the day care center."

"Oh my God." Pennington put his hand on Ken's arm. "Look, maybe they're all right. Ken, my God, I—" Pennington's cell phone rang. "Yes, I'm on my way to the scene right now. Alert the authorities that I'm on my way. Did they send the list of employees from the HR database? Okay, I'll call when I get to the site. Bye."

They rode the rest of the way in silence.

23

The Ayvil complex was a blur of flashing lights piercing the darkness. Police cars—state and local, ambulances, fire trucks, trucks with alphabet soup markings, National Guard trucks painted in camouflage, unmarked cruisers and SUVs, and refrigerated trucks. The kind used to carry away bodies. Bulldozers and backhoes were starting to move the debris as searchers pulled out bodies for processing and transport to the makeshift morgue, a little city of tents farther out on the property away from the building. Helicopters chattered deafeningly overhead, sending spotlight beams into the steaming, charred wreckage of the building. A piercing, acrid, burned stench filled the air.

All approaches to the building were cordoned off with yellow tape. To one side were packs of news vans with their microwave antennas raised, a small forest of twelve-foot steel arms wrapped in coiled wire pointing toward the heavens. Officers were herding a growing crowd of distraught family members and keeping them corralled to the other side. Police, fire, and other officials talked on cell phones and walkie-talkies. Orders were shouted in all directions. People were screaming, people were crying, reporters with microphones were talking to their cameras in the glow of floodlights.

Pennington's car was halted by two state police officers at the barricade by the big white Ayvil sign.

"I'm here from the company," Pennington said through the car window.

"You Pendleton?" one officer asked.

"Penning— yes," he said, then mumbled, "close enough."

The officer squawked into his radio, "Tell the Incident Commander that the guy from the company is here." Something crackled in his earpiece. He motioned the car onward.

Another officer, a local cop with a radio headset, was waiting. "You from the company?" he asked as he opened the rear door.

Noise exploded into the backseat. "I'll bring you to the IC." He spoke into his radio, "I've got the management guy here. We're headed for Unified Command Post. Over."

Ken and Pennington got out of the car and followed the officer.

"We've got police from a dozen towns here plus state police," he explained over his shoulder, "fire from all over Monroe County, and National Guard. We've got the MEs from two counties. And everyone is stretched beyond the limit. We've got the NDMS on the way to handle—"

"What's that?" Pennington asked innocently.

"National Disaster, uh," the officer paused angrily, "National Disaster Medical Systems Mortuary Opera— Uh, extra refrigerated trucks to handle all these dead people. We're still combing the wreckage for survivors. So far, we haven't found any." He paused for a moment and shivered. "Never seen so many dead bodies in one place, all burned and pulverized," he muttered to himself. "Follow me, I'll take you to the Incident Commander. He's with the fire marshal and the men from OSHA and the EPA. They've all got questions for you."

He led them through the chaos to a telecommunications van parked on the grass, a microwave dish sticking up from the roof. Two technicians sat inside surrounded by a jungle of consoles. Hayward, the state police captain, and Evans, the fire marshal, stood by the open doors, wearing headset radios. They were burly men in their fifties. Hayward and Evans wore their everyday uniforms. A third man in an ill-fitting business suit paced beside them.

"This is the management guy," the officer announced perfunctorily, and walked away. Evans nodded then turned his back on the group and talked intently into his mouthpiece.

"Mr. Pennington," Hayward snapped, "this is the worst mass casualty incident I've ever seen. How did this happen?"

"I-I don't know, I just got here," Pennington said, knowing he sounded lame.

The man in the suit jumped in. "Where are your inspection certificates? Your paperwork? When were your last inspections? Were your people handling any materials they weren't supposed to?"

"I'm sorry, who are you?" Pennington asked.

"I'm from OSHA! And your company has a shitload of questions to answer."

Evans finished his radio call and joined the angry circle around Pennington. "How were your guys handling their feedstocks? What the hell did they do to blow this thing sky-high?" he asked. "We need plans of the building to investigate the wreckage. Where are your plans?"

"And how come nobody got out?" Hayward barked. "That's what I want to know."

Ken was paying no attention. He was surveying the scene under the floodlights. "My wife and daughter are in there," he said to no one in particular. "My wife, my daughter."

Hayward turned to Ken. "I'm sorry, sir," he said with mechanical sympathy. "We are going to start processing the bodies for identification tomorrow morning." Then he turned angry again. "Were *you* in charge? Huh, were you? Because if you were, you have a shitload to answer for. Don't you dare leave town, you hear?"

Under the floodlights and search beams of the helicopters, Ken could begin to recognize what parts of the wreckage were what. "The wing where the daycare center was," Ken cried urgently, "it's all gone!" Ken pointed at that corner of the smoking debris. He saw cameras flashing and body bags being carried away. "My wife and child were in there. My wife and baby!"

"Please, Officer," Pennington said quietly to Hayward, Evans, and the man from OSHA, "can we please continue our discussion privately? I'll answer everything I can."

Ken let out a scream then broke into a furious run in the direction of what had been the day care center.

"Stop him!" Hayward shouted.

24

Ken outran the three cops for the first hundred yards. His heart pounded. His legs flew. He was adrenaline on fire.

Then he stumbled in a rut, fell down, rolled over, and jumped back to his feet. It was enough to give the cops the chance to catch up.

As Ken neared the floodlit corner of wreckage where he had seen the cameras flashing and the body bags being carried out, the cops grabbed him in a flying tackle maneuver and brought him to the ground with a thud.

"Get off me!" Ken shrieked. "Get the fuck off me!" He was on his feet again and struggling. It took all three cops to restrain him.

"That's off-limits!" the lead cop said, gripping Ken around the shoulders.

"My wife! My daughter!" Ken wrestled against them, screaming. In the distance, he could see adult bodies and little child bodies, charred black. A pile of them huddled near what had been a doorframe. The technicians were all in haz-mat suits and gloves and masks. They took pictures and rolled the sticks of dead, blackened meat into body bags, zipped them up, and carried them away.

Ken strained to see. "My wife! My daughter!"

The cops lifted him off the ground. He kicked his legs furiously in the air. They turned him around and carried him away.

Ken howled, "Sandy! I'm here! Sandy!" Had he seen their bodies in that pile? No one could breathe inside those bags! Of course not—they were for dead people and dead people did not breathe. If Sandy and Sara were dead, Ken had urgent questions. Why am I still alive if you are not? But if I am alive, you can't be dead. We are all alive together. This is our life. This is not happening! This cannot be happening!

"I told you," the lead cop shouted, "you can't go in there!"

"Sandy, Sandy," Ken repeated as they dragged him away.

"Somebody take this guy home," the lead cop said.

"Tell that guy he better not leave town," Hayward barked over the radio.

"Yes, sir," the cop said into the mike clipped to his shoulder. He looked at Ken, who had lost his fury and just looked dazed.

The cop spoke into his mike. "I don't think this guy's going anywhere."

"Take this guy home," the lead cop said.

A young police officer stepped forward and took Ken by the arm. "Where do you live, sir?" he asked gently.

"Edgehill Street in Beaver Creek," Ken muttered.

The cop put his arm through Ken's arm and walked him to his cruiser.

They rode in silence.

When they pulled up to the darkened colonial at 26 Edgehill Street, Ken got out.

"Is there a relative's house you'd rather go to?" the cop asked.

"No," Ken said flatly. He walked up to the front door, got out his keys, and let himself in. The cop waited until Ken closed the front door and turned on a light. Then he drove away.

25

Ken walked through his house, turning on lights. He walked through every room on the ground floor, looking. Just looking. The message light on the answering machine was blinking furiously. The readout said that eighteen messages were waiting. Ken walked past it. He went upstairs to the bedrooms where he and Sandy and Sara had slept last night and awakened just this morning. In the master bedroom, he gazed at the unmade bed, the sheets holding the wrinkles their bodies had made when they rose to start this day. He picked up Sandy's pillow, pressed it against his face and inhaled. It was her scent, her living scent, her essence, her presence. Her. For the first time since he heard Cliff Reynolds on TV in the Cleveland airport, he started to cry. Softly and steadily like a gentle rain.

He walked into Sara's room. Her pink Hello Kitty pajamas were on the dresser beside her crib. He picked them up and inhaled. He could feel her tender baby skin in the scent. He took one more deep breath of Sara and walked downstairs.

He wanted to lie down but could not figure out where. He tried the couch in the living room. But his mind flooded with memories of a thousand everyday events that happened on that couch. He jumped up as if the couch were electrified. Every place he tried to sit or lie down felt haunted. Finally, he found a piece of neutral ground—the little hallway between the dining room and the kitchen.

He lay down on the floor in the narrow space. He liked the cold, hard wood. He lay on his side and curled his knees up into his chest. He wrapped his arms around his knees and hugged them tightly. He cried in waves. He felt nothing but an empty pit in his belly he knew would never go away.

26

When Justin Hildreth heard the news, he stared up at his butler with disbelief. Alejandro had run upstairs to the library of the red-brick Georgian town house on East Sixty-fifth Street on Manhattan's Upper East Side, sputtering about the television news. "They keel the workers," he said in his Argentine-German-Italian accent. Hildreth had just settled in to thumb through his priceless collection of Rembrandt etchings and listen to a new recording of the late Beethoven string quartets.

"Don't be ridiculous, Alejandro," Hildreth said as he looked up from the gilt leather box containing the black-and-white masterpieces. "You're making no sense. Now tell me again what you saw."

Hildreth's butler, a courtly man just a few years younger than his master, picked up the remote, turned on the TV in the wall of mahogany book shelves, and clicked on American News Network. There, under the title DISASTER IN OHIO, was Kat Pierce.

"It's a tragic scene of mass death. Inside this factory building here on the outskirts of Dayton, an estimated one thousand workers have died in what officials are calling the worst industrial accident in American history."

Hildreth gaped at the television.

Kat continued, "That's all we have for the moment. We're told there will be an official update sometime in the next few hours and we will bring that coverage to you. This is Kat Pierce for ANN at Ayvil Plastics outside Dayton, Ohio."

The telephone rang. Alejandro walked across the library to the Chippendale desk Hildreth had inherited forty years before, along with this town house, another town house in Georgetown, an ocean-front mansion in Southampton, and two hundred million dollars.

"Hildreth residence," the butler said in his heavy accent. "Just a moment, please. I will check." He covered the mouthpiece. "Mr. Hildreth, is Mr. Pennington. Is calling from Dayton."

Hildreth bounded across the room and took the cordless phone from the butler. Alejandro took a step toward the door. "No, Alejandro," he said, cupping the receiver, "please stay. I may need you."

The butler nodded and stood at attention, pretending, like a good servant, not to be listening to the phone conversation.

"Tom! I just saw the report on television."

"It's horrible." Pennington stood at the command post talking into his cell phone.

"Is the situation under control? Do you have it under control?"

"Yes, I believe so. It looks like all the workers are dead." Pennington's voice quivered. "Including the mothers and children in the day care center."

Hildreth took a deep breath. "Is Arch Paulson still in China?"

"He's on his way back."

Noise from the disaster scene filled the background.

"They're going to hold a press briefing in an hour," Pennington said.

"Our most important priority is the families of our people." Hildreth looked up at Alejandro. Alejandro made eye contact, knowing when his master wanted him to be a silent part of a conversation. "We will be judged on our decency and generosity in the face of this tragedy."

Alejandro nodded.

"Tom," Hildreth said softly into the phone, "this disaster could destroy the company."

27

Tom Pennington had just scribbled a few words on the back of a business card when his turn came to face the cameras. It was long past midnight. Captain Hayward read a short, carefully worded statement, reiterating what everyone already knew. An explosion and fire had destroyed the building. An estimated one thousand employees were dead, including twenty preschool children in the day care center. There appeared to be no survivors. The cause of the accident was under investigation.

Pennington stepped up to the forest of microphones on the lawn in the Joint Information Center. Cameramen and correspondents jockeyed for position, shoving and elbowing each other. Floodlights glared, flashes from still cameras popped on and off ceaselessly, the racket of helicopters came and went clamoring above.

Pennington looked deeply into the glass eyes before him and took a deep breath. "I'm Tom Pennington, Executive Vice President of Ayvil Industries. I'm in charge of Ayvil Plastics and several other divisions of the company." He stopped and cleared his throat. "I don't know how to express the shock, horror, and grief we all feel. It's, uh"—he sighed—"beyond the power of words." He cleared his throat again. "Our safety policies and procedures are second to none. Those of us who knew the people who died here, well, we may live on after this horrible event. But we will never fully recover. Never."

Pennington stared deeper into the cameras. "This business was in trouble, but we were in the process of turning it around. We were confident that the future would be good for Ayvil Plastics and the people who worked here." He shook his hand in the air; the gesture looked more defeated than defiant. A single tear began to trace a path from the corner of his right eye down his cheek. It glistened in the harsh light of the television cameras. He brushed the tear from his cheek.

"We cannot bring back our friends. But we can tend to the living. We can fulfill our human and corporate responsibilities. Ayvil Industries will establish a foundation, to be headquartered here in Dayton. That foundation will provide for the needs of the families and children and grandchildren of these Ayvil employees for the next twenty-five years. Let it serve as a living memorial to their enterprise. God speed this investigation and God rest their souls."

Pennington turned to leave. The reporters were shouting, "Mr. Pennington!" like a chorus of lunatics. They pushed and shoved, clamoring for attention. Pennington shook his head sadly. "Please. It's very late. Thank you." He turned and walked out of the spotlights into the dark.

28

At once, the mob of news crews scrambled to separate so that the reporters could do their individual wrap-ups. The reporters took their places just a few feet from each other, far enough apart not to interfere too badly with each other's microphones. They talked intently to viewers they could not see, staring deeply into their cameras.

Kat Pierce brushed her luminous bleached-blond hair back from her forehead and gave her cameraman his cue. "Okay, big fella, let's roll," she said, and winked. In the next instant she switched on her serious on-air voice and knit her beautiful brows into an expression of gravity. "We've just heard the first official briefing here at the scene of the Ayvil Industries disaster. An estimated one thousand employees, including twenty preschool children, are dead in an industrial accident. Ayvil Industries Executive Vice President Tom Pennington announced that his company would set up a foundation to provide for the surviving family members of the dead employees for the next twenty-five years. Mr. Pennington appeared visibly shaken and made a very emotional speech. From my vantage point very close to him, I could see that he had tears in his eyes as he spoke. I have covered a lot of executives from major companies under many different circumstances, and I can tell you that is the first time I've seen one of them cry. This is Kat Pierce for ANN at this scene of tragedy in Dayton."

29

Justin Hildreth pointed the remote at his television and clicked it to MUTE. The ANN newsroom appeared and offered bulletins-to-come on the TRAGEDY IN DAYTON.

"At least they're not calling it the Ayvil Tragedy," he said half to himself, half to Alejandro. The cordless phone rang. Hildreth grabbed it.

"Hello?"

There was a shower of static on the other end.

"Justin? Hello, Justin?"

"Arch? Is that you?"

More static. "Yes, it's me. Can you hear me?"

"Just barely. Go ahead."

"What the hell's going on there?"

"It's terrible. Just terrible." Hildreth looked across the library at Alejandro. "This could be worse than Bhopal was for Union Carbide."

"This was Pennington's fault!" Paulson barked. "He endangered the workers. He relaxed the standards. Pennington let this happen." More static.

"I'm losing you. Maybe you should call back."

"What did you say?"

"Just come back. Tom Pennington is on the scene."

Over the static from Paulson's end. "I told you, it's Pennington's fault."

"What?" Hildreth shouted. "I can barely hear you." More static. "Just come home." Hildreth pushed the button on the phone and handed it to Alejandro.

30

The Holiday Inn in Fairborn just off I-675 near the factory had never seen anything like it. The cash register rang and the liquor flowed as it never had before. Reporters and crew jammed the bar area and packed every booth.

Kat Pierce and her two crewmen sat crowded into one side of a booth. Another television journalist—a handsome, lantern-jawed man from CBS—and his two crewmen were packed in opposite them. The on-camera personalities, with their TV cheekbones and hair, looked like creatures from another planet beside their partners, the lumpy camera operators and soundmen.

"Can you believe the energy here at this ungodly hour?" said the CBS newsman.

"Reminds me of every war zone," the cameraman beside him said, slugging back his Scotch. "The more death there is, the noisier the boys get." He raised his empty tumbler to his mouth. "And, uh, the girls," he added, nodding at Kat.

"Kiss my ass," Kat said. The cameraman smirked. "In your dreams, buddy," she said, "in your dreams." She held her green Heineken bottle by the throat and took another long gulp. Just like one of the boys.

The CBS journalist looked at Kat and asked, "So what do you make of that guy Pennington? The tears, the humanitarian stuff. Do you buy it?"

"What's to buy?" she asked. "He was counting on those people to make him a hero. And now they are dead and his company is fucked like no other company has ever been. I think he gave us the real thing."

"Well the camera sure loves him." The CBS guy shook his head.

She smiled and said, "Yeah, he is awfully cute." Across the table, the cameraman coughed into his glass. Kat mused, "I could do a great segment with him. That'd give me a shot at an anchor spot in New York. Get me off the road and out of shit holes like this."

The cameraman looked up at a commotion by the door. "Speak of the devil," he said. "Guess who just walked in?"

31

Like the Red Sea under the command of Moses, the crowd parted to make way for Tom Pennington. The room hushed. He stopped and stood for a moment. His jacket and tie were long since discarded; the sleeves of his white shirt were rolled up.

"Guys, please," he announced sheepishly, "I'm off the record now, okay?" He walked up to the space in the center of the bar. The noise of the crowd resumed.

"Grey Goose on the rocks," he said quietly to the bartender. He put down a twenty-dollar bill.

"You want to run a tab?" The bartender stared at Pennington, comparing the real man with the image he had seen on TV.

"No thanks," Pennington said. "Just make it a double, please. And keep the change." The bartender filled the tumbler with ice and poured to the rim. Pennington sipped, closed his eyes, and held the liquid in his mouth. Finally, he swallowed. When he opened his eyes, Kat Pierce stood before him, a little rumpled but still glamorous in her sleek gray Donna Karan pantsuit. She was five-four to his six-one.

She raised her bottle. "I'm not here. You're not here. This never happened. Journalist's honor."

"*Journalist's* honor?" Pennington asked.

Kat smiled. "How about scout's honor? I earned lots of merit badges."

He smiled back. "Well, in that case, here's to not being here and not having this conversation." He touched the rim of his glass against her bottle and took another sip.

"I'm Kat Pierce," she said, extending her hand.

"Oh yes, I know who you are," he said, taking it. "I've seen you on TV. I'm Tom Pennington."

"I've seen *you* on TV, too." She held their handshake a moment longer than necessary. "I was very moved by what you said tonight."

Pennington looked down.

She touched his arm gently. "No, really."

He looked up. "I-I tried to do what was right under the circumstances. But you never know how things will come across."

"Don't worry. You came across."

"Really?" he asked hesitantly.

"Really." She examined him closely. In just a few minutes of contact, she had seen Tom Pennington, the rich handsome corporate power player. She had also seen his tears of grief, felt his warm sexy smile, his desire to be a nice guy, and now his boyish vulnerability.

Pennington's shoulders drooped. "I'm so tired, but I just couldn't go to sleep."

Even his exhaustion looked good. This man just kept getting better. Kat raised one pretty eyebrow and took his hand. "I hope you don't mind my being so blunt. But after being in so many war zones, you realize that life is shorter than you think. Let's go talk in the lobby. It should be quieter there."

"Good idea." He finished his drink in one long gulp and followed her out.

They found two chairs in a dark corner. Kat left her shoes, sleek but practical Prada pumps with a low heel, on the floor and curled her legs up under herself.

"So tell me about Tom Pennington," she said.

"Why don't we start with Kat Pierce?" Pennington said, stretching out his legs. "After all, she's usually the one asking the questions. How did you become a famous TV journalist?"

"Semi-famous," she said. "The network tells me I need to work on my Q scores." She was referring to the Performer Q surveys that rate fame and likeability. "Let me give you the *Reader's Digest* condensed version." She brushed her hair back with one hand, a gesture that she knew was at once crisp and sexy. "Kat's short for Katherine, which I hate almost as much as Kathy. Uh, small-town girl, blue-collar family. Washington State, the arid eastern half where nobody goes. State university, journalism major. First job at a newspaper then at the local TV station. Then one local news job after another, one Podunk place to the next. Always sending out that tape of your best stories in hopes of a job in a bigger market. Try to get seen by a network. Finally, in Billings, Montana, I got the call from ANN to become a junior correspondent. From there, it's a blur of airports, wars, and disasters." She gripped an imaginary microphone. "This is Kat Pierce reporting live from another godforsaken hellhole for ANN."

"And the personal side?" Pennington asked hesitantly.

"Nah, hardly any. Total workaholic. Oh, I married right out of college, but it was a disaster from the first." She winced. "We were both so relieved when it was over, we actually parted friends. Well, sort of. It's like we lived through this terrible nightmare together and couldn't believe we escaped with our lives. Imagine divorce as a bonding experience."

Pennington smiled.

"Okay, Tom Pennington, now it's your turn."

"It's amazing," he said, "you and I are so alike. We're like two peas in a pod. I see myself in so much of your story." Kat sat up attentively. "I, too, grew up blue collar in another middle-of-nowhere place. Mine was Scranton, Pennsylvania. I was the chronic over-achiever. Won scholarships to get the hell outta there, but I would have jumped on a freight train if that hadn't worked."

"Where'd you go?" she asked.

"Mm, uh, a prep school then college and the business school."

She knew that people who said "the business school" meant Harvard. "Come on," she teased, "out with it."

Pennington lowered his eyes and mumbled, "Hotchkiss, Princeton, and Harvard."

Kat whistled. He was also not impressed with his pedigree. Quite a change from the usual Manhattan alpha males and their Ivy League braggadocio.

"Listen, I was the kid on financial aid who worked two jobs and studied his ass off. Working too hard, always proving myself. Sound familiar?"

"Uh-huh," Kat said. Then they said in unison, "Two peas in a pod."

Kat lifted Pennington's left hand; he wore no wedding band. "Are you, uh?"

Pennington sighed. "I met Katherine junior year and we got married just before graduation. She worked to put me through business school. I landed a job with a big consulting firm. We felt like we were finally going to make it. We took off the last week in August to visit her family on the coast of Maine."

He took a deep breath; his voice faltered. "That was eighteen years ago. We went for a day sail. One of those squalls blew in out of nowhere. You know the weather up there. We crashed on the rocks, the rigging snapped, the boom went flying and slammed into Katherine's head." He paused again. "She died there in my arms." He looked away. "She was two months pregnant."

Kat took his hand again.

"Since then I've been married to my work. Like you." Pennington sat up straight. "Thanks, Kat, I think I can get some sleep now." As he let go of her hand, he dragged his fingertips gently across her palm and fingers, just barely touching. As the very tips of their fingers touched, he held the touch for an extra second. It was electric and very seductive. "I'm really glad we met, Kat Pierce."

"Me, too, Tom Pennington." She reached up and stroked his cheek. It was a frank, grown-up invitation. "Remember what I said about living in a war zone?"

"Sure do," he said.

"I'm room 418," she said.

"Will I see you tomorrow at the site?"

"If you want to."

"I want to."

"Then you will."

32

Ken woke up on the floor and knew that everything in his house was about to cause him pain. Every chip in the woodwork, every spot on the upholstery would rekindle a memory. And the more intimate and ordinary the item, the more deeply it would sear his soul. He knew as he headed for the shower that the sight of Sandy's razor and collection of shampoos and conditioners would be excruciating. Her toothbrush next to his in the porcelain holder above the sink was a knife in his heart. The everyday things we leave in their places, not knowing that this will be the day we die, torture the ones we leave behind.

He showered and shaved and thought about whether or not he should begin to clean up the objects his wife and daughter would never come back to use. He decided to leave everything exactly as it was.

He passed through the kitchen and felt no need for coffee or breakfast. He bent down and took one long drink of water directly from the kitchen tap and walked outside. A white rental car was parked in the driveway. Phil Lambert stood beside it.

"I called over and over again," Phil said matter-of-factly. "You never picked up."

Ken thought, That's because I didn't know what to say after murdering my wife and child. But all Ken said was, "Oh."

"Are they . . . uh?" Phil asked.

"Gone," Ken whispered. "Everyone. They said so." He stood face-to-face with his former brother-in-law. He looked into those big dark eyes and saw a flash of Sandy. Phil wrapped his arms around Ken.

Ken's voice cracked as he said, "Phil, I was in charge."

Yes, Phil thought, you *were* in charge, and I should probably kill you. But I'll give you the benefit of the doubt because Sandy would want me to—but only for a while. Phil let go and motioned to his car. "Get in," he said. Ken did as he was told.

33

The cop at the barricade by the big white Ayvil sign stared at Ken's ID keycard. He crosschecked Ken's name against a list in his clipboard. Then he stared at Ken as if he had seen a ghost. "You . . . you're, you're on the list of people who died."

"Uh, I was out of town yesterday," Ken explained.

"Jeez, you are one lucky man," the state trooper said.

Ken was about to say something, then thought better of it. A blue refrigerated panel truck passed them. Ken and Phil and the cop watched it in silence. Then the cop waved them through.

Phil found a space on the field where they were directing vehicles. The air was as acrid as the night before. As Phil and Ken were walking toward the trailers that looked like command headquarters, they met a sixtyish woman who had just come from the line of family members being processed by aid workers and cops. "How could this happen?" the woman asked the air. "They put some new idiot in charge. I heard he wasn't even an engineer. Terry told me they were making cuts and trying all sorts of new things. Now look what that idiot went and did!" She started to cry.

Ken felt nauseated. The woman retreated into her grief and walked on.

Then Ken saw Pennington, freshly changed and perfectly groomed, talking to the state police commander he vaguely remembered from the night before. He walked across the grass to the command center. Pennington, Hayward, and Evans were deep in conversation. Ken saw that Evans and Hayward had not been to bed, or at least had not bothered to shave that morning.

"Tom," he said loud enough to be heard as he neared the two men. Pennington excused himself and walked toward Ken.

He put his arm around Ken's shoulder and walked him to the side, out of earshot of Evans and Hayward. "Ken, did you, uh . . ."

"There was nothing left. Just bodies."

"Oh, Ken. I am so sorry. What a nightmare. Have you had any sleep? Oh God, what you must be going through."

Ken shrugged.

"What strength you've got. I can't say I'd be so self-possessed."

"D-d-do they, do they know what happened?" Ken stammered.

"It looks like an accident," Pennington said softly. Then he looked at the man beside Ken. "Tom Pennington," he said, introducing himself to Phil.

"Family," Phil said.

Ken looked out at the wreckage, still smoking and steaming. The destruction was far worse than it had seemed at night because now you could see how little was left. Pennington grabbed Ken's arm and pulled him closer, both to get his attention and to whisper in his ear, "Ken, *how* on earth did this happen? We never had any safety vio—"

Hayward jumped in and grabbed Ken roughly. "Yeah, that's what I want to know! If you were in charge here, how in the fucking hell did this happen?"

34

Arch Paulson's town car turned north onto Sixth Avenue from Fifty-first Street. A herd of journalists waited in the plaza in front of the office tower.

"Shit," Paulson said. "Jackals."

"Yes," said Lew Simons, "but you can't let them know that's what you think."

"We'll make Pennington pay for this—you wait and see."

"Arch," Simons pleaded, "please. Not now. Please. Just read the statement. The lawyers have gone over it, word for word. It lays the groundwork for everything you asked for. Just stick to the script. Please, Arch. Then leave them to me. You go on to the board meeting."

"Okay," Paulson grumbled, "goddamn jackals."

The car pulled over. The mob ran across the plaza. As Paulson and Simons stepped out, the journalists and their crews surrounded them.

Paulson and Simons stood side by side, a big bear looming over a little weasel, as the reporters shouted questions. Simons raised his hand. The mob quieted and a dozen microphones were shoved in front of him.

"Mr. Paulson has a brief statement. Then he has to go to an emergency board meeting." Paulson stepped forward, blinking at the flashbulbs. He shuffled back and forth from one foot to the other, holding the sheet of paper. He cleared his throat, took a deep breath, and began to read. He barely looked up.

"At a moment like this, words cannot do justice to our thoughts and emotions. We are shocked and saddened by this terrible accident, an accident that has no precedent in our company's history. Our prayers are with the families of those who died. Our lawyers are preparing more detailed statements that will be made public later this morning. As Chief Executive, I plan to lead a task force, working closely with the authorities, to find out exactly what happened and why. Furthermore, I will personally lead a corporate-wide safety audit of all our operations all around the globe. Our purpose is to do everything humanly possible to ensure that nothing like this ever happens again. This initiative will take some time to complete, but I am committed to seeing it through for the sake of everyone in this great company."

Paulson lowered his script, folded it, and put it in the inside pocket of his suit coat. He looked up and was silent. In a meeting of subordinates, this would have been their signal to retreat because the boss was done. The journalists did no such thing. They started shouting out more questions, one louder than the other. Paulson looked annoyed and a bit alarmed.

Simons raised his arm again. "Please! Please! I'll take your questions." He gestured to one side of the crowd to indicate they should let Paulson go through. "Thank you, Mr. Paulson," he said to his CEO as he pushed him gently toward the opening. Paulson smiled an awkward, nervous smile. With a burst of light flashes, the cameras captured it. Paulson then lumbered away into the lobby of the glass-and-steel tower.

35

High above the plaza, Macmillan and Czerwinski stood looking out Macmillan's window on the forty-second floor. It was directly below Paulson's office but was less than one-third its size and had none of its opulence.

"The reporters look like they're going to eat poor old Lew alive," Czerwinski said.

"Can you believe this is happening?" Macmillan rubbed his temples. "Donna kept me up all night. She's got the TV on, all upset, crying about the people, the children, how could this happen in my company? I said to her, Jesus, what about the stock? What about my bonus? She got mad and asked how could I talk about money at a time like this? And I said, how could I not?"

"We could be really fucked, you know," Czerwinski said, "like Johns Manville with those asbestos claims."

"Yeah, I know. Take all that nice Ayvil paper and wipe your ass with it."

They stood in silence for a while. Sounds of the crowd below echoed distantly.

Macmillan went back to the chair behind his desk. "How do you think it happened?"

"How should I know?" Czerwinski sat down facing him. "I heard Arch is looking to crucify Pennington for it."

"Well, crucifying Pennington sounds good to me," Macmillan said. "It was his division, after all."

"Know what I think?" Czerwinski asked in a whisper.

"What?" Macmillan leaned closer.

"I think Arch is secretly happy it happened."

Macmillan snorted. "No way! A thousand employees dead?"

"It's tough shit for them," Czerwinski said, "but it's the opportunity he was hoping for. I'm telling you, he's going to put on this serious face about industrial safety and all that. But underneath he's think-ing, 'Wow, I can't believe my fucking luck.' "

"Come on," Macmillan snapped. "Arch is a miserable son of a bitch and a ballbuster, I'll grant you that. But he's not that kind of monster."

Czerwinski shrugged. "Oh yeah?"

36

Paulson was surprised at the message light on his private line. He dialed voice mail immediately to listen to the message on the line that hardly anyone knew existed.

"One unheard message," the system's friendly female voice announced, "sent yesterday at two fifteen P.M." A male voice made wobbly by the cell phone signal said, "Mission accomplished." Then a click. Paulson instantly coded in DELETE and looked nervously around his empty office. "Message deleted," the friendly woman told him.

He surveyed the pile of news stories and transcripts of broadcasts on his desk. "Get me Pennington on his cell in Dayton, would you, please," he barked at his intercom.

"Mr. Paulson," the secretary said over the speaker, "his cell phone is ringing, but it sounds busy and he's not picking up."

"Let me try," Paulson fumed, "give me the number." She recited it and he dialed his own phone. It rang and rang and at the end of each ring there was a little beep, indicating that the line was connected but engaged in another call. He hung up and tried again. Same thing.

"Get me Justin Hildreth at home, please." He waited impatiently. "So? Where is he?"

"I'm sorry, Mr. Paulson. I'm not getting through. It rings, but he won't switch lines to pick up, either. It just rings and rings."

"Keep trying!" He pounded his desk. After a few more minutes, the secretary came back. "I got his butler. Mr. Hildreth is on his way over. He's in the car. He'll be here soon."

Paulson reached for the videocassette beside the press notices. It was labeled with the date, the time aired, 1:45 A.M. EDT, and the notation JOINT INFO CENTER/T. PENNINGTON. He picked it up, walked into the private den beside his office, popped it into the VCR, and, remote in hand, sat down on the couch to watch. It was the same five-minute piece that was running on all the stations everywhere. Paulson watched it three times through. Each time he got angrier. He watched the Incident Commander make a dry, factual statement. Then he gazed at handsome Tom Pennington crying. As he watched Pennington finish his speech for the fourth time, he barked out loud at the TV screen.

"A foundation? A foundation to take care of them for twenty-five years? Who gave you authorization to make a stupid fucking promise like that?"

A voice from the doorway answered. "I did."

It was Justin Hildreth.

"Oh, Justin," Paulson said, trying to recover his composure, "of course. Please come in and sit down." Paulson walked into his office and sat behind his desk. Hildreth waved away the offer of a chair and paced back and forth.

"I knew Pennington's methods were going to lead to no good. I just knew it. From the minute he sprang that stupid turnaround idea on us."

Hildreth stopped suddenly and turned to face Paulson. "You told me the turnaround attempt was *your* idea, not his."

Paulson looked down. "I did. I did. It, uh, *was* my idea. It's Pennington's methods I object to. All that touchy-feely New Age crap. Jesus H. Christ! In an industrial company, you've got procedures and protocols you follow. I gave him too much rope. Now look what he went and did."

Hildreth looked out the window. It was a beautiful summer morning, the sky was cloudless and radiant blue, the skyscrapers glistened like temples of success. The air had not yet turned smoggy.

Hildreth talked to the view. "In the months ahead, this company is going to be fighting for its life."

"And I'm going to be leading that fight." Paulson got up from his desk and stood beside Hildreth. "I've never needed your support more than I do today. For the sake of the company we've built together, for the sake of the principles and values we share," Paulson rested one hand on Hildreth's shoulder, "I need your support in cleaning up this mess my way."

Paulson lowered his voice and tightened his grip on Hildreth's shoulder. "I would never say this in the board meeting. But between you and me, we should prepare to sacrifice Pennington to the wolves. First, because he brought this trouble on us. But, more important, because we're going to need to deflect the blame away from the company."

Hildreth stared out the window. "Well," he said. "You *are* the CEO."

37

"I am *not* going to let an Ayvil situation happen here!" the man from the Nuclear Regulatory Commission barked at Michael Guillaume and Howard Polski, Vice President of Quality Management from General Industries' Power Systems division. The three men were in the tiny windowless office just down the hall from the control room at Perry's Bend.

"Gerald," Guillaume said, "that's not fair. That was an accident in a plastics factory, we're not—"

"First of all, it's *Mr.* Davenport to you," Gerald Davenport, resident NRC inspector, said. "And second, I'm talking about things that are my responsibility to prevent. Pre-vent! There's a lesson for us all in what just happened there."

Davenport stared at Guillaume over the edge of the reading glasses perched on the tip of his nose and did not like what he saw. Guillaume, with his taut ebony skin, dramatic angular features, and still-athletic build, looked like a man in his early forties, although he was actually fifty-two. The only sign that might betray his age was the slightest beginning of a sag beneath his strong, determined jaw.

"This plant," Davenport said, "has been plagued with problems, all of them well documented. Like the defective gasket in the turbine trip oil system, inadequate maintenance of the backup diesel generating system, corroded cables leading to it, delayed activation of the Emergency Operating Facility, inadequate root-cause analysis in the inspection methodology, which led to the tube failure we just witnessed. Plus a history of valve seals and temperature sensors not being replaced on schedule."

"But all that happened under the old management from Dynergetix," Guillaume said.

"Your company bought Dynergetix. You bought their problems. I don't care whose fault they are, they belong to you now."

"That's why we put Howard Polski in here," Guillaume said as he motioned toward his colleague. Polski was a broad-shouldered forty-five-year-old engineer with a wide pale face and a brush cut. "Howard spearheads Quality Management for our entire Power Systems division. Nobody has more experience than Howard."

"I'll believe it," Davenport said, "when I see the results myself. I don't care what anybody has done elsewhere."

"Yes, of course, Mr. Davenport, you are right." Guillaume knew that his job at this moment was to suck it up. Guillaume also knew it had been a mistake to wear a business suit to this meeting. Polski had the nuclear engineer's uniform down—tan Dockers and a permanent press shirt that had never seen an iron, let alone an expensive hand laundry service, and no sport coat. And around the neck a plain inexpensive tie and the lanyard with his photo ID and keycards. Guillaume's original instinct to bring a change of casual clothes on the corporate jet was the one he should have followed. But the day had been so hectic. The 7:00 A.M. breakfast with Wall Street analysts in New York, the lunch in Cleveland with the Jobs Council of the manufacturers' association, the flight to Perry's Bend for this meeting, then back on the jet for dinner in Chicago with a panel of institutional investors, all in one day.

Yes, he should have brought a change of clothes for this meeting. He realized it the minute he sat down in front of the beat-up old desk in the cramped little room.

He watched Gerald Davenport, federal bureaucrat, watching him. Gerald Davenport, fat, pasty white man nearing sixty. Polyester shirt from Sears or Wal-Mart. Gerald Davenport, sizing up Guillaume's meticulously hand-tailored suit of fine Scottish wool—lapels perfect, seams flawlessly following the lines of Guillaume's form, real buttonholes at the cuffs of the suit jacket, hand-sewn with a care and attention to detail no factory-made garment could ever have. Yes, Guillaume realized, when you added up his shoes from Lobb's of London, his custom-made shirt from Jermyn Street and bespoke Savile Row suit, his Rolex President and the gold cuff links, he was wearing more than Davenport made in three months.

Davenport was also regarding him with a look Guillaume had seen before—the look an angry, frustrated, low-rent white man reserves for a successful black man. Guillaume could feel it. And he knew, given his corporate responsibilities, his job was to sit here and take whatever abuse Gerald Davenport felt like dishing out.

"Now, I want to see your supervisor at the prehearing."

"The hearing?" Guillaume asked. "Who said anything about a hearing? Why would you escalate this into a hearing? We are one hundred percent in compliance."

"I didn't say hearing. I said *pre*hearing. To ascertain whether or not we will need a full hearing."

"Excuse me," Guillaume said with the humility he knew was expected, "I'm not familiar with a prehearing."

"I'm afraid you do have a lot to learn, Mr. Guillaume. A prehearing is off the record, informal. It is my prerogative and, for your information, I'm doing it to protect your company's record as well as the public's safety. Now who is your supervisor at General Industries?"

"Why, I report to the CEO, Harry Warren."

Not looking up from his clipboard, Davenport asked, "Good, can you arrange for your supervisor to be at the prehearing?"

"Mr. Davenport, he is the *chairman* of General Industries. His schedule is—"

Davenport cut him off. "According to Article Two in my QMS documentation, the CEO of General Industries—" Davenport ruffled through sheets to get to a page near the bottom of the stack in his clipboard. Finding it, he read aloud. "—'the CEO defines the overall quality policy and promotes a culture of conformance to requirements, customer satisfaction, and continual improvement, and is ultimately responsible for its implementation, through appointed representatives.' " He looked up. "That's what it says and that's what we're here to work on."

Guillaume sighed. "Yes, I can arrange for Mr. Warren to attend."

"Excellent." Davenport smirked at Guillaume. "That would be a very," he paused, "a very *affirmative* action." Davenport looked down again. "Thank you, Mr. Guillaume, that's it for now. We'll see you at the prehearing."

Guillaume and Polski stood up to leave. They exchanged looks. Guillaume thought about saying something. Anything. Then, as he had learned to do so effectively in corporate life, he thought again. And said nothing as he and Polski walked out.

38

Hayward was grilling Ken with angry questions. Phil stood in the background, watching. Behind them, the technicians of death and disaster picked through the ruins of the charred Ayvil building.

"But you have no direct experience handling those chemicals yourself, do you?" Hayward asked.

"No," Ken said, cringing, "I'm from marketing."

"But your mission *was* to shake up the business and try new things? Isn't that right?" Hayward asked.

"Yes," Ken said, "but not where safety was concerned."

Hayward ignored him. "You have any idea how bad this is? There were bodies piled up around the doorways. Incinerated. Crushed by the blasts then burned by the inferno. It looks like people couldn't open the emergency exit doors. Are you familiar with your Magnalock system? Are you?"

"Uh, yes."

"Then what about the dwell time setting?"

"What?"

"I thought you said you understood one of the most important safety and security systems in the building! Huh? Dwell time, dwell time! That's the time it takes for the door to unlock after someone touches the handle in an emergency." Hayward folded his arms across his chest. "It's fifteen seconds, no more, by law."

"Uh, that was Al Darling's department." Ken was struggling to sound competent. "He was a top man in facilities management and security systems."

"You mean you had *one* man doing *both* jobs? Security is a complex function these days. Isn't that stretching your people a little thin?"

"Captain Hayward, please," Pennington interjected.

Evans jumped in for his chance to pile on. "Tell me, Mr. Olson, why did they put the system on test again?"

"What do you mean?" Ken asked.

"They put all the alarm systems on test," Evans said angrily. "Why? Can you tell me *why*?"

Ken looked blank. He was ready to be arrested, even eager. He was sure he would be convicted. If he got the death penalty, it would be a mercy. Then again, maybe he didn't even deserve that.

"On test means," Evans explained in a huff, "the central station will ignore any and all signals it receives from the facility. Police and fire, too."

"Hey, Charlie!" Another officer burst into the group. "This case is getting stranger by the minute." Catching his breath, the officer blurted out the story in chunks. "Cops in Nelsonville. Two stiffs in a mobile home in the woods. Shot in the head. A burned-out SUV from Ayvil Control Systems, in the trailer, plans of this building. Plus, get this—" He had his breath now and was ready for the big news. "—agriculture permits for ammonium nitrate. About two hundred pounds of it!"

Hayward jumped to his feet and pulled the officer aside.

"Agriculture permits?" Ken asked Phil.

"That's how you make ANFO," Phil said, shaking his head. "Mix ammonium nitrate with diesel fuel. Like the Oklahoma City bomb. This place was blown up with a bomb, a big one."

Ken looked like he might crumple; Phil grabbed him by the shoulders. Whatever had happened here, it was not his brother-in-law's fault. This is the man Sandy loved. And he would need an ally now. Phil whispered into Ken's ear, "Just hang on, bro. I'm with you."

Hayward turned back to the group and pointed a finger at Ken. "Let's go. *You!* Maybe you can ID them. Just remember, you guys have no fucking rights at my crime scene."

39

The clearing in the woods was strung with yellow tape and teeming with cops. Technicians worked inside the mobile home and around the burned-out SUV. Ken, Phil, and Pennington stood around as they waited for Hayward to summon Ken. Phil helped fill the time by explaining what the various experts would be doing at a crime scene like this—like a sports commentator but grimmer.

"These guys are in way over their heads," Phil said to Ken while Pennington was on one of his many cell phone calls.

"Well, they sure know how to bully," Ken said.

"Professional bluster," Phil said, "one part testosterone and two parts bullshit. Every guy in a uniform has it. Believe me, the Feds will push them aside soon as they get here. This is their case."

Ken gave him a puzzled look.

"Somebody paid professionals to plan and execute this," Phil explained.

"But who would bomb a plastics factory?" Ken's mind was reeling. Phil shrugged.

Hayward finally approached. "This heat," he said, waving his hand, "really cooks them. You ready to see if you can identify them?"

Ken nodded.

"Cover your mouth," Hayward said. Pulling a handkerchief from his pocket, Ken followed. They stepped inside the sweltering little space.

Everything was as Houghton had left it, except for the police chalk marks, tape, and notes. The two men lay in their death poses, their wounds gone black, flies swarming in and around them. Their skin had gone gray and was starting to puff up like grisly inflated blowups of once-human creatures. In death, the enzymes and microorganisms that power and feed the body turn on us and start to feed *on* the body, reducing us to a gassy balloon of noxious fluids and bone, a banquet and breeding ground for insects and their larval young.

Ken coughed into his handkerchief and held his breath against the stench. He stared at the bodies. Yes, it was them. He nodded. He saw the building plans unfurled on the table. From behind his handkerchief, Hayward shot Ken a look that asked if he had seen enough. Ken nodded and followed him out into the sunshine.

"That's them!" Ken said.

They walked up to Pennington and Phil.

"That's them. The men who were working on the HVAC installation. I don't remember their names, but you'll find them in the logbook. They signed in every day."

"*If* we recover the logbook," Hayward said.

"There were two more—another guy, I don't remember his name, and the boss."

"Did you ever check them out with the company?" Hayward asked.

"I don't think so, why should we?" Ken answered defensively. "We exchanged e-mails, invoices, phone calls to and from their offices at Control Systems. This was a relationship between two sister companies."

"That's probably what somebody went to a lot of trouble to make you think," Phil interjected.

Hayward shot him an angry look and turned to Ken. "Now what about this guy, their boss?"

Ken tried to recall the man in as much detail as he could. "His name was, uh, Hower, I think, maybe Howard. No, Houghton. Yeah, Houghton."

"That's what *he said* his name was," Phil said.

"He was six feet tall, maybe a little taller," Ken said, "solid, big-boned. I'd say early forties. Had a goatee, glasses, short hair. Kind of pale white skin. A funny accent." Ken tried to visualize Houghton in detail. "The goatee, the glasses," he said, turning to Phil, "it was all a disguise, right? Like his name?"

Phil nodded. Hayward grunted.

Ken was angry at himself. At the time, he had not paid much attention to the man. Now he wanted to have a clear picture of him in his mind. To be able to recognize him someday. And kill him. Ken had never felt that before. Suddenly he ached with the desire to choke the breath out of another human being.

"Now get this," Hayward said, "there was a cell phone near one of the stiffs. The last call it made was yesterday, a few hours after the incident. To a number at your company's headquarters in New York. Turns out it's the private line of your chief executive, Archibald Paulson."

Ken's mouth fell open.

Pennington groaned.

"Well, we can sit back and relax," Hayward said with a mixture of resignation and disgust. "Fibbie's coming. The Feds will be here soon."

Ken looked at Phil, who gave him a knowing nod.

40

The FBI team treated the local cops like children. The agent-in-charge, Ted Decker—forty-five, tall and gruff, with a widow's peak, flat nose, and gray eyes—flaunted his contempt. After inspecting the crime scene with his own team, Decker had his second-in-command talk with Hayward and Evans. Then he led the caravan of cruisers, government sedans, and rental cars back to the Ayvil plant. The group gathered at the new central command post, a communications van far more elaborate than the Ohio State Police van beside it.

Decker announced to no one in particular, "Our technicians found traces of ANFO right off the bat." He shot a condescending look at Hayward and Evans. "What's more, it looks like they had more ANFO charges planted all around the building. That's why it blew so high and burned so fast. If you gentlemen had just analyzed the blast pattern, it was all right there. All you had to do was look for it."

Hayward sniffed and turned his head.

Evans said defensively, "We were working on it. We knew it didn't all add up. That was on our list of possibilities."

Decker looked at the circle of civilians and stared at Lambert.

"Decker," Phil said as he stepped forward.

"Lambert," Decker said curtly, "I thought that was you back at the trailer. What brings you here? You're not still—?"

"No," Phil said. "Retired. I'm with Medusa now."

"Go for the gold, eh?" Decker said.

"You two know each other?" Ken asked.

"We worked together," Phil said, "a long time ago."

"Yeah," Decker said, "a *long* time ago."

Phil gave Ken a look that said, *I'll explain later.*

"Agent Decker," Pennington said, stepping forward, "there's something I think I should share with you."

"What's that?" Decker asked impatiently.

"A voice recording."

"Of what?" Decker asked without interest as he made another call.

Pennington walked back to the town car where he had left his briefcase. He came back holding a microcassette player. Decker looked up from his call, only half paying attention to Pennington.

"When I decided that a turnaround was worth trying," Pennington explained, "I knew I was risking my job. So, I, uh, well, based on what I've seen with employment law and terminations and all that—"

"Yes?" Decker asked impatiently.

"Well, I started taking a recording device with me into my meetings with Mr. Paulson. It was concealed. I wanted to be sure that I had a record of exactly what transpired. In case it came up in a legal proceeding if I were terminated."

Nervously, Pennington passed the little tape player back and forth between his hands. "At the time I didn't think anything of the strong language Arch used. We all use dramatic figures of speech sometimes. But now, well—"

Decker tapped his foot.

Pennington cued up the microcassette player. He listened and jockeyed the cassette backward and forward a few times to find the right spot. "This was right after Arch saw the video of me at the town meeting where I had publicly committed to the turnaround. I told him I had a report that provided the rationale," Pennington said as he pushed the PLAY button.

The first voice was Pennington: *"Arch, it's all in the report. I think you'll find it very compelling. You'll see. I've done exactly what you asked me to do."*

The next voice was Paulson: *"Well, that may be true. But you did not do what you goddamn well knew I expected you to do! Which is to close down that operation and get it off our goddamn books! Why is that so hard to understand? What's this about a turnaround? Turnaround, my ass! What are you doing giving those people hope? Their business is dead. Those people are dead. Now, if you don't know how to go in there and kill them off, I'll go in myself and show you how it's done."*

Pennington pushed the STOP button. "It's too incredible to think about. The chief executive of—"

"Nothing is incredible in my line of work, Mr. Pennington," Decker said. "I want a copy of that."

"Certainly." Pennington handed the machine in Decker's direction.

Decker waved Pennington away with a dismissive gesture. "I've got to go to New York and ask that guy Paulson some questions," he said, looking at his watch. "I guess I'll recognize his voice now."

"I have a private jet at the airport," Pennington offered. "You're welcome to use it."

"So do I," Decker said arrogantly, and turned to leave.

"Uh, Agent Decker," Phil said to the FBI man's back, "maybe you should check for any large wire transfers to offshore banks."

Decker stopped in midstep and almost turned his head back to look at Phil. "Gee, thanks, Lambert," he grunted, "I never woulda thought of that. Not in a million years." Decker smirked and walked away.

"How do you know him?" Ken asked Phil.

"Long story, long time ago. Joint operation that didn't go so well. Bad decisions by our so-called superiors."

"Phil," Ken asked, "can the FBI bring whoever did this to justice?"

Phil had a flippant answer on the tip of his tongue but stopped himself. "They'll try," he said.

41

The sun was setting over Ayvil Plastics. The media vans were in their designated area, with reporters from all over filing stories from what was at that moment the most famous business location in the world. The FBI and police and fire and Red Cross types were hunkered down for an extended stay.

Ken was waiting for his turn at the makeshift morgue. All the waiting family members had registered and been given numbers. "Like a bakery," one of the grievers had quipped with bitter irony. Pennington and Ken sat on folding chairs on the lawn near one catering truck, having coffee in Styrofoam cups.

"Ken, I meant what I said about you heading up the foundation. You're the only continuity we've got after this tragedy. We also need a strong manager to dismantle this business and help the company move on. Just think about it. Give me your answer when you're ready."

"Tom," Ken asked, "do you think Arch Paulson really—?"

"It can't be possible. It just can't be." Pennington shuddered. He stood up to leave. "I've got to get back to New York. There's nothing more I can do here."

Pennington shook Ken's hand, then reached forward and took him in a warm, manly hug. Ken closed his eyes inside the protective embrace. Pennington gently patted his shoulders. Pennington let go and held him by both arms, as if keeping him from falling over. He turned to leave then turned back. "Uh, Ken, one question?"

Ken nodded.

"What were you doing in Cleveland?"

Ken felt like Pennington had grabbed him by the throat. "Uhhh," he stammered, "uh, I, uh, had family obligations."

Pennington nodded. "Strange, the ways of fate . . . So strange."

Pennington walked toward the cluster of TV vans. A couple of reporters who were hanging around their trucks tried to get his attention.

He gently waved them away. He had given his share of statements over the course of the day; there was nothing else to talk about. As he neared the two ANN vans, he raised his arm in a wave, hoping to catch the eye of one person in particular. He succeeded.

Kat Pierce was conferring with her camera crew. When she saw Pennington from afar, she waved back eagerly. It was as if an excited high school girl bubbled up from inside this tough reporter and waved back at the handsome football captain. She had to slow her feet to keep from running to meet him.

"I'm glad I got to be with you last night," she said.

"Me, too," Pennington said. "Just to be with you."

"Yeah, imagine that," she said.

"Yeah, imagine that."

"Tell me, Tom Pennington, could you, uh, imagine more?" she asked.

"Oh, definitely," he said.

"Well, maybe we should stop imagining."

He brushed the palm of her right hand lightly with the tip of one finger.

"You going back to New York now?" she asked, and returned the gesture, just barely touching his hand with her fingertip. They walked toward his waiting Lincoln.

"You have to catch a plane?" she asked.

"No, actually, the plane leaves when I'm ready."

"Well then, could I persuade you to delay your departure just a little?"

Pennington stopped and smiled at her. "Yes, I could be persuaded."

"Room 418," she said as she pulled the hotel keycard from her purse and put it into his hand. "Right after I finish my report."

Pennington smiled as he got into the backseat of his town car.

42

Kat Pierce stared at her best friend, the camera. The spotlight glared in her beautiful face as she talked into her microphone.

"Here in Dayton the sun has gone down on an incredible day of human tragedy. Since the predawn hours of this morning, families were lined up for the grisly task of identifying the bodies of their loved ones."

She relaxed her perfect posture slightly as the network fed snippets of her earlier reports into her story. Scenes of the families in line, tearful individuals, confused children. Scenes of grief-stricken people. Then back to Kat live. With a hand signal from her producer, she straightened up again and looked into the camera.

"Here at Evil Industries, this is Kat Pier—" She caught herself and stuttered. "—I mean, Ayvil Industries. *Ay*-vil Industries. Sorry, uh, this is Kat Pierce for ANN."

The instant the light went off, she held her mike down and cringed. "Oh, shit! I said Evil Industries, didn't I? Jesus, guys, I am tired. Sorry. Evil Industries? What a jerk." Then to herself, she whispered, "He's gonna kill me. He's absolutely gonna kill me."

43

Kat started apologizing the minute the door opened. "Oh, Tom, I just caused you so much trouble. I said 'Evil, Inc.' All the other reporters picked it up. It was a slip of the tongue. I am so sorry. I never flub words like that on camera. Really, Tom, can you ev—?"

To silence her, he took her by the shoulders and kissed her on the lips. She accepted the kiss and returned it. From there, making love seemed natural and easy. They spoke not a word; there was no need. They were two exceptionally successful people made lonely by ambition and drive, drawn to each other's physical beauty and worldly powers. They shared passion and tenderness and, with sophisticated technical skills on both their parts, satisfied each other's lust and curiosity.

She lay on his chest amid the bed linens, making lazy circles with one finger up and down his abdomen.

"I have no words," he said softly.

"You are very expressive without them."

"So are you." He smiled.

Kat said, "You had something important to ask me? Have I, by chance, already answered it?" She tickled him.

"Well, yes, on the first count. But no on the second." He sat up. She sat up beside him, her legs wide apart. "This is serious," he said. "It's about us and this awful tragedy and your career and mine."

She shook her head. "Well, you've certainly got my attention."

"Kat, there's a side to this story that has not been reported. That's by design of some powerful people. But it needs to get reported. And soon. But I can't be the one who leaks it. Now I can give you the lead, but you're going to have to choose. Because if you want the story for your career, there can never be an us. Understand? But if you can see that the story gets reported by someone else—and not from ANN—then you can do some good and we can be together. And someday soon not in secret."

"Wow," she said, "you make life complicated."

"No, life makes life complicated."

"I have to choose right here and now?"

"If I can't leak the story to you, I've got to make other plans. And fast."

She leaned forward and took his face in her hands. "Tom Pennington," she said, staring hard into his eyes, "you are something."

"So?"

"I'll plant the story with another network."

"Good," he said, and gave her a long, deep kiss.

"Now, tell me," she said, "what is it?"

44

Agent Decker looked around Paulson's office. He took it all in—the forty-third-floor panorama, the mahogany splendor. He was unimpressed. "What exactly can you tell us about what happened at that plant in Ohio?" he grunted.

Paulson snapped back, matching the agent's machismo. "Just what I told you on the phone. Nothing. I don't know anything about it. I was in China."

"Who called you on the cell phone we found on the dead man?"

"I have no idea. I assumed it was a wrong number."

"Then the caller left a message?"

"I deleted it."

"I see." Decker looked around again. He imagined Paulson's offices under construction, just raw plywood and Sheetrock waiting for the thin veneers of power and money. "You say you have nothing to hide?"

"Absolutely nothing."

"Then may we search your office?"

Paulson thought for a moment, drumming his fingers against the surface of his desk. Then he stood up. "Certainly. Go ahead. Be my guest." He made a sweeping gesture with open arms. "I told you I have nothing to hide."

"And your computer? Can we image your hard drive?"

"Go ahead."

"And your PBX computers?"

"What's that?"

"The company phone system."

"Absolutely. Have at it. You will find what I have already told you you'll find. Nothing."

Decker pulled his cell phone from his belt clip and pushed a speed-dial number. "Send in the team. He gave us permission." He snapped the phone shut and stood. "Thank you, Mr. Paulson, for your cooperation."

"No problem," Paulson said, barely hiding his anger. He walked toward the door.

"And Mr. Paulson," Decker said to the CEO's back, "don't go too far."

Paulson did not turn his head to look at the FBI man. "I will be in my conference room just down the hall," he said through gritted teeth.

45

"You don't you really think he did it?" Macmillan asked Czerwinski as they sat in Macmillan's office with the door closed.

"Well, I heard from my contact in corporate security that the FBI put a freeze on our voice mail hard drive. They want to get all the messages and data off it," Czerwinski explained. "Apparently there was a call from the cell phone of a guy connected with the bombing— a little while after it happened. Made directly to Arch's personal line, with a message and all. And they want to check Arch's hard drive for his bank account transactions."

"You mean," Macmillan asked, "like he might have paid somebody to—?" He left the unthinkable thought hanging.

"Hey, the FBI didn't come here to pay Arch a social call," Czerwinski said. "Security told me they were talking tough. No fucking around."

Macmillan shook his head with disbelief. "Oh, come on!" he said as he paced around his office. "But sabotage? Murder? *Mass* murder?"

"I don't know," Czerwinski said unemotionally. "Wouldn't you say that Arch has been getting stranger and stranger these past few years? More isolated. More lost in his own personal la-la land?"

Macmillan sat down. He shrugged.

"These guys are here to get evidence against him. You know, probable cause and all that," Czerwinski said.

Macmillan stared at the floor.

"I think it's possible he's gone over the edge," Czerwinski said. "Really, I do. Just look at him." He held up one stubby finger. "For one thing, he's got more money than God. And with that CEO benchmarking the board does, he keeps getting more and more every year—just for showing up. These guys get paid like rock stars and they live even better. Hell, the company picks up the tab for just about everything. I'd say that could give you a pretty distorted view of your place in the universe."

Czerwinski held up a second finger. "Two, except for the board who bust his chops only occasionally and the odd wacko investor once a year at the annual meeting, he lives in a world where he has total control. Everybody he talks to tells him 'Yes, sir, yes, sir, three bags full.' And anybody who doesn't, well, he never talks to them again. Between the BBJ he takes everywhere and the limos and the mansions, the guy's feet never really touch the earth. Forget all that talk about his humble origins. Arch is used to getting whatever the hell he wants, however the hell he wants it." Czerwinski snapped his fingers impatiently like a potentate ordering the servants around. "I think that'll give you an even more fucked-up view of the world and your place in it." Czerwinski leaned forward. Macmillan stopped pacing. "I'd say Arch has always been a little bit crazy about power and control. Wouldn't you?"

Macmillan nodded.

"And he was feeling threatened? Right? He said that to us, remember?"

Macmillan nodded again.

"Okay, then," Czerwinski said, "is it not at least conceivable? I said, at least conceivable, that Arch really did do this? *And* that he could convince himself he could get away with it? It sure as hell looks like the FBI thinks so."

Macmillan jumped to his feet. "Shit!" he cried. "Everyone associates us with Paulson. We've been his guys all these years."

"I know, I know." The men fell silent. Macmillan paced back and forth.

Finally, a lightbulb seemed to go on inside Czerwinski. He asked quietly, "Don't you think the FBI needs to know about Arch's stated desire to do something terrible in Pennington's world?"

"Let's think it through," Macmillan said. "Three of us were witness to that conversation. If nobody mentions it, it's like it never happened. Right?"

"Right."

"But if one of us does," Macmillan said, "the others look like they've been holding back."

"Okay," Czerwinski said, "but if *we* don't say anything, why on earth would Arch? It would only make him look worse."

"But what if he got backed into a corner?" Macmillan asked. "He could say that he made the suggestion to us without realizing we would ever actually *do* something about it. Then who looks like they've been trying to hide something? They could play us against each other."

"They sure could." Czerwinski took a deep breath. "The shit from this thing hasn't even begun to hit the fan. If there'll be one thing worth preserving, it'll be our integrity."

"You said it, preserve our integrity."

Czerwinski clapped his fat hands together and stood up. "I think Paulson's finished, one way or the other. It doesn't matter what he did or didn't do."

"I agree," Macmillan said.

Czerwinski reached for the phone on Macmillan's desk. "You mind?"

"No."

"I'll call the receptionist upstairs," Czerwinski said as he dialed. "I don't think the FBI guy should leave without talking to us."

46

Decker invited Paulson back to his office a few hours later. Paulson took his place behind the desk. Decker sat facing him. "May I ask you another question?"

"That is why you're here," Paulson said curtly, "isn't it?"

"I mean a personal question."

"Ask away."

"What would a man in your position consider a lot of money?"

"This is a very big company. We deal in billions every day."

"No, I mean for you personally."

"Let me tell you something, Agent Decker. I have been working since I was fourteen years old. I was orphaned as a teenager and I put myself through Michigan State, working days, nights, and weekends. Nobody ever gave me anything. I have transformed Ayers & Vilmont from a sleepy domestic manufacturing company into Ayvil Industries, a global force across dozens of industries. Believe me, I know the value of a dollar. And I have earned every penny I call my own."

"That's very inspirational, Mr. Paulson. But let's talk about here and now. You are a big-time corporate CEO. That makes you a very rich man, doesn't it?"

"Very rich? I wouldn't say so. It all depends on what you compare yourself to. A lot of people make a lot more than me. You know, the board pegs my compensation at the seventieth percentile of my peer group. Take a look at hedge fund guys, venture capitalists, LBO guys, real estate developers. Let's just say there are a lot of men out there who make me look like a piker. Believe me, a lot of them. I'm surrounded by them in Greenwich."

Decker looked at his notes. "My colleagues from the SEC tell me you made over twenty million dollars last year."

"Well, technically that's true. That's what's reported. But that's not all in cash; it never is. A lot of that is from instruments that have been accumulating for years, along with long-term incentive plans, and so on. It's very complicated, executive compensation."

"Yes, I'm sure it is," Decker said. He leaned forward in his chair. "How much actual money do you have, Mr. Paulson?"

"I-I have no idea. It depends on the markets, where my investment managers are deploying funds, where those investments are relative to—"

"Well, then, how much cash can you put your hands on? On short notice?"

"I don't know, a few million, if I had to. Where is this leading?"

"What's a few?"

"Two, three, four million. It depends. I'd have to liquidate some instruments."

"Do you do any offshore banking?"

"Yes, actually, I have an account at the Royal Bank of the Caymans. I own a home down there and I'm a partner in some real estate investments—a golf course and some condos. That's all public knowledge." Paulson seemed to review his financial statements in his mind. "Let's see, I got into a fund run out of Bermuda, a currency fund run out of Isle of Man. You know, these kinds of things that aren't for the general public. Minimums are a million and up."

"I wouldn't know," Decker said. "Mr. Paulson, you've had a lot of activity in that Caymans account recently. Can you explain why?"

"What are you talking about? I haven't had any transactions there in—I don't know—a year, maybe eighteen months. Not since I bought the interest in the golf course."

Decker reached into a folder and extracted several sheets of paper stapled together and handed them across the desk to Paulson.

"You've been e-mailing your New York brokerage firm for the past week. Looks like you cashed in a pile of options. Then you sent instructions to transfer two million dollars of it to your account in the Caymans. From there it was transferred into another account at the Royal Bank of Grand Cayman, an anonymous numbered account. This was all done on instructions sent by you on this computer." Decker pointed to the PC behind Paulson's desk, its large flat screen flashing a scrolling screen saver with the Ayvil logo. Then he held up the folder filled with printouts. "It's all right here."

Paulson stared at the paper then at Decker. "This is wrong. This didn't happen. First of all, I have given no instructions to send even a nickel to the Cayman bank, let alone two million. Second, I have been in China conducting negotiations. I gave no such authorizations to move these funds."

"I'm afraid you did, Mr. Paulson. All the passwords, all the redundant levels of security identifications were provided. Not only were these transfers certified kosher, they are all right here in the history. This money went to the Caymans. We called the bank and told them that we would have a court order soon enough and would they just help us fast-forward the process. So they agreed. In that numbered account, there were standing orders to move your two million to other numbered accounts in other offshore banks. It was your money, it was laundered, and now it's gone."

"That's ridiculous. That can't be."

"Now about the phone call to your private line from that cell phone in the trailer. The message you deleted. The wrong number?"

"Yes?" Paulson tried not to look worried.

"We retrieved the message. You know, they don't really get deleted for some time. They just get pushed over to a sort of parking lot on the hard drive until they get overwritten." Decker tried to read Paulson's expression for fear or weakness. He thought he saw Paulson flinch. "The caller was a man. He said, 'Mission accomplished.' We can play it for you."

Paulson stood up and put both hands on the desk. To keep himself from falling over. "We are done," he said angrily, his false bravado transparent. "I want to talk to a lawyer."

"That is your right."

"This is all a goddamn lie, some kind of crazy conspiracy. Are you accusing me of being a mass murderer? Is that what you're doing? Because if you—"

"Mr. Paulson, I'm not accusing you of anything. But I am going to have to ask you not to leave the country while we investigate."

Paulson glared.

Decker looked at him blankly. "Thank you, Mr. Paulson," he said almost cheerfully. "I'm sure your office will tell us how to reach you when we need to talk again." He stood up and walked out, closing the big mahogany door behind him.

47

Pennington sat in the library of Hildreth's town house. A silver-haired gentleman sat beside Hildreth. They listened to Pennington give his account of everything that had happened in Dayton. The afternoon sun poured in. The towering windows were open to the walled garden with its flower beds, ivied trellises, and tinkling italianate fountain. The noise and grit of Manhattan were worlds away.

"I wanted us to meet in private," Hildreth said. "And I wanted Ben Toland to be here. Ben and I have served on the board longest." Toland, a pale chubby man in his sixties, looked like an old-fashioned bank president. "I'm afraid the corporate offices are just too exposed right now. I never imagined I would ever find myself living through an experience like this. Did you, Ben?"

"No," Toland said, "this world of ours has gone crazy."

"But," Hildreth said, "times of crisis show what we're really made of. Tom, your instincts and your actions have been superb. I told the board I will put your name forward to become the new CEO. The board is prepared to follow my recommendation."

"No question about that," Toland said.

"Well," Pennington said, taking a deep breath, "this is not the way I wished that would happen."

"No one did," Hildreth said solemnly. He stood up and paced across the library. He stopped at a slightly smaller than life-size bronze head, Auguste Rodin's masterpiece, *Man with a Broken Nose*. He patted it nervously. "Tom Pennington, this could be the worst job in the world. It may be impossible for any man to succeed, given everything that's happened."

"That is a possible scenario," Pennington said quietly, "but not the only one."

Hildreth turned from the statue and studied Pennington carefully. "Do you consider yourself up to this challenge?"

With his eyes locked on Hildreth's, Pennington said confidently, "Yes."

"Then it's settled." Hildreth looked at Toland, who nodded in agreement. "I think everyone agrees that Arch Paulson could not possibly have committed this crime. But that is not what counts. Appearances alone could destroy the company. The Cayman bank connection, the phone call, it's appalling. I put in a few calls to Washington, asking to please keep these things out of the press as long as they can. Fortunately, I still have friends there."

Hildreth stared out into his garden. "I told Arch he should resign, but he wouldn't hear of it. I'm going to try once more with him. I think you should accompany me. I'm going to his house in Greenwich tonight. You should accompany me."

"Certainly, I'll clear my calendar," Pennington said. He reached for his briefcase. "Let's assume we can get the company through this."

Hildreth nodded. "All right. None of it matters if we can't."

"There's something we should start working on immediately." He reached into his briefcase and pulled out two tabloid newspapers, the *New York Post* and the New York *Daily News,* and put them on the ottoman in front of Hildreth. There, on the two front pages, were similar black-and-white photos of the Ayvil Plastics building with an inset of Paulson looking at the reporters with his stupid smile and (much to the chagrin of the two competing editors) the same bold-face headline in quotations with multiple exclamation points: EVIL, INC.!!!

Hildreth shook his head. Toland groaned.

Pennington said, "We must change the name of the company."

The network anchorman on the NBC midday news said, "And this just in, related to the fatal explosion at the Ayvil Industries plant outside Dayton, Ohio. Police from Nelsonville, east of Dayton, have found two men dead of gunshot wounds in a trailer in the woods. Engineering plans of the Ayvil plant were found with them. And in the hand of one of the dead men, they found a cell phone. According to a well-placed source, the last number dialed on the phone was a call made to the personal line of the office of Ayvil Industries CEO Archibald Paulson. We will keep you posted as this tragic—and strange—story unfolds."

49

Pennington and Hildreth met at Paulson's estate early that evening. Their town car parked in the driveway just inside the newly constructed eight-foot-high fieldstone wall that separated Paulson's grounds from the traffic of North Street. There were new walls like this all up and down the roadways of Greenwich. Costing anywhere from $200,000 to over $1 million, they were considered every plutocrat's essential, if pointless, lawn accessory.

Across the road were a TV news van, a local Greenwich police cruiser, and an unmarked Crown Victoria with Decker sitting in the front passenger's seat and another agent at the wheel.

When Paulson's white three-story wooden house was built in 1890, it was considered comfortable but not grand. It was a fine house for a prosperous family to call home, not a mansion. Since Paulson had bought it in the early eighties, he had added enough wings and ells to triple its original five thousand square feet. The house had lost its pleasing form and proportions and become a sprawling architectural octopus with fat tentacles of wood, stone, and glass reaching out in all directions. The house, along with the four-car garage, indoor and outdoor pools, paddleball court, and pitch-and-putt green, made the four-acre plot feel cramped. The ancient elms looked threatened, as if they might be sacrificed at any moment to make way for the owner's next expensive whim.

Yet Paulson's lavish displays of wealth were neither unusual nor especially conspicuous for this once sleepy town of Greenwich, Connecticut. His manse looked modest in comparison to the new crop of gigantic fake French chateaux, Italian palazzi, and English manor houses built mostly with giddy new wealth from hedge funds.

"He won't budge," Hildreth said to Pennington. "He's got attorneys, private detectives, and computer experts. He says he's going to prove that he never authorized the money transfers, that he's not connected in any way. And he refuses to resign or even take a leave of absence. When NBC broke the story about the cell phone call this afternoon, all hell broke loose. He says he will sue everyone from the networks to the federal government to Ayvil and its board. He says if he goes down in flames, everyone will go with him."

"Have you seen him yet?" Pennington asked.

"No, we got this from the lawyers." Hildreth lowered his voice. "I'm afraid there's something else the FBI knows. Something very serious. I'm afraid it's not just incriminating. It shatters Arch's credibility. I've used up all my chits in Washington to keep the FBI from hauling Arch away before we got the chance to talk to him."

Pennington looked a bit confused. "What?"

"Testimony from Czerwinski and Macmillan. It seems that Arch tried to enlist their help in cooking up some kind of scheme, a serious crisis that would damage you and the Plastics division. The purpose was to let Arch rush in to save the day and have the board demand that he stay on past retirement age. They say they didn't give him any ideas, but they were convinced he was serious in his intent."

Pennington looked stunned. "Does Arch know you know about this?"

"No." Hildreth gestured toward the walkway of Belgian paving stones that led to the front door. They approached the towering pseudo-Palladian portico of white columns. Before Hildreth could push the doorbell, a small Filipina woman in a maid's uniform opened the door. "Meestah Paulson in gunroom," she said, and ushered them inside. She led them through the grand foyer, past the baronial library with its huge collection of unread antique volumes, and down a set of stairs into an underground complex. She directed them to a heavy paneled door. She opened it, revealing the soundproof lining on the inside, and closed it as she left.

50

Paulson sat on a small leather couch. He wore lime green golf slacks, a white golf shirt bearing a country club crest, shiny brown alligator loafers, and bright yellow cable-stitch socks. On the walls around him were glass cases filled with shotguns and hunting rifles. Spotlights built into the ceiling lit the cases of firearms like works of art. Beyond the denlike sitting area was the shooting range, a long tunnel with paper targets on pulleys at the far end. On the table before Paulson was a gleaming new shotgun with a silver panel on the butt, engraved with Paulson's initials. A box of shotgun shells sat open beside it.

"Hello, Justin," Paulson said flatly. He looked angry and tired, with circles under his eyes. "I sent Mary down to Jupiter Island," he said, referring to Mrs. Paulson. "I put her on one of the G3s. But don't worry. I paid for it. Wrote a personal check to cover all costs. I just couldn't risk her flying commercial under . . . under these circumstances." He gestured for them to sit in the chairs facing him.

"Can I offer you a drink?" he asked after an uncomfortable silence.

"No, thank you," Hildreth said.

Paulson looked at Pennington.

"No thanks, I'm fine," Pennington said with unease.

They sat in silence. Finally, Paulson leaned forward and pushed the shotgun in Pennington's direction. "See that?" he asked. "Purdy's of Jermyn Street, Mayfair, London. Two hundred fifty thousand dollars. Custom-built for me. I had to wait three years for that gun. Three years! You know what three years means when you're my age? I could only dream about a gun like that when I was your age, Pennington. Go on, pick it up."

Pennington did not move.

"Go on. Pick it up and hold it. Feel the grace and balance of it. One hundred percent machined by hand. Go on!"

Hesitantly, Pennington picked up the shotgun and held it uncomfortably.

"That, Pennington, is a thing as close to perfection as you will ever hold in your hands."

"Uh, I'm not much of a connoisseur of rifles."

"Shotgun. It's a shotgun. Hand it to Justin. He knows firearms, don't you, Justin. How many times have we been hunting together? Maine, Canada, Scotland, Kenya. How many times has it been, Justin?"

Awkwardly, Pennington handed the shotgun to Hildreth, who held it for an instant, then promptly "broke" it, opening the gun at the hinge.

"Jesus!" Hildreth cried. "It's loaded."

"Well, of course! I came down here for some target practice." Paulson stood up as if to go somewhere, then changed his mind and sat down again. "You know, under the law, a man is innocent until proven guilty."

"I am not a prosecutor," Hildreth said. "It is my responsibility to protect the interests of the company. Arch, there's something I have to ask you."

Paulson crossed his arms across his chest. "Ask away."

"Did you make plans to create a crisis in the corporation?"

Paulson sat back as if he had been struck in the face. "Do you mean am I a mass murderer? Is that what you're asking? Jesus! I am the chief executive of this company. That's the most ridiculous thing I've ever heard. I am the CEO."

Hildreth sighed. "I'm afraid Paul Czerwinski and Keith Macmillan have told the FBI otherwise. They say you asked them to help you dream up a terrible crisis. The objective was to push back your retirement. That's what they told the FBI, and that's what they will testify to in court."

Paulson's eyes narrowed, his face began to redden, the fingers of both hands twitched nervously. "Czerwinski and Macmillan, huh? *My* guys?"

"Arch Paulson," Hildreth said softly as he put the opened shotgun back on the table, "I can't say whether you are innocent or guilty. But I do know with absolute certainty you are unfit to be chief executive. If you don't resign here and now, the board will fire you first thing in the morning."

"Listen, I can explain," Paulson said. "I can explain everything. You know how it is inside a big company. Sometimes in corporate life, you've got to play a little rough, you've got to protect your political flank. It's just part of the game."

"You consider mass murder a game?"

"No, of course not. What I did was—"

"But you did take actions to harm one of your divisions?"

"It wasn't murder, just let me explain."

Hildreth stood up. "I've had enough."

"All right," Paulson said, staring at the floor. "I lied a little. When it looked like the explosion was an accident, I took advantage of the situation. I went for it. Who wouldn't? But I didn't arrange it, you've got to believe me."

"What about the phone call to your office? You tried to cover it up!"

"I didn't know what was really going on."

"The FBI and the U.S. Attorney's office think that the hit men you hired double-crossed you to prevent you from ever naming them. Evidently, this kind of thing happens all the time in criminal circles."

Paulson sat upright and shouted, "I am not a criminal! I didn't pay to have those people killed!"

"Arch Paulson, you are through. Have you gone so crazy amassing your *rewards,*" Hildreth said with a sneer and looked around distastefully, "that you have forgotten that the rewards are in exchange for responsibility? I leave you to the criminal justice system. You should know that young Pennington here will be appointed the new CEO and will try to clean up the mess you have created."

Paulson stood up, suddenly defiant, staring down at Hildreth, emphasizing his height advantage over the old Brahmin. "Yeah, well I've got resources to throw at this, too. I'm a rich man, a powerful man. I'm vice chairman of the American Business Council. I'm a director of four other Fortune 500 companies. I've been to Bohemian Grove every summer for fifteen years. I don't need you anymore, and let me tell you—"

Hildreth ignored him. "Even if you are proven innocent, which I doubt, no company, no board, no club will have you. You will never go back to Bohemian Grove, I promise you. And *I* am a man of my word."

"Justin," Paulson said, suddenly pleading, "you were born rich. You don't know what it's like to fight your way up the ladder in a big company. Come on, we've been friends for twenty years."

Hildreth said quietly, "You were never a friend. You were hired help." He walked to the soundproof door and opened it. "Tom, I'll wait for you upstairs," he said over his shoulder, and left without closing the door.

51

Paulson picked at his fingernails.

Finally, Pennington said, "Tell me what you *did* do."

"What do you mean?" he mumbled.

"You know, the thing you said you did."

"Why should I?"

"Because it's the right thing to do. Because it will help us prevent further harm to the company. Because underneath it all, you're still a decent man with a deep sense of responsibility." He was waiting for Paulson to look at him. When Paulson finally met his gaze, he said, "Because you're Arch Paulson, that's why."

Paulson looked away. "I don't owe you a fucking thing."

"I'm not asking for me; I'm asking for the company. The company *you* built."

Paulson drummed his fingers on the arm of the couch. He spoke softly, barely opening his mouth, hardly moving his lips. "Phantom suppliers. Bank account in Bermuda. The auditors should pick it up next quarter. It'll look like it's been going on for months and months, long before your stupid turnaround. Got your boy's name all over it. Nielson."

"Olson?"

"Yeah, him."

"Why?" Pennington asked.

"To make you look bad. Like you promoted a crook to be your right-hand man."

"How did you do it?"

"Huh?"

"Arch, how did you do it? How did you direct payments to the phantom suppliers?"

Paulson looked at Pennington with hatred.

"Come on, it'll come out eventually."

Paulson looked down at the floor. "E-mail. Freelance hacker hired another hacker who got into Olson's e-mail address. Nothing traces to me. Looks like he ordered the payments, validated the supplier, and supplied invoices. No paper necessary. Not these days."

Pennington gave a sigh of relief. "Thanks, you did the right thing. I knew you would."

Both men stared at the floor for a while. Finally Pennington spoke.

"I heard you make a speech last year. You spoke about the need to be able to accept rapid change and adjust your worldview accordingly, rather than clinging to old beliefs about the way things were, even ten minutes before."

"I give a lot of speeches," Paulson said listlessly.

"Well, I remember this one. You were very convincing."

"I usually am," he sneered, making a feeble attempt at his old arrogance.

"I suggest you take your own advice and accept your world as it is right now. Your life is over, no matter what happens in your trial."

"You can't talk to me like that."

"Arch," Pennington said softly, almost sympathetically, "you're not a CEO anymore. You are a poor man in desperate trouble he will never get out of."

"I never give up," Paulson said. *"Never."*

"You might as well come clean," Pennington said with pity in his voice. "Why did you have those poor people murdered?"

"Fuck you!" Paulson growled. He grabbed the shotgun, snapped the barrels into place, and stood up. He took the firing position, with the barrels in Pennington's face, his fingers nervously caressing the two triggers.

Pennington sat frozen. His mouth went dry.

"I didn't do it, you little fucker," Paulson said, the shotgun shaking ever so slightly.

Pennington saw. "Go ahead and shoot me. It will only prove your guilt."

The gun quivered again.

Suddenly, a shriek filled the air. "Meestah! Ayeee!" The maid stood in the doorway.

"Shit," Paulson said, lowering the gun. "What is it, Dora?"

"Meestah, ah, meestah," the maid chattered, her chest heaving, "Meestah Hildreth ask me to get Meestah Pennington."

"Go on, then," Paulson said, talking to the floor. "Get out."

Slowly and carefully, Pennington stood up, took the maid by the arm, and ran upstairs. Hildreth, Decker, the other FBI man, and two local Greenwich cops were waiting in the grand foyer.

Suddenly, an explosion sounded from downstairs.

Everyone jumped. The maid started screaming again.

They found Paulson slumped across the couch, mouth agape, the back of his head blown away, the shotgun in his lap, one hand still gripping it. His face, with eyes wide open, wore a blank, almost surprised expression. A huge puddle of blood surrounded the remains of his exploded head. On the wall behind, a dark red starburst covered the silk wallpaper. Chunks of bone and brain were dripping downward, making sickening little noises. Paulson's jaunty yellow socks and elegant alligator slip-ons made an odd counterpoint to his hideously disfigured corpse.

52

Cap Mistral was a fortress of luxury and indulgence, built at the northern tip of Mahé, the main island of the Seychelles archipelago, the legendary tropical paradise a thousand miles east of Kenya in the Indian Ocean. The resort sat on a peninsula protected by mountains covered in forest on one side and rocky cliffs and crashing waves on the other.

The guests were an international assortment of princes and despots (some deposed, some not), billionaire businessmen (some legitimate, some not), plus the odd arms dealer, drug lord, rock star, dissolute heir or heiress, and their entourages. They paid thousands per night to indulge themselves in Cap Mistral's exceptionally private, lavishly appointed villas.

The man called Peter Houghton sat naked on the edge of the plunge pool in the courtyard of his villa. Three naked and very drunk young women frolicked beside him. Above them the moon glowed brightly; a line of tiki torches lit the patio. He no longer had a goatee or black horn-rimmed glasses or dark hair. He was hairless from head to toe. Naturally so. And he was no longer called Peter Houghton.

He was Stephen Hodes, a businessman carrying a Dutch passport, who had discreetly put a roll of twenty American C-notes into the concierge's hand upon arrival at the resort. The concierge, a bland German Swiss named Ackermann, was famous for providing, in exchange for large dollops of cash, absolutely anything guests requested with secrecy and the complete absence of moral judgment.

"Of course, Herr Hodes, it would be my pleasure," Ackermann said when Hodes mentioned he was in a mood to entertain some beautiful women in his bungalow.

"I have one friend already coming from town, a pretty brown girl," Hodes said, slipping another roll of hundreds into Ackermann's hand, a gesture so practiced by both men, it was barely visible. "I would like two more, one of each of the other local colors." Meaning white and black.

"Certainly," Ackermann said with a hint of a smile. Never once looking down, he felt the bulk of the bills in his hand, knew there was enough money for two more girls and himself, and slipped the money into the drawer of his desk.

"And would you like the dinner buffet style? By your pool?"

"Yes, good idea."

"Of course," Ackermann said, noting to himself to include, under one of the silver domes on the buffet table, the standard collection of condoms, lubricants, and sex toys he knew guests liked to have handy for such occasions.

Apsara, the pretty Indian woman in the pool, was the receptionist at the bank. Hired for her good looks to greet the parade of rich foreigners who came to visit their money in this tropical paradise also famous for its banking-secrecy laws, Apsara had only a vague notion of the transactions that went on in the offices behind her. It was a good job for a girl from a poor family. It let her make use of her looks and gave her the chance to meet foreigners with lots of money.

Hodes was delighted to see such a pretty woman working in the bank. He invited her to dinner at the resort. Apsara understood that she was engaging in a transaction with the man, but a friendly one, with a little intimacy yielding a lot of cash. She had done it before when the men seemed friendly and generous enough.

She was not surprised to arrive at his villa and see two more girls already there and drinking champagne. After more champagne and courses of rich food fed playfully into each other's mouths with their fingers, and still more champagne, the skinny-dipping came naturally. After that, little bouts of sex play with the generous man seemed harmless enough in their tipsy haze.

"One more little game," Hodes called to the girls. He sat down at the edge of the lounge chair. He pulled a wad of hundred-dollar bills from the pocket of his bathrobe and waved them in the air. "Come stand over here by me." The girls giggled as they climbed out of the pool. They took the bills and divided them up among themselves. They made a line in front of him. "Now turn around and bend over." Tittering, they did as he asked.

"Now close your eyes, girls. Remember, eyes closed."

They closed their eyes and waited for the game to begin.

From a Louis Vuitton overnight bag by the chair, he produced a seven-inch GLOCK Field Knife and removed it from its scabbard. Designed for slashing, stabbing, and cutting just about anything, the blade had a jagged sawtooth along its spine; the cutting edge was sleek and razor sharp, ending in a menacing upturned point. He reached for the first girl in the line, the white girl. Steadying himself with his free hand on her cheek, he pressed his face close to her. "Now just hold still. Very, very still."

Gently and carefully he dragged the tip of the blade along the small of her back where the *V* of her tailbone met the crack in her cheeks. The soft downy little hairs that grew there collected along the edge of the knife.

"Hare," he whispered to himself in Afrikaans, *"jy, het hare oral."*

"What did you say?" the girl asked nervously, feeling something but not daring to look behind and see.

"Hair," he said, "everywhere. You people have hair growing all over you, don't you?"

The girl giggled nervously. She held her breath until he finished. Then he moved to the black girl and dragged the blade ever so lightly across the small of her back, adding her darker, coarser hairs to the edge of the blade.

The girl held her breath. He inhaled her noisily. "Oh, the cuts," he muttered to himself. The girl quivered; he held on tight. He thought of what he could do with the tiniest flick of his wrist: the blood, the pain, and the pleasure it would give him. If he wanted.

But not here. Not now.

"Now don't move," he cautioned and reached for Apsara's butt, using his free hand to spread her cheeks apart. He shaved her tailbone area, watching the little crop of her fine dark hairs collect on the knife blade along with the blond down and black hairs from the other girls. Apsara turned her head and saw the horrible blade in his hand. She yelped and shuddered out of his grip. He yanked the blade away to avoid hurting her and cut his finger in the process.

"Vokkin' etter," he sneered in Afrikaans. Fucking cunt.

Apsara ran to the deck chair nearby. She scooped up her clothes and fled naked from the villa, crying.

The party was over.

Silently the other girls collected their things and got dressed. "Can you call us a ride?" the white girl asked over her shoulder. "It's a long walk down to the great house."

Hodes grunted and walked to the cordless phone on the buffet table, strewn with the wreckage of their champagne and lobster feast. He pushed the auto-dial button marked with the concierge symbol, two crossed keys.

"Yes, Herr Hodes?" It was Ackermann.

"Send a golf cart up for my guests."

"Right away, sir." Pause. "Herr Hodes, I trust everything was to your liking?"

"Yes, just fine." He stared at the smooth surface of his fingertip (he had had his fingerprints removed years before) and the drop of blood forming from the cut. "Tomorrow," he said into the phone, "I think I would fancy meeting some of your local boys." He raised his hand to his mouth and tasted his blood. "Yes, some boys."

"Certainly, Herr Hodes, whatever you would like."

53

Kat Pierce strode nervously back and forth behind the video editor's workstation—a jumble of dials, meters, and computer drives. Suddenly she stopped, turned, and stared at the bank of television monitors mounted above.

Kat's exclusive one-on-one interview with Tom Pennington was just about ready. Various frames of the two of them were frozen on the screens above.

"I've got another idea, Stan," Kat said. "Run my intro to the news clip where he cries again, will you?"

Kat appeared on the center screen. "Let's go back to that night," her videotape said, "and the statement you gave." Stan pushed the button. Kat's image froze with her mouth partially open.

"Where do you want me to pick up his statement?" Stan asked.

Kat thought for a second. "From the end of his speech. Where the camera starts to move in on his teardrop."

On another monitor, Pennington's statement at the impromptu news conference flew by on fast-forward. Stan pushed a button and it froze just as Pennington's face was growing larger in the frame.

"Yeah, that's the in-point," Kat said, "right there."

Stan typed instructions into his computer and the image of Tom Pennington backed up and then started to move at normal speed.

"We cannot bring back our friends and colleagues who died here," Pennington said gravely. The camera moved in and picked up the tear streaming down his cheek. "But we can tend to the living. We can fulfill our human and corporate responsibilities to those they leave behind. Ayvil Industries will establish a foundation, to be headquartered here in Dayton. That foundation will provide for the needs of the families and children and grandchildren of these Ayvil employees for the next twenty-five years."

"Okay, stop it right there," Kat instructed. "Let's cut in a reaction shot of me."

Stan pushed a button. The image of Pennington froze.

"Which one?" the editor asked.

"Let's go to the B-roll."

The editor typed on his keyboard. Above, on another large monitor, solo shots of Kat flew by on fast-forward. The sequence, shot after she had finished interviewing Pennington, showed her asking the same questions she had asked while Pennington was being taped, along with faked reactions to the answers he had already given. There was Kat looking concerned, Kat listening intently, Kat leaning forward, Kat nodding with affirmation at the empty seat beside her that was just out of frame. None of it was journalism; it was all acting.

"That's good," she said, "right there."

"Looks like you got something in your eye," Stan said about the scene in which Kat lowered her head, closed her eyes, and brought her right thumb and index finger up to her eyes.

"I did, it was a fleck of dust," she said, "but I think it'll play well with that big emotional moment."

"Let's see." Stan typed in the new cuts. On the first big monitor, Pennington was rewound and said his heartfelt words again.

Then Kat Pierce filled the screen, lowering her head, closing her eyes, raising thumb and forefinger, not to remove a speck of dust as she had a moment ago, but to respond with profound emotion to Pennington's tearful speech.

"That's good," she said.

"Yeah, it really works," Stan agreed. "This interview is going to be gangbusters."

Kat nodded proudly. "That," she whispered to herself, "is why they're going to pay me even bigger bucks."

54

After months of scenes like this, Ken was about to run out of patience. Since Paulson's suicide, he had been repeating this moment with grieving family members again and again. "You see, Mrs. Bartlett, it's an annuity. It's been carefully figured out by actuaries. It guarantees you and your children regular payments equivalent to what Clyde would have earned had he lived and finished his career at Ayvil. This is in addition to his company life insurance and AD&D policy."

He put down the worksheet prepared for the heirs of Clyde Bartlett, determined not to let his exasperation with her naive questions show. He looked around her modest living room and fidgeted in his chair, wondering if this was Clyde's chair when he was alive. On the end table was the usual collection of Kodak moments of the marriage of Clyde and Amy Bartlett, from their wedding thirty years before through the childhood of their two boys to a recent camping trip with Clyde and two strapping college-age sons posing by a stream.

"Mrs. Bartlett," he asked, "would you like to show this to your accountant? I'm sure he can help you—"

"She," the woman said curtly. She was not being snippy; she was just upset and confused.

"I'm sure *she* can help you understand it," Ken said soothingly, "the retirement benefits, the 401(k), the lump sum pension settlement, and all."

"Maybe I should take it to her. You know, Clyde did all the finances and wrote all the checks. I'm afraid this is Greek to me. You've been very patient, I'm sorry."

"It's quite all right. I'm afraid I'm not much of an insurance salesman. Any questions, please don't hesitate to call me. That's what I'm here for."

She reached across the coffee table and patted his hand maternally.

"You're a very kind man," she said. "It must be very draining for you, reliving this with families, especially, uh," she stammered, not wanting to say what she was thinking about Ken's own losses, "well, er, I would hope that a nice young man like yourself would be thinking of moving away from Dayton now that, er . . ." She was digging herself in deeper and was unsure how to get herself out.

Ken smiled at her and patted her hand in return. "It's okay. When the time is right. For now, I've got several important jobs to do, and this is one of them."

"Can I pour you some more coffee?" she asked.

"No thanks," he said, collecting his papers into his briefcase and standing up. "You have my card. Please don't hesitate to call if you need anything. Anything at all." Ken started to move toward the door. When he saw that Mrs. Bartlett was making no such move, he sat back down. He had seen this before. Now was the time they wanted to talk about It.

"Why do you think he did it?" Mrs. Bartlett asked.

"You mean Paulson?" Ken offered.

"Yes, why on earth did he do it?" She was calm even though tears were welling up in her eyes. "Why? He had millions and millions of dollars, more than anyone could spend. He had all the power a man could want. Why did he do this to innocent people who were just trying to do a good job?"

"I don't know the answer, Mrs. Bartlett. I just don't know."

"Clyde used to say that Ayvil was a good company. He was proud to work there. He said the bosses at headquarters deserved their money because they carried the weight of the whole company on their shoulders."

She was starting to cry. Ken reached across and held her hand.

"But Paulson never took responsibility for the losses at Plastics," she said through her tears. "Clyde used to say, 'Headquarters steers the business. We just pull the oars.' Paulson acted like it was the fault of the people like Clyde. But *they* made the decisions. If the business wasn't doing well, it was *their* fault, not Clyde's. Paulson never came home and told his wife that he might have to take a pay cut or lose his job because Plastics wasn't doing well."

Ken almost smiled at her unintended irony. "No, I don't think so."

"But if the business wasn't doing as well as it should have, why did Paulson keep getting his millions and blaming *us* when *he* should have been the one getting the blame?"

Ken nodded sympathetically, unable to counter what she was saying.

Tears were streaming down her cheeks. "I hate Paulson," she said in a cold whisper. "I hate him for killing my Clyde. I hate him for killing everyone who worked at Ayvil. I hate him for thinking he could blame us and make us pay for *his* mistakes and get away with it. I hate him for the millions he made off our backs. And I hate him for killing himself. If Clyde had to die, I wanted Paulson to go on trial, I wanted Paulson to pay the price like any criminal."

Her face went red; she pulled her hand away from Ken's and started shaking her fist at the air. "He was a murderer, a thief, a coward! That's why he killed himself, the bastard. I hate him. God, I *hate* him. He never paid the price for anything. *We did!*" She fell back in her chair, sobbing hysterically.

Ken rose, walked quietly to the front door, and let himself out.

55

That night, the words of Bartlett's widow rang in Ken's head. He started shouting at his empty house. "Fucking, fucking Paulson!"

Suddenly, his right fist took on a life of its own, searching the room for something to smash. He charged to the stairwell and pounded the banister. His arm bounced back as the hardwood pole quivered from his impact.

He searched for a better target.

He slammed the wall once. He felt the stud behind the plaster-board resist his blow and bruise his hand. He slammed the wall again a few inches away. This time, he punched a hole in it. Plaster chips, dust, and blood. He punched another hole. He punched again and again and again shouting, "Fucking Paulson!" with every blow.

Broken bits of plaster began to cake together with blood. The pain felt good; the damage felt satisfying. He caught his breath. He was panting the way he used to after sex. Holding his right hand high like a bloody trophy, he took his car keys off the hall table with his left hand and drove himself to the hospital.

56

Lew Simons pointed the remote at the television set in the corner of the empty conference room at Ayvil headquarters. Pennington and Hildreth sat on opposite sides of the large table. It was dark outside and the rest of the building was mostly empty. The TV popped to life and filled the room with the irritating jingle of a commercial. Simons quickly muted the sound.

"You know, Tom," he said, "you are the first CEO I've worked for who arranged a prime time interview with a top journalist on his own."

"I believe in maintaining close personal relations with the press," Pennington said. "It's good for the business."

"It's great. You're doing my job for me."

"Don't worry, Lew," Pennington said, "if I'm a bust, I'll take the blame. If this does any good, you get all the credit."

"Well," Simons said, "we've got an army of pollsters ready to start calling and tracking our image ratings as soon as the show is over." Simons crossed two fingers and raised them in a good-luck gesture.

The commercial ended and the show began. Simons switched off the mute. Music, all jittery and serious, came on under the computer-generated stainless steel logo. The announcer said, "ANN presents *Prime Time Focus,* an in-depth look at the people shaping important events of the day. Tonight, Kat Pierce talks to Tom Pennington, chief executive of embattled Ayvil Industries. Then, Len Jolles talks to Dag Ahlander, Sweden's controversial foreign minister."

Kat Pierce appeared, looking beautiful and deadly serious. "Good evening and welcome to *Prime Time Focus.* I'm Kat Pierce. Tom Pennington could have the toughest job in corporate America. He became CEO of Ayvil Industries following the explosion that killed nearly one thousand employees at the company's plant in Ohio this summer. The monstrous crime was apparently engineered by CEO Archibald Paulson, who committed suicide soon after. Now Tom

Pennington has the job of trying to pick up the pieces of this shattered company."

The shot widened to reveal Kat sitting across from Pennington. "Mr. Pennington," Kat asked solemnly, "can a company ever rebound from a tragedy as unthinkable as this?"

"I promise you, Kat," Pennington said, "it can and it will. Out of this tragedy and loss, we will forge a new vision. We owe it to the memory of those who died, to their families, to our employees around the world, the communities they live and work in, and, of course, to our shareholders. I can't reveal all the details right now, but we will make a new start with a new strategy and a new vision."

Pennington watched himself impassively. Simons watched eagerly, hanging on to every word. Kat asked tough-sounding questions. Pennington responded with understated confidence.

"And then," Kat asked as they were retelling the story of Paulson's last minutes, "he raised his loaded shotgun and pointed it right at you?"

Pennington shuddered. "Yes, I related all this in my testimony at the inquest."

"I know, but please, tell it again here tonight for the benefit of our viewers, if it's not too painful."

Pennington took a deep breath. "Well, Mr. Paulson was clearly very distraught."

"Did you fear for your life?"

"When he put that shotgun in my face, I had every reason to believe he was capable of pulling the trigger."

"Did he reveal any of the details of the mass murder?"

"No. He rambled on. He was very erratic, in a panic, and very angry."

"Do you think he had suffered a psychotic break?"

"Kat, I have no training in psychiatry. But he seemed pretty crazy to me, whatever that means. I'm convinced that if the maid had not come down to get me when she did, I wouldn't be here today."

Kat shook her head and changed the subject. As the interview went on, Lew Simons's mood brightened. With each skillful answer Pennington gave, Simons looked back at his boss and smiled.

As the segment was heading toward its conclusion, Kat asked, "That night at the plant, Mr. Pennington, the cameras caught you with tears in your eyes. Isn't that unusual behavior for a Fortune 500 executive?"

"Not at all," Pennington said. "This was a devastating human tragedy. And I responded the way a human being should. Values are the only basis for leadership. I think business needs more humanity in order to serve the greater good."

The video of Pennington that night in front of the plant appeared on screen, the tear glistening against his cheek. Up to now, Pierce had been the tough-talking, skeptical journalist. Then, just after Pennington's tear, the camera cut to Kat leaning forward to wipe the tears from her own eye, her armor finally punctured by the charismatic, feeling executive. Cinematic technique turned illusion into absolute reality for twenty million viewers.

The segment ended with Pierce thanking Pennington and Pennington saying, "No, Kat, thank you for the chance to help us all with the healing process. I believe we can emerge from this with a more human-centric corporation and a more humane outlook for the business world."

"I'm sure our viewers hope so, too. This is Kat Pierce for *Prime Time Focus.*" Simons hit the Mute button as the commercial came on. He gave Pennington the high-five sign.

"Lew," Hildreth said to Simons, "be sure to put copies of that interview into the hands of every analyst on Wall Street, whether they cover us or not. This should become a watershed moment, not just for our stock, but for the whole business world."

"Yes, Mr. Hildreth," the PR man gushed obsequiously, thrilled that the powerful old aristocrat had spoken to him by name, "a watershed moment for the whole business world." He jotted Hildreth's phrase onto his legal pad. He had the hook for the press release.

57

The ringing telephone pierced Ken's painkiller haze. He squinted against the sunlight and looked at his watch. Half past noon.

"Huuulllo," he mumbled. It felt odd to hold the phone in his left hand, but his right hand was bandaged into what looked like a first baseman's glove made of gauze.

"Olson, this is Peter Fairchild, chief auditor. From Ayvil headquarters. You have to come to New York to go over some things ASAP."

"Send one of the Gulfstreams to pick me up," Ken said, surprised at his sarcasm.

"This is serious. We've got you booked through Cleveland to La-Guardia on United. You're staying at the Ramada Midtown. Eight thirty sharp tomorrow. Eighteenth floor. Peter Fairchild, extension 7230. Oh, FYI, we are not business casual here at corporate. And don't forget to bring your ticket. It's *our* receipt." The man hung up.

Ken looked at his watch again. He had never slept this late in his life. He had no idea what they might want. Surprised at himself again, he realized he did not care.

He showered awkwardly, with a plastic garbage bag over his bandaged hand, shaved badly, got his suit pants, dress shirt, socks, and shoes on, then draped a tie around his collar. Throwing his jacket over his shoulder, he grabbed his wallet and keys and headed downstairs for the car and the airport.

58

Peter Fairchild, a man so colorless and corporate he was almost invisible, was taking Ken through the documents. "You see this e-mail here?" he said, and handed a copy across the conference room table. "This is where you first set up a payment number for Alliance Systems, Inc."

Across the table, three men stared at him grimly—Fairchild the auditor, Leonard Begley the chief legal counsel, and Lew Simons.

Ken stared back in wonder. "No, I didn't. I have no idea what you are talking about. I've never heard of Alliance Systems, I don't know what they do, and I never instructed anyone to pay them anything."

Fairchild said, "These are *your* e-mails. They come from your computer. Look, here's Alliance. Here's Bannister Manufacturing. You made these requests and had the funds sent to this account in Bermuda." Fairchild spread out a pile of documents on the conference room table. "Here is the history. And here is the statement from the bank in Bermuda, the account with your name on it. It's all here, Ken. Everything you did. You started this months before your promotion, and it only got worse afterward."

"Except I didn't do it. None of it." Ken was confused and angry.

Fairchild ignored him. "Now there must be at least a third phantom vendor because Alliance and Bannister got paid a total of three million and there's five million in the account. Alliance? Bannister? *A, B*. Was the third one a *C*? Unfortunately, the records coming out of Dayton are kind of a mess because of the, you know, disaster. But we're working on finding out the names of the others you faked. We'll have them shortly. So why don't you just come clean and get it over with?"

Ken sat upright, as if about to get up and leave. "I have to talk to Tom Pennington," he said. "Tom and I worked very closely on the turnaround. I need you guys to escalate this to Pennington's level. You'll see. He knows me, he trusts me, and he'll back me up." Ken squirmed in his chair and felt his injured hand throbbing.

His accusers exchanged glances. Then Fairchild spoke. "We *have* taken this to Mr. Pennington."

"And?" Ken asked.

"And," Fairchild said, "you're finished."

"What are you talking about?" Ken stood up. "Do you have any idea what I have done for this company? What I've contributed? What I've gone through? Not just before Arch Paulson went off the deep end but since then? I have been Tom's right-hand man, his lieutenant."

Fairchild cut him off. "I said you're finished here. Mr. Pennington's orders."

Ken sat down. He racked his brain for an explanation and a plan. He came up blank. Then a lightbulb went on. "Wait a minute, if you're going to be pressing charges," Ken said, "shouldn't there be someone here to arrest me or something? And shouldn't I have been told to have a lawyer with me? Isn't that what you do in those cases, Mr. Uh . . ." He looked at the lawyer, a smug, pale little man.

"Begley," the counsel replied. "Yes, that would be the procedure. But we are not pressing charges."

"I'm confused. You just told me I am guilty as sin and you've got the proof. Why aren't you going to try to put me in jail?"

Begley cleared his throat. "Mr. Olson, the evidence is very good but not ironclad. Unfortunately, these electronic trails are not only newer than old-fashioned paper trails, they are more, shall we say, more ambiguous from an evidentiary standpoint. Furthermore, while you almost certainly did move the money, you did not spend any of it, which, while curious, is also convenient. It means that we will be able to get the money back with interest, so the harm to the corporation is more an inconvenience than a loss. In addition, there are extenuating circumstances resulting from both your situation and the situation of the corporation at this particular moment in time."

"What the hell are you talking about?" Ken asked.

"Public relations issues," Lew Simons said urgently, "very complex public relations issues. We want to make this ugliness just go away. Mr. Pennington wants us to put the past behind us."

Simons looked at Begley, who picked up again in his haughtiest tone. "What we do not want is a highly visible court case about a company that no longer exists and will not be part of the new corporation in any case. Now, since all the money is still there in Bermuda, we propose three things. One, sign these documents, which will turn the money back over to the corporation. Two, sign this consent decree, which says, in effect, that even though you did not embezzle these funds, you promise never to do it again. Three, sign this termination agreement that says you are voluntarily resigning from the corporation, accepting this rather generous severance package, and will hold the corporation harmless now and in the future. You should have an attorney review these documents. Also, here is a package of your handiwork, printouts of the invoices, the bank statements. And here are the files on CD. A souvenir of your exploits, if you will." He handed a thick manila envelope across the desk.

Ken held up his slim briefcase. The fat envelope was too big to fit. "Can you send it to my house?"

Begley nodded.

"Just one thing," Ken said. "I want to see Tom Pennington in person, one-on-one."

"Look," said Simons, "this is a good deal, a fair deal. Actually better than fair, all things considered."

Ken stared at the flack and, to his own amazement, said in a calm, cool voice, "Fuck you."

"Mr. Olson, please," Begley said, "let's be professional about this."

"Yeah," Ken sneered, "very professional. I want to see Tom Pennington. In fact, I insist on it." He saw that he was shaking his bandaged fist in the air. He stopped and lowered his hand to his lap. "I'll sign your goddamn documents and crawl back under my rock. I just want to see Tom Pennington face-to-face."

59

The giant projection TV screen dwarfed the figures seated on the dais. The life-size Tom Pennington stood at the podium at the front of the stage. Behind him, an immense projected image of his head and shoulders mirrored his every motion.

"We are here to announce a new beginning for a new corporation. With a new mission, a new strategy, and a new name." Pennington's image dissolved to black and letters appeared on the screen. "Humanifit," Pennington said proudly. "Let me say it again." He enunciated with exaggerated clarity: "Hyoo-MAN-iffit." The letters doubled in size, filling the entire screen. "It means exactly what it says. That humanity benefits from the things we do."

Applause filled the packed hotel ballroom. A stirring musical score came up, not quite military, not quite religious. The logo shrank to the bottom third of the screen and a montage appeared above it. Happy workers in factories, happy workers in offices, happy truck drivers making deliveries, happy scientists in labs, happy people all around the world working happily for this new corporation called Humanifit.

"A great corporation has no other purpose *but* to serve humanity," Pennington said, "to serve its shareholders, its customers, its employees, and the communities where it lives and does business. To do so, it must earn a healthy and consistent profit. That's the other *f-i-t* in Humanifit. *Profit,*" he said emphatically. "Without profits, the corporation cannot exist. It cannot serve humanity. It cannot serve the greater good. Therefore, the mission of this company called Humanifit is simple and to the point: Profits for the greater good."

The Humanifit logo moved up to the middle of the screen and PROFITS FOR THE GREATER GOOD appeared below it. In the background, the moving images of happy workers froze in place.

Pennington's voice filled the ballroom. "Together, we have been tested and taught by the past. Together, we have endured unimaginable tragedy. We will never forget the colleagues we have lost. We will preserve their memory and dedicate our new efforts to them. I am humbled by the challenges and heartened by the opportunities of being your chief executive officer. I cannot do this job without the support of our employees around the world. I am asking for each and every one of you to commit yourselves to our shared vision. To our common interest and to the greater good."

Pennington gestured at the men seated at the dais. "Here at headquarters, I have asked Justin Hildreth, our most senior board member, to assume the title of chairman of the board of directors. And I have added two new inside directors to the board. They are my partners, my colleagues, and my trusted confidants, Keith Macmillan and Paul Czerwinski, the two co–chief operating officers of Humanifit."

As the three men stood and waved, their images filled the giant screen and waved behind them. More applause sounded. As the clapping subsided, the music came up again. Tom Pennington leaned into the microphone and spoke over the music. "Ladies and gentlemen, colleagues, shareholders, customers, community leaders, stakeholders of all kinds around the world, welcome to our shared future. Welcome to something more than a new company. Welcome to a new *kind* of company. Welcome to the future. Welcome to Humanifit." As the music filled the ballroom, the audience rose as one and applauded thunderously.

60

"Lew Simons waited anxiously in the anteroom just behind and below the stage. Ken Olson stood beside him, suitcoat slung over his bad right arm, and, beside him, a 275-pound security guard wearing a cheap suit and an earpiece. As the presentation ended, Simons turned to Ken. "Now, we agreed. Five minutes of Mr. Pennington's time, that's it. And no funny business." He nodded his head in the direction of the guard who loomed over Ken like a stone wall covered in gabardine.

As applause and music rumbled in the background, Tom Pennington came down the stairs and entered the small waiting room. He stopped when he saw Ken. Simons bounded over and took him by the arm protectively. "Tom, I told him just five minutes and no funny business."

"It's okay, Lew," Pennington said gently, and walked over to Ken. "What happened to your hand?"

"Oh, nothing."

"Looks pretty serious from here."

"Cut the small talk, Tom," Ken sputtered. "What the hell is going on?"

Pennington radiated confidence, serenity, and warmth. "Ken, you evoke such a complicated array of emotions in me. Admiration, respect, sympathy, pity, and now, disappointment. Actually, it's worse than disappointment, much worse. Everything I thought I knew about you, all the faith I invested in you, I-I . . . Listen, Ken, I will always feel your pain. Your loss is unimaginable to me. But at the same time, what you did was unforgivable."

Ken wanted to explode but stood silent.

"Ken, the one value that separates the business world from the jungle is trust. And trust is what you violated. We've cut you the best of all possible deals. Now what you should do is focus on the future.

Go find a place to start a new life. I think we've given you justice and then some."

Ken wanted to repeat the word *justice* and demand how Pennington could dare to call this justice. But when he opened his mouth, only air came out.

Justin Hildreth appeared at the top of the stairs. "Tom," he called, "the analysts from Morgan Stanley and UBS are very positive. The rebound is officially under way."

"I'll be there in a second, Justin," Pennington called. Then he turned back and put his hand on Ken's shoulder. "Please accept the settlement. It's more than enough to let you start a new life. Others in this company don't feel you deserve it, but I do. Believe me, I do." Pennington started to leave then turned back and leaned forward to whisper in Ken's ear, "Alliance, Bannister, Cambridge. *A, B, C.* I can't believe I didn't catch it back then." In a flash, he was up the stairs and gone.

At the same instant, Ken felt something like a vise grip squeezing his shoulders and lifting him onto his toes. The security guard escorted him out of the room down a dingy corridor past hotel kitchens, pantries, laundry rooms, and onto the loading dock at the hotel's service entrance. The racket of boxes being unloaded and trucks beeping in reverse gear filled the air.

"I'm supposed to leave you out here," the guard said gruffly, "and tell you not to bother anyone from the company again. D'ya unnerstand?"

"Sure," Ken said, pulling his arm away from the goon's grip, "fuck you very much."

The giant glared at him and raised one arm threateningly.

"Have a nice day," Ken said as he walked quickly toward the sidewalk.

61

Park Avenue in front of the Waldorf-Astoria after lunch hour was quiet. Light traffic and few pedestrians. The sky was cloudless and the temperature was cool. Ken started walking north on Park Avenue.

"Well, Sandy," he muttered under his breath, "that's it. I've lost everything there is to lose." After a few blocks he stopped and stood at attention.

"Alliance, Bannister, Cambridge. *A, B, C. C?* Cambridge! Holy shit. Pennington knew what the *C* was, but Fairchild didn't."

Holding his suit coat with his bandaged hand, he reached into his inside breast pocket and extracted his cell phone. "Fairchild was 7230," he said, dialing the number. It rang twice.

"Fairchild here," the gruff voice said.

"Ken Olson here."

"Olson? What do *you* want?"

"You found out what the *C* was yet?"

"You gonna volunteer some help?"

"Then you haven't found it yet. The *C.*"

"What do you care?"

"You haven't found it yet, have you?" Silence. "Found any *D*s or *E*s?"

"That supposed to be some kinda clue?"

"Maybe," Ken said, and hung up. "Je-sus. Pennington knows and the auditor doesn't. Sandy, I need your help on this one."

No one noticed Ken Olson heading for Central Park. He was just another businessman with his suit coat and briefcase in one hand, bandages on the other, talking to his dead wife.

Ken sat on a bench beside the picturesque lake at the southeast corner of the park. He was talking softly, making points with one hand then the other. Just himself and Sandy.

"Okay, since Pennington knows all about the embezzlement, he must know I didn't do it. Now maybe he embezzled the money. But to a CEO like him, that's chump change and not worth risking your career over.

"So he's not the embezzler. But he's still withholding the truth about this from his own company. Why would he do that?

"Because, uh . . . maybe because the embezzlement is covering something bigger.

"Like what?

"Like murder?

"How?

"Don't know yet.

"Okay. What have we learned about Pennington today?

"That he's an ice-cold liar.

"Okay, what else could he have lied about?

"How about everything?

"Okay, everything he ever said was a lie.

"He said he wanted to save the business.

"Lie.

"He said a turnaround was viable.

"Lie.

"He said he was heartbroken when everybody was murdered.

"Lie.

"He cried on national TV.

"Lie."

Ken stopped his two-sided monologue, took a very long, very deep breath, and spoke very slowly. "He . . . said he . . . wanted to install . . . a new . . . ventilation system to make the building . . . more comfortable."

He could only mouth the word, "Lie."

His hands dropped to his lap. His shoulders slumped. He spoke to the air. "Sandy? Sara? What did I do to you?" His eyes filled with tears, but the tears would not fall. He wiped his eyes dry, and that was that. It was strange. After all these months of weeping, he could not cry anymore. He even wanted to this time. He just could not.

Ken felt cold and empty inside. Yet relieved. At last he knew the full and final weight of the guilt and regret he would carry until he himself died. He knew exactly what he had done, what he could never undo. He also knew what he might do to try to make up for it. He reached for his cell phone and speed-dialed Phil Lambert's office.

62

"I've got the money," Ken said, "I can afford Medusa. Those bastards just paid me off. I might as well use their money against them. What else am I going to do with it?"

Phil Lambert looked up from his desk in the shabby, mouse-gray offices of Medusa Worldwide on Third Avenue and Fifty-third Street. "Gee, Ken, our retainers start at five thousand a month."

"No problem." Ken said. He was animated—angry and cheerful at the same time. "I want to hire *you*," he pointed the index finger of his uninjured hand emphatically, "my ex-brother-in-law, to be my very own private investigator."

Phil gave him a skeptical glance.

"I'm prepared to pay whatever it takes for you to dig around and come up with the evidence to nail Tom Pennington. That was *your* sister he murdered and your one and only niece."

Phil sighed. He was thinking, Poor guy hasn't a fucking clue what he's walking into. Not a fucking clue.

"Did you hear me?" Ken asked impatiently.

"Ken, I want their killers brought to justice as much as you do. But they had an inquest, findings, the whole nine yards, and nobody even hinted at Pennington. They established that Paulson paid for the bombing. And he shot himself when the chickens came home to roost. Paulson sent Houghton the money. Then Houghton double-crossed Paulson and sent the trail right back on him, *and* killed his own partners in the process. Very slick."

"There's more to it than that. There *has* to be, Phil."

"Ken, sometimes things are exactly what they seem. Paulson had the motive, he said so in front of witnesses. And as a big-time CEO, he had the means. You have to accept his guilt as a real possibility. It could be that the crime has already been solved. That's what the FBI and the criminal justice system concluded."

"Oh, come on, Phil! You believe everything the government says? *You* of all people?" Ken was steaming. "You think there are no unanswered questions about the murder—murder!—of *your* sister and her child and all those innocent people? Do you? *Huh?*"

Phil was silent. Of course, Ken was right.

"Huh? Answer me!"

"No," Phil said sadly, "of course I don't. It's just that sometimes it's better not to . . ." His voice trailed off.

"Phil, they made me a free man today. I'm going to put the house on the market and move to New York. So I can be near Tom Pennington day and night. And I'm going to hire a savvy investigator to help me nail him. I've got the money and God knows I've got the time. Now, is the investigator who gets justice done for Sandy and Sara going to be you? Or some stranger? I'm going to make it happen, Phil, one way or the other. Who's it going to be? *Who* is it going to be?"

"Ken," Phil said, "I don't think you understand. There are no good guys out there. There are bad guys and worse guys. Big government, big business, they're all in bed together. If they covered this up, they did it for a reason."

"Yeah, like what?"

"Like the reason no one is supposed to know about. That's why they used private military muscle. Ken, did you know that the USA, our government and our great big respectable corporations, are at the top of the list of customers of PMCs? More than Columbian drug lords, more than third-world dictators, more than illicit arms traders, more than all the vicious, murderous low-lifes out there put together. And do you know why?"

Ken shrugged.

"Because they can get their dirtiest work done and keep their distance from it." Phil bent down and reached into the file drawer of his desk. He fished around for a moment and pulled out a folder. He flipped through its contents and landed on the stapled sheets he was looking for. "Ken, this is a hundred-billion-dollar global industry."

Phil handed him the pages, a single-spaced list of corporation names three pages long with their countries of registry. Many of the names were American companies he recognized—famous consulting firms, oil companies, defense contractors, and manufacturers of all sorts. Others were names of ancient warriors or battles or mythological heroes. Some were just acronyms or names like Protection Services, Ltd. The countries of origin stuttered with repeats like South Africa, Canada, Angola, Israel, United Arab Emirates, Russian Federation, Uganda, France, Belgium, Zimbabwe, and, with the most repeats of all, United States and United Kingdom.

"This is the marketplace," Phil explained. "Any kind of military expertise or muscle you could imagine is for sale. Believe me, anything. Think gene splicing is hot? This, bro, is a growth industry and it's really and truly global."

Ken shook his head. "I never knew this existed."

"Because you're not supposed to know!" Phil lost his cool. "When I tell you I have seen really ugly shit done by really horrible people, I mean just that. And I was working for the *good* guys. This is what you're up against, Mr. Crusader for Justice. And your severance settlement and the profit on your house doesn't amount to shit compared to the millions your former employer is ready to use to keep whatever their dirty secret is secret."

"What about Sandy and Sara?" Ken asked in a whisper.

"What about them?" Phil's voice cracked slightly.

"You and I let them down while they were alive. True?"

"True," Phil said and looked down. "But nothing we can do can change that. Or help them."

"No, but what about us?" With his good hand, Ken took his brother-in-law by the shoulder and shook him. "What about *us*?"

Phil yanked his shoulder out of Ken's grip. "What do you mean?"

"Phil, what can *we* do to make things right?"

Phil took a deep, weary breath.

Ken asked, "Deal?"

"Deal," Phil said reluctantly. And, he thought, My poor dear brother-in-law has no idea what kind of deadly things we could find under this rock he wants us to lift. No fucking idea.

Ken offered a high five.

Phil did not return the gesture. He spoke glumly. "You have

officially engaged me as your Medusa investigator. I'll clear it with my bosses and get an engagement letter drawn up."

"Good. Now tell me, where do we begin?"

Phil took out a yellow legal pad and began making a diagram, circles with connecting lines, like a complex chemistry equation combined with a diagrammed sentence. Phil's pen went back to the top of the diagram. "We start with the guy called Houghton. We know he's a vicious killer who has a knack for technology and complex project management. That makes him a valuable guy in the world of private military corporations. He's got to have a reputation."

Phil drew more lines on his chart. "This guy is known *somewhere*. And sooner or later, he takes his money out of his dirty bank accounts and spends it. So we can work on the man's professional trail. And his money trail." He circled the lower half of the chart. "That's where the international banking system and the banking havens come in."

"Like the Caymans, where Paulson's dough went," Ken said eagerly.

"Uh-huh. Like the Channel Islands, Mauritius, Panama, Pakistan, like the Bahamas, like Vanuatu."

"Vanu-what?"

"Island in the middle of the South Pacific. French bankers there ask no questions as long as you transact in French. Everybody's got to get paid, you know, but it's best if no one knows where, how, or how much. There are shell corporations inside shell corporations set up by lawyers in Belize who front for lawyers in Fiji who know nothing about the shell company in Andorra that holds the untraceable bearer shares from the British Virgin Islands."

"You lost me," Ken said, looking confused.

"That's the idea." Phil winked.

"Good. So you're really on board."

"I was never not on board, Ken," Phil said hesitantly. "It's just that—"

"What? *What?*"

"You think that a has-been DIA agent working privately for an unemployed middle manager can take on the secret dirty tricks department of big business? With all their guns and lawyers and billions? Do you really think justice has a snowball's chance in hell?"

Ken swallowed hard. "Yes, I do," he said, mistaking his determination for confidence, "abso-fucking-lutely."

63

Kat Pierce liked the missionary position best. After a long day of political maneuvering at the network, it was a relief to lie back and let someone else do most of the work. Besides, after trying just about every position and kink, she had concluded that if a man wasn't worth having sex with face-to-face, he wasn't worth having sex with.

When the phone rang beside her bed, she whispered, "Ignore it." She covered her eyes with one hand to keep from losing her concentration and raised her hips to rub her pubic bone gently against her lover. She closed her eyes and concentrated on keeping the rocking motion slow and controlled.

"This is the answering machine," her friendly male computer-synthesized greeting announced, "please leave a message after the tone." The machine beeped.

Over the speakerphone, the voice of Ken Olson hemmed and hawed. "Uh, this is Ken Olson calling for Kat Pierce. I've spent the last couple of days calling all around the network, trying to get this unlisted number of yours. I, uh, hope this is Kat Pierce of American News Network, the, uh, TV journalist, uh, because I've got something very important to tell you. If this is not the same Kat Pierce, then I guess you can, uh, I don't know. Ms. Pierce, I've seen your reports on TV. And especially last spring, your reports about the mass murder at Ayvil Industries. You may remember me. I was the plant manager. Well, I'm calling you because I've got a story you can help me make public. Uh, Ms. Pierce, I have information about the murder, about who really did it. It wasn't Arch Paulson, the CEO who committed suicide. It was just set up to look that way. It was Tom Pennington. That's right, Tom Pennington. I can prove this to you, Ms. Pierce. That's why I need your help. You can use your power as a journalist to help see that justice is done. Please call me on my cell phone. I'm here in New York for a while then I'm moving back for good. So I'll be available to meet at your convenience. Any time, really." He gave her his number and hung up.

Kat Pierce lay still, her hips no longer grinding. Tom Pennington withdrew his now semi-erect penis, shiny with her vaginal juices.

"That's ridiculous. He's delusional," he snapped. He composed himself then added in a more sympathetic tone, "He's sad and pathetic, actually." Pennington sighed and lay down beside his fiancée. "This poor, poor man. Oh, Kat, he has such a heartbreaking story. . . ."

On the floor beside the bed was the new issue of *Fortune* magazine. On the cover, bigger than life, was handsome, smiling Tom Pennington. Beneath his movie star chin, the headline proclaimed, "A more humane face for corporate America."

64

The CEO of General Industries arrived without fanfare. Harry Warren made sure he and Guillaume drove themselves in a modest rental car from the GI Gulfstream to the Perry's Bend Nuclear Power Plant. Michael Guillaume had suggested that they might go business casual for Davenport's benefit.

"Horseshit!" Warren had said. "We wear suits to important business, and this is important business." Harry Warren was a short bald man whom no one remembered as short or bald. He filled every room he entered with his energy and personal magnetism. "We'll give this Davenport guy the respect his position deserves, even if the man himself doesn't deserve it. Besides, he's from the government," he added with a smile. "I want to let him know that we'll only go so far to suck up to him."

Howard Polski, who flew in on another GI jet from another Dynergetix facility in South Carolina, met them at the plant. The three men sat in a big empty conference room in Building 4 at Perry's Bend. They sat obediently while Gerald Davenport harangued them with excerpts from a seventy-page draft report on the tube-rupture event months before. The report was to be a multiagency report, compiled by Davenport and his NRC people, General Industries, the state Department of Public Services (DPS), the state Emergency Management Office (EMO), the state Department of Health (DOH).

But for this meeting, his so-called prehearing, Davenport sat alone at a long table facing the other long table at which the three GI executives sat. The conference room was pointlessly large for such a small gathering.

"As you know," he said, reading aloud from his papers, "DPS, EMO, and DOH will jointly decide whether a larger proceeding will be necessary to determine whether the event could have been prevented, what the root causes were, and how to address them. Key to this will be an assessment of the failure of Dynergetix to thoroughly assess steam-generator-tube degradation and provide NRC with clear and complete information." Davenport looked up from his report and stared at the men facing him. "This failure may be symptomatic of more widespread problems undetected by Dynergetix management."

"But Mr. Davenport," Guillaume said deferentially, "Dynergetix no longer owns or operates the plant. General Industries has brought in all new management under the supervision of Howard Polski. And we have begun a new top-to-bottom quality management process along with equipment upgrades and replacement, where indicated. Howard Polski's team has been providing documentation every step of the way. We are deliberately exceeding all guidelines and specifications."

Davenport ignored Guillaume. He looked directly at Harry Warren. "Mr. Warren, may I ask you a question?"

"Certainly, Mr. Davenport. That's why I'm here."

"Why did your company buy Dynergetix in the first place?"

Warren smiled. Like a slugger who sees a juicy fastball coming straight down the middle. "Strategy," he said. "Dynergetix was an undervalued asset. Undercapitalized and undermanaged. We could buy it at a good price and, by investing in it and managing it better, bring the business up to its full potential value. We're already starting to show results."

"You an engineer?" Davenport asked.

"No, I'm not. But having spent my life at GI, I have been surrounded by engineers. Really fine ones. Mike Guillaume, my right-hand man here, is an engineer." Warren reached out and put his hand on Guillaume's shoulder, like a proud father. "First in his class at MIT. Isn't that right, Mike?"

Guillaume nodded awkwardly. Davenport remained stone-faced.

"And Howard here, Howard was tops in his class at Cal Tech."

"Third, actually," Howard said.

"And what, may I ask, do you do with all those employees of Dynergetix?" Davenport's eyes never left Warren.

"We evaluate them for their specific competencies. And we do so quite scientifically. If they have what it takes to perform at the level we demand, they stay. If they're not up to our standards, we provide them with severance packages and outplacement services. We try to give them as soft a landing as possible."

"That's damn white of you," Davenport said with a smirk. He looked directly at Guillaume.

Polski grimaced. Guillaume shook his head.

"Mr. Davenport," Warren said sharply, "this plant and public safety are the agendas here. I don't know what your other agendas might be. But they do not belong. I am offended by that racial slur and others I have heard about. It is hateful. It is unhelpful. It is beside the point. And, for a government employee like you, it is illegal. My colleague is too proud and too polite to play that card, even though it would be his right to do so."

Warren stood and raised his right arm, his index finger pointing at Davenport. "But I am not nearly the gentleman he is. Mr. Davenport, if you make one more remark like that in front of me or my people or in front of anyone remotely connected to any of us, I promise you, I will have your ass deep-fried. If there's one thing I can afford, it's lawyers. Lots and lots of lawyers."

Davenport stared at Warren in shock.

Warren was on a roll. "Now, if we are going to talk about fixing this plant, let's get on with it. If not, this meeting is over." Warren picked up his briefcase. Guillaume and Polski sat still and silent.

Davenport looked down into his papers and mumbled, "I, uh, am recommending that there will be no need for a formal hearing. That will be all."

65

Ken studied the view from his new Manhattan apartment. It was on the ground floor of a shabby building on West Ninety-fourth Street between Columbus and Amsterdam avenues. It was one of those undistinguished mid-rise apartment buildings from the 1950s, a plain upended shoebox of dirty white brick that ruined the block of elegantly detailed nineteenth-century brownstone town houses. Ken's one window on the world was behind bars, looking out on the sidewalk at a sunless slice of street and a scrawny, stunted old tree. It suited his mood perfectly, including the unreasonably high rent.

His apartment was a monk's cell. A narrow single bed and bureau against one wall, plus a small bedside table jammed with twenty framed photos of Sandy and Sara and the three of them together—a shrine.

No other furniture and no decoration, except by the window, the desk and computer that had been in the study in his house and, on the floor, a large color laser printer. On the wall surrounding the window were dozens of clumps of pages pushpinned from floor almost to ceiling. The results of many Internet searches about the life of Thomas Pennington—from his prep school accomplishments to the recent articles about his transformation of Ayvil into the hot stock called Humanifit. It, too, was a shrine, but of a wholly different kind.

Beside the Pennington papers were two sheets of paper pinned to the wall. One was the cryptic diagram Phil Lambert had drawn on his legal pad a couple of months before, showing how they would track down Houghton and his money. The other was a sheet on which Ken had drawn the outline of a man's head, hairline, ears, glasses, and goatee but no other facial features. Above the head, he had written "Peter Houghton" followed by six angrily scrawled question marks.

Ken flipped open his cell phone and dialed Phil's office. The secretary put him through at once. "You back from that banking assignment?" Ken asked.

"Last night," Phil answered.

Ken was angry. "We lost time while you were away."

"I racked up enough billable hours to double my bonus from last year," Phil said. "A man's got to make a living."

"I'm a paying client, too, you know," Ken snapped.

"Ken," Phil said, determined not to sound defensive, "I'm afraid you are not the chairman of the bank in question and the college roommate and lifelong friend of the chairman of Medusa Worldwide."

"I see," Ken said coldly.

"So," Phil's voice turned bright, "you all moved in?"

"I've been a New Yorker now for almost a month."

"Congratulations. How do you like it?"

"It's easy to figure out life here in the Big Apple," Ken said, looking around at his grim apartment. "Everything is way too expensive and a royal pain in the ass."

"You're getting the hang of it," Phil said, "except that no one who lives here calls it the Big Apple. Listen, Ken, I can see you tomorrow at eleven. We can get the investigation rolling. Can you make it?"

"Uh, let me check my calendar." Ken made a lot of noise shuffling papers next to the phone. "Yes, I think if I move a few meetings around. Yes, yes, I think I can do it. Yeah," he called as if talking to a secretary some distance away, "my secretary says I can make it."

"Wiseass," Phil said, and hung up.

Ken looked around the little apartment, trying to decide what to do next. He clicked on his music file on the computer and selected the song "Scar Tissue" by the Red Hot Chili Peppers. With time on his hands and a broadband connection, Ken had discovered all sorts of music he never knew about in his past life. The Chili Peppers' brand of rough and raucous Los Angeles funk rock was one of his favorites. This particular song grabbed him with its opening line, "Scar tissue that I wish you saw." Boy, did he know about scar tissue. The drawling, melancholy beat resonated with his mood and he found himself singing along with the refrain, "With the birds I'll share this lonely view," over and over again.

As the music filled his little apartment, he thought about the handgun he had bought before leaving Ohio. He usually kept it in the back of his bottom drawer. Today, he had it out on a pile of books on the floor beside his desk. He had joined a gun club where he practiced, and was becoming proficient with it. He knew that the compact, small-caliber pistol was good only at very close range. But that was fine with him. He knew he would use it at close range. The question was whether he would ever have the satisfaction of using it to kill one or both of the men who killed his family. The Chili Peppers sang another line toward the end of "Scar Tissue" that resonated even more powerfully with his state of mind: "I'll make it to the moon if I have to crawl."

Ken's reverie was shattered by the harsh metallic buzzing of his doorbell. In the weeks since he packed up and moved to Manhattan, no one had come calling except delivery men bearing cheap take-out food. He turned off the music, walked to his door, and was about to unlock it when he remembered this was New York. He stopped and peered through the fish-eye lens of the peephole. There stood an attractive young woman in jeans and sneakers. Late twenties, early thirties. He thought she looked familiar, but he couldn't quite place her. She had dark hair and dark eyes, like Sandy. She was fidgeting from one foot to the other.

He unbolted the door.

"Hi," she said with some embarrassment, "I live upstairs. I've seen you a couple of times in the building."

"Oh yeah," he said, now recognizing her, "I've seen you, too."

"I heard your music playing. Sorry to bother you. Listen," she said, wincing slightly, "my lock is jammed. Again. The super's not around, naturally. And I," she lowered her voice, "I *really* have to use the bathroom. Could I trouble you? I'm sorry."

"Oh, sure." Ken smiled and waved her inside. "Please. Be my guest." She dashed across to his bathroom and closed the flimsy door. The hard surfaces of the bathroom combined with the hollow door to act like an echo chamber, magnifying the sounds that spilled out into the apartment. The toilet seat dropped violently, an explosive and very long rush of pee hit the water in the bowl, a little fart, the sound of toilet paper being yanked off the roll, then the roar of the toilet flushing and water running in the sink. She opened the door looking embarrassed and relieved.

"Thank you so-o-o much." She wiped her hands on the seat of her jeans and crossed the room toward him. "Well," she said, trying to smile her way out of her uneasiness, "these New York apartments. You hear everything, don't you? Jeez. I guess we're kinda like an old married couple now. And we haven't even met. I'm Cindy, Cindy Morse. I'm sorry to barge in on you like this." Before extending her right hand, she wiped it again on the seat of her jeans. It was still slightly wet when he shook it.

"No, I'm sorry," he said, "no hand towels. I wasn't expecting guests."

"Listen," she said, motioning her head upstairs toward her apartment, "I hate to—"

"Pee and run?" Ken couldn't believe what he said. She winced again, hands cupped protectively in front of her crotch, her thighs clenched together. "No, that's not what I meant, I'm sorry. I meant maybe you don't have to run off right this second. I just thought—"

"It's my lock. Upstairs. The key is jammed, and I can't open it. All my keys are up there, stuck in the door."

"No problem," Ken said, thinking quickly. He held up one finger to tell her to wait while he rummaged through his closet past shoes and boxes. He found the toolbox he used to keep in the garage in Dayton and fished out a yellow spray can of WD-40. He inserted the long, thin plastic straw designed for problems like locks and held it up to show her. "This should do it," he announced.

"Great," she said, and motioned for him to follow her upstairs. Checking his pocket to be sure he had his keys with him, he followed her past the elevator to the stairwell and up two flights to the door of her apartment. Her key chain was in the top lock.

First he squirted oil around the keyhole, jiggled the key to spread it, and pulled it out. He handed the key chain back to her. "Step one," he said, suddenly enjoying himself. He squirted more oil into the keyhole, reached his free hand back toward her like a surgeon, and said, "Key, please."

She handed him the key chain, the key in question first. He squirted the length of the key again and slowly worked it into the lock. It jiggled, he turned it, and the lock opened with a snap. He unlocked and locked it several times to make sure it was working. "There you go. One less tip for the super you can never find."

"Yeah, tell me about it," she said. "Thanks a lot, I really appreciate everything."

"Oh, my pleasure, really."

Cindy backed into her doorway then stepped out into the hall again. "Listen, I, uh, would you like to go have a coffee or something around the corner? You know, the Starbucks?" She cocked her head to one side and smiled.

Ken hesitated then said, "Sure, I'd like that. Cindy, is it?"

"Yeah, Cindy." She gave him a questioning look. "And?"

"Oh, of course," Ken said, stumbling on her cue. "I'm Ken Olson." They shook hands again.

"Hi, Ken Olson," she said, "give me ten minutes to pull myself together. I'll come get you and we can go to Starbucks." She hesitated before closing her door. "You new in New York?"

"Brand new."

"I thought so."

66

Ken and Cindy sat side by side in the crowded Starbucks overlooking Columbus Avenue.

"It's Thursday afternoon," Ken said, "and this place is packed. Tell me, how do all these people support themselves without regular jobs?"

"I don't know. We all get by, I guess. We do different things. Freelancers, creative stuff. Me, I'm a special ed teacher."

"Really?"

"That's work. But it's not nine-to-five in an office," she added emphatically.

He decided he liked her, and not just because she looked vaguely like Sandy.

"Actually," she said, "I have a dual identity. I take acting classes and go on casting calls whenever I can. I'm an actor." She turned her head as if talking to someone beside her. "No, I'm a teacher." She turned her head to one side then the other, back and forth. "Actor, teacher. Actor, teacher. Teacher, actor." She shrugged. "I guess people come to New York to try things they could never try back where they came from."

"And where would that be?" he asked.

"Fall River, Mass. How about you?"

"Umm," he thought for a moment, "Ohio."

"And you're . . . a writer?"

"What makes you say that?"

"Well, I noticed your computers and all your research papers on the wall, so I figure you must be writing a book or an article or something like that."

"Yeah, something like that." The last thing Ken wanted was to explain himself.

"And you're . . . recently divorced," she said with a bit of pride in her powers of detection.

He looked at her quizzically. She took his left hand in hers and pointed to his third finger. "See? The indentation and white shadow from your wedding ring are still there. You stopped wearing it just a short time ago. Am I right?"

"Well, yes and no. I did stop wearing it about a month ago." Ken was not sure how much of the story he wanted to get into. "But . . . my wife died. Very suddenly. A terrible accident. Last summer. Along with our daughter." Ken looked down at his lap.

"Oh my God! I'm so sorry. You poor man! How awful! I didn't mean to pry. I am so sorry." Cindy took him by the shoulders, just short of hugging him.

Ken gave her a half smile. "Thanks, I'm pretty okay," he said. "I have good days and . . ." His voice trailed off as he glanced out the window.

She let go of him. They drank their coffee in silence. When she finished, she asked, "Would you like to try a real New York adventure?"

"Sure, what kind?"

"A walk in Central Park." She looked at her watch. "If we walk across to the East Side now, I'll have just enough time to get on the Lexington Avenue subway and get to my class downtown."

"Love to," Ken said, and smiled for the first time in a long time.

67

The man called Houghton, then Hodes, was now blond and letting himself into Ken's apartment with the keys he had made from the superintendent's master set two days before.

The hooker had been easy to hire. For a thousand dollars she was happy to seduce the building's superintendent in the middle of the day while his wife was out and the kids were at school. It was easy to sex him and drug him just enough to convince him that he was Superman. Long enough so she could give the big blond man the building's keys for an hour. Long enough for him to make copies of the front door key and Ken's keys.

The big blond man looked like just another repairman or installer, with his metal tool chest and Panasonic TV box strapped with bungee cords to a chrome suitcase wheelie. He could have been from the cable company or Con Ed or the company that services the coin-operated washers and dryers in the basement. Except for the walkie-talkie headset and the watcher down the block, the man who had been called Bill Hunt in Ohio. He was waiting to alert him if Ken and Cindy should return ahead of schedule.

The big blond man paid little attention to Ken's things. Except for the outline sketch labeled "Peter Houghton" with all its question marks on the wall. He stared at it for a moment and snickered. Then he yanked it from under the pushpin, folded it, and put it in his pocket. Then he saw the pistol on top of the pile of books. He picked it up. It practically disappeared into the palm of his hand.

Stupid little pop gun, he thought. A gun for a girl to keep in her purse. *"Vokkin' slap poes,"* he muttered. Fucking weak pussy. He might use it to kill someone who did not matter. Like his watcher on the street, Hunt or whatever his name was, the man he would use for maybe another job or two—until he knew too much and had to be eliminated.

He put the little gun in his pocket and set to work on Ken's apartment.

First, he unplugged Ken's computer and printer from the surge protector connected to the wall socket. He opened the Panasonic box and lifted out what appeared to be the shell of a television set and set it on the desk beside the computer monitor. Then he got a different surge protector from his tool kit and connected all the electronics to it. He dropped Ken's surge protector into the empty television carton. Then he got another device, apparently a small transistor radio but with several wires coming out of it, and walked over to the old gas stove in the cooking alcove of the one-room apartment. He set the "radio" on the stove, went back to his toolbox, and got a flashlight.

"Anybody coming?" he asked into the mouthpiece of his walkie-talkie. "Over."

"Nope," Hunt's voice crackled, "nobody. Over."

"Watch for any man–woman couples. In all directions. Over."

"Nothing so far. Over."

"Over," the blond man said, and bent over the back of the stove to look for the gas line.

68

Ken and Cindy walked diagonally across Central Park, headed south. They passed busy softball fields and tennis courts, patches of forest carefully landscaped by Frederick Law Olmstead and Calvert Vaux 150 years before to grow into natural-looking primeval woods, the way they did today. They walked around the Great Lawn and by the side of Turtle Pond where Belvedere Castle loomed with its stone turret housing the weather station.

At some point in the walk—Ken had not noticed when—Cindy put her arm through his and there it stayed. They passed the equestrian statue of the medieval Polish king with his swords drawn, crossed the Park Drive, and headed down Cedar Hill past dog walkers and expensive English and German nannies with their old-fashioned prams toward the stone gate at Fifth Avenue and Seventy-ninth Street. The sun had almost set in the sky behind them.

They had been chatting effortlessly about little things—likes and dislikes, favorites of this and that. The casual physical contact was warm and easy. Not romantic. Just friendly. The noise of Fifth Avenue broke their bubble of intimacy. Their locked arms finally separated.

Ken was feeling rather jaunty. He realized that, other than shaking hands, he had hardly touched or been touched by another person since the morning he said good-bye to Sandy and Sara at the airport.

"Behold," he said, gesturing like a tour guide at the line of exclusive apartment buildings across the street, "the co-ops of Fifth Avenue, home to the densest concentration of multimillionaires in the world. I know this from my research," he added parenthetically. "Did you know, Cindy, apartments over here routinely sell for twenty million and up?"

"Really?"

"Oh yeah, I've read all about it. But here's the good part. These co-ops are so exclusive the buyers have to put down one hundred percent in cash. No mortgages allowed, thank you."

"Jeez."

"But that's not all. In order to get approved by the co-op board, they've got to show a liquid net worth at least ten times the purchase price of the apartment. That's two hundred million *after* you've plunked down twenty million to buy the damn thing."

Cindy looked up at the cream-colored stone façades and the impeccable canopies quietly announcing the building numbers, like 980, each one a proclamation of immeasurable status to those in the know. "I don't worry about this stuff, Ken," she said. "I have trouble with my monthly Visa payment. And I still owe a couple of thousand for the furniture I bought last year. In fact, my roommate just moved out, and I've got to get a new one if I'm going to make the rent."

They stood on the west side of Fifth Avenue and watched the scene. Town cars, limos, Mercedes-Benzes, Rolls-Royces, Bentleys coming and going. The doormen, many wearing white gloves, dressed in military parade splendor, ushered privileged residents and visitors in and out of the buildings.

They were approaching a newer apartment building. Jarringly modern and gray, it stood out from the cream color of the older limestone buildings around it.

"That's some fence," Cindy said as they approached the building. Enclosing the narrow strip of plantings between the building and the sidewalk was an elegantly sculptured, antique cast-iron fence ten feet high. Every black post was a sculptured spear ending in a long-pointed tip encased in shiny gold leaf.

"Sure is," Ken said, "the builder ransacked it from an old mansion up the Hudson. Like that Vanderbilt wrought-iron gate at the Conservatory up at Hundred-and-fifth Street and Fifth. This fence came from the mansion next door, the Van Hootens or some such. Now it's at nine-seven-seven Fifth." Ken read the numbers on the canopy as they passed underneath it.

They stood and looked into the cavernous lobby. The walls were towering slabs of polished gray stone. Doormen in gray uniforms were scurrying about. At the far back wall, a waterfall cascaded down a polished stone slab, hiding the elevator banks from sight. A line of very spare modern crystal chandeliers hung from the twenty-foot ceiling, one after the other. The effect was very grand and very austere.

At that moment, a group of six people appeared from behind the waterfall. The men were in tuxedos, the women in glittery evening dresses and high-heeled sandals. They were laughing, looking perfect and glamorous. Even at this distance, Ken could recognize them. There was Tom Pennington. At his side, ANN's Kat Pierce was touching him fondly. Ken winced at the thought of his naiveté in contacting her with his suspicions months before. From the handle-bar mustache, he recognized Ed McCabe, the aging billionaire founder of American News Network. Beside him was an elegant fortyish woman who was probably his latest wife. And with them was Doug Welch, Hollywood's hottest director-of-the-moment, and Kristi Burnham, the female lead of his last action movie, her neckline open down to her navel. Ken froze, watching them get closer and closer. They paid no attention to the world around them. Their private joke, whatever it was, made them oblivious.

Ken clenched his lips. Cindy touched his shoulder. "Hey, what's wrong?"

He watched them approach, just a few feet behind the glass wall and the revolving door. The starlet looked ahead and made eye con-tact with him. He turned his head in a panic. They were about to reach the revolving door.

Ken took Cindy's hand urgently and pulled her out from under the lit canopy to the near darkness of the sidewalk beside it. As the group of six began to file through the revolving door one by one, he threw his arms around Cindy and pressed his face against her cheek, twirling her around so he could watch them entering the waiting limousine over her shoulder. When the doorman closed the limou-sine door and the car started to pull away, he let go of Cindy. She kept her hands around his waist.

"What was that about?" she said.

"I'm sorry."

"Don't be," she cooed, not letting go of him.

Ken pulled her hands off his waist and started speaking rapid-fire. "*That* was the CEO I used to work for. It was no accident that killed my wife and daughter. That bastard had a thousand other people blown up at our plant in Ohio! And I came to New York to nail him and—"

"I remember that!" she said with a flash of recognition. "On the news! The bombing. Oh my God!" Cindy took him by the shoulders.

Ken squirmed himself free. "Uh, listen, I, uh, shouldn't we be getting you to your subway?"

"It's okay, I can skip class." She touched his arm again, gently. "You're all alone here, aren't you?"

Ken looked down.

"Well, not anymore." Cindy put her arm through his and pulled him toward the crosswalk. "Let's go back to the West Side. I want you to tell me everything. Everything."

69

"Tom, what is it?" Kat Pierce asked with annoyance. She had to lean over and whisper loudly into his ear to be heard above the music and racket. They were at Table 1 of the grand ballroom of the chic new hotel in TriBeCa. Ultraexpensive and themed with puzzlingly sparse modern artworks, The Minimalist was this season's favorite venue for charity fund-raisers. Kat and Tom were seated with Ed McCabe and wife and Doug and Kristi and two other luminaries at the fifty-thousand-dollar-per-table dinner.

"You've been looking at your watch all evening," Kat snapped. "It's ten after ten, if you've got to know."

"It's nothing," Pennington said. "I'll be right back." He mumbled excuse me and walked toward the bathrooms. Kat fidgeted in place. Her fifteen-thousand-dollar sequined Michael Kors dress was turning clammy from the long hours of stuffy heat and the vinyl upholstery of the hotel ballroom chair. McCabe, who sat beside her, turned to face her. Farther down the arc of the round table, McCabe's wife and the Hollywood couple were engrossed in show business gossip.

"That's a nice little rock he got you." McCabe took her left hand and held it up to the light. "What's that, six carats?" He reeked of booze.

"Eight," she said flatly, and removed her hand from his.

"I stopped buying big engagement rings two wives ago. Too much trouble on the back end. I just add an extra five hundred thousand into the prenup and call it a day."

"How romantic of you." Kat looked away, feigning interest in something across the ballroom.

"So when are you two tying the knot?"

"September," she said curtly.

"Ah, perfect! Perfect! Right after you tape the season kick-off of *Prime Time Focus*. I've got high hopes for that show. Everyone at

ANN does." Kat turned back to face him because he was talking business again. McCabe never really got drunk, but his conspicuous public boozing gave him the license he wanted to make mischief and say things other people would swear he would never remember. "Kitty, my dear Kitty, we've come a long way, haven't we?" He took her hand again; she took it back. "Remember when I brought you to New York from that affiliate in Butt Fuck, Montana?"

"One, it was Billings. Two, don't call me Kitty." She turned her head for a moment of relief from his breath, a pungent blend of Scotch and the Cuban cigars he had smoked during breaks outside at the curb. "And three, you had to bid against CBS to keep me."

"Oh yeah, the good old days. You know, Kat," he said, putting special emphasis on the final *t*, "way back in medieval times, the lord of the manor had a special privilege. He got to enjoy all the brides in his realm the night before their wedding." McCabe reached under the table and put a hand on Kat's knee. Taking advantage of the slit in her elegant dress, he moved his fingers upward several inches and squeezed gently. "The French called it *dwah de senyerr,* didn't they?"

Calmly and deliberately, Kat reached down, took his hand off her thigh, and placed it on the table.

"You had your turn down there," she said coldly. "That was then and this is now. You're lucky I don't have my lawyers all over you."

"Now, Kat, Kat, why would you do that? We have a very productive, mutually beneficial business relationship."

"Yes, we do, Ed. And now I'm engaged to be married."

"This number three?" he asked leeringly.

"Number two." She was curt and businesslike.

"Hey, who's counting? Let me commend you. You've hooked yourself a winner. If they had such a thing as a trophy husband, this boy would be one. I watched him in action at the Modern Leaders retreat in Sun Valley. Believe me, your puppy can run with the big dogs. He more than holds his own. He's a player." He patted her knee gently, just enough to touch the inside of her thigh, and quickly withdrew. "You done well, Kat, you done really well."

"I always do," she said with an icy smile. "Don't I, Ed?"

The old billionaire nodded and sat back. He glanced at his wife and the movie couple as if looking for an entry point back into their conversation. Deciding against that world, he turned back to Kat.

"Now, Kat, my gut tells me something. Tells me Tom's working on something big. A big deal."

"I don't know what you mean," she said with no intonation.

"Aw, come on. Your boy has been playing the market like a virtuoso. Just look at him. He takes the most damaged company on the stock exchange and gives it an extreme makeover. And just look at the bounce-back. That stock's doing better than it ever could have as the old company. The market loves a comeback. Because it's such a great story. Nothing sets off a feeding frenzy like a really good story. Now, for his next move, I think your boy is shopping his company around, looking to get acquired. Now's the time, of course. Contrary to what they say about buying low and selling high, people love to pay a lot, especially for a stock everybody wants a piece of. He'll negotiate a hefty acquisition premium on his already overvalued stock price. Figure I could make a quick ten or twenty million on a deal like that." He looked at her intensely.

"Ed," she said coldly, "you know better than to ask that kind of question. Even if I knew anything, which I don't, I couldn't and wouldn't tell you."

"Of course I know that," he said with a wide grin. "I just wanted to watch your face while you said it." He touched the inside of her thigh again, just for an instant. "Thanks, Kitty."

She turned her head as if she had been slapped. Or felt up, which she had been. Smugly, McCabe folded his arms in front of his chest and settled in to watch the fashionable people all around.

Pennington returned to the table but did not move to sit down. He touched Kat on the shoulder. "We have to be going," he said. Kat looked relieved and stood up to get away from her employer.

McCabe poked his wife's arm to interrupt her conversation. "Hey, Tom," he announced, "the night is young. Why do you and your bride-to-be have to leave? The fun's just beginning." Mrs. McCabe and the Hollywood couple looked up and voiced loud insincere regrets.

"Sorry," Kat said, reaching across McCabe to offer her hand to Mrs. McCabe. "Thanks so much, it was lovely."

"Oh yes," the ageless face-lifted socialite said, extending her wrinkled hand across her husband, bracelet and rings glittering blindingly, "it was. Will we see you in Aspen and Palm Beach?"

"I hope so." Kat smiled.

"Thanks again. Night, everyone," Pennington said as he escorted Kat toward the door.

"Tom, do you know how rude it is to keep looking at your watch all night?" Kat barked as they snaked through the crowd.

"Come on, stop busting my chops."

"Well, do you?"

"I had business I needed to complete."

"And did you?"

"Yes."

They stepped outside. Pennington motioned for his limo waiting down the street. "Thank God." She sighed as she tottered toward the open back door in her thousand-dollar Jimmy Choos. "I want to get out of these shoes, take a shower, fool around a little, and go to sleep."

70

After a long dinner, Ken and Cindy walked north up Columbus Avenue. The streets were dark, quiet, and mostly empty. Until they turned onto West Ninety-fourth Street.

Down the block near their apartment building were two fire trucks parked on the curb. Their lights were flashing, hoses snaked all over the sidewalk. Smoke hung in the air.

"Holy shit!" Ken gasped. "That looks like our building!" He broke into a run; Cindy followed.

The firefighters were cleaning up, replacing their hoses and equipment onto the fire engine. Ken's window was a blackened empty hole. The rest of the building appeared to be untouched.

After a bitter argument, the fire marshal convinced Ken that he could under no circumstances go back into his burned-out apartment. The other firefighters finished checking the rest of the building and directing other tenants back into their apartments. "Show's over," was their refrain.

"You sure it was an accident?" Ken asked the fire marshal for the umpteenth time. "You really goddamn sure?" Ken looked like he was ready to punch him out.

"Like I told you before," the marshal said, pushing his helmet back and wiping soot from his rugged face, "your surge protector was way overloaded. Unsafe. Your equipment just fried and you had a bad hookup with the gas line. That should get your landlord a violation. Jail, if I had my way. You know, you guys are lucky. Lucky you weren't there when the gas blew from the sparks of the electrical fire. Lucky for the rest of the building you didn't have all that much to burn. And lucky we're only two blocks away."

"I'm telling you," Ken said in a loud angry voice, "there are people out there who would like to see me d—" He started to say *dead*, but stopped when Cindy squeezed his arm.

He pulled free of her. "I'm going to call the FBI," he said insistently. "They need to know about this."

"Ken!" Cindy said, taking his arm again.

The marshal gave Ken a skeptical and very tired look. "Right. The FBI director will be here any minute now." His patience was now officially at an end. "Sir, we've got work to do."

"Ken, come on." She pulled him toward the door to the vestibule. "Thank you so much."

"There'll be a report?" Ken asked.

"Att's right," he said, and looked at his men packing up. "We'll contact you at your girlfriend's, right?"

"That's right," Cindy said, and dragged Ken through the door, "you've got the number."

The radio squawked and crackled with static. The fire marshal turned and raised his sleeve to his mouth to answer into his microphone. He was off to his next disaster.

"Come on, Ken, there's nothing more you can do," she said, and pulled him inside. "Let's go to my apartment."

"This was no accident," Ken muttered. "Good thing I'm seeing Phil Lambert tomorrow. He'll be very interested." He followed her inside and up the two flights to her door.

She undid the locks and walked inside. "Be it ever so humble," she said, and tossed her jacket onto a chair beside the small kitchen table that doubled as a desk. The apartment had a smallish living room furnished with a combination of Ikea, Crate & Barrel, and Goodwill. Her drapes were brightly colored, with intricate feminine patterns. Facing the couch was an old television and VCR on a rolling wicker table.

Ken stood in the doorway.

"Come on in," she said, kicking off her shoes and stretching her arms wide. "Whew! What a night."

"He can slow me down, but he can't stop me," Ken said through gritted teeth. "Good thing I'm seeing Phil tomorrow."

"Guess what, Ken? It's already tomorrow. And I don't know about you, but I need to get some rest. If you want to go off to a hotel room, you can. I just thought—"

"No, no, I'd rather stay here."

"Then come inside and shut the door."

He did as he was told.

She walked over to him, took him by the shoulders, and shook him. "Ken, look at me. You can't do anything right now. Now come on, take a deep breath and hold it." She demonstrated. He followed her lead.

"Now exhale," she said like a yoga instructor. "Again." They breathed in and out together. The tension began to seep out of him.

He turned from angry to exhausted. "All my stuff is gone," he whispered. "My computers, my research, my evidence."

"You can look tomorrow. Maybe not all of it got burned."

"All my stuff from home, all the stuff I cared about." Suddenly, he gasped for breath. "All my pictures of Sandy and Sara, all the negatives, all our videos. I had them packed in four moving boxes in the closet."

"Poor baby," she said.

"It's all gone," he whispered. Suddenly, he pulled away from her. He grabbed his wallet from his back pocket and flipped it open, hunting frantically for something. From inside the mess of plastic cards, he pulled a dog-eared photo of Sandy holding little Sara at her first birthday party. He stared into their happy faces and studied the details of their kitchen in the darkened background. He was angry at the bent corners of the snapshot. The scratches on the coated surface stung like knife cuts. "I've still got this," he said.

Cindy walked him over to the couch and eased him down onto it. She took the wallet and the snapshot from him and set them on the coffee table. She propped the photo up against the wallet so that it stood facing Ken.

Keeping his eyes on the photo, Ken cupped his hands under the pillow and pulled his knees up toward his chest. She walked to the end of the couch and pulled off his shoes. Then she got the bedspread from her bed and covered him over. Ken was already asleep.

She walked back into her bedroom, leaving her door open.

71

"Breakfast!" Cindy announced. "From the Greek coffee shop on Columbus. The Five or Six Brothers, you know that one."

"Yeah," Ken said, half asleep, "all those brothers and not one decent cook." He peeled back the bedspread and looked around. It was late morning. He had not slept this late since, he thought, since . . . then decided not to think of when it was.

He stared at the photo of Sandy and Sara on the coffee table for a while then looked over at Cindy. She was unpacking toasted English muffins, scrambled eggs and home fries, two cups of fresh orange juice, and four tall cappuccino cups. She spread the breakfast out on her table by the kitchen alcove at the far end of the living room.

"You went down for the count." Cindy motioned for him to come over and eat. "Boy, you are one sound sleeper. I've been up for hours."

"Did I snore?"

"It was fine. I don't like living alone."

He joined her at the table. She passed him an orange juice. He gulped it down. They said nothing while they ate up everything she had bought. "Oh," she said, wiping her mouth after her last bite of eggs, "I went to the Duane Reade on Broadway." She produced a white plastic bag from the floor and put it on the table beside him. "I got you a toothbrush. I hope you like the toothpaste I use. I got you a guy's razor and shaving cream and some Right Guard. That okay?"

"Yeah. Sure that's okay. I mean that's great. Thank you." He was still disoriented. "Jeez, thanks. Thanks for everything."

She blushed.

"No, really, I was just thinking about it. You were the one who said we should have dinner out. And thanks for letting me stay here."

She touched his hand briefly. "It's okay. There's a clean bath towel in there. I hope my shampoo and body wash are okay. They don't smell too flowery."

"No, sounds great." He stood up.

He walked into the bathroom and closed the door. It was the same landlord's bathroom he had had downstairs, but it was filled with all the female products and accessories he had not lived with since Sandy. He undressed and hung his clothes on the hook on the back of the door. The shower gave him immense relief and pleasure. He felt he could stay under the hot stream all day, maybe forever.

Finally, he turned off the water. He shaved and brushed his teeth. Standing with the towel wrapped around his waist, he looked at his wrinkled clothes and wondered what to do next.

"Uh, Ken," Cindy called from the other side of the door, "before you get dressed, I, uh, well, my mom always made a huge deal about clean underwear. So I got you a three-pack in the Duane Reade. All they had were tighty-whities. Kinda goofy. I'm sorry. Open the door, and I'll hand them to you."

He opened the door a crack and took the package. When he emerged from the bathroom, Cindy was cleaning the table with a sponge. "You're welcome to stay here until you figure out what to do," she said without looking up. "I've got the spare bedroom, you know. Like I told you, my roommate moved out."

Ken stood looking at the apartment for the first time in daylight. It was a somewhat larger version of his studio downstairs but facing the back courtyard. Cement yards, the backs of brownstones, a few scrawny trees, but more sunlight, thanks to the slice of open sky. He could see into her bedroom; she had replaced the bedspread that had been his blanket. The door to the second bedroom was open. Cindy motioned toward it. Ken went over to see.

It was a small oblong room with nothing in it but dust kitties and grit on the gouged, battered hardwood floor. A narrow window looked out on a brick wall of the building next door. At least the window did not have bars over it like the window of his studio downstairs.

"She took everything when she moved out. I mean everything."

Ken considered his options. "How much is the rent?" he asked.

"No," Cindy said, "I'm just offering you the—"

"Don't be silly, I can pay, it's no problem. And I can be right here in the building while I figure out what to do with my place."

"But you shouldn't be paying two rents."

"Really, it's no problem. I can buy some furniture. Hey, I have to, anyway." Ken looked at his watch. Almost eleven. "Oh, jeez, I'm going to be late for Phil."

72

Phil listened to Ken as they sat in his office at Medusa. "You know," Phil said, "the fire marshal could be right. The wiring was original with the building?" Ken shrugged. "And you had too much stuff plugged into one outlet?"

Ken shrugged again. "Yes, but I had a surge protector."

Phil waved away that thought. "They're worthless after one power surge, and we get surges all the time. And how old was the stove in your apartment?"

"I don't know. Looked original with the building. Sixty years old? Seventy?"

"And how's the maintenance?"

"What maintenance?"

"I repeat," Phil said patiently, "you are one lucky son of a bitch."

"Phil, I'm telling you—and I'm not being paranoid—they are out to get me."

Phil chuckled at the irony Ken could not hear in his own plea. "My dear brother-in-law," he said, trying not to be condescending, "let me tell you something as a man with my professional background. If they, whoever *they* are, wanted to kill you, they would have killed you. You are not dead. That leads me to think this really was an accident. What else did you have in the apartment?"

"Well, I sold the house furnished and junked most of what the buyer didn't want. I brought my computer equipment and boxes of family pictures and videos." Ken choked for a moment on the thought of losing all his images of Sandy and Sara, then regained his calm. "I brought a few sticks of furniture from Dayton, but not much. My clothes, but that's it."

Phil was thinking, making notes on his legal pad. "You said when they fired you, they sent you a CD with the incriminating invoice files on them."

"That's right."

"Where's that CD now?"

"In the apartment," Ken said hopefully, then thought for an instant and said, "but probably fried with the rest of my stuff."

"That's too bad."

"Why?"

"Because the metadata would tell us who created those files and when."

"The meta-what?"

"It's a record the file keeps every time someone works on it. Who did it, how long they worked on it, how many changes they made and when. It's all embedded in the file. Our forensic computer guys discover all sorts of things when they dig back into the history of a file. They can even recover data on hard drives that have been burned or dropped out of airplanes. It takes more time, but it's amazing what they can reconstruct. Think we could recover any of your equipment?"

Ken shrugged.

"We should try."

Ken leaned forward in his seat. "Listen, Phil. I'm a paying client, right? So what exactly have we got going for this investigation? Don't you give me a status report?"

Phil pointed at his computer, as if that did all the work. "Monthly. It's coming, just like all our clients get."

"Come on, Phil. Out with it."

Phil grabbed the manila folder that was Ken's case; it had only a few sheets in it. He flipped through them as he spoke. "Well, later this week, I've got an appointment to see Decker. The FBI saw where that money went when it left the Caymans. They just never followed through because the case closed when Paulson killed himself. He can't tell me anything officially, but maybe he can point me in the right direction. I remember that Decker wasn't too chickenshit about the rules. Or he might tell me to fuck off and get lost. It's worth a visit, though. And I've already started making some calls to PMC contacts of mine."

"That's good," Ken said, "that's good. Now tell me, what can I do from my end? Do you want me to do some espionage with my old contacts at the company? I could maybe get some of my old buddies to feed me files. You know, confidential stuff. I could follow Pennington around, watch his movements, see who he talks to, bribe his door-man to let me go through his trash. Know what I mean? I'm here in New York now, and I've got time and money to play with."

Phil shook his head emphatically no. "Listen, Ken, can we talk? I'm no therapist or anything. Like Sandy said, I'm not even much of a family member. But I do know two things. One: I know that this investigation we are going to do, and believe me, it's going to be a real, honest-to-God professional investigation, is going to be tedious, boring, and full of detailed technical process that often leads nowhere. And it will be *very* time consuming. So, you, brother-in-law, had better just calm down, relax, and chill out. This will take time. And no, I do not, repeat *do not,* want you running around play-ing junior G-man." Phil raised his voice and leaned over the desk. "Under no fucking circumstances, do you read me?"

Ken nodded.

Phil was angry. "You could get hurt, get in trouble, or fuck up the whole investigation! None of which, if you can think clearly for half a second, you would want to do. Agreed?"

Ken nodded again.

"I do this shit for a living, and I'm goddamn good at it. If you're going to get in my way with amateur antics, let's call the whole thing off right now. Okay?"

"Okay," Ken said quietly, "now what's thing two?"

Phil tried to smile his way out of the angry head of steam he had built up. "Ken, Ken, if *I'm* still fucked up about losing Sandy and Sara the way we did, can you even begin to imagine how fucked up *you* must be?"

"Well, that's my—"

The anger in Phil's voice returned. It was the only way he knew to express concern. "Of course, you can't imagine because you're still so fucked up with your grief and mourning and all that. *You* can't see it in you, but *I* can." Phil paused and took a calmer, more sympa-thetic tone. "I've seen this with widows of guys we lost in the DIA, but I'm guessing it's not much different for widowers. Here are the facts: You may not realize it, but you're off balance. It's a physical thing as well as mental. It's not your fault. It's just going to take some time."

Phil shook his finger accusingly. "And that's *another* reason I *do not* want you running around pretending you're James Bond. *You are not hitting on all cylinders!* You won't be for a while. So don't try anything stupid, because, because," he was fishing angrily for the words, "because you'll end up doing something . . . stupid. You're my sister's husband, for Chrissake, I gotta look out for you!"

Ken smiled at Phil. He could see glimpses of Sandy in his flashing dark eyes and hear her furious, protective, angry love in his ranting. "Okay, I hear you."

"You had fucking better hear me good," Phil said, spitting out the last of his ire and folding his arms across his chest.

The men sat in silence while the air around them calmed down.

"What are you doing to fill up your time?" Phil asked finally.

"You mean besides playing junior G-man and tailing Pennington?"

"Yeah," Phil smirked, "besides that."

Ken raised one hand in a mock karate chop. "Martial arts classes."

"Good, that's very good. Keep it up. Take more classes. Okay? Try them all. You know aikido? I think aikido would suit you."

"Okay."

"What else? What other activities?"

"I run around the reservoir in Central Park."

"Excellent! Keep track of your time. Try to shave some off every week. Compete against yourself."

Ken considered mentioning the occasional shooting lessons at the downtown gun club, but quickly dismissed that thought. He shrugged. "Hey, I just moved here, got any suggestions?"

Phil took a deep breath. He was not practiced at giving of himself. He was near the end of what he was able to offer this man who meant so much to the sister he had let down in life. "Here's my two cents' worth. You're a business guy, with business skills, right?"

"Right," Ken said, "or at least I was."

"And you are still in the middle of, uh, you're still, you know, grieving for your wife and daughter, right?"

Ken nodded.

"Jesus, I am no good at this," Phil muttered as he reached into his desk drawer and pulled out a brochure. "Here, I know these guys from referrals in the old days. And I also know that their New York office is really fucked up, business-wise. They could use a business-savvy volunteer to help sort out their finances, management policies, all that stuff. And since you happen to be from the idle rich and can afford to hire Medusa, you could be just the volunteer that could save their business and help with the good work they do."

Ken took the brochure. It was from the American Grief Counsel, New York City Chapter. "You could help them with *their* business," Phil said gently, "and they could help you with *yours*." Phil stood and offered Ken a handshake to end their exhausting interview. "We'll meet tonight at your building. See what our guys can recover from that charbroiled CD and your hard drive."

73

The steel jaws crunched as the Dumpster full of Ken's charred, waterlogged possessions was swallowed into the bowels of the private garbage truck.

"Hey, what are you doing?" Ken asked the building superintendent, who stood by the garbage man working the lever that closed the electric jaws. Two crewmen stood by, all sooty from the cleanup job they had just finished.

"Landlord wants you out," the super said to Ken. "You made a big fuckin' mess."

"Well, it was his fucking fault! Ask the fire marshal."

"I don't ask nobody nothing," the super said, "they tell me to clean out your shit, I clean out your shit."

The last of the burned debris tumbled out of the Dumpster into the container. The driver pulled the lever that hoisted the Dumpster securely over the lip of the giant, now shut, jaws.

"Hey!" Ken protested as the garbage crew climbed into the cab of the truck. "You can't take that away. That's evidence."

The driver of the garbage truck waved to the super as he slid the truck into gear. Ignoring Ken, the super waved to the truck with his right arm while he felt, with his left hand in his pocket, the roll of twenty one-hundred-dollar bills the driver had given him in exchange for his cooperation.

Ken did not recognize the driver beneath his soot-streaked cheeks, sooty coveralls, dingy baseball cap pulled low over his forehead, and greasy black locks of hair running down the back of his neck. How could he? He looked nothing like Peter Houghton. He was just another indifferent stranger heaping another indignity on Ken Olson.

Ken reached in his pants pocket for his cell phone. He pushed Phil's number on speed dial. When he heard no sound, he looked down at the phone. The battery was dead. And he realized that his charger had just vanished with the rest of his possessions in the garbage truck. He raised the cell phone in an angry gesture, as if he might throw it across the street or smash it on the sidewalk. Then he took a deep breath and slowly replaced it in his pocket. From his other pocket, he took the spare key to Cindy's apartment and headed upstairs. As he walked into the building, he told himself that the first thing he would replace from his lost possessions was his computer. Then his handgun.

74

Brilliant sunlight flooded Justin Hildreth's courtyard. The soothing sound of the fountain poured into the library.

Hildreth sat with Pennington and Lew Simons. "It's an inspired merger, Tom," Hildreth said. "When the deal is completed and Humanifit becomes part of General Industries, it will create the fifth-largest corporation in America."

Simons was excited to be in the inner circle in such rarified surroundings and anxious to make a good impression. "Forbes is calling it 'the merger of the decade,'" he said eagerly. He looked back and forth between Pennington and Hildreth, hoping for an acknowledgment of some kind. "I let the reporter think he came up with that, but I planted the phrase with him, word for word." He got nothing from either man.

"Tom," Hildreth continued as if Simons did not exist, "you have made us all very proud. You embraced responsibility at a moment when common sense would tell most men to flee. I warned you at the time. Becoming chief executive of Ayvil could have been a one-way ticket to oblivion."

"Not with the senior board member I had as my advisor," Pennington said with a smile. "All I can say is, thank God I'll have you on the board of General Industries, too."

Hildreth lowered his head modestly just as Alejandro brought in a silver tray with tea service for the three men. Alejandro poured and distributed each man's nearly translucent antique Spode teacup and saucer with sterling silver spoons crafted in London before the American Revolution. Then he disappeared.

Rushing to finish his tea, Simons spoke up first. "You know, Mr. Hildreth, Tom's empowerment philosophy of downsizing is getting a lot of play in the business press. It's making its way into the business schools as one of today's greatest management innovations."

Hildreth looked over the rim of his teacup and offered Simons a faint, condescending smile. Hildreth took his time drinking his tea, leaving Simons to fidget, trying to think of something else he might say in his desperate attempt to engage his superiors.

Hildreth finally finished and set his cup and saucer down. "Tom, you have been true to your own mission statement. You really have served the greater good. You rescued a company, preserving thousands of jobs and the savings and investments of countless others. You gave that company a new identity and a new life, increasing its value dramatically for all. And with this merger, you have created wealth for many people on a scale few could have predicted. Although *I* knew it all along."

"Thank you," Pennington said, "but no chief executive does anything alone."

"Don't be self-effacing," Hildreth said as he reached for the teapot. "I predicted that you would change the history of business, and you have." Teapot in hand, he looked at Simons. "More tea, Lew?"

Delighted to be noticed, Simons thrust his empty cup under the spout of the teapot. "Gee, thanks, Mr. Hildreth, I'd love some more."

Hildreth poured for Simons then looked at Pennington. Pennington gave a small shake of his head. Hildreth poured himself a refill and put the teapot down. Balancing his cup and saucer on his lap, he said, "I am proud that shareholders of Humanifit will become shareholders of General Industries at this very handsome but very fair price."

Simons jumped in eagerly. "A lot of analysts said we could never command that kind of multiple. I guess we really showed them."

Pennington nodded. Hildreth raised his cup to his lips.

Simons babbled on, thrilled that he finally held the spotlight. "With the run-up in the stock we've had since Tom became CEO, there was some real money to be made." He looked around at the town house. Everything was fabulous, expensive, authentic, and in perfect taste. This was the kind of taken-for-granted opulence that only generations of big money could buy. It was like a movie set, only real, Simons thought. "I had this crazy fantasy," Simons chuckled, "that I kept a secret off-shore account for trading in our stock. With what I knew and some leverage, boy, I could have made one hell of a killing."

Hildreth suddenly inhaled as he swallowed. He coughed for an instant and quickly put his cup down. He covered his mouth with the linen tea napkin and coughed a bit more to clear his throat.

Simons barely noticed. "Of course, if I got found out, I'd be a fugitive. But I hear there are still a few nice warm places where you can live the good life and not worry about extradition." He laughed nervously.

Hildreth put his napkin down. "That is not funny, Mr. Simons," he said sternly.

"No it's not," Pennington agreed. "You of all people should know better than to joke about that kind of thing. We have all been working for the greater good."

"Exactly," Hildreth said. "The greater good."

"Of course, uh, the greater good," Simons said meekly.

Without looking at the watch on his own wrist, Pennington turned to Simons. "What time is it, Lew?"

"Ten thirty," Simons offered quickly, hoping to regain favor however he could.

"We'd better head over to the GI building," Pennington said. "We've got a rehearsal for the announcement meeting with the team this afternoon. Lew, did you get everything you need from Justin for the press release?"

"I think so." Simons looked hesitantly at Hildreth, hoping for a sign of forgiveness. "Anything more you want to add, Mr. Hildreth?"

Hildreth flashed an exaggerated smile at the flack. Simons knew that Hildreth had written him off.

"Then we're off to General Industries," Pennington said as he got up to leave.

75

Decker consented to see Phil for ten minutes. He listened to Phil's recap while taking a break from the piles of papers and folders on the desk.

"I don't know what you expect to find," Decker said, standing up. "The case is closed. Besides, I thought you left government to make money at Medusa. Sounds to me like you're trying to be Sir Galahad on some kinda crusade for truth, justice, and the American way."

"That was Superman," Phil said.

"Huh?" Decker had turned his back and was fishing around in the file cabinet behind his desk.

"Truth, justice, and the American way," Phil said, "that was Superman's line."

Decker looked idly at his watch and spoke to the window. "That's ten minutes, Lambert. We are officially done here."

Phil did not move from his seat.

Decker turned around and reached for the folder on top of the pile. With his face buried in the folder, he said, "You got a problem with English comprehension? I said we are done."

Phil sat still. "No, we're not."

Decker spoke without looking up. "I said, case closed. Now go find your billable hours someplace else." He snapped the folder shut and turned his back to Phil, diving once again into his file cabinet.

"That guy Olson," Phil said, "is not what this is about."

Decker started humming to himself, signaling that he was beyond ignoring Phil.

Phil went on. "His wife and daughter were in the day care center that day. They died."

Decker raised the volume of his little tune and dived deeper into his paperwork.

Phil waited for Decker to get to the end of the song. Then he said, "She was my sister."

Decker stood up straight and closed the file cabinet drawer. "I see," he said, and bent down to open a lower drawer. He fished briefly in it, then found what he was looking for—a plain manila folder stuffed with papers to a thickness of about an inch. He started thumbing through it, talking to Phil without looking up.

"I don't know what I could possibly do, Lambert," Decker said, his voice brightening. "The case was closed when Paulson confessed and killed himself. My superiors were satisfied that justice had been served. And in their wisdom, they directed men like me to other matters." He paused and looked out the window. "Now, a few people who saw the particulars of that case felt that maybe, just maybe, it all got wrapped up a little too neatly. But not me. As you know," he said, with a truckload of sarcasm, "*my* faith in the wisdom of my superiors knows no bounds."

Decker paused. "Ah," he said, finding a particular document. He pulled it from the middle and slid it to the front position at the top of the folder. "I don't know how you could possibly track the money trail out of the Cayman bank. You see, we had court orders down there, so we were able to see the accounts where the money was sent after it left the second Cayman account. But that is privileged information. You'd also need the signed traveler's checks we located around Dayton. The goons used them to pay for equipment and rentals. The serial numbers are all from the same sequence. We have copies signed by all three of the dead men. You'd need those. And, of course, you'd need the one example of Peter Houghton's signature from the burned logbook we found in the steel desk at the guard shack. If you could work with a handwriting expert, you might be able to match this guy's handwriting with a signature card at some foreign bank. And maybe even find another one of these traveler's checks with his handwriting on it somewhere. That would definitely link him to the mass murder. But as a private investigator, you'd never be able to get your hands on any of this. It's really a shame."

Decker closed the folder and put it on the desk. Then he turned around and reached back into his filing cabinet. "Jesus, Lambert, sometimes I think I'm drowning in paper. Just fucking drowning in it." He bent over the file cabinet drawer as if he were planning on spending some time there. "Now where did I put that report they just called me about? You know, sometimes I take out a folder that

I need and, with all this mess in here, I can't find it again for an hour or so. Must be Alzheimer's creeping in."

Phil leaned forward and opened the folder on the desk. The top sheet was a Xerox copy of wire transfer instructions from the Royal Bank of the Caymans, complete with bank names and account numbers. It was the advice that moved the millions from the numbered account in the Caymans to three other accounts in three other offshore banks. The first receiving bank was in the Channel Island of Guernsey. The second was New Hebrides Bank of Vanuatu.

Son of a gun, he thought, recalling the way he cited Vanuatu to Ken. Although at the time, he was merely using Vanuatu as an example of how far-flung international money laundering could be. The third bank was the Development Commerce Bank of the Seychelles. Beneath that were copies of the signed traveler's checks, behind that a copy of the burned logbook page with Peter Houghton's signature.

Phil took the folder, put it in his briefcase, and stood up to leave. Decker still had his back to him.

"Well, if your superiors closed the case," Phil said a bit too loudly, "it's because they knew best. After all, that's why they are your superiors."

"I'm glad to hear you say that," Decker said with his head buried in the cabinet. "Funny how files disappear and then I find them an hour later."

"Listen," Phil said from the doorway. "I gotta run to the bank before it closes. I'll be back in a bit, if that's okay."

"Sure," Decker said, "I'm not going anywhere." Phil was already gone.

76

"Ken, meet Henry Mills," Phil said. "He's Medusa's in-house forensic document examiner." Mills, a brawny, energetic man in his late forties, handed Ken his business card. Along with the usual information, it said that Henry Mills was certified by the American Board of Forensic Document Examiners and four other forensic document academies. Ken read the crowded little card and looked up with a puzzled expression.

"I'm the handwriting expert," Mills said.

"Ken," Phil explained as he spread out the papers across his desk, "we've gotten an unexpectedly good start on tracking the money that paid for the Ayvil operation."

Mills picked up one sheet. It was a copy of a page from the charred remains of the logbook that Mack the security guard kept in his steel desk at the guard shack. The page it had been copied from was singed on one side. Someone had highlighted one signature in yellow.

"Look at Peter Houghton," Mills said, pointing.

Ken stared at the signature. It was big and confident, with a couple of odd flourishes.

"Note the letter forms," Mills said, "the single scoop of the capital *P*. The unconnected lowercase *e*'s in *Peter*. The loop of the lowercase *g* that does not sweep to connect to the top of the letter. This is definitely not an American-trained writer. It is European or European-influenced. Northern European, not Mediterranean."

"He had an accent, right?" Phil asked.

"Yeah," Ken said, "kind of British but not quite."

"Well," Mills said, "it looks British-influenced to me. But British Commonwealth, not native British. Could be Australian, New Zealander, Caribbean, South African maybe. We need to get more samples of his handwriting."

"But Peter Houghton is not his real name," Ken protested.

"Everyone's handwriting is unique," Mills said, "if you know what to look for. This signature here will be our standard, the exemplar, for this man, whoever he is. We've got a number of automated ways to analyze writing samples. Like FISH."

"Fish?" Ken asked.

"Forensic Information System for Handwriting. And a few other computer programs. Combine them with a trained eye, and we can spot a unique individual, no matter what name he signs or what he's writing."

"Even numbers," Phil said, "right, Henry?"

Mills nodded.

"This admissible in court?" Ken asked.

"Yes," Phil said confidently.

"Most of the time," Mills added.

"What do you mean?" Ken asked.

"The courts go back and forth," Mills said, "but with proper documentation and testing, we *can* put someone away with it."

"Now after the Paris Air Show, I'm going to Guernsey," Phil said, pointing to the first bank on the copy of the wire-transfer instructions from the Cayman bank. "The first million went to this account held by a company registered in Panama called Whitelaw, S.A. I've got some British contacts from my government days who might be able to help me get around the banking secrecy rules."

"How?" Ken asked. "You told me those rules are spelled out in black-and-white. And we don't have a court order."

"Yeah," Phil said, "but the real world operates in gray areas. For instance, we're not supposed to have these documents. And yet, here they are." He smiled proudly.

"That's right," Ken said suspiciously. "How did that happen?"

Phil scooped up the documents and closed the folder. "What documents?" he asked.

Ken smiled. "You know, I'm starting to like the color gray."

77

Ken's single bed dominated one wall of Cindy's spare bedroom. Crowded along the other wall were a chair and a cheap desk with a big flat-screen monitor. The CPU tower and a big color printer were on the floor. Papers and files were piled everywhere inside the narrow little cell. All by itself on the sill of the little narrow window was that last snapshot of Sandy and Sara, duplicated and enlarged with the scratches retouched away. It was mounted and matted professionally, protected by UV-filtering Plexiglas, in a beautiful frame.

After two months as roommates, Ken and Cindy had fallen into routines like an old married couple. In the evening, they sat at opposite ends of the couch with their own magazines, half-watching television and hardly speaking, except to ask the other if it was okay to change the channel.

"Anything happen at your job today?" Cindy asked. They called his part-time volunteer work at the grief center his job.

"No," Ken said, "just the usual."

"Come on, tell me a little," Cindy said.

"You know, business things. I'm straightening out their accounting. Helping organize their call center. Stuff like that. Not very interesting."

"Do you ever," she paused, "do you ever, you know, use their services yourself?"

Ken looked directly at her. "Why do you ask?"

"Well, you know, I figured that was part of, you know, your healing process. I mean, they've got all those counselors right there."

Ken mumbled something and turned back to the TV.

"You know," Cindy said cautiously, "I've noticed a change in you since you started working there. Really, you seem much more, I dunno, together. Do you get to talk about it? Do they help you work it through?"

"Yuh, sure," Ken grunted.

"You want to talk about it?" Cindy reached out and touched his arm. "I've noticed a change. I really think they're helping you."

"No," Ken said brusquely, "I don't want to talk about it."

"I understand," Cindy said, "but if ever you need to—"

"I said I don't want to talk about it." Ken reached for the remote and turned up the volume. "But thanks," he added, "thanks for asking."

Cindy took her hand back. "Men," she grumbled.

"And now," the too-loud announcer said, "our nightly business report with Ralph Colin." Ken sat up with interest. "A merger of gigantic proportions was announced today," the business reporter said. "General Industries, makers of everything from dish drainers to nuclear reactors, is acquiring Humanifit, formerly known as troubled Ayvil Industries, in a deal valued at over fifty billion dollars."

"Holy shit!" Ken cried, bug-eyed. "He pulled it off!"

"What?" Cindy asked, looking up from her magazine.

"Sssh! Just a sec."

The television reporter droned on over video of the press conference. "GI's chief executive Harry Warren announced the merger today. Analysts generally applauded the deal, saying it is priced a bit richly. Shareholders of Humanifit, the company whose stock was battered by the mass murder arranged by its former CEO, has recently made a rebound under the leadership of new CEO Tom Pennington. GI's Warren said this merger completes his vision for the company he has transformed over his twenty-year tenure. He is to retire next year when he turns sixty-five.

"With Warren were the two executives most likely to succeed him, the new vice chairmen—Michael Guillaume, long his right-hand man, and Tom Pennington. Guillaume has had management rotations through many of GI's diverse businesses. Pennington is credited with doing the impossible, rescuing Ayvil Industries.

"Handicappers of corner office contests say the race will be too close to call. On one side, Guillaume, age fifty-two, is a lifetime GI executive and a highly visible symbol of African-American success in corporate America. On the other, Pennington, only forty-two, has become a corporate superstar with his innovative ideas about humanitarianism and big business. As with most mergers, this one will probably lead to thousands of lay-offs."

Ken leapt off the couch and started pacing. "Holy shit, holy shit! That son of a bitch Pennington probably just made fifty million on his change-of-control provisions. No, more than that. A hundred. Two hundred. Who knows? I'll check the filings."

"What are you babbling about?" Cindy asked.

"I need to think. Please!" He tapped his chin and scratched his head as he paced. "Let's see, Warren's retiring. Two-man horse race. Pennington and Guillaume. Ten years' age difference. Board looking to the future. Pennington versus Guillaume. Guillaume versus Pennington. Pennington won't wait to see if he is chosen. Why should he?"

"Ken, what on earth are you talking about?"

"Pennington's modus operandi. He's going to fix the race. He's going to do something horrible to discredit Guillaume. Pennington told me himself, he is all about the next thing. And his next next thing is going to be eliminating Guillaume! I've got to give Phil a heads-up. I'm going to stop the bastard before he does anything."

Cindy jumped up off the couch and stood close to him. "Can I help you?"

"Huh?"

"You know, help. I could be your sounding board. I see you working in there all by yourself. Don't you need somebody to try your ideas on? Help you think things through? Doesn't everyone need that?"

"Well, yeah, sure."

"We could be like, like, like Nick and Nora Charles in *The Thin Man*." The aspiring actress in Cindy was getting excited. "Or Bogie and Bacall in *To Have and Have Not*. Or Bogie and Bergman in *Casablanca*. Yeah, like them!"

"Yeah, just like in the movies," Ken said sarcastically.

"I'm serious, Ken. Let me help you. You can't just talk to yourself all day. And I can be really smart about a lot of things. You'll see. You'll stop this bad guy, and I'll help you." She opened her arms to him. "Deal?"

"Deal!" He grabbed her in a friendly victory hug.

78

At Le Bourget Airport, the Paris Air Show was in full flower. Every afternoon the latest and greatest aircraft put on shows, circling the airfield and saluting the crowds, shaking the conference room tables and nearly knocking over drinks as they roared right overhead. The newest fighter planes, commercial passenger jets, corporate jets, attack and troop transport helicopters, and private helicopters. In the booths and pavilions, every kind of missile was on proud display. Surface to air, air to air, antimissile, antipersonnel. Plus every kind of bomb. Smart bombs, cluster bombs, guided and unguided. It is the planet's most complete display of creativity at killing and destruction.

The customers came from all over the world, dressed in suits or flowing robes and headdresses, or a mixture of Western and exotic attire. They came from governments, governments-in-exile, would-be destroyers of governments, private companies, private empires, private armies, and all the people and organizations who do business with and for all of the above.

There among the crowds, moving from booth to booth, inquiring about private military contractors, was Phil Lambert. He came with three sets of business cards from three fictitious corporations. He was asking questions about a brawny, tech-savvy mercenary with an odd accent.

At the end of the show's last day, Phil returned to his airport hotel room and called Ken with a change in plans. "I've got some leads on Peter Houghton."

"That's great," Ken said, resting his cell phone against the pillow in the dark of his narrow bedroom. It was 2:00 A.M. on West Ninety-fourth Street. Ken had told Phil to call at any time of the day or night. "Who is he?"

"There are two. And one of them, a guy whose name—names, actually, he's got a lot of different passports and identities—keeps coming up when I nose around and describe him and his particular expertise. If I can get on another airplane after Guernsey, I think I'll be able to nail it down."

"What are you waiting for? Go, spend the money. Do it."

"Good," Phil said, "just checking."

"Where you off to?"

"Guernsey to London, London to Johannesburg."

"So that's where that accent came from?"

"Maybe," Phil said, "we'll see. I'm off now, bro."

Ken said good-bye and they hung up.

Phil had something more. But he did not want to report it to Ken. Not yet. It was the other line of questioning he had pursued at the Paris Air Show—about an American executive who used to attend this show when he worked for Paragon Industries. Tom Pennington.

79

McCabe came to Kat's office first thing in the morning. This was unusual because, first, he never came down to any employee's office, and second, it was first thing in the morning and McCabe only showed up after lunch, if at all, these days.

He stood in her doorway and leered at her like the sugar daddy he had once been. "I've got something ve-ry bi-i-i-g," he gestured with arms wide, "that's going to make you ve-ry happy."

Kat tried not to look up from her desk. "Christ, Ed," she snickered, "are you forgetting that I've seen it in all its glory? I promise you, on its very best day it was never that big and it never made me all that happy." She looked down again at her work, pen in hand.

"You are one tough bitch, Kat. That's why I love you." He went on blithely. "Far more important, that's why America loves you. Now I want to show you a preview of the fame and riches you are about to enjoy."

Kat looked up at him.

"See?" he said playfully. "I knew that'd get your attention."

"What are you talking about? I have to tape my *Prime Time Focus* debut in less than a week and I'm sweating bullets right now to try to make it perfect. I'm busy."

He sat on the corner of her desk, pushing her papers aside. "This is going to be your breakthrough. I just feel it."

Kat looked up into McCabe's face. He wasn't such a bad guy, after all. He had been, and continued to be, good to her. Truth be told, he was not all that bad in bed; what the old guy lacked in prowess he more than made up for in enthusiasm and attentiveness. And he had not balked at her new multimillion-dollar contract. "Thanks, Ed," she said, finally letting some warmth come into her voice, "I really appreciate that. You've been great."

"Now for your surprise," McCabe said brightly, "I want you to go down to the plaza on Fiftieth Street. Felix is parked in my new

Maybach. You seen it?" He was referring to his new $320,000 Mercedes limousine, an immense tanklike salon on wheels, nearly twice as long as a normal sedan and half again as wide.

"Yes," Kat said, "it's hard to miss."

"Well, Felix is waiting for you. Just get in. He is going to take you on a short drive with the curtains closed. Don't peek until he tells you it's okay. Promise?"

Kat frowned. She really was busy.

"Come on, indulge me. You're going to like what you see."

McCabe got off the corner of the desk and started helping Kat out of her chair like a maître d' in a fancy restaurant. "Listen, I'm the boss and I say you can spare ten minutes for a little preview of coming attractions."

"Okay, okay," Kat said, reaching for her purse, "I'm on my way."

McCabe put his arm through hers and escorted her out of her office.

"You're in a good mood," Kat said as she got on the elevator.

As the doors closed, McCabe waved to her and grinned. "Another divorce finalized. Another new beginning."

Downstairs, Kat walked toward the silver behemoth, parked conspicuously unticketed in the no-parking zone in front of ANN Plaza. McCabe's driver Felix opened the gigantic back door. The curtains were drawn across the windows.

"I know, I know," Kat said, "no peeking until you say so."

"That's right, Miss Pierce. Boss's orders."

Kat fell back into the huge leather seat and let herself feel like a celebrity. After all, she was one of the boldfaced names now. Her picture, sometimes with Pennington, sometimes without, appeared regularly on Page Six of the *New York Post,* in the party columns of *New York* magazine, *W, Variety,* and even *People.*

When Felix stopped the car in Times Square and gave her the go-ahead, she drew the curtains aside and gasped. What she saw was a towering new billboard. It was ten stories of Kat Pierce, backlit on a quarter-acre sheet of translucent plastic, looking sexy and serious behind her news desk. The headline above read: PIERCE TODAY'S HEADLINES. Beneath her: KAT PIERCE NOW ON PRIME TIME FOCUS. And in smaller type at the very bottom: WEDNESDAYS AT 9 ON ANN, THE NAME TO TRUST IN NEWS.

At first she gasped. Then she felt a surge of pride. She looked at herself in the mirror of this monstrous limo then at her other self on the monstrous billboard. She stared up at the perfectly retouched image of the golden blond media star named Kat Pierce. She wondered if that poised, confident, ten-story woman could be the same Kat Pierce from the boondocks, the awkward girl with mouse-brown hair and every reason to feel inadequate.

She reached into her purse for her phone and called Pennington on his private line in the office. "Tom, oh, Tom, I've got something to show you," she cooed. "Something big. Can I come pick you up, honey? Please? McCabe let me borrow his limo. Come on, it'll be fun. You'll see me in a whole different light." She gazed up at herself again. "And I'll have you back to your office in no time. Promise. Tom, honey, you gotta come see," she said in a breathy whisper, realizing that the thrill she was feeling was in no small part erotic.

"I can't," Pennington snapped, "I've got wall-to-wall meetings. I'm in the middle of one of the biggest mergers in history."

"I know you're tied up, honey. But I want you to see this. Let me come get you. You won't believe this car." Now, as she felt her life coming together so brilliantly, she wanted to share this moment with her picture-perfect man.

"Kat," he said curtly, "I've got to go." And he hung up.

Kat looked up at herself, covering half a building, and sighed. She thought about how she had beaten the odds by never giving up, by doing whatever it took—whether it was outsmarting rivals, shamelessly sucking up, or using her body to get what she wanted from powerful men like McCabe. Yes, she was tough. And toughness had made her a winner. When she told Felix they could return to the office, she felt little tears running down her cheek. Uncertain about what could be making her cry, she decided it must be happiness.

80

Pennington sat with Harry Warren and Michael Guillaume in Warren's conference room atop the General Industries building in Midtown. It was a plain room, except for the view, which was a breathtaking sweep of Manhattan from the fiftieth floor. Together, Guillaume and Pennington made a striking pair, two handsome knights on the corporate chessboard. One black. One white.

Guillaume spoke first. "As I see it, the first order of business is to trim down and eliminate our redundancies. I think we've got to show Wall Street the right kind of efficiencies of scale."

Warren nodded approvingly at his protégé. "Mike knows the way to my heart, Tom. He and I have been at this game together for some time now."

Pennington smiled and said, "But never with an acquisition of this size."

"Dynergetix was pretty close," Guillaume answered confidently. "When you've got your operating principles in place, you can scale them however you need to." He looked at his boss. "Right, Harry?"

Harry nodded again.

"I agree absolutely," Pennington said, "but I think what I can bring to the party is some of the out-of-the-box thinking we've been doing at Humanifit. I think, as we start making the cuts, we've got to get out there and show our employees how important they are to making this merger work. Michael, I think you and I need to get on our airplanes and go press the flesh. Plant walk-throughs, town meetings. Nonstop. Just as if we were running for office. What we're campaigning for is the commitment of each and every employee we plan to keep and the support of all the communities we touch."

Warren jumped to his feet and bounded over to the window. "Tom is right," he said. "And so are you, Mike. Together, you two men have everything we need."

"What's more," Pennington said, "I think it's vital that we bring video crews with us. The employees we don't touch personally we've got to touch with the next best thing. The war for the hearts of two hundred thousand employees can't be won with memos."

"Good point," Warren said thoughtfully.

Guillaume worked hard at not showing how miffed he felt, being upstaged by the newcomer. "Harry," he said, "once the deal is approved, we won't have the time to be away from the office."

"You men put your heads together and show me a plan. Show me your best thinking. Collaborate." Warren left without saying anything more.

Pennington and Guillaume sat in silence.

"You know, Michael—," Pennington began.

"Please, it's Mike," Guillaume said in a formal but friendly tone.

Pennington smiled. "Of course. Thanks. You know, Mike, I think you and I have more in common than most people would think."

Guillaume gave him a quizzical look.

"Really, I mean it." He looked into Guillaume's eyes and tried to reflect what he thought he saw there. "Look, nobody in my family ever saw the inside of a boardroom or a conference room like this. Hell, when I was growing up, my father punched a clock in a factory and my mother waited tables. I went to school on scholarships and worked two jobs the whole time. Even now, there's a part of me that can't believe I'm here. I look at these men like Justin Hildreth and Harry Warren and I wonder, how did the kid I used to be get to be here with men like that? I know that our job is to be pillars of strength and leadership. But sometimes I get the feeling that I'm a stranger in my own life. Know what I mean?"

"Yes," Guillaume said cautiously, "I do know that feeling."

"I thought so," Pennington said. "You know, as we get to work together, I think you're going to find we have an awful lot in common. On the business side *and* the personal side. I wouldn't be surprised if you and I start thinking of ourselves as two peas in a pod."

"Really?" Guillaume smirked. Then he reached his arm forward and put his dark hand on the table beside Pennington's white hand. "Two peas in a pod? That's got to be some kinda pod," Guillaume said.

"You'll see," Pennington said with a smile.

81

The bank buildings on the Isle of Guernsey looked innocent, Phil thought. Stone gothic town houses three or four stories high, all together on a block that resembled a university campus. Except that they held the secrets behind billions and billions of untraceable money from all over the globe.

Phil sat across from the manager in the cozy walnut-paneled office. The manager was very pale and very British—exceptionally polite and utterly impossible to read.

"Yes," he said in his BBC English accent, "Alban Reade told me you would be calling here. Alban and I served together in the Falklands. RAF."

"I know," Phil said. "Alban and I worked together on several joint operations when we were in intelligence services."

"Ah yes," the banker said, "more fine examples of British-American cooperation."

"Well, you Brits are our closest and most loyal ally." Phil was not sure if this would get him anywhere with the banker, but it was worth a try. "What would the world be like without our united efforts?"

"You are," the banker paused to inspect Phil more closely, "no longer in the intelligence services?" Phil nodded. The banker held Phil's Medusa business card up to the light, as if he might see a hidden message on it. Not finding anything to decode, he put it on the old-fashioned leather-framed green blotter on his desk. "You understand that our banking industry exists because of our protection of client privacy."

"Yes," Phil said, "I understand completely. But, as I'm sure Alban told you, this is an exceptional case." Phil extracted a loose-leaf notebook from his briefcase and placed it on the desk, facing the banker. "The FBI traced a million dollars that came from an American brokerage account to a bank in the Caymans and then to your bank. It was wired into the account of a Panama-registered corporation called Whitelaw, S.A. Then their investigation stopped."

The banker sat stone-faced.

Phil opened the notebook. It held plastic sleeves with full-page color photographs inside. Crime scene photographs of employees lying in their death poses at Ayvil Plastics. Phil flipped through the pages for the banker, giving him a tour of the horror. Piles of charred bodies all around the wreckage and, finally, the day care center, with dead children and mothers burned and crushed.

The banker looked at the pictures blankly.

"We have every reason to believe," Phil said, "the man who did *this* is the beneficial owner of Whitelaw, S.A."

The banker closed the notebook and handed it back to Phil. "When the bank has the proper orders from the judiciary, we extend the full cooperation required by law."

"This is a very special exception," Phil said, opening the notebook again and letting some passion enter his voice. "That's why I called in a favor from Alban. In hopes that you could extend a little special cooperation. This owner of Whitelaw, he must have a signature card on file here, even if it's just a number. We have a handwriting expert on the case. If there has been any other unusual activity in the account, or if there have been any wire transfers to other banks, it could help us find this criminal. Please. Is there anything you can help us with? In the spirit of justice? In the spirit of Anglo-American cooperation?"

The banker gave Phil his blank stare. "You know perfectly well that I cannot. If the FBI knew where the money went, why didn't they follow through on the investigation?"

Phil had no answer. Because the answer was the morass of government, politics, influence, and bureaucracy. The answer was convenience, finding a highly visible bad guy like Paulson to feed to the media. And helping all the vested interests move on.

Phil put the notebook in front of the banker again and flipped to a pair of grisly photos. "I'll be back eventually with court orders. You can help us speed that process."

The banker closed the notebook and stood. "Maybe there is something I can do, uh, in the spirit of Anglo-American cooperation."

He motioned Phil to the sitting area outside his office. Phil sat for ten minutes. Then the manager's office door opened. "I can tell you this much," he said from his doorway. "The Whitelaw account was closed three weeks ago. All the money was withdrawn in cash." As he closed his door, he added, "But you did not hear this from me."

82

Cindy interrupted the usual boring evening of TV with a little cupcake on a dinner plate. One lit birthday candle stood in the center of the frosting top.

"Happy anniversary," she said coyly, setting the plate in the middle of the coffee table.

Ken forced a smile and gave a shrug of confusion.

"We've been roommates for three months," Cindy said.

"Seems like forever," Ken blurted. "Uh, what I mean is—"

Cindy leaned forward and touched his arm. "It's okay, I know what you mean. It's because we're so comfortable together. It's easy, us rooming together, don't you think?"

"Yeah," he said, "I guess it is."

"Come on, make a wish," she said, motioning toward the half-burned candle.

Ken leaned forward and inhaled, about to blow out the candle.

"Wait," Cindy said, clutching his arm more firmly, "we should make a wish together, shouldn't we?"

"Sure, why not?"

Without letting go, Cindy slid right next to Ken and pressed herself against him. "Come on, one, two, three!" She pulled Ken forward with her as she leaned in to blow. They exhaled together. Their faces were close together, their cheeks just touching. Cindy leaned in a few inches and gave Ken a soft unhurried kiss on the lips.

"It's okay," she said, patting his hand, "I know."

"Know what?"

"The *real* anniversary was last week, wasn't it?"

"What do you mean?" he asked, pretending not to know.

"The anniversary," she said as she squeezed his hand, "the anniversary of your loss."

Ken looked at the floor.

"I heard you crying that night. That's the only time I've heard you cry since we moved in together."

Ken nodded. He did not pull his hand away from hers.

"They say it takes a full year to complete the mourning. That's what your literature from the grief center says. You left it lying around. I hope you don't mind my reading it." She waited, just holding his hand. He did not move. She placed her other hand on his. "You had a loss most people can't even imagine. But I've seen you getting stronger every day. Really."

He looked at her.

"Really," she said. "Ken, it's time for you to come back to the world of the living." She let go of his hands and slid her arms around his chest. "Sandy would want you to. It's time."

Ken let her hug him. She rested her face against his neck. "You can do it," she whispered into his shoulder, "it's time." She stared up into his eyes, her lips just slightly open, inviting a kiss. When Ken hesitated, Cindy moved in and kissed his mouth ever so lightly— once, twice, three times, each time her lips lingering longer against his.

"Uh, we shouldn't," Ken said, drawn to his pretty roommate and hesitant at the same time.

"Ken," Cindy purred, planting little kisses between her words, "you need to live. To feel alive. Sandy would want you to live. She would want you to feel alive. I'm a woman. I know."

"I don't think I'm ready." He tried to let go of her.

She held on tight. "If you don't start living again now, when will you?" She made a circle of kisses around his mouth.

"Not now," Ken said.

"Now is all we have," she said.

That stopped him.

"Now is all we have," she repeated. Then she placed her lips on his and whispered through soft kisses, "Did you miss any 'nows' with Sandy? Tell me, Ken, did you?"

He thought of many. A painful list of chances for happiness with Sandy that he missed, bungled, and threw away. "Yes," he said quietly.

"Now is all we ever have," she said insistently, "don't you see?"

He nodded.

"Then kiss me back," she whispered. She took his head in her hands and showed him just how he should do it. "You remember how, don't you?" This time, her lips drew his lips apart.

"It's all right," she said comfortingly, "it's all right, Ken. You deserve to feel alive again."

He started kissing her back, at first hesitantly, then more urgently. She moved one of his hands onto her breast. He pulled it away. "Don't you want to touch my breasts?" she whispered. "Don't you?"

He answered with a hungry hand.

"My ass?" she whispered with her tongue in his ear. "Don't you want to reach down and touch it when we're standing in line in Starbucks and you think no one is looking?"

"Yes," he said breathlessly.

She took his hand off her breast, kissed his fingertips one by one, and gently traced lines up and down his palm. Then she took his hand and put it between her legs, where it was warm. Warmer than he remembered. "Don't you want my—" She paused and spoke even more softly. "—don't you want my pussy?"

"Yes," Ken whispered, his heart pounding, his breathing forced as if there were a lead weight on his chest.

"Then take me," she said, piercing his mouth with her tongue, "take me now." She stood up and walked him into her bedroom. They stood by her bed. Ken took her head in his hands and locked his mouth on hers. They fell onto her bed. She helped him as he pulled at her clothes. When she was down to her satin bikini panties, she lay back on the bed, stretching out her legs and parting them just slightly. He stared hungrily at her breasts, her tummy, and the rough outline of her bush pressing against the smooth satin. Every detail of her body was electrifying. It was like his first time with a woman. As he reached for the elastic at the sides of her hips, she raised her legs and folded them back to help him slide her panties off faster. He held the little ball of cloth in his hand, suddenly riveted by the wet spot in the center. Her odor flooded his nostrils. It was rude, insistent, intoxicating. He yanked his clothes off and gave in to the power of sex.

Ken buried his face between her legs, thrilled to rediscover the messy oblivion of a woman. But he could not wait for her. He desperately needed release. He climbed on top. She jammed a condom into his hand. He tore at the wrapper and slid it on. He entered her and came at once.

Then, just moments later, he was hard again.

"Whoa, cowboy," Cindy said, removing the first condom with a ball of Kleenex and expertly sliding on the second one. "There's no need to rush. We've got all the time in the world." This time, she led him through a slower tango, riding on top of him and straddling him like a saddle. She got her own climax first, rubbing herself against him just the way she wanted. Then she guided and teased him to his second orgasm, making it slower and bigger than his first.

They lay back in the narrow bed, suddenly aware of how cramped it was. As Ken's breathing began to slow, he felt a light, floating feeling. He thought he ought to find a way to cuddle with this woman, if only because that was what one was supposed to do. He tried but she would not let him.

"No, that's okay," Cindy said. "I'm not big on spooning." She pulled her legs together and sat up against her pillow in a way that clearly separated her body from his. The coupling was over.

"Well, uh, Cindy . . . we, uh . . . ," Ken stammered.

"Well what?" Cindy said brightly. "Did you like?"

"Oh, yes, I, uh . . . ," Ken said, still not sure if there was some kind of declaration of affection that was appropriate at this time.

"Good." Cindy smiled. "Me, too. Listen, I've got an early class." She motioned with her chin in the direction of Ken's bedroom. Seeing his puzzlement, Cindy gave Ken a hug and said, "Poor dear." She gave him a formal, closed-mouth smack on the lips. "We'll keep it cool. And every now and then hot. Nick and Nora, fighting the bad guys, okay?" She tousled his hair fondly as if he were a boy. Then she turned and reached for the paperback book on her bedside table.

"Okay," he said, and climbed out of bed. He stood naked in front of her, letting himself get used to this feeling in front of a woman who was not Sandy. He looked at their clothes piled together on the floor and wondered if he should pick up the items that were his and take them back to his room. He stood still for a moment, taking stock.

Yes, he liked Cindy and found her attractive. But he felt no deep emotional connection to her. Still, he felt better than he had felt in months. Alive again, vibrant, pulsating.

Was that enough?

Yes, his body told him resoundingly, it will do just fine.

He thought of the photo of Sandy waiting for him on his windowsill. Then he remembered the night, one of far too many, when he was too busy to make love. He could hear her voice clearly, making her plea for the life force. "*Everybody* deserves to be gettin' some," she said. "We've only got so many chances before we die." Maybe Sandy would forgive him. Just maybe.

He felt himself getting hard again. He cleared his throat to get Cindy's attention. "Uh, Nora?" he said playfully.

She looked up and smirked. She put her book down, peeled the sheet back, and reached into the drawer for another condom.

83

The sun was setting over Lyford Cay in Nassau, the Bahamas. Here, along the priciest shorefront strip of this gated community of the super-rich, the water of Clifton Bay was afire with glorious colors, making the eight-figure price tags routinely paid for Lyford Cay properties seem almost reasonable.

Harry Warren and Justin Hildreth, dressed in linen slacks and sport shirts, looked out over the water from the veranda of Hildreth's yellow stucco mansion, situated on the choicest waterfront lot in the cay.

"Thanks," Warren said, eagerly taking his second daiquiri from Alejandro, who always accompanied Hildreth as he made the rounds of his houses. "Justin, I've been down to Lyford Cay before. Played the course, naturally. But I must say, this property of yours, your view"—he gestured at Hildreth's grand home, with its ocean-to-bay expanse of beach—"well, you're really in the catbird seat here. You do have an eye for real estate."

"I wish I could take the credit," Hildreth said. "My late wife's father was one of the original investors in the cay. He picked this spot when there was nothing here but landfill and a speck of reef. This house was his present to us. Of all our homes, this was Margaret's favorite. When she became ill, she spent her last days here."

Hildreth gazed out over the sunset. Alejandro stood beside him, tray in hand. Without having to look, Hildreth reached for the crystal glass of sherry waiting on Alejandro's tray. He took a small, delicate first sip then downed the rest in one draft. Then in a seamless hand-off, Alejandro took the glass from Hildreth.

Hildreth cleared his throat. Alejandro nodded as he took the tray and vanished back into the house. What Warren could never have guessed was the signal Hildreth and his manservant had just exchanged.

Since Margaret's agonizing death from colorectal cancer, Hildreth had become terrified of his own gastrointestinal tract. He insisted on having his stool tested for occult bleeding every time he had a bowel movement, even though his doctor said this was overkill. Hildreth gave Alejandro the chore of preparing the test smear to be sent to the laboratory. Now, when Hildreth finished defecating he did not flush. Instead, he would signal Alejandro, who would take the sample smears from his master's turds, prepare the slide for mailing, then flush.

When Hildreth first told Alejandro of this additional responsibility, he thanked him warmly. "I'm sure you won't mind," he said confidently. And in a way, Alejandro did not mind. He believed that, with patience, the day would come when he would even the score with his master. The more points Hildreth accumulated on the debit side, the more points Alejandro would be entitled to exact from him when that sweet judgment day finally arrived. Alejandro had lowered his head obediently and replied, "No, Mr. Hildreth, I do not mind."

"You know, I could retire to a place like this," Warren announced. He clenched his hands around an imaginary putter and gave it a short stroke. He watched the pretend ball roll across the green and nodded triumphantly when it dropped into the cup that was not there.

"When I retire, I know it will be here," Hildreth said. "As I like to say, I'll learn to practice the arts of comfort and serenity. But not for a while, I hope." Hildreth cleared his throat as if to erase the prospect of his retirement. "Harry, if you don't mind my saying so, I think you might enjoy expanding your network. From what I can see, apart from some very admirable charities, your board positions are all in the business world. I think you could cast a wider net."

"Business is my whole life."

"I realize that. But your retirement is just a year away. It's a tough transition for CEOs. I've seen it before." Warren nodded thoughtfully. If thoughts of Arch Paulson occurred to either man, they showed no sign of it.

Hildreth went on. "There are a number of boards I can think of— museums, hospitals, international organizations—that would benefit from your talent and energy. I'd be delighted to put your name forward and make some introductions. I can think of several of my clubs, too." He paused. "Like the Maiden Rock Club." Hildreth said the name slowly and quietly, romancing each syllable in his best lock-jaw accent. He was referring to the ultra-exclusive, old money country club in Southampton. Many tycoons applied for membership at Maiden Rock only to be put on its famous waiting list. There they would wait and wait, grow old and die, never to be called from the list to the first tee. "Would that interest you?" Hildreth asked, knowing full well that Warren would covet the prestige of such a membership and thrill to be able to play the legendary course whenever he wanted to.

Warren looked down into his drink, ill at ease being the receiver, rather than the grantor, of largesse. But the world of access and prestige that Hildreth dangled before him was irresistible, even with all the money and power he had amassed as CEO. In the presence of the polished aristocrat, Harry Warren, the monarch of General Industries, still felt like the bricklayer's son that he was. And Hildreth knew it.

"Yes, it would," he said softly, appreciating the favors Hildreth promised and resenting them at the same time. "Thank you," he said with some difficulty.

Warren took a deep breath and stood up. For that instant, he towered over Hildreth. "Justin," he said, trying to regain the upper hand, "now that I have made you our most senior board member, I need your support in something very important."

"Certainly."

"I want Mike Guillaume to succeed me as CEO. I've been training him for more than a decade."

Hildreth sat silent for a bit too long. Finally, he spoke. "You know, Tom Pennington has an exceptional talent for leadership. I'd say he was born to run a company like GI."

"But he's not a General Industries man. Guillaume is."

Hildreth stood. "Harry," he said, looking down, "as chairman of the succession committee of the board, I think it is in the best interests of the company that we have a horse race. This merger will be the course. Let's see whose leadership emerges. I believe *that* is what is best for the company. I'm sure the rest of the board, and you, as chairman, would agree."

Harry Warren clenched his jaw. "Yes, of course."

Hildreth patted Warren on the shoulder and said brightly, "I'm delighted to add General Industries to my list of boards. I'm preparing to live another twenty years at least."

Alejandro appeared in the doorway. "Mr. Hildreth, Mr. Guillaume and Mr. Pennington are back from the club."

"Show them out here, please."

A moment later, Pennington and Guillaume appeared, a little rumpled after their game.

"Who won?" Harry asked eagerly.

"We did," Pennington said.

"Huh?" Harry looked confused. "I thought you men were going mano a mano."

"We ended up playing in a foursome," Guillaume explained. "With Gary Lankford of Dalton Aerospace and his CFO."

"Good old Gary!" Harry barked enthusiastically. "I haven't seen him since last summer at Bohemian Grove. I didn't know he had a place down here. So you beat Lankford's ass, eh?"

"Of course," Guillaume said with jock arrogance.

"Alejandro," Hildreth called, "can we get these men a drink, please? They must be very thirsty." Alejandro appeared in a flash with tray, pitcher, and chilled glasses. He served the drinks and vanished again.

"So did you have any money on the match?" Warren asked.

"Nah," Pennington said, "we figured it was enough to let them lose with dignity. We didn't need to decimate their net worth, too."

The four men shared a laugh. Then Guillaume turned to Warren. "Harry, you'll never guess the name of Lankford's CFO."

Warren shrugged.

Guillaume said, "Davenport. Gerald Davenport!"

Warren burst out laughing.

"What's so funny?" Hildreth asked.

"Oh," Warren said with a snicker, "same name as a friend of ours. Actually, he's more Mike's friend, right?"

"Yeah, right," Guillaume said.

"Let us in on the joke," Pennington said, "come on."

Guillaume smirked. "Gerald Davenport is the NRC inspector at the Perry's Bend nuclear plant, the one we inherited in the Dynergetix acquisition. We were in there cleaning up the mess the old management left behind, and this guy is busting my chops. I mean really busting my chops."

"Well, of course he is," Warren interjected. "He's got to be the Grand Dragon or whatever of his local Ku Klux Klan. He's a screaming racist bigot. And because he knows it's Mike's job to take whatever crap he dishes out, he really dishes it out. Shameful. A nasty little bureaucrat with a big bat."

"That *is* a shame," Hildreth said, "in this day and age."

"Cost of doing business," Guillaume said, shaking his head.

Hildreth looked over at Pennington as he spoke. When Pennington met his gaze, he nodded ever so faintly. Pennington acknowledged him with an even fainter nod and a lowering of his eyelids.

It was a minute interchange that neither Warren nor Guillaume noticed.

84

It was well past midnight when Pennington joined Hildreth for a walk along the beach. The full moon shone like a second sun. It cast strong, dark shadows and created a glittering silver highway of reflections that stretched from the beach out over the waves to the horizon.

"Harry Warren wanted my vote for Guillaume to succeed him as CEO," Hildreth said as they padded over the sand. Hildreth wore sandals and his Lyford Cay outfit of white linen slacks and pastel polo shirt. Pennington wore sneakers, running shorts, and a runner's tank top.

"I'm surprised he waited this long," Pennington said.

"I'm not," Hildreth said, "Harry is aggressive. But he is also measured and patient. I'm sure he's an excellent chess player."

"What did you tell him?"

"I made a trade. In exchange for clubs and boards he would never in a million years be invited to join, he will let us have a horse race. You versus Guillaume."

Pennington nodded.

"I've never liked horse races. I can't stand uncertainty." Hildreth stopped and looked out over the waves. "It's ironic, the access I can give a man like Harry. This world of mine is vanishing; I'll be able to keep it as a bargaining chip in my lifetime. But its power is eroding every year. The flow of new money is washing it away."

"But hasn't the flow of new money *always* kept changing who holds the power?"

Hildreth raised his chin in the gesture people interpreted as him looking down his aquiline nose at them. "I beg your pardon?"

"Oh, come on," Pennington said, "old money always resents new."

Hildreth looked at him with mild surprise. "I hope you're not accusing me of being a snob."

"I had snobbism rubbed in my face. Remember, I was the poor kid on scholarship at Hotchkiss and at Princeton and—"

Hildreth put his hand on Pennington's shoulder. "Tom, the people you met at school, the ones who took the accident of birth as proof of their superiority, were just lucky idiots. Money ends up in the hands of the most unlikely people. On the other hand, you have reached your position in life, not because you were destined to be rich, but because you were destined to *lead*. That's what I spotted in you. I'm interested in the men who are superior by nature—the natural elite of the human race. They have the right to *get* more because they know how to *do* more."

"You mean like . . . ," Pennington asked with a mischievous smile, ". . . a master race?"

"Well, to be perfectly blunt," Hildreth said, "in some ways they had the right idea. But in the end, the Nazis were ham-fisted bullies. And more to the point, they had their criteria all wrong. The idea of racial or tribal superiority is archaic and unworkable. Bloodlines and family trees can't prevent your relatives from growing up to be idiots. In fact, it often guarantees it. Witness our English cousins and their aristocracy. No, I'm talking about an aristocracy of ability."

Hildreth started walking again; Pennington followed. "Look at Harry Warren. He is very capable but very common. He measures everything with money. As a result, he misses the larger point. Or Michael Guillaume. Guillaume is exceptionally talented, but he does not qualify either. He is too conventionally good." Hildreth said "good" with contempt. "He is bound by the rules that keep ordinary men ordinary. He will remain second-tier his whole life. He will be proud of it and never know better."

"Whereas I, Tom Pennington?"

Hildreth stopped and looked back over his shoulder to see if Pennington was following. When Pennington folded his arms across his chest, Hildreth turned and came back beside him.

"You, Tom Pennington, have cold, clear intelligence and the unblinking willingness to act. Hotchkiss, Princeton, and Harvard gave you a taste for life at the top and deprived you of it at the same time. It bloodied your raw ambition and polished you—an exceptionally useful combination. You learned what great kings and presidents know—that rulers make decisions that shatter some lives and benefit

others. Different rules apply to those who truly understand power."
Hildreth put his hand on Pennington's shoulder in a fatherly gesture. "After an appropriate time as CEO of General Industries, it
will be time for you to apply your talents in higher office. As I've said
before, you are what they used to call 'presidential timber.'"

Pennington smiled. "Of course. But for now, tell me how we take
the uncertainty out of this horse race?"

"First, we need to collapse the time. A year is far too long to wait.
We need to hasten Harry's retirement."

"You don't mean?" Pennington asked.

"No, that would be dangerous. And too obvious. We need to
weaken Harry Warren, not destroy him. He rules that company and
its board with the force of his personality. If we can neutralize that
charisma of his, that's enough. He has a bad heart, you know."

"Yes, I know."

"Well, our government, in its pursuit of science, has formulated
chemicals that can shock the heart and weaken it without killing it.
And leave no trace. It's been, uh, field-tested abroad by our agents.
The Washington connections I have given you should get you what
you need."

"Yes, I know who to contact."

"Whom," Hildreth said.

"Yes, whom," Pennington said obediently.

"The next step, I believe, is the nuclear option."

"I beg your pardon?"

"They gave it to us this afternoon," Hildreth said. "Their problems at the nuclear power plant. That nuclear business is a potential
trump card for Guillaume. That's why Warren expanded their nuclear presence by acquiring Dynergetix. The government is finally
giving back those billions to the private sector in a form of power we
don't have to buy abroad. Once the subsidies from Washington start
pouring in to build and refurbish nuclear plants, it will create a
mighty river of money, a mother lode of earnings. The bonanza of
nuclear power will make the biggest defense contractors turn green
with envy. And of course, those plants also double as centers for
bomb-fuel technology, although we don't like to say that in the
press, do we?"

Hildreth started walking again. Pennington followed this time.

"We need to turn Guillaume's strength against him. A small incident, well timed, should do it. Shortly before the day of the board's vote."

"A nuclear accident," Pennington said, "would mean more deaths."

"A small amount of collateral damage would be acceptable," Hildreth said. "In fact, a minor disaster with fatalities will be a boon to our policymakers. It will only underline the need to award more contracts that much sooner. You'll be able to make brilliant, impassioned speeches on the subject, I'm sure. Can you arrange that? The plant they mentioned is already a sore spot and has had some press."

"Yes," Pennington said confidently, "I have just the man to do it."

"Same fellow you used in Ohio?" Hildreth quickly raised his hand. "Wait, I don't need to know. Tell me, is this enough to get you started?"

"Yes, I can work out the rest." Pennington reached down, grabbed his sneaker, and pulled up one leg to stretch it in preparation for his run. He stretched for a moment and released. As he pulled up his other leg, he spoke in an idle, offhanded tone. "Say, Justin, can I ask you a question?"

Hildreth nodded.

"We've taken this stock on one of the most profitable rides in history. I don't know how you might have done it as an insider, but I do hope you have been able to get your share of the gains." Pennington winked at his mentor.

"Gentlemen never discuss their personal finances," Hildreth said curtly, and turned his back to Pennington. Pennington cut short his stretch and jogged away.

85

"I've got two candidates to be Peter Houghton," Phil said as he closed the door of his office. "I may have come up empty in Guernsey, but we hit pay dirt in Paris and Johannesburg."

Ken had just about sprinted from Ninety-fourth Street to Midtown when Phil called.

"Now, the last time you saw this guy who called himself Peter Houghton," Phil said, "he had a goatee, mustache, and black horn-rimmed glasses. Right?"

"Right," Ken replied, his foot tapping furiously. "Please, Phil, don't make me wait. Who is he? Please!"

Phil had two thick manila folders. He extracted the top sheet from one folder then from the other. Ken stared down at black-and-white photos of two brawny, big-jawed white men about age forty. The photos had the grainy look of images that had been copied from the Internet, edited, and enlarged. The backgrounds were fuzzy and out of focus. The man on the left was clean-shaven with close-cropped dark hair and eyebrows. The man on the right was completely bald and somehow odd-looking. Ken stared at the face, trying to figure out what made him look strange.

"This guy's got no eyebrows," Ken exclaimed.

"He's got no hair," Phil said.

"You mean on his head?" Ken asked.

"I mean no hair. Period. Anywhere. He had a disease as a child and he lost all his hair. Left him as the human equivalent of a hairless Chihuahua."

"But I don't recognize either guy," Ken said, his voice distraught.

Phil handed him a soft-lead drawing pencil. "Go ahead, add the goatee and glasses."

Ken took the pencil to the first face. He stroked lightly against the paper, tentatively scribbling in the glasses and goatee as best he could remember them. He shrugged when he was done. "Now he just looks like any guy with a goatee and glasses. I guess it was a good disguise."

"Yes," Phil said. "Corny but good. Now do the other one."

Ken scribbled on the second image. "I don't remember what his eyebrows looked like because of the glasses," he said.

"Or even if he had eyebrows," Phil added.

"The fucker," Ken said as he stared at his scribbles. He struggled to put these images together with his fuzzy recollections. "I don't recognize either one. Shit."

"Hold on," Phil said, producing two new printouts from his folders. "I've got a buddy who's good with Photoshop." He put them on top of the sheets Ken had marked up. This time the glasses, goatee, and hair were real and retouched convincingly onto the faces. "Now clear your mind and look again."

Ken shut his eyes. Then stared again.

Rumblings like distant thunder sounded in the back of his mind. Sensations from that morning in the conference room with Al Darling came back to him—his own hand on the big table, the sound of the unrolled paper of the building plans as the curled edges fought against the staplers and notebooks that were holding them down. The sound of the goateed man's voice. The look in his eyes from behind those glasses. Ken stared at the retouched photo on the right and remembered moments forgotten until now.

"Yeah," Ken said, tapping the retouched face on the nose, "that's him!"

"You sure?"

"Yes, I'm sure."

"I mean, are you really, really sure?"

"Jesus, Phil, I told you yes. I am goddamn sure!"

"Good," Phil said, "I wanted you to be sure you identified him first."

"What do you mean 'first'?"

Phil produced a copy of two documents, one signed Grant De Waal, the other signed Jan-Willem Fredericks. He put them beside the copy of the Peter Houghton signature from the Ayvil logbook. "Because Henry Mills has also identified him."

Ken stared at the handwriting samples. Even to Ken's untrained eye, it looked like the same handwriting.

"He's South African," Phil explained, "an Afrikaaner. His real name is Grant De Waal." He pronounced it gutturally in the back of his throat. "Chhhraaant De Vaaahl."

"The accent!" Ken cried out.

"Uh-huh," Phil said, "not quite British, not quite German. It's more Dutch, although the Dutch in Holland consider Afrikaans a primitive and rather embarrassing version of their language."

Ken stared at the face in the picture and shook his head.

"His nickname is Bles." Phil pronounced it "blaiss." "Short for *bles kop*, meaning 'bald head.' De Waal got this rare fever as a child that screwed up his endocrine system. Developed the condition called *alopecia totalis*. Lost all his hair. Hence the nickname Baldy. There's a pop singer down there called Bles Bridges who has lots of hair, so the name's a little in-joke. De Waal grew up on a poor farm in the northern Transvaal, an area they now call Tzaneen. Started in a white supremacist hate group called the White Lions under Apartheid. That's where he learned to kill, mastered the basics of explosives and bombmaking. At first it was to stop the blacks and teach softhearted whites a lesson or two. Then he joined the South African Defense Force. Rose to lieutenant in one of the 'rec' units—the rangers who used to go into Namibia and Angola and make preemptive strikes against Communists." Phil paused. "And women and children and anyone else they could butcher. Found he had leadership abilities—in a deadly sort of way. When Apartheid collapsed, he joined Executive Action like other SADF. That's where he learned that you could go on killing rampages for fun and profit. Even working for the occasional black tyrant who could pay in cash or gold bullion or diamonds."

"Executive what?" Ken asked.

"Executive Action. Private army. They worked in Angola and Sierra Leone to put down the rebels, make the country, ahem, safe for democracy. And secure the oil and diamonds while they were at it. There were rumors they had a hand in Uganda, Zimbabwe, and Ethiopia. De Waal was part of EA's first force sent to Papua New Guinea later on, but he quit before the company was officially shut down in '99 when South Africa passed an anti-mercenary law."

"And Executive Action?"

Phil smiled. "Dispersed into a network of companies around the world. They now provide everything from heavy equipment rental to computer software to adult education."

"And Grant De Waal? Bles?" Ken asked slowly, mimicking the throaty pronunciation Phil had used. After a year of not knowing, he savored the ability to speak the name of Evil.

"Executive Action gave him the training and connections he needed to go freelance. He was a clever organizer of missions and good at getting the most out of experts in technology. Here are some of his finer achievements." Phil handed Ken more photos. There were shots of burned-out villages in jungle clearings, piles of butchered black bodies and body parts in a mass grave, more villages where dozens lay dead around their huts.

Ken stared in horror.

"These are shots of De Waal, taken on various operations," Phil said. "As you can see, he looks different wherever you see him. The hairless condition makes him strange and too easy to remember. So De Waal protects his identity with the arts of hair and makeup. He lives all over. Roams from one exotic island to the next, probably visiting his money in those anonymous accounts. He has multiple passports, multiple identities. The guy is good." Phil caught himself. "I mean, effective."

"So is this enough to show Decker and get him back on the case?" Ken asked.

"I'm afraid not. Remember, we were not supposed to have a lot of this evidence in the first place. We haven't pieced enough of the puzzle together yet. You see, Decker is going to have to go back over the things we get in the gray area and get them again in legal black-and-white, with his court orders and his official channels."

Ken grunted.

"All we have done is given Peter Houghton a name. Which may be something the FBI already knew from their investigation and may not prove anything new."

"That's fucking dandy," Ken said. "What now?"

"Get a more complete picture of De Waal's network, before and after the Ayvil operation. Find out who paid him and how. Look for more of the traveler's checks they used in Ohio. Traveler's checks are a good way to launder money, almost as good as cash. We've got to be very deliberate and not miss any—"

"What about getting to fucking Pennington?" Ken asked angrily.

"Remember, Ken, you promised me you could accept the possibility that Paulson really did do it. Remember?"

Ken glared.

Phil remained calm and professional. "I think we're on the verge of breaking this open. I'm going to try the bank in Vanuatu next. We just need a little more patience. These things are complicated. They take time."

"I'm afraid," Ken said, "time may be the one thing we don't have much of."

86

Pennington read the IM screen on the cell phone: D257P.

He waited outside 977 Fifth Avenue and watched the medallion numbers on top of the passing taxis. When he saw D257P heading toward him down Fifth Avenue, he pretended to flag it down. As the cab pulled to the curb, he opened the back of his cell phone, removed the SIM card, and flicked it into the gutter.

He got in and said nothing to the driver, a large swarthy man with black hair and a scruffy beard. The driver turned on the meter and pulled away from the curb. Pennington offered no destination; the driver did not ask.

Pennington looked at the plastic ID card in the slot in the divider screen. "Ali Khalil," he said, reading the name aloud. "You from Pakistan?"

"Same village as you, sahib," Grant De Waal said, putting on a theatrical Pakistani accent.

"You look very convincing," Pennington said, leaning forward to get a better look.

"I always do," De Waal said coldly. The cab slowed as it approached the bottleneck at Sixty-sixth Street where the crosstown traffic spilled onto Fifth Avenue from the Central Park Transverse.

"So you have a plan?" Pennington asked.

"Yah," De Waal said. "Been consulting with Russian friends. Lot of their nuclear engineers are out of work. It's a shame."

"How much have you spent so far?"

"Two hundred thousand, including my travel and hotels."

"Jesus, Bles, where do you stay when you travel? The Ritz?"

De Waal turned around and looked at Pennington through the open window of the bulletproof barrier. "Where do *you* stay when you travel?" he sneered. "I'll bet it's not Motel Six, yah."

"How much more do you need to set up the operation?" Pennington, the canny financial executive, was annoyed.

"Another three hundred thousand." De Waal found a hole in the traffic and was skillfully driving the taxi through it.

"What?"

"You heard me," De Waal said as his burst of open field driving came to a stop at the next knot of stalled traffic at Grand Army Plaza at Fifty-ninth Street.

"I don't understand," Pennington protested. "You did the Paragon operation with ten thousand in setup expenses."

"For that job, all I needed was a laminated ID card to get into the hangar, a blue jumpsuit, and a toolbox. And that was five years ago. We were younger then. Life was simpler."

De Waal slammed on the brakes for no reason other than to shake up Pennington. Pennington was thrown forward against his seat belt. "After all I've done for you"—De Waal pretended to sound hurt— "are you going to start nickel-and-diming me now? Huh? These things cost what they cost."

Pennington rubbed his shoulder where it had been bruised against the belt. "All right," he said.

"Don't you want to begin with the objectives and strategy," De Waal asked, "like we usually do?"

Pennington said, "To repeat, the objective is an embarrassment in the boardroom, not another Chernobyl. Just a small number of deaths. Now what's your strategy?"

"A simple plan." De Waal cleared his throat. "Now, a nuclear power plant is nothing but a giant plumbing operation. You move tons and tons of water and steam around, yah? Heating it, cooling it, pumping it from the reactor to the generators and back again. Nuclear fission?" De Waal shrugged. "That just makes the heat. Water, that's where the power is. That's where we fuck them up."

De Waal smiled into the rearview mirror.

Pennington smiled back.

This was what made De Waal such a valuable find. As an executive, Pennington prided himself on his ability to spot people with talent and deploy them in roles where they could grow and have ever greater impact. De Waal, although outside the normal corporate sphere, was clearly one of his best "hires." Pennington had helped him grow and develop from a simple bloodthirsty thug into a highly sophisticated manager.

De Waal was trying to get the cab out of the stinky wake of the bus ahead. He returned his gaze to the road and began jockeying the cab out of the lane. "Now in order to know what is happening in the plant," he said, "you have to know the temperature of the water as it moves from here to there. And for that you need a simple, low-tech device available at just about any plumbing supply store for under fifty dollars." He announced proudly, "A temperature sensor."

He had the cab out from behind the bus. "It's a little metal collar that fits into the pipe and is wired into the control room. Now temperature sensors, like all measuring devices, are subject to error. And it's not uncommon for manufacturers to get reports of flaws in sensors from a given production run. In which case, to be safe, they have to recall all the sensors that came from the bad lot. Happens all the time."

Pennington spoke up. "So you are going to replace sensors at Perry's Bend with new sensors that you provide. Right?"

De Waal nodded in the mirror. "But wait, it gets better. There's a story behind it that Davenport, the NRC man, is going to love. Why is this lot of sensors defective? Can you guess? Huh?"

Pennington shrugged at the mirror.

De Waal chuckled. "*Vokkin' kaffirs.* Fucking blacks. Your damned government forced us to hire a minority contractor for one of the crucial parts. Comes from a black-owned company. Would you trust your safety to sensors made by blacks, Mr. Davenport? I mean, would you?"

Pennington reached through the divider window and patted De Waal on the shoulder. "You're good, Bles, you are very good."

"No, I'm the best," he said, steering around a stalled taxi. "We replace the sensors that are supposed to be bad with ones we know are bad. The hot water coming out reads as cold, the cold water coming in reads as hot. Soon they don't know whether they are coming or going. The system readings go haywire."

"Then what?" Pennington asked.

"Well, if their procedures are as good as General Industries claims, there will be an automatic shutdown of the reactor. Then they investigate. Davenport will declare an NUE." De Waal paused and shot Pennington a smug look.

"All right," Pennington said, "what's that?"

"Notification of an Unusual Event. General Industries will get instant publicity. Guillaume will have egg on his face and maybe radioactive waste."

"Any way of knowing how this will play out?" Pennington was not asking out of concern, but out of his need to understand the consequences of decision making. He was merely making a mental decision tree to assess probable outcomes, the way he had been trained to do in business school.

"That's the sport of it," De Waal said cheerfully. "We won't know until it happens. As for me, I plan on being long gone."

"When can you be ready to execute?"

"I need another two weeks to get the details worked out. Then, give me forty-eight hours' notice, and we can be at the plant."

"Excellent," Pennington said. "Now tell me, Bles, what's the price for all this?"

"Thought you'd never ask." De Waal paused. "Six million dollars." He slammed on the brakes again, throwing Pennington forward into the belt.

"Six million? That's absurd."

"What's the matter, Pennington, you can afford it. How much did you get in this merger? A hundred million? Two hundred million? If you're worth that much, my percentage to keep you there is chump change. Besides, now that you're so rich, isn't it your social responsibility to spread some of it around? That's what you Americans say, yah?"

"This is highway robbery."

De Waal looked at Pennington in the mirror. "Take it or leave it."

De Waal yanked the steering wheel. The cab swerved to the curb at Fifth Avenue and Forty-fourth Street. "I want three hundred thousand more for expenses now. That'll make half a million. Plus another two and a half up front for a total of three. Now. That'll make half up front," he said. "And half transferred on the day. If I get word that my three million dollars has been transferred, I'll know we have a deal. If I don't, I'll go back home for some target practice in Namibia. Up to you."

"I can't transfer that much all at once," Pennington complained. "It will attract too much attention."

"Half up front," De Waal said curtly. "Half on the day."

Pennington grimaced as he did the math and calculated the risks. "One million now spread out over two weeks," he said, "half a million on the day I give the order, another half million on the day of the operation, then four more installments over a week. That's two million up front and the other four on delivery, taking into account the handling problems with numbers like these."

De Waal thought for a moment then said, "Deal." He unlocked the taxi doors with the switch by his armrest. He did not have to say that it was time for Pennington to get out of the cab.

"Hey," Pennington protested, "aren't you going to take me back to my building?"

De Waal turned around and stared at Pennington through the window of the divider. "What do you think this is? A taxi?"

87

Twenty-seven hours after leaving JFK, Phil saw Vanuatu. Or at least Efaté, the main island of the eighty-three-island nation, a thousand miles east of northeastern Australia and almost two thousand miles due north of the North Island of New Zealand.

From his window seat, he looked down on the towering mountains of rain forests, where isolated peoples still lived in the Stone Age. As the Air Vanuatu jetliner, an old Boeing 727 bought third- or possibly fourth-hand, banked in for its descent to the capital city of Port Vila, Phil reviewed his facts about this country that billed itself as the premier tax haven of the South Pacific.

If someone like Grant De Waal set up a Vanuatu International Corporation, he would enjoy the following benefits: No disclosure of beneficial owners. No tax on offshore profits. No capital gains tax. No income taxes. No exchange controls. Profits made in other countries transferred to Vanuatu, tax free, no questions asked. No government register of directors or shareholders. No audit requirements. No local meetings required. Bearer shares allowed. Privacy guaranteed. And all for an annual government registration fee of $330 American. Corporate bank accounts for a Vanuatu International Corporation could be established with a local Vanuatu bank in as little as two days. The only requirement being that the Vanuatu International Corporation does no business in Vanuatu.

From the information Phil had been able to glean, De Waal had been a satisfied customer of the Vanuatu banking and offshore company system for at least three years. Although Phil had no subpoenas, no court orders, and no badge, he had had a reasonable degree of confidence that he could apply pressure. He had pulled favors from old colleagues at DIA, contacts at Interpol, and even the contact of a contact who knew the Minister of Justice of Vanuatu himself.

After landing and clearing customs, he checked into the Coral Reef Motel. It had been billed as a renovated motel with kitchenettes and views of the harbor, suitable for the business traveler. It turned out to be a shabby harborside wreck with its view of the water blocked by a newer hotel. So much for travel Web sites. Phil cranked up the noisy air conditioner, closed the dingy curtains, and slept for a full day.

The New Hebrides Bank of Vanuatu paid homage to the archipelago's former colonial name. But there was nothing remotely Scottish about it. It was French run, French staffed, and 100 percent French speaking. Phil had an appointment with the manager in his small corner office of the two-story stucco building in the center of the business district of Port Vila. Like all tropical capitals in the third world, Port Vila was an eclectic mixture of decaying colonial architecture, modest attempts at modern buildings of steel, glass, and concrete, and flimsy tin-roofed shacks, all huddled together in a sweaty jumble under the blazing hot sun, with goats wandering the streets.

Phil spoke to the manager in fluent French. "Monsieur Tavarnier, it is encouraging to come so far from civilization and have the comfort and confidence of knowing that we can communicate with the precision and intellectual acuity only French affords," he said, taking the manager by surprise. Even though Phil could rattle his French a mile a minute in a flawless Parisian accent, he chose to speak in a flat, distinctly American tone. It was his way of saying that he had penetrated and mastered the imperious and exclusionary French culture without actually embracing it.

Monsieur Tavarnier was a short dark man with greasy black hair who did not speak much in return. Phil expected as much from a bank manager who dealt in secrets. He presented his Medusa credentials and described his years in the DIA, including his tours of duty in France, Martinique, and French-speaking West Africa. "I have come to get some information on one of your depositors. His company is called Hammersmith, Ltd., a Vanuatu International Corporation."

"We do not reveal information," the bank manager said, "without a court order issued in Vanuatu."

"Of course, I understand that completely." Phil nodded respectfully.

Then he brought out his exhibits. First, the notebook with the ghastly pictures of charred dead people in Ohio. He turned the pages slowly and described what had happened and how, including the deaths of the children and mothers. Tavarnier watched impassively. At the back of the notebook, Phil had added photos of several African massacres credited to De Waal, and as he showed these he went into more of the known details of De Waal's bloody resume.

Tavarnier looked at the notebook as if it were a catalog of auto parts.

Next, Phil showed him the wire transfer copies that the FBI had obtained, with the trail to the New Hebrides Bank of Vanuatu highlighted in yellow, complete with Hammersmith's account number. Then a credit report, obtained by somewhat gray means, from a cooperative banker friend in San Francisco, also indicating large balance increases in the Hammersmith account immediately following the explosion in Ohio. Phil described the discovery of a similar money trail to Whitelaw, S.A., of Panama and made it seem like he had cracked the code there and gotten the information he needed from Whitelaw's bank in Guernsey.

Tavarnier was unimpressed.

Phil invoked the FBI and how they were already at work obtaining court orders around the world. He invoked Interpol and his contacts at DIA. "I have it on good information that there are several investigations ongoing concerning certain practices here at New Hebrides Bank."

Tavarnier did not flinch.

Phil decided to be more overt. "I spoke to Inspector Elster from Interpol," he said, and waited, knowing that the tenacious German had been to the bank just the week before, chasing drug money. No reaction. "I briefed Herr Elster on De Waal and his activities. He, of course, had heard of him before and told me he would look favorably on anyone who could help bring this monster to justice."

Tavarnier began to look bored.

Phil tried what he hoped would be his trump card. "And I have word that Monsieur Natapei, your very own Minister of Justice, is interested in ridding your banking system of customers like this. De Waal, in particular."

Phil did his best to make it seem like a posse of international authorities was about to swoop down on the New Hebrides Bank of

Vanuatu, confiscate De Waal's money, and bring him and everyone who ever helped him to justice. Phil concluded with an impassioned second trip through the notebook of horrors, page by page. He dropped the powerful names one more time. "Monsieur Tavarnier, for all the common interests we share, for all the people we know in common who work so hard to make the world a more honest place, for all that is decent in civilized men like you and me, I urge you, I implore you, to help in this investigation."

Phil sat back.

Tavarnier showed no reaction. Finally, he opened his mouth. "You speak excellent French."

"Now is the time to help us with information," Phil answered, trying to sound a bit threatening, "not when the case is taken over. It will be too late for you then."

"We have no information to give," the banker said. He stood up. The meeting was over.

Phil pointed to the notebook of murder victims. "See what your client did to these people? What about them?" Phil asked, visibly at the end of his rope.

The banker shrugged and said in perfectly British-accented English, "Everyone dies sooner or later." He showed Phil the door.

As Phil stepped out into the blinding sunlight, he thought about calling Ken. Then he rejected the idea. He did not want to discourage Ken. Or admit his failures so far. He had one more lead from the FBI documents—the bank in the Seychelles. He did not have the kind of intelligence or contacts he had brought to Guernsey and Vanuatu. But so what? His intelligence and contacts had produced nothing, anyway.

Phil hoped he would get a break in the Seychelles. He just had to. Then he could call Ken. And maybe even Decker.

88

Ken had papers all around his little bedroom. Strewn over the bed, taped and pinned to the wall, piled high on the desk. He was printing articles off the Internet as fast as he could. And thinking. He knew he was disobeying Phil's orders not to interfere. But he rationalized this work by telling himself that, since this concerned the future and not the past, it was not, strictly speaking, part of Phil's investigation.

One particular pushpin held a clump of articles to the wall on the subject of sociopaths, or the more popular term, psychopaths. Ken had all the diagnostic checklists checked: the lack of conscience and remorse, the cold-blooded treatment of others, the lack of regard for legality, the risk-taking, the charm and manipulative behavior, and so on. Pennington fit the bill, Ken decided, and then some. With his brilliant acting, playing the role of caring humanitarian and benevolent leader while he murdered and plundered, Pennington was a psychopath on steroids.

Cindy was out. Ken never knew whether it was acting or teaching or graduate courses in special ed. Or one of her countless casting calls that never seemed to result in her getting a part. Ken stared at the articles about Michael Guillaume and Tom Pennington and their companies. He was hunting for something—a pattern, a clue, something to lead him to Pennington's next murderous career-advancing move. Nothing popped out.

"Think like Pennington," Ken told himself aloud.

He tried drawing charts the way Phil did. But he did not know what to connect. He could not see where he was going. The exercise produced balls of paper tossed to the floor and a dull ache in Ken's forehead.

"Where is Guillaume vulnerable?" Ken asked the empty apartment. "Think media, right, Sandy?" He glanced at the photo of his wife and child on the windowsill. "Hey, goofball," Ken said using

Sandy's teasing inflection, "Pennington is a fucking media whore. Look for the big story. Headline news that would torpedo Guillaume. That's where he'll strike."

Okay, that's a direction. He stood and walked to the wall of Guillaume press clippings. He read down the column yet again, standing on tiptoes and reading until, finally, he was on his knees reading with his neck twisted. It was a paper-clipped collection of articles on Guillaume and Perry's Bend 2 Nuclear Reactor, the troubled plant GI had taken over when it acquired Dynergetix. There were quotes of Guillaume pledging to fix the problems, Guillaume reassuring the public, Guillaume vowing to exceed regulations, Guillaume taking responsibility for getting the reactor back in operation.

Then an image from deep inside Ken's memory lit up like a flashbulb. The news report on ANN. The handsome black executive at the nuclear power plant. That was Michael Guillaume at Perry's Bend, the guy Ken said was in deeper yogurt than even he was. It all came together. Talk about the circle of life, he thought, quoting one of the song clips from the Disney videos Sara loved to watch over and over.

"That's it!" Ken cried. He's going to zap Guillaume in his nuclear belly, he thought. It's exposed and vulnerable. Guillaume put himself on the line publicly. Everyone is looking to him to fix it: the public, the NRC, the state government and all its agencies, the shareholders, the GI board, and his boss, Harry Warren. One fuckup in that power plant and he's toast. And, of course, standing right there to step in and save the day for General Industries is none other than Tom Mr. "I-Serve-the-Greater-Good" Pennington.

Ken was excited. And worried. What if Pennington already had a scheme in place? What if it were happening this very minute? What if thousands of people had no idea they were living in harm's way, with a nuclear disaster about to blight their lives and the lives of their children and grandchildren? What if he was too late?

Then he thought of something just as bad.

What if he was wrong and Pennington was planning something else?

Or, what if he was wrong and, just as Phil had warned, Pennington was innocent all along? That would be okay. It just meant that Ken Olson was a misguided jerk. And what did that matter? He had nothing better to do and he was, after all, just a misguided jerk.

Ken sat down. In his gut, he felt he had the right idea. He had to trust himself. He refused to second-guess himself. He had it right this time; he just knew it. He stood up and looked around the tiny room.

He decided to go for a run.

He stepped out of his shoes and jeans and got into his running clothes. He was already running in place and humming to himself when Cindy let herself in the door.

"You're in a good mood," she said, sounding weary as she tossed her backpack, kicked off her shoes, and fell onto the couch.

"I figured it out," Ken said proudly. "What Tom Pennington is going to try."

"Really?" She sat up straight.

Ken stopped bouncing and recapped his theory and his memories of Guillaume and the Perry's Bend news story. She listened. "Holy shit," she said. "Really?"

"Well, I can't say with absolute certainty. But I really think I'm right. And I'm goddamn sure it's worth a warning to Guillaume." Ken started bouncing on his feet again, preparing for his run.

"You gonna do the reservoir?" Cindy asked.

"Twice, maybe three times around," Ken said. "Whatever it takes to figure out a way to get on Guillaume's calendar."

Cindy jumped up from the couch and stood face-to-face with him. She mimicked his jogging motions in her stocking feet. "Hey, Nick, it's me, Nora. Remember? I can help you figure this out."

"Go for it, Nora. I'm all ears."

"Well, let's see," she said, "you're not planning to write him a letter, are you?"

"Nope, takes too long and too many other eyes will see it."

"It would also make you look like a nutcase. You send a threatening note like that, you'll come off like you're paranoid. They'll send the cops after you or worse." She pointed an accusing finger at him. "Remember Mel Gibson in *Conspiracy Theory?*"

"Yeah," he said, his bouncing slowing to a mere shifting of his weight from one foot to the other as his enthusiasm dimmed. Cindy mirrored his motions. "Same with an e-mail, too, I guess," he said, starting to look perplexed.

Cindy nodded.

"I could try calling," Ken ventured.

"What are your chances of getting through to him?" she asked.

"Slim to none."

"Uh-huh, and exactly what phone message are you going to leave with his secretary? Do tell us, Mr. Gibson."

Ken stood still. His hands dropped to his sides. "Okay, got any ideas?"

"Give me a sec," she said. Cindy turned and started pacing around the living room. She made a circle around the room and came back to Ken. "Well, every single girl knows, if you want to meet men, you hang out near the men's room."

Ken was puzzled. "Huh? You're suggesting I meet Guillaume in the men's room? You know how tight security is in that building?"

"No, silly! I'm just saying you put yourself directly in his path, where you *know* he has to go."

"Okay, Nora, explain."

"You know where the guy works, right?"

"Right."

"And you know you can't get *in* to see him."

"Right again. So?"

"So," she said with a knowing smile, "where does he *have to go* to get from his secure office building to go, like, well, anywhere else?"

"To his limo?" Ken was still puzzled.

"Right," Cindy said impatiently, "and where does he *have to go* to get there?"

"In the plaza of the building? On the sidewalk? To the curb?"

"Exactly! Just another man going where he has to go. You see," she added proudly, "being a single woman teaches you everything you need to know about the world." She offered him a high five.

Ken slapped her palm and started bouncing on his feet again.

"Twice around the reservoir?" Cindy asked.

"Make it three," Ken said as he headed for the door.

"Oh, Ni-i-ick," Cindy called to him. "Come back nice and sweaty. Nora will be waiting for you."

89

The next day, Pennington found Guillaume at the elevator bank on the fiftieth floor. It was five thirty, and both men were leaving for the day.

"Half day?" Pennington asked sarcastically, seeing Guillaume's briefcase in hand.

"Board meeting. That kids' charity," Guillaume said. "I'm not getting home till past midnight tonight. You can't imagine how they like to argue. Somehow, they've got more time than we do." Guillaume reached in his pocket for his key ring.

"Allow me," Pennington said, and produced his own key. He walked to the elevator call button and inserted the key into a discreet brass-covered keyhole, turning the switch that would summon the private elevator that only the CEO of General Industries and his top lieutenants could use.

"Listen, Mike," Pennington said, "I'm glad I ran into you. There's one piece of unpleasant business from the past I need to tell you about. So you don't get blindsided."

"Shoot."

The car whooshed into place. The doors opened. The two men got in. They began their express descent, all alone, in the wood-paneled cabin.

"There's this man named Ken Olson. He was at Ayvil Plastics. I put him in charge of the turnaround. Poor man lost his wife and child in the bombing; they were at the day care center. He was out of town that day. It was logical that I put him in charge of the foundation for the families left behind. Then it turned out he had been embezzling. Millions. Right under my nose. Long before the tragedy."

Guillaume shook his head sadly.

"We were able to get all the money back. So rather than prosecute, given his circumstances, we just let him go. He signed a consent decree and a hold-harmless. We gave him a generous settlement.

Very generous. I mean the poor man, misguided as he was, had lost everything. Anyway, it seems that now he's really gone off the deep end. Become something of a crank and a stalker."

Guillaume listened.

"Anyway, he's got all these crazy conspiracy theories, some of them with me as the evil mastermind. Fact is, he's just a lost soul. Last I heard he was living here in New York. Wouldn't surprise me if he tried to contact you."

"What's his name again?"

"Olson, Ken Olson. Seemed like a good enough guy. I certainly thought so. He had me fooled for the longest time. Apparently, he rants at anyone who'll listen about the company, about me, the FBI, the works. I just wanted to give you a heads-up, in case."

The elevator whooshed to a stop on the ground floor and the doors opened.

Out in the plaza, Ken Olson watched from behind a magazine.

90

Ken had been at the General Industries plaza for forty minutes, walking around trying to look purposeful, making pretend cell phone calls, walking in, walking out, looking at his watch as if expecting someone at any minute. He wore a gray business suit, white shirt, and a blue tie. He carried a small briefcase and the latest copy of *Business Week*. In his corporate soldier's uniform, he was as good as invisible.

He had his eye on the farthest bank of elevators. There was a uniformed security guard, a paunchy older black man, sitting on a stool at a small desk. Armed with his clipboard and walkie-talkie, he was guarding access to a single set of doors—the doors to the private elevator. Finally, the private elevator doors opened. To his horror, he saw Michael Guillaume *and* Tom Pennington step out together, engaged in conversation. Ken panicked for an instant and froze, then turned his back.

"Thanks for the heads-up," Guillaume said to Pennington as they exited the car.

"No problem," Pennington replied. He was about to say something more when Guillaume turned his attention to the security guard.

"Hey, man," Guillaume said jovially and offered the man a high five, "what's good?"

"How 'bout them Yankees?" the guard said, and held up the tabloid sports page proudly.

Pennington stood by, looking for a natural place to insert himself into the conversation. He could not find one.

Ken saw two Lincoln Town Cars waiting at the curb in front of GI plaza. If the two men walked out to their limos together, he would have to try another day and maybe another way. All he could do was watch out of the corner of his eye.

"We've got the hitting and the pitching," Guillaume said to the guard. "We just have to be careful not to blow it by getting cocky."

"You said it."

Pennington inserted himself, ignoring the security guard. "Uh, then I'll see you tomorrow, Mike."

"Right," Guillaume said, turning his head, a bit surprised Pennington was still there. "And thanks again for the heads-up."

Ken was preparing to abandon his hope of catching Guillaume alone.

"Listen," the guard said to Guillaume, "thanks again for those tickets. I mean, first-base line, extra innings, and we won. It don't get any better than that."

Pennington headed for the main revolving doors and his waiting limo. Fortunately, Ken thought, he was walking at a brisk pace.

"My pleasure, man," Guillaume said to the guard. "Had to teach my boy a lesson after he blew that math exam. Told him the seats should go to someone who actually deserved them."

Ken breathed a sigh of relief and hoped that Pennington would continue to walk faster. And that Guillaume would spend more time talking to the guard.

As Guillaume turned from the guard's desk, he raised his chin in a subtle farewell nod. "Later," he said to the guard.

"Later." The guard nodded in return.

Ken watched. Pennington had a long lead on Guillaume. He was almost at his limo as Guillaume passed through the revolving doors.

Ken held his breath.

He was thrilled to see Pennington climb into the backseat and close the door. He was unhappy to see Guillaume walking briskly toward his limo. Pennington's driver shifted from Park into Drive. Ken wanted to scream at the man to take his foot off the brake and pull the hell away. Afraid that he would lose his chance if he waited for Pennington's car to be gone, he decided to gamble. He put the strap of his empty briefcase over one shoulder and walked slowly into the plaza, his eyes darting from Pennington to Guillaume and back again.

Guillaume was getting closer to his limo.

Ken sped up. Then a cab stopped in front of Pennington's limo, blocking its way. The passenger, an old man, opened the door of the cab. Slowly. He fished through his wallet. Slowly.

Ken wanted to explode. He kept walking, hoping Pennington

would not look in his direction. Before he got too close, Ken stopped and looked down at the ground. Pennington was reading papers from his briefcase.

Ken looked up. The old man in the taxi did not need change. Mercifully. He finished climbing out of the cab and shut the door. The impatient cabbie tore away into the traffic. The old man walked behind Pennington's limo to get to the curb. Pennington's driver sped off just as Guillaume reached for the door handle of his shiny black Lincoln.

Ken started walking again. Very fast.

"Uh, Mr. Guillaume, Mr. Guillaume," Ken called a bit loudly and out of breath.

Guillaume turned around. "Yes?"

Ken hurried the last few feet. "Mr. Guillaume, I have something very important to tell you."

Guillaume looked at him quizzically. "I beg your pardon?"

"Please, sir, if I could have just a moment of your time."

Guillaume looked confused.

"My name is Ken Olson." He stopped and took a deep breath.

Guillaume took his hand off the door handle and faced Ken, sizing him up. "Oh, I know who you are."

"You do?" Ken asked.

"Yes, I've been warned about your conspiracy theories. I'm sorry for the losses you have suffered. But I am very busy. Please."

Even though Ken had rehearsed this moment carefully in his mind, when the real moment arrived, the words just spilled out. "A nuclear accident at one of your plants would be devastating for your career, wouldn't it?"

Guillaume's body tensed. "Are you making a threat?" He turned to reach for the car door handle again.

"No, please, Mr. Guillaume, I'm not threatening anyone. I'm trying to protect innocent people."

Guillaume turned to face him.

"First of all," Ken said with relief, "I'm not a crazy person. I'm trying to prevent more harm. I am not suggesting that you get paranoid. Just exercise extra vigilance. If I turn out to be wrong, I'll be the first to admit it. But if it turns out that I was right, I wouldn't be able to live with myself if I hadn't given you this warning." Ken raised his hands with palms open as if to show he was unarmed and innocent.

Guillaume's driver, a burly Irish man with weightlifter arms bulging under his suit jacket, came around the car. "This guy bothering you, Mr. Guillaume?" he asked.

"No, John. Thank you."

John went back to the driver's side and got in. Guillaume opened the back door, tossed his briefcase onto the seat, and closed the door. He stood facing Ken, his arms folded across his chest. "Go on," he said.

"Mr. Guillaume, I was the general manager of Ayvil Plastics. Tom Pennington put me in that job."

"Yes, I know all that."

"That was an accident that turned out to be no accident at all. Now there are—"

Guillaume looked at his watch. "Mr. Olson, where is this heading? I have a board meeting to get to, a charity that means a lot to me. Please get to the point."

"These days, you have to be on the alert for terrorists, especially in your nuclear facilities, don't you?"

"I don't have patience for this kind of thing, Mr. Olson."

"Please, bear with me." Ken wanted to scream, to grab Guillaume by the lapels and shake him. But he knew that would get him nowhere. Instead, he forced himself to speak in a flat, rational tone. "Mr. Guillaume, you are in a competition with Tom Pennington to become Harry Warren's successor. Fact?"

Guillaume nodded.

"Now if someone were to sabotage one of your facilities, it would probably ruin your chances of becoming CEO." Ken raised his eyebrows in a question.

Guillaume was expressionless.

"I won't even try to sell you my conspiracy theory about Tom Pennington."

Guillaume turned his back and reached for the handle of the door.

"Mr. Guillaume, you had problems at Perry's Bend. I saw you in the news reports about it. The very morning of the bombing at Ayvil."

Guillaume took his hand off the door handle but kept his back to Ken.

"Mr. Guillaume, you've got to be vigilant anyway, because the world's so dangerous these days. But be extra vigilant now. Just in case, just in case I'm *not* crazy." Ken held out one of the business cards he had made for himself at Kinko's, with his cell phone number, not the landline number he shared with Cindy.

Guillaume turned around. "What do you want, Mr. Olson?"

"Someone out there murdered my family and a thousand other innocent people. I just want to protect others. That's all."

Guillaume took the card. "I'm going to have someone call you," he said. "His name is Howard Polski, my VP of Power Systems. He's the hands-on executive for all our nuclear power plants."

Guillaume turned and opened the car door. Over his shoulder, he said, "Just so you know, I don't believe you for a second." Guillaume removed his suit jacket, folded it carefully, placing it beside his briefcase, and climbed in.

Guillaume closed the door, fastened his seat belt, and put Ken's business card into his briefcase. He had complete faith in Polski's ability to handle this nutcase. And all the other problems that came with running nuclear power plants.

91

Phil landed in the Seychelles after an eternity on airplanes. He flew from Vanuatu one thousand miles south-southwest to Brisbane then west across the entire Australian subcontinent to Perth. Then west across the Indian Ocean to Cape Town. Then another 1,400 miles due northeast over Madagascar to the main Seychelle island of Mahé.

He took a room at another so-called business motel, shabby and in need of remodeling, and slept for another whole day.

The Seychelles are famous as a happy place, where three races—African, Indian, and white—live peacefully together, marrying and blending as they like. The capital city of Victoria is a busy tropical port with a deep harbor and a growing industrial zone. Although tourism is by far the dominant industry, the Seychelles also do a booming business as an offshore tax haven. Over three thousand IBCs, International Business Companies, are registered in the Seychelles. Phil was certain that Grant De Waal's Lion's Mane GmbH was one of them. He just needed some proof.

He awoke the next morning and prepared his not-so-successful dog-and-pony show for offshore bank managers. He was starting to feel like the hapless Bill Murray character in *Groundhog Day*, reliving the same events over and over again.

"But, monsieur," the manager of the Development Commerce Bank told him, choosing English over the other national languages, French and Creole, "this is the privacy that you would demand, if you were a client of the bank." The manager was a small man with the black skin of an African and the fine angular features of an Indian. With his accent a mix of British and French, it seemed that all the island's influences had been blended together in this one person.

Phil held up a photo of De Waal in his full bald state. "This is the man with the account in the name of Lion's Mane. Do you recognize him?"

"Monsieur," the manager said, "the information of beneficial owners of IBCs is kept in the Registered Agents' Office and is not open to the public. This is the basis of our industry. Surely you can understand that." He picked up a book, presumably a law book, and read aloud to Phil. "No information will be disclosed to third parties except by order of the local court relating solely activities which are criminal under the laws of the Seychelles."

Phil pointed again to the scrapbook of horrors. Was murder on this scale not criminal under the laws of the Seychelles?

The bank manager shrugged. Phil pointed to the picture of De Waal again. "You're sure you haven't seen this man transacting in your bank?"

"I cannot say." Then an idea occurred to him. "No, *I* cannot say. Our laws forbid me from even considering it. However, people who visit our wonderful islands usually stay in one of our fine hotels. And our government has passed no such laws for that industry."

"And which hotel might a man like this stay in?" Phil asked.

"I do not know," he said. "But many of our most substantial and influential clients stay at Cap Mistral. It is famous for its luxury and privacy. It is possible that this man stayed there." He quickly added, "If indeed, he has ever visited the Seychelles."

Phil looked out the window of the manager's office onto the street. His taxi driver was waiting, leaning against his thirty-year-old Peugeot 404, eating a slice of coconut from a pushcart vendor.

"Your driver knows Cap Mistral. Everyone does," the bank manager said.

"Thank you," Phil said, collecting his things, "thank you very much."

"I have done nothing," the manager said insistently. "Please remember, I have done nothing, which is what I am required to do."

92

Harry Warren took his time addressing the ball at the third tee of the Maiden Rock Club in Southampton, Long Island, now *his* club, since Hildreth had fast-tracked him to the membership. The legendary course had been created in the 1890s, sculpted out of gently rolling grasslands by the windswept dunes at the shore. The sprawling shingle-style clubhouse, with its fluted white columns, wide porches, and stark lines, remained an icon of American aristocracy, unimpressed and unchanged by the waves of newly rich who came to the Hamptons to splash their wealth and jockey for social position. This was Justin Hildreth's club on Justin Hildreth's home turf, a timeless world of mansions guarded by towering privet hedges and inherited fortunes.

Harry Warren wiggled the cleats of his golf shoes into the soft grass and brought the head of his driver down to the ball without hitting. Slowly and deliberately, he pulled back several times, recalculating critical parts of his swing. Finally, taking a deep breath, he pulled the club slowly back and followed through, making a solid *thwack* as he connected.

The ball soared upward, flying straight and true in the direction of the green. The sky was cloudless, the southwest ocean breeze was gentle this morning. Warren's golfing companions—Michael Guillaume, Tom Pennington, and Justin Hildreth—mumbled admiration of his nearly perfect shot.

"You don't leave your competitors much room," Hildreth said. "I'm glad I'm not playing against you, partner."

"I compete strictly against myself," Warren said. "I don't worry about making it tough on anyone else, just myself."

Guillaume teed up his ball, collected himself for a moment, then took his swing. His shot rose into the sky and landed a little ahead of Warren's.

"Nice shot," Pennington said as he walked up to the tee. Pennington took his time preparing to hit. He bent down and fussed with the process of putting his ball on the tee. He stood and shook his arms and shoulders before gripping the club to address the ball. He took several deep breaths as he stared down at the ball with arms extended. He moved his fingers around slightly, searching for the perfect grip. He looked up at the fairway one more time then locked his eyes down again on the ball. Slowly, he raised the club into the air and came down gracefully, almost in slow motion. His shot did not soar the way Warren's and Guillaume's did. It flew like a line drive—and flew and flew, landing just ahead of Guillaume's ball, rolling upward onto a small rise in the center of the fairway.

"You're the man to beat," Warren said jovially. "You hit like you were born with a golf club in your hand."

"Hardly," Pennington said. "Every shot is like starting a new job."

"Allow me to provide some comic relief," Hildreth said as he teed up. "Golf is something I've spent a lifetime practicing without ever getting beyond, well, practice." Hildreth addressed the ball with the air of a man resigned to his fate. He pulled the club backward and chopped down on the ball. The sound of the club head striking the ball was muffled. Hildreth punched the ball high into the air, too high. It veered far to the right and landed at the very edge of the fairway, half as far as the drives of the other men.

"You should take a lesson or two," Warren said as the four men approached their waiting caddies, "your swing just needs a little work."

"Nah," Hildreth said good-humoredly, "too old."

"Nonsense," Warren said, "you're never too old to keep learning and refining your game."

As the men handed their drivers to their caddies, Pennington reached into his golf bag and extracted a pack of M&Ms that had already been opened. Pennington poured a few candies into his hand. He took a red one for himself and popped it into his mouth. He extended his hand to Warren. "M&M, Harry?" Pennington asked. "They say the blue ones are lucky."

"I don't believe in luck," Warren said.

"Neither do I," Pennington replied with a smile.

Warren took a blue M&M from Pennington's hand and popped it in his mouth.

Pennington extended his palm to Hildreth, then Guillaume. Hildreth took a couple of candies, Guillaume took one, thought about it for an instant, and took another. Pennington took another red one and replaced the yellow pack into his pants pocket. The four men walked toward their second shots, their caddies following just behind them.

Once on the green, Warren was farthest from the cup, so he was first to putt. Hildreth's caddy held the flag down so that it made no fluttering noises. Warren knelt down on one knee to inspect the topography of the green. When he stood, he reeled backward slightly on his heels and placed his hand against his belly.

"What's the matter, Harry?" Hildreth, who was nearest to him, asked.

Warren shook his head and exhaled uncomfortably. "It's nothing," he said as he bent over his putter and prepared to take his shot. He brought the putter back and sliced awkwardly at the ball, sending it bouncing away. When he looked up, he was pale and struggling for breath. "I don't feel so good," he said weakly. He leaned against the putter like a cane. His head rolled back.

At once Hildreth, Guillaume, and Pennington bounded over to him. "Maybe I better sit down," Warren said apologetically. He was sweating. Guillaume put his arm around Warren's shoulder and walked him off the green to the bench nearby. Hildreth and Pennington followed. The caddies picked up the abandoned balls from the green as the whole group gathered around Warren and Guillaume on the bench under the trees.

"It's nothing," Harry said unconvincingly, looking paler, his breath short. His glazed eyes rolled back. He was losing consciousness.

"Call an ambulance!" Guillaume said urgently to his caddy as he held Warren around the shoulders. "My phone's in the top pocket there," he said, motioning at his golf bag.

During the ten minutes it took for the ambulance to arrive, Harry nodded in and out of consciousness, growing ever paler.

"It looks like it could be a heart attack," the EMS technician said as he and his partner slid the gurney carrying Harry Warren into the ambulance. They had an oxygen mask over the CEO's nose and mouth and IV drip in his right arm. "We'll find out for sure at the hospital."

"I'll ride with him," Guillaume said as he climbed in behind the gurney. "Can I have my phone, please?" he asked his caddy. "I'll call Jeanette at home and tell her where to meet us." Guillaume climbed into the back of the ambulance.

Hildreth watched them drive away. "This is terrible," he said gravely and loud enough to be sure that the caddies standing by would hear. "Nobody appeared to be healthier than Harry. Tom, I'm afraid this means the board will have to consider naming Harry's successor sooner than we thought."

Pennington nodded sadly.

93

De Waal handed Davenport his counterfeit paperwork. Since De Waal's hacker had been able to penetrate the servers at the Verimeter Corporation, the papers he gave Davenport in his office at Perry's Bend were not merely as good as the real thing, they *were* the real thing.

Davenport reviewed Form 18.B, the D-4, the DD-780, the equipment certifications, and the test reports detailing the failure rate of the Verimeter CS-22XB sensor, the one used up and down the length of the twenty-four-inch water pipes in the Perry's Bend reactor. "That's interesting," Davenport said thoughtfully. "But we haven't had any problems with them."

"At least not yet," De Waal said. Today, he was Martin Volkenberg, a Dutchman with receding chestnut hair, walrus mustache, and wire-rimmed glasses. Beside him was his assistant, formerly William Hunt, now Stewart Cox.

"Based on when they were installed and our experience elsewhere," De Waal explained, "it should be a few more weeks before variances start registering. We're doing everything we can to prevent problems before they occur."

"Isn't that what we all try to do?" Davenport mused.

"Mr. Davenport, can we talk frankly?" De Waal looked cautiously around Davenport's little office as if someone might be snooping. "There's a reason these sensors are failing, and it's not something Verimeter has any control over. At least not at the moment. It's confidential."

Davenport was interested.

"I think," De Waal went on hesitantly, "well, I think it's fair to say, uh, just between us white men—"

Davenport smiled. "Please, go on. I'm with you."

De Waal smiled back. "Those sensors were made originally for the government. You know those regulations requiring us to buy from minority vendors, even when their products are no damn good? The problem here is this one part in the sensor. We were forced to buy it from, from a black-owned factory."

"Tell me more, Mr. Volkenberg."

"Please, it's Martin."

"And it's Jerry to you."

"Thanks, Jerry. You know, I came to this country because I believe in initiative. The Dutch government snuffed that out years ago. So when I see this affirmative action stuff, it gets me so angry. Companies like this one would go bankrupt if they didn't have a government tit to suck on. When I think of the decent white people that must have been put out of work. Well, it makes me mad. Just mad as hell."

"You said it, Martin," Cox added.

Davenport opened up to his new friends. "I see it all the time. It's like the company that bought this plant, General Industries. Get this! The executive in charge of all their nuclear power is a black man. Got there on affirmative action. Another one getting a free ride on the backs of decent white men."

De Waal said, "Well, you'll be happy to know that the new sensors have no tainted parts."

"That's good," Davenport said. "When do you want to schedule the installation?"

"How about tomorrow or the day after?"

"Sorry." Davenport looked into his Day Runner. "We are flat out until Friday."

"Uh, I was planning on tomorrow or Thursday at the latest," De Waal said. "The team, the schedule. Wednesday is really optimal."

" 'Fraid not," Davenport said, sounding genuinely sorry. "Friday's the soonest."

De Waal thought about it. He did not know why Pennington had been so insistent on Wednesday or Thursday. Something about a board meeting. If Pennington missed by one day, so what? *Vokk* him. Fuck him. "Friday it is, Jerry," De Waal said.

"Been a pleasure meeting you both," Davenport said. "See you Friday."

94

Phil's sunset cab ride through the mountains to Cap Mistral was hot, perilous, and beautiful. Leaping out of the cab at the porte cochere, Phil headed straight for the reception desk in the Great House.

Phil had been to many of these small super-posh resorts in tropical paradises from the Grenadines to Penang. The intense luxury had a dulling sameness that he disliked. After a few days it was hard to tell whether you were in the Grenadines or Penang, and you did not care.

When he asked for the general manager, he was told he was away on holiday. The reception desk sent him to the concierge, a distinctly European man who spoke English with the flat accent of the German Swiss.

Phil introduced himself to Ackermann and gave him his Medusa business card. Tired and discouraged, he skipped the small talk and presented him immediately with a picture of Grant De Waal.

"I am looking for this man in connection with an important investigation. I have reason to believe he has been a guest here sometime in the last few months."

Ackermann managed to combine abject servility with absolute condescension. "Why, Herr Lambert, our policy of discretion forbids us from talking about our guests," he said. "That is why they come here."

Phil remembered another reason he disliked these kinds of places—men like Ackermann. "If you were a guest here," Ackermann went on, "this is the discretion I would provide for you, too."

Phil began his mental calculations. How much does a rich, returning guest tip this little prick upon arrival to ensure a happy stay? How much does he tip for individual services? How much more does he tip to have his worst habits and vices indulged? How much on top of that to ensure that it all stays secret?

Phil had told Ken that a certain percentage of his expenses would be in cash and unaccounted for in detail. "Audio-visual equipment rentals and miscellaneous," he said, "that's what we'll list it as. It will be for bribes. Maybe it will produce results; maybe it won't. But just kiss it all good-bye. It's going into the ITLS, International Transaction Lubrication System."

Phil guessed that a man like De Waal greeted a concierge like Ackermann with fifteen hundred to two thousand dollars. Phil figured it would take at least three thousand for him, as a stranger and non-guest, to get into the game.

"Pardon me for a moment," Phil said. "It was a long car ride to get here. I'd like to use the bathroom. Please study that face." As he walked toward the men's room, briefcase in hand, he added, "Perhaps it will jog your memory."

When he returned, Ackermann sat serene as the Buddha, the picture of De Waal in the same place Phil had left it. In a gesture he had learned in his world travels, Phil reached toward Ackermann's hand resting on the desk. Ackermann saw it coming. Gracefully, effortlessly, and barely noticeably, the roll of C-notes passed from Phil's fist to Ackermann's. Ackermann's fingers seemed to "weigh" the cash and calculate its value. Almost invisibly, Ackermann opened his desk drawer and deposited the money.

"I do seem to remember Herr Hodes now," Ackermann said, "a most distinguished gentleman from Holland, I believe. And very generous."

That meant Phil's three grand had merely opened the door. "Well, you see, Mr. Ackermann," Phil said, "Mr. Hodes seems to be missing, and his family is very concerned. But they would want me to be very sure that it is the right Mr. Hodes." Phil reached into his pants pocket, cupped another two-thousand-dollar roll of C-notes, and handed it off.

"And how," Ackermann said, "could I give you that assurance?"

"His handwriting," Phil said, "his handwriting is very distinctive. If I could bring a copy of his signature back to the family, it would help them confirm that it was really him. I'm sure he signed the register, didn't he?"

"Oh yes, all our guests sign the register. But that, too, is confidential."

Ackermann wanted more money.

"I see," Phil said, reaching for another roll of C-notes. "But the family is very upset, very upset." Another hand-off, another two thousand dollars.

"Well," Ackermann said with relief, "in matters of family we can make an exception." The concierge rose to go to the back office. "You realize that I cannot show you the actual register itself."

"Oh yes, of course. A Xerox copy of the signature is what I need. Can you make a really good, clean copy?"

"Yes, we have a brand-new Canon copier. How many copies would you like?"

"Five."

"Please," Ackermann said, indicating the chair beside the concierge's desk, "I'll be just a few minutes."

He returned with five copies of the page containing the signature of Stephen Hodes. He handed the papers to Phil and took his seat behind the desk. Phil stared at the page. All the other signatures from that day were blacked out.

Phil was thrilled with what he saw. Even though he would need Henry Mills to confirm it, he was certain it was the same handwriting. "Thank you, Herr Ackermann," he said, adopting Ackermann's preferred German usage in hopes of ingratiating himself. The seven-thousand-dollar investment was paying off.

Seeing the handwriting whetted his appetite for more. "Herr Ackermann, by any chance did Herr Hodes cash any traveler's checks while he was here?" Phil knew that good hotels often kept copies of cashed traveler's checks for some time.

Ackermann looked stumped. Now that was a very difficult question. He looked around the lobby, as if he might spot the answer in a far corner. Phil had one roll worth three thousand dollars left. The rest of his collection of large bills was back in his motel room, sewn into the lining of his suitcase. If Hodes had signed any traveler's checks and if they came from the Ohio series, it would link him to the bombing. That would be enough to contact Decker and get him back on the case with the court orders Phil did not have.

Phil asked himself if a man like De Waal could make a little mistake like that? Just how far is Beaver Creek, Ohio, from the Seychelles? More than the twelve thousand miles it appeared on the map, he thought. It might as well be on another planet. Phil decided it was worth three grand to find out.

He made one final hand-off across the table, this time placing his hand on top of the back of Ackermann's hand and letting Ackermann turn his palm around to face Phil's downward-facing palm. Again, barely visibly, the money changed hands. This time Ackermann stole a downward glance as he placed the roll of C-notes in his drawer.

"I do seem to remember Mr. Hodes cashing some of them. He said he was running low on small bills and didn't feel like making the trip into Victoria to visit his bank."

Phil was electrified by that revelation. "*Did* he eventually visit his bank in Victoria?" he asked, trying not to sound too eager.

"Yes, he did."

Phil felt as if he had won the lottery.

"Were there other people at the hotel who talked to Mr. Hodes? People I could talk to. The family is looking for any type of clue, really." He hoped that Ackermann would treat him to a freebie.

"I'm afraid he kept very much to himself. Most of our guests do."

Phil did not know if that was a real answer or a demand for more cash.

Ackermann rose. "It will take me a while to find the traveler's check records and make copies." He motioned for Phil to follow him, but instead of walking toward the front desk and the office, he led Phil toward the door of the hotel bar, an elegant outdoor pavilion under palm-frond canopies. Ackermann made a welcoming gesture to show Phil into the bar. He snapped his fingers to get the bartender's attention and pointed at Phil when the bartender looked up.

"Allow us to treat you to a drink while you wait," he said.

Phil was encouraged.

"You might ask her about Herr Hodes," Ackermann said, indicating the beautiful young Indian woman seated alone at the bar. "Go on, I'll find you here in a while."

Phil sat down beside her and set his briefcase on the floor. "Hello," he said, "the concierge recommended that I talk to you."

The woman smiled and lowered her eyes demurely. "My name is Apsara."

Realizing how misguided his opening line was, Phil quickly slapped down his business card. "Er, I'm Phil Lambert, a private investigator.

He said you have met the man I'm looking for." He reached into his briefcase and put the picture of the bald De Waal on the bar. "Do you remember him?"

She recoiled when she saw the face. "Yes."

"What do you remember about him?"

"He was a bad man."

"Did he hurt you?"

"No," she said, "I ran away before he could. He had a big knife. He used it to cut our hair—" She paused and lowered her eyes. "—down there. He talked about body hair. He was—what's the word? A creep? Isn't that what you say?"

"Yes, that's exactly what you say."

She stared at the picture again and asked, "Why *does* he have no hair?"

"Childhood disease," Phil said, and quickly got out the grisly scrapbook. "This is what he does for a living. He kills innocent people for money."

She shuddered at the contents and closed the notebook. "I knew he was a very bad man. Are you trying to capture him?"

"Yes," Phil said.

"How can I help?"

"I'm not sure," Phil said hesitantly, not imagining how a pretty bar girl could help him with his international banking problems. "I'm trying to get a copy of his signature from a bank in Victoria."

"Really? Which bank?" she asked.

"Development Commerce Bank."

"That is good," she said cheerfully.

"Why?"

"I used to work there. I was the receptionist. I still have friends there."

"Do you have any friends at the wire transfer desk?"

She nodded.

"Really?" he asked, overwhelmed by his potential luck. "And do you know the person who keeps the file of signature cards?"

She nodded again.

Phil gasped. Even if you signed up with a number instead of a name, the bank has your handwriting on file. Phil did not dare to ask. So he dared to ask. "Do you think maybe?"

The girl raised a finger to her mouth to shush him. "I will get what you need tomorrow."

Phil pulled out a document from his briefcase. He tore the lower third off and circled "Lion's Mane GmbH." "This is the company that holds the account in the bank. I need a copy of the client's signature card and as many of his wire transfers as you can get your hands on."

Apsara took the sheet, then took a small pencil from her purse and scribbled an address on the back of Phil's business card. "Meet me in this restaurant at eighteen thirty. My friends will get me what you need."

Ackermann strolled into the bar and cleared his throat. The girl turned to look at him. "Bungalow six," he mouthed to her. She touched Phil's arm again. "Tomorrow," she said as she slid off the stool. Ackermann handed Phil a copy of three traveler's checks and walked away. They were signed front and back by Stephen Hodes. By now the handwriting was familiar. What took Phil's breath away was the serial numbers. Phil had memorized the series numbers of the Ohio checks. These three checks were three serial numbers in a row. Right from the middle of the series. He would not trust himself until he sat with his document file and compared, but it looked like he had De Waal red-handed.

95

The night they spoke again on stolen cell phones, De Waal sat on the bed in his motel room outside Perry's Bend while Pennington was driving his black BMW 645Ci convertible down the FDR Drive along the East River in Manhattan. Pennington was alone and had the top down on this clear, warm night.

"It's going to be Friday," De Waal said without bothering to say hello when Pennington answered the call.

"I told you *Wednesday*," Pennington barked into the cellular headphone wrapped around his ear. "Thursday at the latest. I sent you the money because we specified the day. The board meeting is Friday. We need time for the incident to happen and get in the news. Wednesday or Thursday. Now go make it happen."

"Can't."

Pennington screeched to a stop at a knot of traffic. "What do you mean, *can't?*" he shouted.

"I can't make it happen. My new best friend Jerry Davenport says it's not possible, and he's the AIC at the plant."

"AIC? I thought he was NRC."

"Asshole in Charge," De Waal said with a little chuckle.

"I'm not paying you six million dollars for jokes. That's not acceptable. We have a plan." All day long, Pennington got executives to stretch their goals and accomplish more than they thought possible. This moment was no different. "Make it happen," he said with the finality that usually ended his business meetings.

"Can't," De Waal snapped, "I just told you."

"Bles," Pennington said impatiently, "what I'm—"

De Waal cut him off. "Listen, I pushed as hard as I could. Remember, we're not supposed to raise suspicions, yah? They can't do it. It's Friday. Period. Or I go home right now."

"What about the money I've already paid you?"

"Report me to the Better Business Bureau," De Waal sneered.

"You fuck," Pennington spat into the phone.

"I'll hang up now, yah?" De Waal had killed men who dared to swear at him. He looked down at the newspaper spread out across his bed. It was that morning's *Wall Street Journal* with a front-page feature article titled, "CEO Sign-On Bonuses: Into the Stratosphere." He wondered how many more millions Pennington was about to make.

"No, don't hang up," Pennington said urgently. "Let me think, Bles, just give me a sec." He needed to formulate a Plan B. "I'm in some traffic here. Bear with me." He stopped talking and snaked the sleek convertible around the approach to the Fifty-ninth Street Bridge. The driving maneuvers in the elegant sports car relaxed and distracted him for the minute he needed to redirect his thinking. "Bles, you still there?"

Bles grunted.

"You're in the Rocky Mountain time zone?"

"Yah. Two hours behind New York."

"Well, that helps. When do you start changing the sensors?"

"We arrive at eight o'clock. We go through security. Quite a few levels, you know. We greet our friend Jerry, coordinate with the guys in the control room. I'd guess we start the work around eight forty-five, maybe a little sooner."

"That's ten forty-five in New York. Uh . . . how long before the incident happens? There still might be time before the board meeting ends."

"Probably after lunch."

Pennington was silent, thinking. Traffic noise in the background.

"You there?" De Waal asked. "I said after lunch."

"I said I'm thinking. What time did you say you enter the plant?"

De Waal was annoyed. "I *said* eight A.M."

Pennington's voice brightened. "That'll work." He pulled onto the ramp to the upper level of the bridge. "I know what to do."

"Huh? Repeat that," De Waal asked in case he had missed something due to the traffic noise or the cellular connection.

"I said, that'll work. When you're signed in, text message me— *IN*."

"Huh?" De Waal asked as the roar of the BMW's tires on the open grating of the bridge filled the line.

"We are good to go, Bles," Pennington shouted into the micro-phone. "Just send me the message *IN,* I-N. I'll take care of the rest. You read me?"

"Yah," De Waal shouted, "*in.* I-N!"

The noise of the metal roadway got louder as Pennington's car sped up. He did not hear De Waal's parting shot: "If you get CEO, you owe me an extra two million in bonus."

"Right! I-N!" Pennington shouted as he snapped the phone shut and yanked the earpiece from his head. Manhattan glittered behind him as he crossed the bridge in the far right lane. At the midpoint, he hurled the phone and its wired earpiece over the railing into the East River.

96

Phil called Ken's cell phone from the airport in Victoria. He got the voice mail. "Once Henry confirms what is already plain to see here," he said excitedly, "we can go to Decker with the whole package. We've got his signature in Ohio and the hotel in the Seychelles, we've got his signature on traveler's checks from the middle of the series used in Ohio. And now, we've got a copy of his signature card from his fucking bank account in the Seychelles, plus copies of his transfers in and out. And guess what? That one million of Paulson's two that left the Caymans? Well, it came here later that same day. From an account in Liechtenstein. There's a fair bit of activity with this account. It could be the connection to Pennington we're looking for. Soon as I get back, we'll go see Decker. Henry will be working on the faxes of the handwriting in the meantime. We're finally making some headway. Listen, Ken, we have made it possible for the Feds to reopen this case. Decker has to take it from here."

97

"What do you mean, we've hit a speed bump or two?" Ken asked angrily. He and jet-lagged Phil sat in Decker's office and listened to the FBI man's list of troubles. "The goddamn GI board meeting is this Friday," Ken said, almost leaping out of his chair. *"This Friday!"*

Phil pulled him back.

"A few temporary setbacks, slowdowns," Decker said, groggy from his own jet lag, "just what I said. These European judicial systems take their time. Could be a month or more."

Ken was exasperated. "That will be too late! Jesus H. Christ! Can't you guys do *anything* right? What the fuck is wrong with you?"

Phil turned to Ken and frowned. "Out of line, bro, out of line."

"Okay. All right," Ken said. "I'm sorry. Now what did you say your bosses called Phil? 'A state actor'?"

"I didn't say they *called* Phil a state actor," Decker said defensively, "I said they're concerned that a judge might call Phil a state actor."

"And what exactly *is* a state actor?" Ken asked.

Phil jumped in. "An unofficial agent of the FBI acting for the Bureau. Or operating under Bureau instructions. Which is not the case, right, Decker?"

Decker grunted.

"Isn't it enough that we *know*?" Ken asked. "We know that the bank in Liechtenstein transferred the chunk of Paulson's money from the Caymans to De Waal's account in the Seychelles on the same day. We know that another chunk went from the same Liechtenstein account into the same Seychelles account a few weeks before the Ayvil operation. And we have strong suspicions that Pennington indirectly owns the Gibraltar-based corporation with an account in that same bank in Liechtenstein. And another registered in Belize. Isn't that what counts?"

Decker shrugged. "Sorry, that's not enough. *How* you get evidence is as important, as—no, correction, it's even more important than—*what* you get as evidence."

"You mean"—Ken swallowed hard—"even if we could prove that he directed money into De Waal's account, Pennington could go free?"

"Pennington *would* go free," Decker said, "if the evidence was tainted. That would make it illegal. Absolutely."

Phil nodded sadly.

Ken's head began to throb. He turned to Phil. "You told me the world works in the gray areas. You said you knew the pressure points, the subtleties, the angles. What the fuck have we been doing all along? *Huh?*"

Phil retained his professional calm. "We have been doing what our friends in law enforcement did not have the time, resources, or permission to do. And we have done it well." He looked at Decker again. "Right, Ted?"

Decker nodded and looked down. Then he mumbled, "My, uh, superiors also got a little pressure from Washington to find a way to back off."

"Political pressure?" Phil asked.

Decker kept his head down.

"Surprise, surprise," Ken said with disgust.

Decker looked down at the papers spread across his desk—the copies of signatures, the copies of traveler's checks with numbers from the same series, the wire transfer advices, the trail from Arch Paulson's bank account in the Caymans around the world to the money laundering network of Grant De Waal to the accounts in Liechtenstein that could, should, would connect it all to Tom Pennington. If only they could get the brass at the FBI and the Principality of Liechtenstein to get on board.

Ken sat brooding.

Phil turned to Decker. "Why do your superiors think I may have been a state agent?" Phil and Decker shared a way of saying the word *superiors*. It was full of scorn and bitter irony.

"Because," Decker said, "they noticed that the three banks you checked out just happened to be the three banks that our confidential records proved were connected to the transfers out of the Caymans."

"I see," Phil said, "some fucking coincidence."

"And I see, too," Ken sighed. Phil's inside information had back-fired on them.

"Then," Phil said, suddenly more chipper, "I should give you the *other* records from all those *other* banks I investigated."

"That's right," Decker replied, mimicking Phil's tone, "all of those *others.*"

"All those *other* banks that turned out to be dead ends," Phil said.

"Yeah," Decker said, "every last one."

"I'll get on it right away." Phil stood and put a hand on Ken's shoulder. "Come on, let's go. We've got more work to do."

"But we're running out of time," Ken said.

98

Polski said just two words as he burst into Guillaume's office: "Perry's Bend."

It was 7:30 on Friday, the morning of the GI board meeting. Guillaume looked up from the notes for his speech spread out across his desk. "What about Perry's Bend?" he asked, still concentrating on the task before him.

"Irregularity at Perry's Bend." Polski was out of breath. "We just got word. The plant received an order to replace some of the temperature sensors, a recall of a particular model. We checked with the sensor manufacturer. They don't know anything about it. Looks like it's happening. Exactly what that crazy guy Olson predicted."

"That guy!" Guillaume cried as an alarming wave of thoughts flooded over him. The paranoid accusations, the threats, and even worse, the disturbing coincidence of Pennington somehow knowing that the crazy guy would find him and say what he said. "Alert the police in Perry's Bend at once."

"Ordinarily, Mike, I'd say yes. But not yet. Please."

"Why the hell not?"

"Our men from Technical Services can handle it better. They're better trained, better equipped, and better cared for than any local cops. Police are useless in a nuclear plant, anyway. Our most elite teams from Tech Services are on their way right now. Including men I've got ready at Teterboro."

"What are you going to tell them at the plant?"

"We're from the new General Industries Random Redundant Spot Check Team. RRSC. Integrating security checks into the total quality management program. We've been planning it for months. Time to pilot it a few weeks ahead of schedule."

"Call in the authorities if there's any trouble. Any trouble at all."

"Understood." Polski turned to leave. "Uh, Mike, when I met with Olson, he asked to be a part of this if an incident ever really happened. I said yes to humor him because he was just a nutcase then. But now that it looks like he's not such a nutcase, I'd like to keep my word and bring him along."

Guillaume nodded. Polski rushed out.

Guillaume stared at the points of his speech to the board and knew he had to rethink everything. Was it possible that Tom Pennington was behind this? It was a thought too outrageous, too unbelievable, too paranoid to entertain. But even if Guillaume entertained it, what could he do without destroying his own credibility? Perry's Bend was *his* problem, a problem that could endanger innocent people and destroy his chances of becoming CEO. There was no way he could make accusations. He had no proof. And if he tried, *he* would be dismissed as crazy.

Guillaume felt as isolated today at the pinnacle of General Industries as he had on his first day in the training program. After all he had accomplished and all he had been through, he was still a black man navigating alone in an alien world that gave him only provisional acceptance.

If Pennington really had engineered this dilemma, Guillaume thought, he had done a masterful job. I have no good way out. Except maybe through Hildreth, the whitest white man of all in this rich white men's club. If the old aristocrat really does believe the high-minded words he mouths so convincingly, I might have a chance.

99

Cindy was watching television on the living room couch. She was in her nightshirt, finishing her morning coffee. Ken had his laundry bag and quarters in hand. He was headed for the coin-operated machines in the basement.

He was confused. This was the morning of the board meeting and nothing had happened yet. "If a man named Howard Polski calls," he said, "tell him I'll be right back. Get his number. Please."

"Okay," she called as the door closed.

Cindy flipped around the channels aimlessly. Finally she found an old movie and settled in to watch. A few minutes later, Ken's cell, sitting in its charger in his bedroom, started chirping. Once, twice, three times. She was enjoying the movie and did not feel like getting up. But she knew after four rings, it would go to voice mail. She leaped off the couch and dashed into his bedroom to pick it up.

"Hello," she said, out of breath.

"Who is this? I thought this was Ken Olson's cell." Polski sounded agitated and impatient.

"It is. I'm his roommate. Is this Mr. Polski? He told me you might be calling. Is there a number where he can reach you?"

"Yes, but only for a short while. This is very important. Will he be back soon?"

"Uh, I'm not sure."

"Well, tell him to call me at this number."

She reached for a Post-it pad and wrote down the number.

"It's urgent. Tell him if he is going to be on the plane with me, he's got to call me immediately. Tell him we have an incident. He was right."

"I understand."

"Thank you. Good-bye."

She looked at the readout on the cell phone and saw the number Polski had dictated. Punching through the keys, she erased the number from the phone's memory. She looked at the Post-it with Polski's number and crumpled it into a ball. She raised her arm to throw it at the wastebasket, then reconsidered and put it into the breast pocket of her nightshirt. She walked back to the couch and flopped down to watch the movie.

She lay back against the pillows and turned up the volume. Just when the blonde let out her big scream as she met the killer in the dark alley, she heard Ken's key in the lock. She turned down the volume with the remote.

"You're watching *Murder by Dark* again!" Ken said as said as he bounded into the living room. "Caught you."

"Guilty pleasure," she said, "fewer calories than ice cream."

The muffled scream was followed by muffled melodramatic music.

"You love that old flick, don't you?" Ken walked over to his cell phone in the charger.

"I just find her performance . . . interesting," Cindy said.

"You mean what's-her-name?"

"Yeah, her, the talented blonde who never made it beyond the B-movies."

Ken was nervously checking the log of received calls. He found nothing.

Cindy watched Ken looking hopefully for the call she had just erased. Suddenly, she hated her deception. And herself. The crumpled Post-it in her pocket felt like it would burn a hole in her heart, or whatever she had left of a heart.

"Ken," she blurted out, "you're a really good man. This is all wrong." He concentrated on his phone. "Remember I told you I'm an actor?"

"Yeah, yeah," he said without looking up, "you take classes, go to auditions, I know all that."

"No, no. I mean all this time with you, I've been acting."

"Yeah," he muttered, "whatever."

"Ken," she said urgently, "for Christ's sake, look at me."

"What?" He looked up.

"I am not who you think I am. All this time, I've been acting. It's been a role. A paying role. Two thousand a week in cash."

"Huh?"

"I'm sorry, Ken. I'm really sorry."

"What are you sorry about?" He walked over to the couch and stood facing her. "Who on earth has been paying you? And for what?"

"I don't really know."

"What do you mean, you don't really know? Somebody's paying you two thousand a week and you don't know what for?"

"To keep tabs on you and report on everything you do."

"What the fuck . . . ?" He bent down and grabbed her by the shoulders.

She jumped away and fled to the corner of the living room.

"I told you I don't know," she snapped. "There was some guy I met in acting class. We started going out a little. Not dating—he's gay. Then he tells me about this role. Tells me about the money, from some friend of a friend of a business connection. He set me up in this apartment, upstairs from you. They had it all planned out. That first night, he beeped me when it was time for us to come back here from the East Side. He didn't tell me they were going to burn up your studio. I guess he didn't want me to have to *act* surprised or up-set; I really was. Anyway, I call in a couple of times a week, I get in-structions, keep him posted on what you're doing, he gives me my money. That's all I know." She started to sob. "I'm sorry, Ken. I'm sorry."

He glared at her. "Are those tears an act, too?"

"Fuck you!"

"You're working for Pennington!"

"I've never met the guy or even spoken to him." She sobbed.

Ken thought of his gun, buried in the back of his bottom drawer. The little gun he had learned to use reasonably well. Well enough to kill someone. He stared at Cindy. He was furious. But no, he had not bought the gun to kill her.

"Here," she said, pulling the Post-it from her pocket. "Howard Polski just called. He's going somewhere on the jet. Wants you to join him. Something about an incident. Here's his cell. Said to tell you, you were right."

He grabbed the crumpled yellow sheet from her hand.

"I wasn't supposed to give it to you at all," she said, as if that might entitle her to a bit of praise or a claim to decency.

Ken ran back to his bedroom and dialed the number. "Howard! It's Ken Olson. I just got your message." He listened intently. "So it *is* Perry's Bend! I'll be there right away. I'll grab a taxi." He glared at Cindy, then stormed out of the apartment. The door slammed shut behind him.

Cindy felt a shiver run through her. She walked to Ken's desk, sat, and thought for a while, staring at the wall.

Finally, she opened the top drawer.

Knowing just where to look, she extracted a business card and picked up the phone by the computer. She dialed the number on the card.

As she waited on hold for Agent Ted Decker, she whispered, "I'm in deep shit."

100

At Teterboro, the GI Gulfstream was one of dozens of private jets lined up outside the hangars, waiting to carry executives anywhere on earth at a moment's notice. It was all general aviation here, no commercial aircraft.

Just by identifying himself at the reception desk, Ken was escorted to the waiting jet and whisked aboard. Polski and three very large, very fit men in casual clothes were waiting.

"Welcome, Ken," Polski said as the plane's door closed and it started taxiing. "I'd like you to meet three of our top specialists from Tech Services: Barney Owen, Peter Findlay, and Bill Feigen. Gentlemen, this is Ken Olson. He's a, uh, a consultant I've known for years. I've been telling him about some of our crisis management systems at GI. I felt it would be helpful for him to see us in action in our hands-on mode."

As the plane soared to its cruising altitude, Ken sat back and listened to the GI men talk engineering gobbledygook, an alphabet soup of strange acronyms, systems and subsystems, laydowns, washdowns, annunciator panels—an impenetrable foreign language of mysterious jargon.

"Well, this will be our first RRSC," Polski said. "We'll take a small group to confront them inside, then escort them out for a little, ahem, meeting. Where the rest of our men will be."

"And if they resist?" Findlay asked, massaging his prominent left bicep.

"Where are they going to run to?" Polski asked. "Getting out of a nuclear power plant is even tougher than getting in." The three large men grunted in agreement. Polski went on, "We can be almost one hundred percent certain these guys are unarmed."

"That's for damn sure," Owen added.

"Well, whoever these guys are," Polski said, "they know that if we blow the whistle and alert the plant, they're going straight to jail. So whatever we offer them will be a better deal. And when we discreetly produce these . . ." Polski opened a leather case that held a collection of odd pieces of grayish plastic. Very quickly, he assembled them, locking one piece into another, until he held a convincing revolver in his hand. "Invisible to security and pretty damn persuasive."

"May I see that?" Ken asked. Polski handed him the lifelike revolver. Ken inspected it. It looked and felt real. "But what if they *do* have weapons? De Waal is a professional killer, a soldier."

Owen snorted, "Our men are soldiers, too. Armed and trained. Even if they got in with arms somehow, they're not getting out. Believe me."

Ken thought, This is a private military operation, too. But *we* are the *good* guys.

101

Pennington felt the cell phone vibrate in his pocket.

He looked at the message screen: IN.

The time was 10:10 A.M.—8:10 A.M. Rocky Mountain time.

De Waal was in the plant at Perry's Bend.

In. The plan was under way.

Pennington got up from his desk. He pushed the button on his intercom. "Jill, I'm going to take a walk around a bit before the board meeting."

Before opening the door to his office, Pennington removed the SIM card from the phone and put it in one of his pants pockets. He put the phone in the other pocket. He walked down the hall to the men's room, something he did regularly. He liked to tell people he felt odd having his own private bathroom in his office suite, and that he liked to see and be seen by his colleagues in what he called "the great equalizer." Once inside a stall, he flushed the SIM card down the toilet. He broke the cell phone into two pieces, putting one in each of his pants pockets. Then he washed his hands, greeted a manager who stood at the sink nearby, and went for a walk around the halls. This was another practiced ritual of his, wandering up and down the floors of the headquarters rubbing elbows with "my people."

Taking the elevator two floors down, he went to another men's room. In the stall, he wrapped one half of the phone in toilet paper. Then, waiting for the bathroom to empty, he dropped the wrapped half into the trash under a layer of wet paper towels.

Taking the back stairs between two other floors, he found a Dumpster filled with construction debris from renovations. He dropped the other half into the Dumpster. And took the elevator back to his office.

102

Cindy Morse was upset by the young FBI agent's attitude.

"Well," he said, reviewing his notes, "when Agent Decker gets back tomorrow, I'll go over this with him. And he will contact you directly, if he needs to know more."

"What's he doing in Europe?" Cindy asked angrily.

"Working."

"Can't you offer me any protection?" she asked urgently. "Isn't that what you're supposed to do?"

The agent said, "I will brief him thoroughly as soon as he gets back."

"Don't you see?" Cindy said, getting more anxious. "I was being paid to spy on Ken Olson about everything connected with this big executive Pennington. Who Ken said was really a mass murderer."

"Yes," the agent said politely, "who did you say was paying you?"

"I told you, I don't know. This guy."

"But who was he?"

"I don't know."

"Who was he working for?"

"I don't know, I already told you that."

"And how did you two communicate?"

"I told you, every week, he gave me a new cell phone that I was supposed to use to call him, no one else. When he gave me the phone, his number was always programmed in speed dial on the two key."

"So he had a new number with every phone he gave you?"

"Yeah, I guess so. I never bothered to look." She reached into her purse for her current cell phone. "Here," she said, reading off the number from the memory.

The FBI man put her on hold and dialed it on another line. When he came back he said, "That number has been disconnected."

"What about the Witness Protection Program?" Cindy asked with desperation. "Like on the TV shows?"

He started to laugh but caught himself.

"What's so funny?" Cindy asked resentfully. "I need help, I mean it."

"Ms. Morse," he explained, his patience wearing thin, "it's not like booking a weekend in Miami. It's for people who are in grave danger after providing very valuable evidence against major criminals. And while what you know may be interesting to Agent Decker, it seems like you don't know very much."

"But I told you . . ." Tears were starting.

"Listen, Ms. Morse, my secretary just called Howard Polski's office like you asked. He is *not* on a secret mission to save a nuclear power plant from sabotage. He is traveling on routine company business. And I'm in no position to contradict them. There's no telling where your Mr. Olson is. But I seriously doubt he is on a General Industries jet on a secret mission."

"Goddamn it! I'm in danger." Tears were streaming from her eyes. "Can't you see that?"

"Thank you, Miss Morse. Agent Decker will be in touch, I'm pretty sure."

103

In the GI boardroom, the Succession Committee sat in formal session. Harry Warren, still weak and confined to his hospital bed, was present through the speakerphone sitting on the eighteen-foot-long teakwood table. Justin Hildreth sat at the head of the table. The four other members of the committee—three silver-haired white men and a jowly white woman in her late fifties with hair dyed brown—sat on either side of the long empty table.

"Enough process," Harry said, his voice feeble, "let's hear from the executives one last time so the committee can vote."

"As we agreed," Hildreth said extra loudly at the speakerphone, as if deafness were another of Harry's woes. He nodded at the man to his right, who got up, walked to the door, opened it, motioned, then went back to his seat. Guillaume entered the boardroom followed by Pennington. They sat on either side of Hildreth.

Hildreth cleared his throat. "We are here to choose the man who will lead this corporation in the next chapter of its history. This is not an easy decision, especially coming, unfortunately, more quickly than any of us had planned."

"Oh, balls!" Warren's voice bellowed, in a momentary return to his former strength. Then he coughed several times. When he spoke again, it was with the feeble heart-patient voice. "Justin, let's move this along. Please."

"Thanks, Harry," Justin said. "As the final step before the committee votes, we want to hear from the two CEO candidates briefly. Naturally, we have gone over your CVs in detail and read your personnel files going back many years. We have evaluated your business results, solicited opinions from your colleagues, bosses, and subordinates throughout the organizations you have led. We have talked to key customers and leaders in your communities. But now, we want to hear you describe the vision each of you brings and hear in your own words why you believe you should be chosen. Harry and I decided,"

Justin explained, "that you should draw straws to determine which one of you gets the last word"—he paused and smiled—"so to speak." Hildreth reached into the pocket of his suit coat and produced two white paper straws sticking out of his fist. He held it forward in the center of the table.

Pennington and Guillaume extended their hands toward the fist.

"No, you go," Pennington said to Guillaume.

Guillaume shook his head no. "You go. I insist," he said quietly.

"Okay, thanks," Pennington said as he pulled one straw from Hildreth's grasp. A fairly long piece.

Guillaume reached for the remaining straw. It was the short one. "Mr. Guillaume has drawn the shorter straw," Hildreth announced. "He will speak first."

And, Guillaume thought, Pennington will have the last word.

104

The Gulfstream landed at the small airport and taxied to the side of the modest terminal where two Chevy Suburbans were parked, their engines idling. Six men emerged from the Suburbans, taking bags and briefcases from the steward on the plane and loading them into the back of the wagons.

Polski spoke to the group. "Sabarsky has alerted our plant managers and they're expecting us to pay a surprise visit on our friends. They promised not to tip them off. Four of them showed up this morning; the boss, an engineer, and two installers."

"De Waal," Ken muttered to himself, "Grant De Waal." He pronounced the first name with the rough guttural *ch* sound he had learned from Phil. Ken had become a student of Afrikaans, learning basic words and phrases from a language tutorial he had bought.

"Huh?" Polski asked him.

"Nothing," Ken said, "just talking to myself."

The Suburbans sped away. From the hill just outside of town, the view looked down onto the plant at the bend in the river. It was an immense and sprawling industrial complex, with massive towers containing miles of pipelines, like several oil refineries combined with airplane hangars. From the cooling towers, clouds of steam billowed into the sky. And at the center stood the steel-and-cement towers of the containment buildings, where the nuclear reactors were.

The two Suburbans were cleared at the front gate of the plant. Hutton and Sabarsky waited in the parking lot by the vehicles, their preauthorized automatic machine pistols at the ready.

They entered the complex and were given badges to wear around their necks and white plastic hard hats marked with the GI Power Systems logo. They went through a gauntlet of security checks—from metal detectors to explosive detectors, first in the "owner-controlled area," the large perimeter encircling the entire plant.

Then they passed into the "protected area" immediately around the plant buildings themselves. This was barricaded and blockaded like a prison, with high fences and razor wire. Closed-circuit surveillance cameras were everywhere. Yet again, they were photographed, wanded, and frisked, through checkpoint after checkpoint, signing in at each new security desk.

Once cleared to enter the "vital area," where the reactor buildings, control buildings, and generators were located, they went through another redundant security check. They stopped for a communal bathroom break along the way after the last scanning machine. They assembled their plastic weapons in the privacy of the stalls and hid them in their jackets.

They gathered at the security desk in the small building that served as the connection point between the containment building, where the reactor was, and the buildings housing the control room and the massive generators beyond. This was the huge oil refinery/airplane hangar complex they had seen from the hill above the river.

An armed security guard was sitting at a bank of twenty color monitors. He was a stoop-shouldered older man with a paunch who looked like he had retired from some other career long ago. On the screens were live feeds from cameras around the reactor and the building beside it. Mostly, there was nothing to see. Pipes, pipes, and more pipes for carrying tons of water through the system.

The cavernous room with the reactor pool was empty, protected by the invisible layers of steel and cement surrounding it. The reactor pool looked so innocent and tranquil. A giant metal thermos suspended in a bathtub of blue water. The unimaginable power of an atomic bomb turned into a hot water heater.

While Polski and the plant manager conferred, Ken gazed at the screens.

"What kind of sound does it make?" Ken asked the guard. He pointed to the screen showing the reactor pool.

"What do you mean?" The guard looked puzzled.

"The reactor there," Ken said, "what sound does it make?"

The guard was surprised at the question. "It's silent. The water's pressurized so it won't boil."

"No sound at all?" Ken thought of the world-shattering sound of an atomic explosion and the fury of its hellfire.

"If you get up real close, you can hear a gentle bubbling sound. But that's it."

Ken shook his head in wonder.

Polski and the plant manager talked. "They're working on sensors in the secondary loop," the manager said, referring to the circuit of pipes that drew heat from the superheated pressurized loop of water that came directly from the reactor core. The secondary loop created the steam that drove the turbines that produced the electricity, then cooled the steam back to water and cycled it back to draw heat from the primary loop again.

The manager pointed to two screens showing scenes from the adjacent building. In each, a man was crouched over a water pipe, fiddling with a gadget too small to see. Behind each man, a plant employee stood watching, looking rather bored.

"So they have not been in the containment building?" Polski asked.

The manager shook his head emphatically no. "The equipment and personnel lock is on. No one's allowed in there when we're on full power."

"Where's the boss and the engineer?" Polski asked.

"I saw them in the control room talking to Davenport early this morning. They went down to Davenport's office, I think."

"Let's go," Polski said urgently to the manager. He turned to his men. "You get our friends. Ken, you stay here. We'll bring you someone you've been dying to meet."

"And how," Ken said.

The manager spoke into his walkie-talkie. "Ames, MacLaren, you read me?" He nodded. The two men escorting the installers gave a thumbs-up to their respective security cameras. "The teams from Technical Services have arrived. Don't say anything to the installers. Just let our men escort them out. Let them do whatever they need to do to persuade them to cooperate." The manager sized up the beefy visitors. "But I don't think they'll need any. Follow them back here to security. We'll have to regroup and go back over the sensor installations so far. Over."

Polski and the manager went through the door that led to the control room. The GI Security men went through the door that led to the secondary loop and the bogus installers. Their journeys through the hallways appeared on two of the screens for a moment.

Ken and the security guard were alone. He invited Ken to pull up a chair and watch with him. He called the bank of monitors "Plant TV."

Ten minutes passed. They might as well have been watching paint dry. Then the guard noticed a little drama unfolding on a screen in the center of monitor bank. "There's your men," he said, and pointed to the monitor.

The overhead camera showed the technician unwrapping what looked like a metal ribbon from around a water pipe. The white helmets blocked the view of the man's face. Then Owen and Findlay reached the man who was watching the installer. They spoke, then he stepped back and Owen and Findlay walked up to the man performing the installation. There was another exchange. Then Owen and Findlay showed their "guns." The technician stood up and raised his arms in surrender.

"Holy shit!" the guard shouted. "They've got guns! How the hell did they get guns in there? I've got to sound the alarm." Ken saw him rise up out of his chair and lunge for a red button on the far corner of the desk. Ken jumped up and threw his arms around the guard, pulling him back to his chair. The guard was as old, tired, and unfit as he looked.

"Je-sus!" the guard shouted. "What are you doing?"

"Please," Ken said, holding him even tighter. "Listen to me. They're not real guns. Honest. We're all on the same side. We're here to *protect* the plant!" Ken held the older man down. "Now don't sound the alarm. Promise? And I'll show you the fake gun." The guard took a deep breath. Ken relaxed his grip a bit. "Promise?"

Ken removed one arm from around the man and stepped in front of him in order to block the red alarm button. Ken pulled the revolver from his jacket pocket and put it on the desk.

"Sure looks real," the guard said.

"It's supposed to. Pick it up."

Cautiously, the guard took it. "It's heavy like a real gun," he said.

"Just weighted plastic," Ken said, "so it behaves right in your hand. Now see if you can slide the barrel away from the handle." The guard took the gun in both hands and began tugging and pulling at its parts. After a little experimentation, the barrel slid away. Then he quickly disassembled the rest.

"See? I told you, it's fake," Ken said. Ken and the guard looked at the monitor again. The people were gone.

"Look," the guard said, "there they are."

The scene was another corridor. Owen and Findlay walked on either side of the installer who had just surrendered. A similar scene played out with Feigen and Castelli and the other installer, but not in view of cameras.

Then the guard pointed to another monitor. The screen showed six men walking down a corridor. Everyone looked polite and calm. Polski and the manager came back to the security room with Gerald Davenport. Then the installers and their escorts arrived. They looked like any blue-collar workmen anywhere. Ken prepared himself to face Grant De Waal.

Polski looked at Ken and pointed to the installers. "Is either of these men the one you're looking for?"

105

Guillaume leaned forward, putting both elbows on the table. He spoke softly, as if addressing an old friend in a confidential chat. "I am the outsider. I was not born to this world." He gestured at the richly paneled boardroom. "Since the day I got here and joined the race, I have literally been the dark horse." He paused. As he had anticipated, the directors exchanged surprised glances at his bluntness. "I have had to work my way *into* this great company as well as upward through its ranks. Have I had to work harder? Perhaps. But we are a company of very hardworking people. Have I had to work smarter? Certainly. But you can say that about any executive who rises as high as I have, regardless of where he or she started. I am proud of my work and honored to have accomplished the things I have accomplished. My record at making money for shareholders speaks for itself. My skills as a manager and a leader are extensively documented."

He took a breath. "What sets me apart is not my color." He glanced around the table at the directors. Then he riveted his gaze at Hildreth. "It is my character." Hildreth nodded. "Everyone in this company knows the values I stand for. Because I have lived them and practiced them every day and through every job I've ever held in my years at General Industries. And in all my board work and volunteer work."

He looked at Hildreth again and narrowed his eyes with concentration. "In my world, integrity is all there is. It is the one value that transcends the struggles of ambition and gain." He was focused on Hildreth, playing, he hoped, to what must be the aristocrat's deepest convictions about the responsibilities of privilege. "There are no question marks, no secrets about Michael Guillaume. Call me old-fashioned, but that is more important to me than anything else." Hildreth returned Guillaume's gaze, revealing no emotion, a skill at which Hildreth had a lifetime of practice.

Guillaume moved his gaze around the room. "As we go into the unknowable and uncertain future, I can provide the one, the only known and certain strength that can keep this company on track no matter what lies ahead." He turned to Hildreth again and caught his eye. "That strength," Guillaume said directly to him, "is strength of character."

Guillaume continued staring at Hildreth.

Hildreth stared back, inscrutable, revealing nothing. Then he looked at his watch.

106

Ken walked over to the bewildered men and stared into their faces. They had hair and eyebrows, real hair, their own. They were burly and strong but neither one was Grant De Waal. He was sure of that. He shook his head with bitter disappointment. De Waal had escaped him already.

"Where's your boss?" Ken barked at the two installers. They shrugged. The stupidity of their expressions confirmed the sincerity of their ignorance.

Polski glared at Davenport. "What's the matter?" Davenport asked guiltily.

Polski turned to Owen. "Get one of those new sensors from that guy's tool kit, would you, Barney?" Owen placed it on the table. "Let's see those temperature foils." Polski opened up the metal sleeve. Inside were two shiny strips, paper-thin, and silvery.

"So?" Davenport said.

"That's supposed to be a bimetallic sensor," Polski said accusingly, "right?"

Davenport nodded.

"That means two metals, one to react if the temperature goes too far in one direction, the other to react in the opposite way." Polski handed the sensor to Davenport. "Now look," he commanded, "look!"

Davenport inspected the device. "Both strips are the same metal," he said, barely whispering.

"That's right," Polski said, "so they will react only when the temperature goes wrong in one direction, not the other, which means—"

Davenport raised his hand to stop Polski from making a public declaration of his mistake. Polski ignored him. "Do you realize what would have happened if these sensors had gone online? Do you, Mr. Davenport? Do you have any idea what you might have caused?"

Davenport's shoulders sank. "We need to replace all of these bad sensors immediately," he said, trying to sound officious and still in charge.

"That's not the only thing in this plant that needs to be replaced right away," Polski said. "I'm going to call the regional NRC office and give a complete report to your supervisors, *Mis*-ter Davenport."

Davenport reached for the phone on the guard's desk. He dialed an internal extension and barked into the phone, "Get three maintenance men down here immediately. We've got to replace all the bad sensors that were just installed. Use sensors from backup inventory."

Polski turned to Owen and motioned to the two installers. "Do we know who these guys really are?"

Owen snickered. "They're just local slobs who've worked around plumbing. They don't know jack shit about De Waal or the operation."

"Do you know who hired you?" Polski asked them.

The two men shrugged. The shorter one said, "He paid up front and in cash, that's all I know."

Ken turned to the NRC man. "What is your friend's name, Mr. Davenport?"

"Volkenberg, Martin Volkenberg," Davenport said meekly.

Ken walked up to him and asked, "Is he about six-one? Brawny? With an accent that sounds kind of British and German at the same time?"

Davenport nodded.

"Did he have hair?" Ken asked urgently.

"What do you mean?" Davenport was confused.

"Did he have hair on his head?"

"Yeah, brown. And a mustache. Glasses, too."

"All fake," Ken said angrily.

"Where is he now?" Polski demanded.

"Don't know," Davenport said, sounding lame and apologetic. "When I heard your managers talking about the random spot checks, I gave him the heads-up. I figured this could blow his installation schedule to hell and he ought to be prepared for it. I figured he went down to tell his men. Him and the engineer who came with him."

Ken looked at today's page of sign-ins and -outs.

And there it was.

The handwriting he recognized from the Xerox copy in Phil's office. The same curves, the same foreign style that had written *Peter Houghton* in the logbook at Ayvil Plastics. They had him now. They had De Waal's signature everywhere. Ken pointed to the signature, written twice, signed in and signed out. "He signed out!" he said urgently. "He fucking signed *out!*"

"I, uh, just came on duty," the guard said defensively, "I never saw anybody sign out."

Polski barked into his radio: "Hutton! Sabarsky! The ringleader will be attempting to leave the plant with his accomplice. He's six-one with brown hair, a mustache, and glasses. Do not let them out, repeat, do not let them out!"

Pennington waited a little longer than was comfortable to begin speaking. "Everywhere I have *served*," he paused to let his audience fully appreciate his choice of verb, "I have sought to innovate and blaze new trails. You have all seen how Wall Street has responded with increased share prices and buy valuations, how the business press has responded with admiring article after article. Many of my ideas have found their way into our great business schools and are shaping the minds and methods of generations of business leaders to come."

Pennington smiled his best presidential-candidate smile. "I am not being immodest. Just factual. No executive in recent memory has had this much influence or this much impact on the world of business. And at age forty-three, I am only just beginning."

He sat up perfectly straight. "What *is* a great corporation, anyway?" He paused as if expecting an answer. "It is nothing but a projection of plans and dreams into the future." Another pause to let his words sink in. "That is why I am the right executive to lead this great corporation. Because, if I have proven anything in my career, I have proven that"—another pause—"I *am* the future." Pennington took a deep breath and sat back ever so slightly in his chair.

An awkward silence. Then, over the speakerphone, Harry asked in a feeble voice, "That it?"

"Yes, Harry," Hildreth said.

"Then, thank you, gentlemen," Warren said. "Thank you both."

"Mike, Tom," Hildreth said, "if you could leave us now. It is time for the board to deliberate and vote."

108

All the way to the Starbucks, Cindy was muttering to herself and fighting back tears. If people were staring at her, she did not notice. If she was being followed, just as she had been all along, and all her phone conversations listened to, she had no idea.

She walked down Columbus. By the time she neared the big windows with the green logos on them, she had pulled herself more or less together. She did not notice the big man who bumped into her and vanished into the morning hubbub. But she did feel the little jab that tore the leg of her blue jeans and pricked her thigh.

"Ow!" she yelped, and reached down to grab her leg. That was all she felt. The poison did its job in a flash. By the time her face crashed into the sidewalk, she was unconscious. Several people stopped and tried to help her. One man ran into the Starbucks to get water and a first aid kit.

Moments later, as the life was fading out of Cindy's limp body, an EMS truck pulled up with sirens blazing.

"Wow, that was fast," said the man who had called 911 on his cell phone.

The medical technicians moved quickly, gruffly pushing the good Samaritans aside and surrounding Cindy with their equipment. They swooped her up into the ambulance and drove away.

By the time the real ambulance arrived a few minutes later, the crowd in front of the Starbucks was gone. There was no collapsed woman on the sidewalk to attend to.

Harry Warren's lead secretary approached the closed doors of the
board room. She held the phone message in her hand and paused
before knocking. The man who had just called, the man who said of-
ficiously he was from the Nuclear Regulatory Commission, had insisted that his message go directly to Harry Warren. No, he did not
care if Warren was in a board meeting. No, he did not care if Warren
was calling in on speakerphone from his hospital bed. He was the
Federal government and his job was to protect the American public.
Besides, he was doing General Industries a favor, although now that
he thought of it he could not imagine why. He was going out of his
way, he, the man from the NRC who did not *have* to go out of his
way, to give the chief executive of General Industries a heads-up.
That's right, as a favor, a favor mind you, he was issuing a PNUE.
For civilians that's a Pre-Notice of Unusual Event, and ma'am that's
more than most other nuclear power plant operators would get, so
she had better get this message to Harry Warren, board meeting or
not. Harry Warren needed to know that there was a problem brewing
at the Perry's Bend nuclear power plant and he needed to know *now*.
He was giving them hours of advance notice. Hours they could use
to send their technical services personnel. Hours they could use to
actually prevent the issuance of the real NUE. And ma'am, in case
you think this can wait until later in the day, you and General Industries are sadly mistaken and he did not want to think about the consequences.

She stood at the door, holding the message in her hand. Then she
knocked.

Hutton and Sabarsky cocked their machine pistols and peered around the lot, looking for the two men. All they saw was a pretty young woman headed for the corner farthest away from the guards and the entrance. She wore tight jeans and walked with a sexy swing of her hips.

She headed toward a white Passat. They watched as the woman got in the car and rolled down her window. It was a mild day with a gentle breeze. She turned the rearview mirror toward herself and carefully applied lipstick and fixed her hair. Then she put on sunglasses, turned the mirror back into place, started the car, turned on the radio, and backed very carefully out of the parking space. She drove slowly down the row of parked cars toward the front of the lot. She smiled and sang along with the radio.

Suddenly, there was a loud crack of a rifle shot. The woman's head exploded in blood. She was thrown by the impact to the other side of the front seat. Her foot must have caught on the accelerator pedal because the Passat suddenly barreled ahead and crashed into two cars parked on the opposite side of the exit lane, demolishing them both and setting off car horns and alarms.

Hutton and Sabarsky jumped from the side of their Suburban and ran toward the crash. At the same time, three guards ran out of the guard shack. Seconds later, the five men met at the crash site. All were panting; all had their guns ready.

The horns and alarms were wailing. The men peered into the blood-spattered Passat. A chunk of the back of the pretty young woman's head was gone. Her mouth was open as if she were still singing the last word of the song.

The five men held their weapons in the firing position and scanned the expanse of the parking lot.

"Look!" Sabarsky cried. "Over there!"

A man was running toward the back of the parking lot. He had a pistol in his hand. Hutton and Sabarsky, in Kevlar vests, took off at a full sprint.

The man ducked down behind a minivan, then suddenly he stood stooped over the Miata beside it. He fired two shots at Hutton and ducked out of sight again. One shot blew out the windshield of a Camry, the other zinged into the fender of a Taurus. Two more car alarms starting wailing.

The man made a break, running through three empty spaces then into a knot of vehicles, trying to zigzag his way clear of his pursuers.

He fired again, this time at Sabarsky, who had already found cover behind a pickup truck. Hutton and Sabarsky, crouching low beneath the line of fire, began closing in on the man's left and right flanks. His path forward was blocked by the other armed guards at the crash site. And backward by the security fence around the parking lot.

The man looked up over the trunk of a red Acura.

"Drop it!" Hutton said from the man's left side, his machine pistol braced into both hands, finger on the trigger.

"He said drop it!" Sabarsky said from the man's right side, poised and aiming in the same position. The man who today called himself Cox dropped his pistol on the ground and raised his hands in surrender.

Hutton walked up to Cox, his pistol aimed at the man's head. Sabarsky lowered his gun and took a pair of handcuffs from his Kevlar vest. Grabbing the man's upraised hands, he cuffed his wrists behind his back. Sabarsky pointed his gun at him.

"If you run, you die," Sabarsky said.

Ken and Polski sprinted into the parking lot a moment later, out of breath, meeting Sabarsky, Hutton, and their captive at the crash site. The other Tech Services men bolted for the Suburbans to get their weapons.

They stared in horror at the dead woman in the smashed car.

"He's out there somewhere," Polski said, scanning the parking lot for a clue. The plant security guards scanned the lot and barked into their radios.

Ken stared at the man in handcuffs. "I remember you!" he shouted. "You were at the plant in Ohio! Where's De Waal?" He grabbed the man's arm. "Where the fuck is De Waal?"

"Fuck off," the captive said.

Ken raised his fist at the man. "I said, where's De Waal?"

Suddenly, another rifle shot rang out. Everyone fell to the ground for cover.

"Holy shit," Sabarsky said, picking himself up slowly. Blood was splattered on him and Hutton. The captive, Cox, lay on his back with a hole in his forehead, a pool of blood oozing out underneath him onto the asphalt.

"Who's in the guard shack?" Polski asked as he raised himself on one knee.

"No one," one of the guards shouted.

"The barrier's down," another guard said loudly, "no vehicle can get out."

More security guards arrived. They and the other Tech Services men were fanning out from the Suburbans, waving their guns as they scanned the parking lot.

Only later would the videotapes reveal the image of a big man in a baseball cap and sunglasses running bent over around the perimeter of the fence and crawling under the barrier and out of the plant.

111

As Guillaume approached his suite of offices, his secretary waved to him urgently. "Howard Polski is on hold for you."

Guillaume nodded and dashed for his office.

"Should I put him through?" she asked.

"Yes, please, Kathy," Guillaume said and closed his door.

"He's on line one," Kathy announced over the intercom.

Guillaume scooped up the handset. "Howard," he said urgently.

"Mike, the plant is secure," Polski said, "repeat, secure. The South African murdered a plant employee in the parking lot. And his accomplice before he escaped."

"It was him?"

"Yes, just like Olson said. The FBI is after him now."

"How did he escape?"

"Somebody who wasn't supposed to tip him tipped him off."

"Who did that?"

"Who do you think?" Polski asked.

"Gerald Davenport?" Guillaume said the name with anger and frustration.

"I already reported him to the NRC. He's toast."

"How do we know it was the man Olson said it was?"

"His signature in the logbook. Olson says his investigators have a handwriting expert who can match it to the signature of the guy at Ayvil. They've got a collection of his writing samples from all over. They've been tracking how he launders his money. We've got him on the surveillance videos now—" Polski did not finish the thought.

"It still doesn't prove who hired him in the first place, does it?" Guillaume asked.

"No, Mike. Not yet. But so far, Olson has been right about everything else."

"But have they connected Pennington to any of this? Have they, Howard?"

"Not yet. But Mike, believe me, if you had lived through what I just lived through—"

"Do we have any idea how long it might take them?"

"No, I'm afraid not."

Kathy interrupted over the intercom. "Mr. Guillaume, Harry Warren is on line two."

"Howard," Guillaume said, "Harry's on the other line, can I put you on hold?"

"No need. Let me finish here. I'll see you tomorrow with the whole story."

"Thanks, Howard, come see me first thing." Guillaume took a deep breath before pushing the button for line two. "Harry," he said urgently.

"I'm sorry, Mike," Harry said, his voice weak, "it was a tough decision, with a very divided board."

Guillaume sucked in his breath, trying to sort through the conflicting thoughts and emotions exploding in his head.

"That little telegram from the NRC didn't help matters any," Harry added.

"Listen, Harry," Guillaume said, ready to jump on that, "there's something important about—"

Harry interrupted him. "It's reality, Mike. I can't change it." The voice sounded only remotely like the Harry Warren he had known for a decade and a half. "We could do a post-game analysis sometime."

"Sure," Guillaume said, realizing that there was nothing more he could do now. Or ever, so far as General Industries was concerned.

"You've got other offers, naturally," Warren said.

"Yes," Guillaume said, "Nortex is the one I like best."

"Well, they'll be damn lucky to get you." Warren sounded like he was fading.

"Thanks, Harry," Guillaume said softly, "thanks for everything."

"No, I'm the one who has to thank *you*." Then he coughed. "Good-bye, Mike."

"Good-bye, Harry." Guillaume stared at the phone after hanging up.

112

There was a knock at the closed door of Guillaume's office. The sound snapped him out of his thinking. "Come in."

Tom Pennington walked in. Guillaume stood and stared.

"No, no, please," Pennington said, motioning for him to sit.

Guillaume remained standing.

"Oh well," Pennington said, "whatever you like." He walked up to the edge of Guillaume's desk. He was in his shirtsleeves, tie loosened, collar unbuttoned—the hardworking CEO. "Listen, Mike, I don't have a lot of time."

"Uh-huh," Guillaume said flatly, and folded his arms across his chest.

Pennington looked Guillaume directly in the eye. "You know, ordinarily, we would do an elaborate ritual designed to help you save face. But we just learned something very disturbing. And as chief executive of this company, I am going to have to ask you to leave immediately. We can have the lawyers and the flacks cook up the right stories to protect your public image." He looked at Guillaume and shook his head. "I want you out of this building this afternoon. Do you understand?"

Guillaume showed no emotion.

"You committed a serious breach of trust today. And while I'm not going to fire you for cause or get into any of that legal crap, we can't afford to have a loose cannon like you at General Industries." He paused and stared deeper into Guillaume's eyes. Guillaume gave him nothing back. "I'm talking about this incident at Perry's Bend. All I can say is thank God the plant is out of jeopardy."

Pennington put his fists on his hips combatively. "You never reported this to your superiors. You tried to keep it below the radar in hopes that you could fix it by yourself. It so happens we were lucky. But what about next time? I can't have that kind of cowboy behavior.

This company is a public trust. We are here to serve the greater good. I am surprised at you, and disappointed. My decision is final."

Guillaume spoke slowly and calmly. "You won't last, Pennington. The law is going to catch up with you sooner than you think."

Pennington gave him a puzzled look. "Mike, you are cracking under all this pressure. You are becoming delusional."

Guillaume reached for the Benin bronze statue on the credenza behind his desk. The eighteenth-century masterpiece from the West African kingdom was a royal figure about eighteen inches high attached with a thick iron rod to a stone pedestal. He held it in his right hand and flexed the muscles in his arm against its weight, something he did to relieve tension.

"Mike, Mike," Pennington said with the tut-tut of a parent. "If violence is your answer, go ahead." Pennington lowered his arms and held his palms open in a Christ-like gesture of martyrdom. "It will only make it worse for you." Then he added an aside to himself. "I can't believe this kind of unstable behavior hasn't been documented before. We've got to take a closer look at the GI personnel practices and psychological testing."

Guillaume put the bronze back on the desk. "I wouldn't give you the satisfaction," he muttered.

Pennington said, "You've got other CEO offers in your back pocket, I'm sure. I got some of the same ones. Nortex was my favored backup. Probably yours, too." Pennington turned and walked to the door. "After what just happened at Perry's Bend," he said over his shoulder, "you know damn well I'm doing you a favor."

Pennington exited, leaving the door open.

113

At the celebration at the trendy East Village restaurant, Pennington felt the phone vibrate. Reluctantly, he excused himself and retired to the stall in the men's room. He flipped the phone open and viewed the message screen: U O ME 2 MIL MORE MY CEO BONUS.

Pennington was getting tired of this. All of this. He had set in motion the agreed-upon payments. Now De Waal wanted more. From now on, everyone will figure I am made of money. Got to nip this trend in the bud. If he let De Waal blackmail him now, he would blackmail him forever. It was time to have him deleted, time for the next thing.

Pennington sent his text reply: NFW. No fucking way.

He angrily pried open the phone and removed the SIM card and flushed it down the toilet. He tore the plastic phone apart and broke it into pieces, then wrapped the pieces in two wads of toilet paper and deposited them in the two trash bins on either side of the row of sinks.

He never saw the text message De Waal sent in reply:

FE—fatal error.

He returned to the table just in time for the photographers from *New York* magazine and the *Daily News* to capture shots of that evening's premier power couple, the new CEO of General Industries and his prime-time-star fiancée, surrounded by their "bold name" friends.

114

Kat and Pennington sat naked on his bed in the dark. "It's okay, sweetie," she said, "it happens to every guy." She took his limp penis in both hands and gave the tip a little kiss. "It's no big deal."

Pennington gritted his teeth. Was it De Waal's extortion threat? Was he just tired? Was he getting old? Or was he finally just bored with the looks, feel, and smell of this woman? Was it time for the next "next thing" in his love life, too?

Kat cupped his balls and stroked his shaft gingerly, as if it were a little sleeping pet. "You want to just, you know, go to sleep?" she asked.

"No," Pennington said. He thrust his hips forward. Dutifully, she took him in her mouth and began applying her best technical skills. To no avail.

Finally, she let go and sat up on her knees. "Hey, I've got an idea."

"What?" he snapped at the darkness.

"Go to your porn stash."

"Huh?"

"Come on, every guy's got one. I won't look. Unless," she cooed, "you want me to. Really, it'll be a turn-on for me, too. We'll be a team, me and the girls that get you off in secret." She rolled over and lay on her stomach beside him. "I won't look or anything. Just pretend I'm not here." She put a pillow over her head. "Go on," she said from under it, "I won't look. Pretend I'm not here," her muffled voice told him. "Go on."

Tom slid off the bed, strode over to his cavernous walk-in closet, and closed the door. She rolled over and put the pillows under her back. She lay patiently in the dark, admiring the glittering skyline view and wondering what kind of images Tom was flipping through to turn himself on.

A few minutes later, she heard the closet door open. In the gray shadows she could see Tom speeding toward the bed, his erection bobbing.

"Hey, slugger," she cooed, and offered him her wide-open thighs. He pounced on her and came with a few violent thrusts. She wrapped her arms and legs around him and held him. She kissed his ear and stroked his back. As he lifted himself off her, she whispered, "You're the best, baby, you're the best."

Pennington walked into the bathroom, closed the door behind him, and turned on the jets of his steam shower. When she heard him humming, she knew he would be in there for a while. She popped out of bed and sprinted over to the walk-in closet. She turned on the light, listening carefully for the shower, and began hunting for his porn stash.

Everywhere she looked was the perfect order of Tom Pennington's dressing room. Expensive suits lined up like soldiers at parade review. Rows of handmade English shoes. With eyes darting this way and that, she searched the shelves and built-in drawers for the slightest trace of human disturbance, while keeping her ears on high alert.

Then, beneath a phalanx of suits, she saw one pair of shoes that was ever so slightly ajar. Getting down on her knees, she saw a black cardboard box, its lid not quite down. Paying close attention to its location behind the shoes, she seized the box, put it on the floor in front of her, and removed the lid.

She was expecting cheesy porno magazines with fetishes and kinks Tom would never admit to her. Maybe he had a thing for huge tits or fat asses or feet or bondage or even golden showers? Whatever it was, she could hint at it and joke about it sometime later, playing dumb about how she managed to strike an erotic nerve with him. She was prepared to enjoy this naughty thrill.

Instead, she found a black loose-leaf notebook filled with plastic page holders containing newspaper clippings meticulously preserved. Confused and concerned that Tom would finish his shower and discover her before she could digest the contents, she flipped through the pages quickly.

The articles made no sense to her darting eyes. The first clippings were about the accidental drowning of the junior year class president at Hotchkiss. She scanned the cracking, yellowed sheets torn from the prep school student paper, the *Lakeville Journal,* and the *Litchfield County Times.* Then there were stories from *Downeast Ledger,* the *Bangor Guardian,* and *The Boston Globe* on the accidental death of

Katherine Sprague, Tom's first wife, years before. Several articles about two executives from Paragon Industries who died when their corporate jet suddenly crashed. Then the clippings got fresher, the paper still white.

It was one article after another about the mass murder at Ayvil Plastics. Frantic that he might emerge from the shower, she flipped back through the pages, reading in a frenzy. Next were the articles about the suicide of Archibald Paulson. Then coverage of Harry Warren's heart attack and sudden retirement. Beyond that were empty plastic sleeves, awaiting clippings to come.

She could hardly breathe. Her head was pounding. She knelt in his closet, naked and trembling, flipping through the pages of this notebook, suddenly remembering what that crazy Ken Olson guy had told her that day on her voice mail.

In a flash, she slammed the notebook shut, put it back in the box, slid the box behind the shoes, straightened the telltale shoes, leaped up, turned off the closet light, shut the door, ran back into bed, and pulled the covers around herself tightly in the dark.

Her mind was frozen. Then her body told her what to do.

Ken thanked the driver of the GI town car and got out. His block at 2:00 A.M. was silent and deserted. He had no idea what he would say to Cindy. Several times since leaving Perry's Bend, he had thought about calling her but decided against it. He would tell Decker all about her. She would certainly get arrested for something. He would move out tomorrow. That much he knew.

He stood in the dimly lit vestibule and stared at his mailbox. The little slot that once had MORSE/OLSON on a plastic strip was empty. He turned to the bank of doorbells and checked 3-B. Same thing.

He had been gone one day. One very long day. But just one day. What could have happened? What had Cindy done? Who was she really?

He took out his key. It worked. He walked past the elevator and ran up the stairs. The apartment keys worked. He swung the door open. The lights were still on.

Cindy always left her things strewn around—half-read books, shoes not always in pairs, jackets, notebooks, bras on her bedroom chair. There was nothing. Her bed was stripped down to the bare mattress and box spring. None of her stuff anywhere.

Ken went to her closet. It was empty. He checked the bathroom. Not one of her things remained.

He walked to his bedroom. Everything of his was just as he had left it, including his picture of Sandy and Sara on the windowsill. The apartment was now his. Cindy Morse had disappeared from his life as suddenly as she had appeared.

"Well, fuck her," he muttered as he undressed. He collapsed onto his bed and fell into a deep, dreamless sleep.

Still naked, Kat jumped out of bed and dashed back to the closet. She had a few casual outfits on hangers and in a few drawers Pennington had given her. Quickly she put on jogging pants and a sweatshirt. She was bent over fumbling with her sneaker laces when Pennington appeared in the closet doorway, naked but for the towel hanging off one shoulder.

"You going running at this hour?" he asked.

"Uh, no," she said nervously. "Gotta go back to my place and change. The network called. Gotta leave on assignment, all weekend long."

He looked puzzled. "I thought you were taping *Prime Time Focus* next week."

"I'll be back in time. Right now I gotta pack. Car'll pick me up at six A.M. for the airport, which means I gotta get up at four thirty. You want to sleep, don't you?"

"Yeah, but with you." He took a step toward her with his arms open.

She stepped backward, almost falling over.

"Hey, what's wrong?"

"Tom, I'm a journalist. This is my life. This is going to happen all the time. If you can't accept it, then maybe we shouldn't be together."

He took the towel from his shoulders and wrapped it around his waist. "Where did this come from all of a sudden?"

She stepped past him sideways without touching, like a stranger on a crowded bus. He followed her as she turned on the lights in the bedroom and collected her glittery little three-thousand-dollar Judith Leiber handbag. It looked foolish against her jogging outfit.

"What the hell is going on here?" he asked.

She walked backward, inching for the bedroom door. "It's not you," she said. "It's me."

He took another step forward. She took two steps back. She was in the doorway with one foot in the hall.

"Kat, I haven't felt this way about a woman since Katherine."

She sucked in her breath. "Tom, I have to leave for work."

She turned and hurried down the hallway to the grand foyer, where the elevator doors opened directly. Since Pennington's apartment was the only one on the floor, it needed no front door.

Pennington followed her, reaching out and gently touching her elbow. Slowly, he turned her around and drew her toward him. Close enough to touch the side of her cheek.

She jumped away from him, stroking her cheek where his hand had been.

"What's the matter?" He looked at his hand, as if he might see the cause of her alarm smeared across his palm. Like blood.

He took one step forward. She took one step back.

"Kat," he said soothingly, "we are so good together. Just look at us." He motioned to the large photo in the silver frame on the side table. It was Pennington and Kat and the President and First Lady posed like old friends. "There's no limit to what we can do. We could be such a team. Think of the life we could have together."

"No," she said. *"No!"*

She took the large engagement ring off her finger. "I can't marry you." She laid it on the table beside the presidential photo, then ran to the elevator and pushed the call button.

He moved toward her, a tear forming in the corner of one eye. "Kat, can't you see? I love you."

The elevator doors opened. She dashed in and pushed the Close Door button frantically. In a moment, the doors closed.

Pennington wiped the tear from his eye and smiled. He stopped at the presidential group portrait and pressed the tip of his index finger against Kat's smiling face. "Bad girl," he said to her picture, "you promised not to snoop." He made the motion of firing a pistol and mouthed a little "pow."

117

The morning after the GI board meeting, Hildreth had his usual breakfast of freshly baked croissants from the French bakery on Lexington Avenue, fresh-ground espresso, fresh-squeezed orange juice, and shirred eggs. Every morning, no matter which one of his houses he was in, it was always the same.

Since Margaret's death, Hildreth had become even fussier and more rigid about his breakfast ritual. He always appeared at 6:30 A.M., dressed for the morning's activity. There were always newspapers on the table to the right of Hildreth's place setting. In the Manhattan and Georgetown houses, it was always *The New York Times*, *The Washington Post,* and *The Times* of London. No one in the household staff was to talk to Mr. Hildreth until after he finished.

This morning, Hildreth was dressed in a gray suit, white shirt, and blue regimental striped tie, ready for a morning of hobnobbing with friends, first at the Union League Club then lunch at the Knickerbocker. He always sat at his breakfast table with his suit jacket on. As always, he drank his juice, took a sip of coffee, ate his shirred eggs and one warm croissant before picking up his *New York Times*.

He read the front page above the fold as it lay on the table. Then he picked up the paper, unfolded it, and held it open with both hands. As he did so, a single white sheet slid out of the newspaper and sailed down to the antique carpet at his feet. Annoyed at these ads that spilled out of newspapers and magazines, Hildreth put the *Times* back on the table and reached down to remove the stray insert from view.

But it was not an advertisement for an appliance sale. It was a plain white sheet of paper with a short message in 30-point type perfectly centered on the page:

You and Pennington are murderers.

Hildreth gasped. His eyes darted around the breakfast room to make sure he was alone. No, no one. He crumpled the paper into a ball.

He stood and put the balled-up paper in his pocket. Then he reached for *The Washington Post*. Hesitantly, he unfolded it and held it open at arm's length as if it were contaminated. A new sheet floated down onto the carpet, landing facedown. Hildreth closed the *Post* and put it back on the table. He knelt down and turned the sheet over slowly:

We have proof of your offshore accounts and your insider trading in Ayvil, Humanifit, and GI stock.

Hildreth grabbed the sheet, balled it up, and stuffed it into his pocket. He stood and turned back to the table, staring at *The Times* of London. He reached for the paper with just his thumb and forefinger. He lifted it up. A third white sheet sailed down to the floor.

He dropped the newspaper. It fell in a splattering heap. He could see the printing on the white paper from where he stood:

Justice will out.

He reached down and grabbed it. He balled it up and put it in his pocket with the others. Hildreth looked around his breakfast room. *His* breakfast room. With everything just as he wanted it. And suddenly it looked alien. It was no longer his. This house was no longer his. "Alejandro!" he called frantically. "Alejandro! Come here!" He grabbed the bell and started ringing it, over and over.

"Alejandro! Goddamn it! Alejandro!"

The door to the butler's pantry opened. Alejandro stood in the doorway awaiting instructions. "Jess, Mr. Hildreth?" In that instant, Alejandro nervously lowered his eyes to Hildreth's waist, then raised them immediately.

Hildreth saw the movement and looked down at himself. The

crotch and left thigh of his gray trousers were wet and stained dark. He had peed himself. Once he saw, he felt the wet and warmth.

"A-A-Alejandro," he cried, "the newspapers. Who brought the newspapers?"

"The newsboy, Mr. Hildreth." Alejandro struggled to keep from staring at Hildreth's wet spot. "He come at six today. Like always."

"Are you sure?"

"Jess, Mr. Hildreth. Everything same as always." Alejandro looked at the mess on the floor. "Something is wrong?"

Hildreth bent down to pick up *The Times*. He started collecting the scattered pages and hastily reassembling the newspaper. Ordinarily, he would leave such a cleanup chore to others. "No, nothing is wrong," he sputtered, "that will be all."

Fifteen minutes later, Hildreth spoke to Alejandro on the intercom. "Call the private jet people. We are leaving for Lyford Cay immediately."

118

Ken awoke in his empty apartment and turned on the TV. It was the midday report. He had slept past noon. Oh well, it was Saturday, he thought.

As he was pouring his second cup of coffee, he heard the business correspondent finishing the weekly market wrap-up. "And the big question of who will succeed Harry Warren at the helm of General Industries has finally been answered. Tom Pennington was named the new chief executive, effective immediately. Pennington nosed out longtime GI veteran Michael Guillaume, who . . ."

Ken stared at the television but heard no more of the reporter's words. Noises started going off in his head. He put down his coffee mug, got his key chain by his bed, and unlocked the bottom drawer of his desk. In the back of the drawer under his boxes of checks, right where he had left it, was the Kel-Tec P-32 pistol. He had bought this gun twice, once in Ohio and again in New York after his apartment fire.

"Sandy," he said quietly, "it's time." He picked up the little gun, holding it in his palm. It was so small and felt so comfortable; it weighed only six and one-half ounces. It would nestle invisibly in his pocket until he needed it.

Ken showered, then dressed in the outfit he had carefully planned for this moment: a traditional blue blazer, tan slacks, penny loafers, and a pink polo shirt with the collar rolled upward. He reached for his cell phone on the dresser then changed his mind. He turned off the power button and put it back. He took a long look at the picture of Sandy and Sara on the windowsill. Then he turned to leave.

"Wish me luck, Sandy," he said over his shoulder as he left the apartment.

A moment later, the land-line phone rang. Four times. When the answering machine kicked in, the computerized voice asked the caller to leave a message.

"Uh, I hope this is the right Ken Olson," the woman said tentatively. "I got this number from Information. This is Kat Pierce from American News Network. You tried to reach me some months ago about your suspicions and, uh, accusations." She faltered. "Gee, I'm not sure how specific I should be in a phone message. If this is the same Ken Olson who contacted me, well, Mr. Olson, I'm calling to validate everything you said back then. I'm not exactly sure how we should proceed, but, as you know, I am in a position to help. I don't think I should say anything more in a phone message. If you are the right Ken Olson, all I can say is please call me. I will be out of the country for the next two weeks but you can reach me any time of the day or night. Call me, please." She left the number of the satellite phone on Ed McCabe's yacht and hung up.

The answering machine reset itself.

Then the phone rang again and the machine picked up. Phil's voice filled the empty apartment. "Ken! Hey, Ken! You there? It's Phil. You there? Your line was busy just now. Hey, pick up, guy. Good news, bro, come on, pick up."

Nothing.

Then Phil spoke quickly. "Ken, I tried your cell and got voice mail, so I left a message. I'll leave one here, too. Decker's quickie visit to Liechtenstein paid off after all. They confirmed the money trail between Pennington's shell companies and De Waal. He's getting the warrants for Pennington right now—murder in a zillion counts, conspiracy, bank fraud, wire fraud, you name it. What's more, Decker found other offshore accounts controlled by—get this—Justin Hildreth. Hildreth was secretly profiting from the ups and downs of Ayvil's stock all along. Turns out the old guy was on the edge of insolvency. He may have rigged this whole stock deal in the first place to save his own ass. Decker figured that one out. I told you he was good. He's got Hildreth nailed on insider trading, bank fraud, wire fraud, conspiracy to commit murder with Pennington, the works. Hey, call me when you get this message. And remember what I said. Don't, repeat, *don't* do anything stupid. Okay?"

Phil paused for a moment as if he might get a response. There was none. Then he closed hurriedly. "We're off to the halls of justice."

119

Ken told the doorman at 977 Fifth he was Justin Hildreth. The man looked at him questioningly.

"Justin Hildreth the Third," Ken said with good-humored exasperation, as if he had to explain this all the time. "You've seen my father visiting here. He's Justin number two. Sorry, it's just so boring and pretentious to keep saying 'the Third' like you're a king of England or something."

Ken was dressed for the part of preppy scion, just the way a Fifth Avenue doorman would expect. "Think of us as a movie with sequels like *The Terminator*. I'm like, J-3, you know." Ken smiled. The doorman chuckled. "Just tell him Justin Hildreth. He's expecting me. Really, it's okay."

"Justin Hildreth is here," the doorman said into the intercom handset. He smiled at Ken. Ken winked. The doorman nodded and replaced the handset into its cradle. "It's the elevator all the way in the back on your left. Penthouse B."

"Yes," Ken said cheerfully, "I know. Thank you."

He walked through the cavernous lobby past the stone slab and tinkling waterfall. The doorman controlled the elevator buttons from the desk. The PH button was already lit. The elevator whooshed him nonstop to the penthouse; the doors opened into Pennington's apartment.

Ken stepped into the foyer. Stone floors and walls, domed ceiling and crystal chandelier. To the right, the hallway leading to bedroom suites, to the left the hallway to the kitchen. He could not help but notice the silver-framed picture of Pennington and his media babe with the President and First Lady. Ahead, the vast living room was furnished like the lobby of a small and very expensive hotel. The wall of floor-to-ceiling windows overlooked Central Park. Ken stepped into the living room, curious that Pennington was nowhere to be seen.

"Justin, I thought your message said you were leaving for Lyford

Cay," Pennington called from out on the terrace. He was seated at the table with his back to the apartment. "Come on out, it's such a lovely day."

Ken walked quickly through the obstacle course of overstuffed couches, formal chairs, and antique tables to the open sliding glass doors. The terrace was a railed-in garden in the sky, with meticulously manicured hedges and teak lawn furniture. As the penthouse of the tallest building on upper Fifth Avenue, it was absolutely private, invisible to the rest of the world.

Pennington turned and stood. "Ken Olson, what *on earth* are you doing here?"

Ken walked up to Pennington. "Sit down," he said flatly, "this is not a social call." He pulled the pistol from the pocket of his blazer. "I said, sit down." With his left hand, he snapped the slide back and rested his right index finger against the trigger.

"Ken, what the hell?" Pennington raised his hands. "Put that thing away."

Ken said, "Just sit down."

Pennington obeyed. Ken pulled up the chair and sat next to him, holding the gun with a steady hand. "Ken, this is unnecessary," Pennington said calmly. "Put the gun away."

"No, Tom."

"Don't be foolish. If you shoot me, you'll go to jail for life or get the death penalty. It will ruin your life."

"You already did that, Tom. Mine and a lot of other people's. Just so you could"—he waved the gun in a small arc—"enjoy all of this."

Pennington sat quietly. The only hint of fear was the dry sound his lips made when he opened his mouth. Ken held the gun in place. Finally, Pennington spoke. "What the hell do you want, Ken? Just tell me what you want. Do you want money? I can make you rich. I can give you more money than you ever dreamed of."

Ken nodded as if considering the offer.

"All right, put the gun down and tell me how much you want."

Ken raised the barrel and pointed it at the middle of Pennington's forehead. "No, Tom, here's the deal. You tell me everything. Everything. Talk!"

"If you're going to kill me, why should I? Go ahead. Shoot."

Ken lowered the gun, pointing it at Pennington's heart. "I don't know whether I'm going to kill you or not. First, you'll talk. Then, if you tell me what I want to hear, we can discuss money."

"You're not serious."

Ken raised the gun. "Talk."

Pennington was defiant. "About what?"

"About your career as a murderer. Starting at Hotchkiss. Your opponent for class president, the classmate who drowned."

"Oh," Pennington said dismissively, "that was *so* long ago."

"Out with it!" Ken barked.

"Lucky accident. I just helped him along, made sure he was dead."

"Was that your first?"

"Why do you care?" Pennington was almost bored.

"What about your beloved Katherine?" Again, Ken raised the gun to Pennington's forehead.

"All right, all right. Just put that thing down."

Ken pressed the barrel against Pennington's skull. "Katherine's death was no accident, was it?"

Pennington breathed out slowly. "No."

"Why did you kill her?"

"Her family lost their money. They didn't have that much to begin with, actually; those Mayflower types rarely do. In any case, I'd gotten everything I could from their connections. She wanted to have that stupid baby. She was in the way."

"You're a psychopath, Tom. You know that?"

"I'm effective."

"You fit all the criteria."

"I do what's necessary."

"You're a murderer. No, worse."

"I'm a born leader. I have what chief executives and presidents need to run the world."

Ken shook his head in amazement and horror. "Now, let's talk about the plane crash at Paragon."

"What about it?"

"It was no accident, was it?"

Pennington nodded.

Ken cleared his throat and spoke in a loud voice. "I'm sorry, Tom, I didn't hear you."

"No, it was made to look like faulty avionics. I had to fast-track my promotion to presidency of the division." Pennington gestured for Ken to lower the gun.

He did.

"Now, why did you murder all the employees at the plant?" Ken tried to keep his voice from cracking as he thought of Sandy and Sara. "*Why*, goddamn it?"

Pennington took another deep breath and looked out over Central Park. "It wasn't my idea."

"What do you take me for?"

"Ken, I just told you, it was *not* my idea."

Ken raised the gun to Pennington's temple again.

Pennington pushed the barrel aside again. "Hildreth thought it up."

Ken's mouth fell open. "Hildreth?"

Pennington folded his arms across his chest. "Justin Hildreth never gets his hands dirty with details. Justin Hildreth *commands*. We mere mortals obey. Hildreth wanted to get rid of Paulson and sell the company. He brought me in to execute his strategy. Drive the stock down, pump it again, and sell it off at a premium on top of the high. It was all his idea."

Pennington took a deep breath. "Actually, it was a brilliant idea, even if it wasn't mine. Mass firing? Mass murder? It's such a short step. I'm surprised no one thought of it before. You're killing the poor employees, anyway. You might as well go all the way and finish the job."

Ken shuddered, then asked, "So Paulson fell into the trap you and Hildreth set for him?"

"He couldn't have been more cooperative."

Ken felt his hand getting sweaty around the handle of the little pistol. Pennington continued in an almost chatty tone, "Just as we planned, Arch Paulson thought the accident was a stroke of luck. Then when the planted evidence magically appeared, Paulson stood accused of a crime so heinous that merely being accused was enough to ruin him once and for all."

"And his suicide?" Ken paused. "It *was* a suicide, wasn't it?"

"Oh, yes," Pennington said emphatically. "Paulson did kill himself. I gave him some encouragement, but that's all. It was just an added stroke of luck. He was finished one way or the other. He knew it. His suicide was just, well, when you work hard and plan right, sometimes it all comes together even better than you dared hope for."

"And moving Paulson's money?"

"Easy. Go into his office at night after he left and track his computer keystrokes. Capture his passwords. It's Industrial Espionage 101. Buy a KeyGhost for a hundred bucks and you could do it. Anyone could. When I discovered he had an account in the Caymans, well, the plan sort of invented itself. Paulson thought he was safe and secure running his world from his big mahogany desk. What a dinosaur."

"Tell me, why didn't you have me killed? You blew up my apartment."

Pennington looked at him blankly.

Ken raised the gun again. "I said, why didn't you finish the job and kill me?"

"That would have been simpler, yes. But risky. You were on the FBI's radar. Your death or disappearance would trigger too many questions. So I had you monitored. But I did need to be sure that the CD with the embezzlement files was destroyed. I still can't believe those idiots sent it to you."

"Oh yeah, why *did* you frame me for that embezzlement, anyway?" Ken was surprised at how little that injustice mattered to him now.

"I didn't. Paulson did."

"Paulson? Why?"

"To discredit *me*." Pennington looked directly at Ken. "I couldn't stop it. I had to let you take the blame. I had no choice."

It was almost an apology. Paulson the bastard was something they had in common, almost a bond. It was curious, Ken thought, as he held the gun, fully prepared to take this man's life and accept the consequences, curious the intimacy he and Pennington shared.

"What about Cindy?" Ken asked.

"Who?"

"The woman you put on me."

"Oh yes, her."

"Where is she now?"

"Why do you care?"

Ken raised the gun again. "Where is she?"

"Deleted." Pennington smirked.

"Where did you find De Waal? He escaped at Perry's Bend, but they'll nail him soon enough. Where did you find him?"

Pennington exhaled noisily.

Ken raised the gun again. "I said where did you find him?"

"At the Paris Air Show. Years ago. You can find anything there, if you know where to look. De Waal—you know, I'm not sure what his real name is—he was a real discovery. He combines primitive brutality with an exceptional ability to manage technical experts and large-scale projects."

Suddenly, a deep male voice sounded behind them at the door to the terrace. "Put the gun down."

Ken and Pennington looked up.

"Speak of the devil," Pennington said.

It was a big white man wearing a Con Edison repairman's blue uniform. A shock of curly blond hair and bushy blond eyebrows. He was holding a GLOCK 10 with a silencer. "I said put the gun down," he said more angrily.

Ken recognized him instantly. It was Grant De Waal. De Waal spoke to Pennington. "I want the rest of my money *and* my bonus on top of that, you fuck."

Pennington looked warily at the two guns pointing at him. "I'm afraid you'll have to take a number, Bles. Someone got here ahead of you."

"You fucker," De Waal said as he waved the gun back and forth.

"Ken," Pennington said with icy calm, "this is the man who murdered your wife and daughter. Don't you think you should shoot him?"

Ken kept his gun pointed at Pennington.

"Go on, Ken," Pennington said. "If you don't, he's going to kill us both. You do know how to use that thing, don't you?"

"If you try, you are dead," De Waal said to Ken.

Ken stared at the South African. This was the face he had tried to remember. The cold eyes. The voice with the odd accent. The large thick body. He could not count the hours he had spent hating this murderous creature.

"*Nee nee, Bles,*" Ken answered in the Afrikaans he had learned. No no, Baldy. "*You* are." Ken raised the gun abruptly and, in a well-practiced move, aimed for De Waal's head and fired. The shot exploded; the gun recoiled. De Waal fell backward, a black hole between his eyes. The GLOCK 10 dropped from his hand and clattered onto the tile. Ken's hours of practice at the gun club had finally paid off.

Pennington sat absolutely still.

Ken lowered the gun to his side and took a deep breath, not quite believing what he had just done. He stared at the body, the back of the head where the bullet made the exit wound, a puddle of blood pouring onto the stone terrace.

Ken was disappointed. Disappointed that it was over so fast. Disappointed that he could not make De Waal get up off the stone terrace and shoot him again. And again. And again. Until he had killed De Waal as many times as De Waal had killed the spirit and joy and life force in him. Until he had killed him enough times to bring Sandy and Sara back to life.

"Thank you, Ken," Pennington said almost cheerfully. "That was good work. We should get our stories straight before we call the police. We can use this to our advantage."

"I don't think so, Tom."

"Ken, don't be stupid." Ken did not reply. "Haven't you learned anything about the way the world works?"

Ken stared at De Waal. Satisfied that he was really dead, he took a deep breath and looked at Pennington. "Well, Tom, there is one thing I did learn from you."

Pennington looked puzzled.

This time, it was Ken's turn to smirk. He paused, making Pennington wait for his response. With his free hand Ken patted the breast pocket of his blazer. "Always wear a concealed recording device to important meetings."

Pennington's eyes narrowed, his nose flared with rage. He lunged at Ken. The force knocked him down and sent the little gun flying out of his hand. It skittered across the terrace. Suddenly, Pennington was on top of Ken with his hands on his throat.

Ken wanted to throw Pennington off, but could not. He struggled for air. Then for an instant he stopped trying and closed his eyes. In the blackness an image appeared.

It was their last day of life. When Sandy gave him the necktie. When he and Sandy smothered Sara in hugs and kisses for the last time. He felt their warmth and smelled their soft skin. Both of them as real as they were that morning. Deep in his skin, he felt their presence and knew that nothing on earth could take this away from him.

His body responded with a surge, muscles firing, bones lifting, an angry animal instinctively protecting its life. He caught Pennington by surprise. His knees jabbed into Pennington's crotch. Ken yanked the hands from his throat and leaped to his feet.

Pennington teased him with a smile. Ken responded with his right fist in Pennington's face. Blood exploded around Pennington's eye.

Ken had his back to the railing of the terrace. Pennington lunged for him. Ken let his body absorb the force without resisting. The strategy he had learned in aikido. As they were both about to slam into the railing, Ken's body tightened and recoiled. He dropped to his knees then surged upward, turning the force of Pennington's aggression against him. Ken lifted Pennington off his feet and hoisted him into the air.

Over the railing.

Ken looked at Pennington in the blurred instant—the bloodied face, the limbs in midair, the sky, the treetops of Central Park. Time did not slow down the way they say it does. It was over in an eyeblink.

There were screams from below. The sickeningly meaty thud of tearing flesh, the crunch of shattering bone as Pennington landed, facedown, on the elegant iron fence. The gold-tipped spears skewered him from crotch to head. Six golden spears poked out of his broken lifeless body. The gold leaf was slimy and red from his blood and viscera. The seventh spear was buried in the middle of his forehead. Thomas Pennington, corporate superstar, murderous monster, was transformed into a hideously punctured human shish kebab on the spikes of the aristocratic iron fence in front of 977 Fifth Avenue.

Ken stood holding his throat, every breath burning, the fury slowly draining out of him. As the ambulance and police cars pulled up, another government vehicle arrived. A Crown Vic bringing Decker and Phil and warrants for the arrests of Thomas Pennington and Justin Hildreth.

120

While they were prying Pennington's body off the fence, Justin Hildreth sat alone on his veranda overlooking Clifton Bay. On the table was the little brass bell and a very old, yellowing paperback book with loose, decaying pages.

Hildreth picked up the bell and jingled it.

As he always did, Alejandro appeared with the glass of sherry on the silver tray. He stood silently at attention. Hildreth looked out over the water.

"Ah, Alejandro," Hildreth sighed, "I do hope you like it here in the Bahamas. We are going to be staying indefinitely." Hildreth felt grateful for the lovely setting and the anti-extradition laws of his adopted tropical paradise.

"Jess, Mr. Hildreth, is nice the cay."

"Glad to hear it." Hildreth took a deep breath. "Well, things didn't work out quite the way I'd hoped, but, uh—" He paused and thought the better of what he was going to say. "—we can't always control events as fully as we'd like to. Can we?"

"No, Mr. Hildreth."

"You know, when I was a boy at Hotchkiss, my father put me in a competition against his lead portfolio manager at the Morgan Bank. He gave me a hundred thousand dollars to invest, which was a lot of money in those days." Hildreth did not look at Alejandro as he spoke; he hardly ever did. "My father said I had to beat his money manager and turn in a higher rate of return at the end of the year. The carrot he extended was a million dollars; the stick was leaving prep school, finding a job, and supporting myself entirely. I believed him to be completely serious. He gave me a book to read on how to succeed in this difficult and dangerous world. He told me he never wanted me to take anything for granted."

Hildreth looked at the old paperback on the table.

"After nine months, my portfolio was outperforming the man at

Morgan's. Except for one stock. It was dragging my performance down. It was a very interesting company that was developing technology that would become the smoke detectors we now take for granted. They were superb at product development but weak in capturing attention. And what is Wall Street if not the art of capturing attention?"

Without having to look at Alejandro or the tray, he reached out, took the delicate crystal glass, and held it before him.

"Thank you, Alejandro," he said. "So I decided to take matters into my own hands and help this company get some attention. I had made friends with the janitor of my dormitory. He was a simple man who lived in the city of Torrington not far from Hotchkiss. I made something of a sacrifice of him and his family. But it served my purposes. And the greater good. Today, smoke detectors are everywhere." He sighed with satisfaction.

Alejandro looked down at the floor.

As always, Hildreth took one delicate little sip, then downed the rest in a single gulp. Again, without having to look, he would replace the glass on Alejandro's waiting tray. Their routine never varied.

Until this moment.

The seizure Hildreth suddenly felt buckled him over in pain. He fell off the chair and squirmed on the floor. He was convulsing, drooling, spitting, peeing, and shitting. His wild kicking knocked over the chair and the little side table. The last thing he saw through his panicked haze was Alejandro standing over him, just barely cracking a smile. "You shit for the last time," Alejandro sneered quietly in Spanish.

The crystal glass lay shattered on the floor. The old yellowing paperback book was near it. *Success Can Be Yours!* in screaming block letters was printed on the faded cover. One of the pages that had fallen out had a passage double underlined and highlighted with the immature markings of a teenage boy: *"Start by working harder than others could ever imagine. Then find the courage to take risks others only dream of. And you, too, can ascend the pinnacle of success."*

When he was sure the soiled aristocrat was dead, Alejandro calmly left the house. He walked unhurriedly to town, as if on a routine trip to the market. As usual, he gave a friendly wave to the security guards at the gates of Lyford Cay. At the marina, he boarded a small fishing boat. The boat puttered out of the harbor and headed for Cuba, where Alejandro began a multileg journey on airplanes, boats, and buses, ending in Uruguay in a village near the Argentine border.

Alejandro had a new passport and a new identity. He had earned them so easily, he thought. Just by slipping three sheets of paper into Justin Hildreth's morning newspapers. For Agent Ted Decker of the FBI.

Alejandro settled in the casita he had bought with money stolen from Hildreth, little by little, over his twenty-five years of service.

Here, not far from the land of his birth, he would tell his neighbors that he looked forward to spending his declining years in peace, learning to practice the arts of comfort and serenity.

121

Polski's voice sounded distantly through the intercom. "Ken, come on down. I've got someone who wants to see you."

"Just a sec." Ken felt in his pants pocket to be sure he had his key, a New York habit he still had to think about, then ran downstairs. There, on the sidewalk, was Polski. Beside him was Michael Guillaume in his hand-tailored suit, white shirt, and Hermès tie. Behind them the limo and driver.

Polski bounded up to Ken, gave him a big handshake, and escorted him over to Guillaume.

"Ken!" Guillaume said warmly, extending his right hand. Ken took it. "You did it! You beat the bad guys. You got justice done." He high-fived Ken.

"Yeah, I guess I did."

"Let's have a seat, New York City style," Guillaume said. He motioned toward the stoop of the nineteenth-century brownstone beside Ken's apartment building. The three men climbed to the top of the wide, welcoming stairway.

Guillaume unbuttoned his suit jacket and flung back the tails as he sat. "Been a long time since I sat on a stoop like this and watched the traffic go by. Brings back memories. Come on." He patted the stone step. "Let's talk."

Ken and Polski sat on either side of Guillaume. Sun poured through a break in the clouds; it was turning into a beautiful day.

Guillaume paused for a moment and looked at the street. "I am sorry I doubted you, I want you to know that."

"It's okay, Mr. Guillaume, really."

"Hey, it's Mike."

"Mike," Ken said.

"You know," Guillaume said, putting a hand on Ken's shoulder, "I'm going to need executives I can trust at Nortex. Men with your kind of backbone and intelligence are hard to find."

"Oh, please."

"I mean it. We need people like you."

"No, I could never go back to that life."

"You're missing the upside of what we can accomplish with good people."

Ken shook his head no.

"Come on," Guillaume said, "I know it's got its flaws. Sometimes it's rough and unfair. What happened to you is a tragedy. No one can make up for it. But that was an aberration. Sure, the business world is far from perfect. It's only as good as the people. But it works. It's the best thing we've got."

"Maybe so," Ken said with a shrug.

"Don't be foolish," Guillaume said, "you can make a lot of money working for me."

Ken looked off in the distance, searching for a point on the horizon he could not yet see. He thought about Sandy and Sara and the moments he would never share with them. This was the ache he would never lose, the hole he could never fill.

Then he thought about the life they shared while they had it. And how precious and beautiful and fleeting it had been. This warmed him and gave him an odd sensation he could not quite identify. Through his struggles, *this* feeling had been the thing that hardened his determination and gave him the power to pretend, if only for a few critical moments, that he was not afraid. Maybe, he thought, this was what they call courage.

"What are you going to do now?" Guillaume asked.

Ken stood up and stretched. He felt relaxed and hopeful, although he did not know what it was he was hoping for. "I honestly don't know."

"Where will you go?" Polski asked.

Ken sighed. "Don't know that either. To Starbucks, I guess. I think I've become one of those people who hang out there in the middle of the day. None of us seem to have regular jobs. But somehow we get by."

"Call me any time, Ken," Guillaume said. "If you ever change your mind, we'll have a place for you at Nortex."

"You're a good man, Mike." Ken offered Guillaume his hand. They shook.

"Good luck, Ken," Polski said as they shook hands.

Then Ken went down the steps. Without looking back, he walked along West Ninety-fourth Street toward Columbus Avenue, leaving the corporate men and their limo behind.

ACKNOWLEDGMENTS

Writing the manuscript is a solitary occupation. Bringing the book to fruition is the work of many souls.

Thanks to John Silbersack, my steadfast, undaunted, and indomitable agent. And to Trident Media Group, especially Dan Harvey, another great innovation from the incomparable Robert Gottlieb.

Three cheers for the amazing team at Tor Books—Bob Gleason, Eric Raab, Linda Quinton, Kathleen Fogarty, Elena Stokes, Patty Garcia, Phyllis Azar, and, of course, Tom Doherty. Their creativity, resourcefulness, enthusiasm, and dedication are every writer's dream.

Peter Farago for the dazzling jacket graphics and photography. John Morrison for art directing tirelessly behind the scenes.

John Paine of John Paine Editorial Services (www.johnpaine.com). If I may be so bold as to write a tag line for him—John Paine is the editor to help you get an editor.

Daniel Starer of Research for Writers (www.researchforwriters.com). This really is the ultimate resource (and I would say this even if Dan were not a Bowdoin alumnus).

Experts who shared their expertise: Nick Ward of TPS Consulting in London for assistance in explosives, Curt Picard on HVAC, Jeffrey Fulmer on factory security systems. And to the experts who preferred not to be named, thank you for help in researching international banking, techniques of money laundering, forensic computing, emergency and disaster recovery, criminal prosecutions, FBI procedure, private military contractors, weapons manufacturers, the Paris Air Show, and Afrikaans vocabulary both polite and crude. Any factual mistakes are mine.

Many friends and colleagues in the world of books were extraordinarily generous with help and encouragement. I am ever in your debt.

To Evelyn for putting up with my monomania. And our family and friends for their endless patience and understanding.